KNIGHT EXILED

THE SHACKLED VERITIES

BOOK THREE

TAMMY SALYER

KNIGHT EXILED

ALSO BY TAMMY SALYER

INTRODUCTION

Hello and thank you for being here! Should you enjoy the words on these pages (and I hope you do!), I encourage you to join my Book Club and visit me at:

www.tammysalyer.com

I occasionally send newsletters to my Book Club with new releases, special offers, and other bits of news. As a special thanks to new members, please enjoy a handful of novellas and short stories from my many and sundry universes FOR FREE.

CHAPTER ONE

One singular moment, one unforeseen twist of fate, and a person's life could change completely.

Symvalline Lutair and her daughter Isemay had been trapped under hundreds of pounds of earth and debris from an avalanche on Mount Omina. Straining against the massive weight, she linked her klinki stones into a shield, holding them overhead to keep from being buried alive, as gangling minions of a foreign Verity flanked them. She was sure she and Isemay would never survive, sure her strength would give out beneath the weight of the mountain. And the next moment—

It wasn't the first time she had traveled by wystic arts across a great distance. But it *was* the first time she'd traveled the starpaths to a foreign realm. And it was definitely the first time she'd gone anywhere for reasons other than her own choosing.

Less than a heartbeat passed, though it felt endless—the flashing lights in the darkness, the movement that felt so swift it had seemed she stood still while the Cosmos rushed past her instead of the other way around, and the disembodied hollowness, as if she were made of nothing yet still part of everything, all effects of starpath travel. She had known at once what was happening. She had no idea why.

Then—hard ground lay beneath her, a cool breeze wafted over her, and the sound of a nearby stream tickled her ears. Her eyes flew open.

"Mum, where are we?"

The sound of Isemay's voice, though hesitant and bordering on panicked, gave her a sense of ease that no other thing in the Great Cosmos could have achieved at this moment. Her child, her Crumb, was safe. Now the deed would be to keep it that way. Symvalline sat up and looked around.

Isemay lay curled on her side as if sleeping. They had come to rest in a midsized valley, near a wide and swift river. Symvalline quickly checked herself over, ensuring she was not wounded, then gently touched Isemay's light copper curls. "Are you okay? Have you been hurt?"

Isemay's answer was immediate. "No. I feel a little…tingly, but I'm okay." She pushed herself onto her hands and knees, then stood.

"Wait, don't move. We need to be cautious."

"I know, Mum, but look." She stared into the sky. Symvalline followed her eyes.

Three moons crested the horizon, magnificently large in the dark night sky. Millions of stars gleamed around them, a tapestry of light where every spark seemed to exist specifically to illuminate the three orbs, one blue, one red, and the last pale and colorless. They spanned a quarter of the sky from one side of the horizon to the other.

Symvalline had read deeply into Vaka Aster's Scrylle and knew immediately where they were. "Arc Rheunos," she said aloud. "The realm of the Verity called Mithlí." Why and how in all the wystic wonders had they come to be here?

"I've never seen anything so beautiful," Isemay said. She turned her head back, her gray eyes, like her mother's, reflected light in the stars' glow. "How are we going to get home?"

Always the precocious, blunt, and obstinate one, her child never left a thought in her head unspoken or in need of interpretation. But Symvalline wasn't paying attention.

"Quiet," she said urgently, barely above a whisper. "Get behind me."

Twenty paces away along the riverbank, several sets of eyes caught the light, watching them. She reached for her back, where the sack she'd carried Ulfric's sword Light Spell had been hanging, but it wasn't there. Had she lost it on Mount Omina? When the avalanche had started, everything had been chaos. She could remember falling, getting up… but little else besides reaching Isemay just in time to activate her klinkí stones and keep the mountain from coming down on their heads.

Whoever's eyes they were, they remained still, mostly in shadow, but Symvalline could make out something strange about the beings. Their forms suggested they were like her and Isemay, people, but darker shadows rose from their backs over their heads…

Automatically, Symvalline's hands extended as she called through her Mentalios lens for her klinkí stones. To her incalculable relief, the eight crystals rose immediately and came to a hover, glowing a wystic cerulean, over her upturned palms.

"We are not a threat," she said calmly in Elder Veros. "We are lost travelers from…far from here."

Instantly, there came a hushed chorus of whispers and several of the bodies shifted closer together, as if conferring. The tones sounded excited, if fearful, to Symvalline. "Stay very quiet, Isemay. Don't scare them. They are likely more frightened by us and the manner in which we arrived here than we are of them."

Isemay nodded, silent and obedient, as she'd been before she'd reached her adolescence.

After a moment, the whispers stilled. A figure stepped a few paces closer. "Plague-bringers," the voice said in an accented Elder Veros. "Get away from us."

After more than seven hundred turns, Symvalline knew every manner of tone, emphasis, and inflection that a voice could make, and this man's could not hide his uncertainty, or his lack of authority. If her guess was correct, he was a youth, perhaps not much older than Isemay.

"We carry no plague," she assured him, speaking slowly to be understood. "We are travelers, and we aren't sick." Did she dare risk it?

Telling them where they were from? Would they even know of the other realms?

"Plague-bringers!" He waved something threateningly. "Go back to where you came from!"

"Put your hand on my waist, Isemay," she whispered over her shoulder, "and stay close."

"But—"

"Shh!" Symvalline slowly paced a few steps forward. "Look into my face, friend. Hear my voice. Am I ill? Is my daughter?" She reached back and pulled Isemay up beside her until she was visible, all the while allowing her klinkí stones to remain circling just over one hand. "We are in need of help. We need to return to our home. Will you, can you help us?"

She saw the speaker clearly now. She'd been right, a youth. His hair hung below his collar bones and was twisted into braids. He wore a top and trousers of an unidentifiable cloth or fiber and carried a large satchel that hung just below his waist, held by a strap over one shoulder. But it was the wings on his back, spread halfway open and towering above his head, that held her gaze. Isemay gasped in surprise.

The rest of the stranger's assembly were whispering again behind him, some alarmed, others curious. But one voice hushed them all with a "Quiet." The new speaker, this time feminine-sounding, moved up beside the youth, then past him, brushing away the outstretched hand he tried to stop her with. Symvalline hadn't seen her at all a moment before, and she seemed to have materialized from the night air itself.

"Salukis," the new person said. "Move over. They're not the Minothians, and they came by starpath. If they were here to spread the Waste, they wouldn't be friendly about it." She stepped up to Symvalline and Isemay and eyed them with unhidden fascination. "Where in all the Cosmos did you strangelings come from?" Her eyes dropped to Symvalline's klinkí stones. "And what are those?"

In the starlight, the only things with discernable color were the three moons and Symvalline's stones, but even in such muted circumstances, Symvalline could see there was something unique about the woman's coloring, though she couldn't put her finger on what it was.

The woman seemed to be older than the youth, but not by much, and her tone did not lack the authority his did. What stood out most was, unlike the boy, she had no wings, nor did she seem to have a single strand of hair anywhere on her visible features. Nevertheless, her eyes shone kindly, if warily.

"May I see them?" she said, lowering a hand and turning her palm up to invite Symvalline to give over her klinkí stones.

Symvalline was willing to accept the risk of palming the stones but not of giving them to the stranger. As she closed her fingers around them and their blue hearts dimmed, she said, "They are called klinkí stones, powered by the spark given to me by my Verity, Vaka Aster."

The woman lowered her own hand, seeming to accept Symvalline's refusal to pass them over. "Then you must be from the realm of Vinnr. Why are you in Arc Rheunos?"

So she is learned about the five realms. A good sign. "I'm sorry, I can't say why we're here." *Because I don't know.* She decided not to share her uncertainty. "All I can say is that we need help returning. We—"

"Were you exiled by your Verity?" There wasn't an accusation in her tone, only curiosity.

"No, at least, I don't think..." She stopped, lacking any explanation that made sense.

"You're in some trouble, I see. The Verities can be...difficult to understand. Let us take you to Archon Raamuzi. She, I think, will be able to help you."

"Mura," the youth said, alarmed, "what are you—"

"Mum, what is that?" Isemay cut in, her hand tightening on Symvalline's waist.

She glanced at Isemay, then followed her wide-eyed stare. On the other side of the valley, a dark gap loomed amid the mountains. From that darkness, small torch-sized lights emerged and began moving fast across the valley toward them. Some were ground-level, others seemed airborne, and there were over a dozen.

Symvalline's attention turned back to the woman when she felt her hand on her arm. Her eyes were round with fear. "Deathless Guards! We must run! Follow us!"

Based on the sound of running feet and swishing grass, the group of Arc Rheunosians had already begun to speed away. Those with wings launched into the air, their silhouettes standing out in the starlight. Most of them were much smaller than the two she'd spoken with, and she could hear more, but she could not seem to see any others in the darkness.

Skirmishes with rebellious factions or overzealous Verity worshippers had been common in Symvalline's early years as a Knight Corporealis, and she was no stranger to fights. But it had been many turns of Halla since she'd had to face an enemy with sword or bow, and she did not want to begin her stay—however, involuntary—in a new realm with one.

"Isemay, don't let go. Come on." She grabbed her daughter's hand in one of hers and released the klinkí stones with the other, letting the stones fly ahead and channeling her vitality into them to enhance their glow and light their way.

Sprawling foliage and the rock-covered ground sloped upward from the river, threatening their footing. Symvalline could make out nothing that resembled a path, and the only guides she had to follow were the uncertain glimpses of the flying Rheunosians, who were speeding away too quickly for her to follow.

She chanced a look behind and felt her first glimmer of fear since the gangling Battgjaldics had stalked her and Isemay on Mount Omina. The pursuers were gaining on them, their lights already passing over the river.

Isemay stumbled beside her and cried out. Symvalline stopped instantly. "Crumb! Are you okay?"

"Yes, it's just my knee." She jumped up, but then lurched to the side. "Ow!"

Symvalline glanced behind once more. They were getting closer. Leaning down, she helped Isemay reach an arm around her shoulders and stood upright. "I've got you. We'll run together."

They kept going, slower now, but determined. In moments, they crested the rise and reached a meadow that spread before them. They'd be able to run faster through the relatively flat area—but so would their pursuers. Symvalline thought she could see grasses and night-blooming flowers bending aside, as if someone were running through them, but she could see no other Rheunosians besides those who flew above. Starlight illuminated another slope at the far end of the meadow, and above that, dark towering forms that suggested a forest. A forest in which they could hide.

"Keep going. We're nearly safe."

Halfway across the meadow, she glanced back again and saw their airborne pursuers already cresting the edge of it. They were large forms, their wings wider than Symvalline was tall. Their faces were lit by the lights they carried, their features pale and hardened.

As her breathing grew ragged and began tearing through her throat, she realized she and Isemay were not going to reach the safety of the forest.

"Where is she?" a woman's, no, a child's voice cried. "Where is Neeka?!"

The voice was distant, seemingly ahead of them. Some of the Rheunosians must have made it to the tree line. Symvalline kept running—but her feet suddenly came up against something soft and she tripped, flailing through the air and coming to rest on her knees and elbows. Her wystic stones dropped to the earth, and Isemay fell in a heap beside her. She began to scramble to her feet but caught a glimpse of what she'd run into.

A small Rheunosian child, no more than seven or eight turns in Vinnric age, lay huddled on the ground in a ball, too terrified to move. Symvalline crawled to her and put a hand on her arm. It was cold, and the girl was shivering. "Come, child. Can you rise?"

"Mum, Mum, they're getting close," Isemay panted.

"Isemay, go! I'll catch up."

"No, Mum, I'm not leaving you."

She didn't have time to argue with her. She swept up the trembling child and stood. "I've got her. Come on."

But it was too late. Symvalline felt something hard and rough strike her in the back, and she went down again, this time curling her body around the child's to keep her from impact. The child let out a cry of terror. They were in a net.

"Mum!"

"Run, Isemay! Keep going!"

It was like talking to a stone. Isemay was beside her, tearing against the ropes binding her and the child, saying, "What do I do, what I do?"

"Stand back," she commanded and reached out for her klinkí stones. They flew to her, but not before the pursuing Rheunosian had reached them.

The man landed a few strides away. Symvalline and Isemay grew still, watching him. The child whimpered. She could hear their pursuer breathing, see his pale, slack face in the glow of the light he held. The torch wasn't lit by fire. Rather, it was a bulb of light resembling the illuminate orbs that lit most of Vinnr's indoors. He was gaunt, slightly stooped, and his eyes were a colorless void. He looked to her like the creatures brought by Balavad to Vinnr. Like the Raveners of Battgjald.

"Get behind me, Crumb," she whispered.

The creature stalked toward them.

From somewhere near the tree line, she heard the voice of the youth she'd first spoken with. "Neeka!"

She glanced over her shoulder, and the young man was speeding through the air toward them. Their pursuer's gaze shot to him, and he withdrew a sword. The Rheunosian Ravener flapped his powerful wings and rose into the air to meet the youth, who, as far as Symvalline had seen, carried no weapon. He would be slaughtered.

Without a second thought, she waved her hands and sent a barrage of klinkí stones into, and through, the Ravener. He plummeted to the ground in a heap, emitting a whistling screech that scoured her eardrums like hot wires. Though he hit the ground hard, amazingly, he stood. Glistening ichor poured from the holes in his clothes. He leaned forward, his movements sluggish and drunken, and swept his elongated, gaunt arms through the meadow grass in search of the sword he'd dropped.

"Crumb, can you reach the dagger in my boot?" Isemay's hands reached through the net's holes at her feet, searching and finding the dagger Symvalline kept in one. "Good, quickly, cut the ropes and get me free."

Isemay did as she was told, wasting no movement, and Symvalline rose clear of the net in moments. She stepped to the Rheunosian Ravener, her stones hovering. "Leave that sword where it is and move away," she commanded.

The creature turned its cold solid-gray eyes in her direction. His lips parted in a thin sneer, and that screeching wheeze, more muted this time, passed between them. The sound wasn't words, but she could understand the threat in them nonetheless.

It shouldn't have been possible for him to move, not with eight neat holes piercing from one side of his body to the other. Yet he was more than moving. He was planning to attack again.

Something flashed in the corner of her eye, and she saw with a glance the Rheunosian youth hovering beside her, staring at her in shock. "You!" she called to him. "Take the child and see my daughter to safety. Go!"

The youth quickly dropped down to sweep up the little one, who was still tangled in the ruined net. The Ravener had found his sword and was leveling it at her for another attack. Symvalline sent two more klinkí stones into his arm, and the sword fell.

"I can carry two of you," the Rheunosian said. "But not all three. We'll be safe in the Churss. The Minothians can't follow us in there." He pointed up to the hilltop where the towering forms of strange-looking trees loomed in darkness.

"No need," Symvalline responded. "I'll slow them down. Now go. I'll follow when you're safe." Isemay began to protest, but the command in Symvalline's voice stopped her short. She would not be spoken against this time. "I am a Knight and your mother, Isemay, you are still a child. You will do as you're told." She caught the youth's eye and gave him a short nod. "Go."

They both saw the Ravener once again retrieving his sword, like a drunken man who couldn't think beyond one simple action at a time. The creature gripped the weapon in both hands, looked toward them, and spread his wings wide, preparing to launch himself at them.

The youth said, "Hold on, Neeka, like an urzidae cub." The child hugged herself to his body, and he took Isemay underneath the arms. With a flap of sturdy wings, he rose up.

Her daughter's eyes never left hers, and she could see the defiance mixing painfully with love in them. The youth swept toward the forest, and Symvalline turned back to the Ravener. With a hurricane-strong barrage of her klinkí stones, she ensured he would not rise again. After one last glance toward the retreating Rheunosian and Isemay, she looked back to the valley and faced the oncoming horde.

THE TROOP of Rheunosians approached quickly. Symvalline didn't know if she could stop them all, but she would try. Whatever feud might be going on in this realm was not her concern. Her daughter was the one thing that mattered, and she would end anyone who tried to harm her.

Four more flying Rheunosians halted and came to a hover before reaching her. It might have had something to do with the massive spinning vortex of klinkí stones she held out as a shield as tall and wide as a house. The blue of the stones' hearts blurred the night, like a carnival of cerulean fire.

Through the shield she watched them hesitate. Three of the four were the same pale, gaunt Ravener-types, but one looked more like the Rheunosian man who had taken Isemay. Less pale and misshapen, more like the youth who'd helped Isemay escape.

"Hold!" the non-Ravener one commanded. "Wait for Archon Tuzhazu."

She had a moment to be thankful that her plan had worked. The pursuers would be stopped long enough for the others to get away.

As they stood at an impasse, the typical-looking Rheunosian gaped at the dead Ravener who lay near her feet, his expression of shock enough to show he was unused to being confronted with death. She held her shield and her silence, waiting for them to make the next move.

Soon enough, the steps of large animals coming over the rise reached her ears, and moments later saw what was making them. Seven massive thick-furred creatures with heads bearing a single horn, gleaming black eyes, and heavy jaws marched toward her. Astride their saddles sat more Rheunosians. Some were winged men, but a handful were the smooth-skinned, hairless women, all muscular and kitted like soldiers.

The foremost stopped his mount before her shield. She noted that he, aside from the non-Ravener-types, was the only one armed with a sword, which he'd drawn. Most eyed her with expressions not of malice, or at least not completely, but with more of the same surprise as the first Rheunosians she'd met.

"Who are you?" he asked in a resonant baritone that nevertheless crawled to her ears like a spider.

She said nothing, her focus flitting in each direction, trying to keep account of them all. He only waited moments before he spoke again.

"I asked you a question, starpath traveler. Tell me your name and your realm. Who sent you and from where?"

"It doesn't matter where I'm from. I am no threat to you or your people."

His eyes dropped to the dead Rheunosian Ravener that lay nearly at his mount's feet. "A liar, then. That tells me who you are, but it doesn't tell me why you're here. Or why you slaughtered this one."

"He threatened my—" She stopped herself. She wouldn't tell them of Isemay. Her daughter was safer if she was secret.

"Your?"

"The Rheunosians who tried to assist me."

"Archon Tuzhazu," a soldier near him said. "She could be a plague-bringer."

The leader held up a hand, and the woman who'd spoken fell silent. He smirked at Symvalline oddly, a look she couldn't read. "Is that what you are, liar? A traveler from another realm who brings us the wasting death?"

Symvalline glanced over her shoulder, reassured that she could no longer see Isemay or the other Rheunosians. She hoped that meant they were safely away. It was time for her to be as well.

"Yes, a traveler," she said. "And now I'll be leaving. Whatever quarrels you have are none of my concern or doing."

"No," the one called Archon said. "I don't think you'll be on your way just yet." He heeled his mount, and it began to lumber toward her obediently.

"You've seen what I can do with these stones," she warned. "I don't want to hurt you."

He gave her that smirk again and reached into a pouch at his side, withdrawing something fist-sized, a darker shadow in his hand that seemed to repel the light.

Somewhere not too far distant behind her, closer to the forest, there was a sound. Small, no louder than a subdued chuckle—but it sounded more like a cry. The Rheunosians heard it too.

"Archon, there's movement," one of the mounted women said.

The leader gave a short nod, and the woman spurred her creature and bounded after it.

Symvalline wanted to turn to look. If one of the Rheunosian children was still in this meadow, they would need her help. Yet her attention was fixed on what was in the Archon's hand.

He followed her eyes and said, "Let me take a closer look at those stones you control."

He held out the thing in his hand as if offering it to her, and she felt a sudden and irresistible *tug* in her mind, as if her very thoughts were being pulled toward his beckoning fingers. The sensation was so unique that it caught her off guard. And like that, all eight of her stones were sucked through the air. The came to rest hovering in a much smaller circle around his outstretched palm, as if the thing he held was a magnet.

Alarmed, Symvalline recovered immediately and called back her klinkí stones through the Mentalios. They jutted toward her for a moment, but then sprang back to circle the Archon's fist. His smirk turned into a grin of triumph.

Without time for a heart to beat twice, Symvalline raised an arm and drew back her sleeve, launching a dart from the wrist-mounted crossbow she wore like a vambrace. The darts in the bow on her right would incapacitate a person for hours. Those from her left would kill them instantly. She chose the right. She hoped to avoid further bloodshed, though this leader of Raveners had brought this retaliation on himself with whatever powerful wystic weapon he wielded—and she feared she knew exactly what it was.

The dart struck the Archon in the neck. His face flushed with surprise, and he toppled from his mount into a motionless heap. Calling back her stones, Symvalline had them back in her control and spinning in the air once more before her still-raised hand. "No one move. I'm not here for trouble. It was you who brought it to me. Now I'm leaving. Do not follow." She'd already begun to back away as she spoke, hoping for even the tiniest bit of Verity-given clemency.

A groan emitted from the Archon, and to her astonishment, his hand shot up and grasped a stirrup. He began pulling himself to his feet as she hurried her own backward steps, never taking her eyes from him. The dart would have laid out a Vinnric for half a day, but here, in Arc Rheunos, their bodies must be different. And, she cursed, he was an Archon, a servant of Mithlí with his own Verity spark. She had no options but to kill him or outrun him.

He heaved himself up. The soldiers surrounding him seemed confused and hesitant, unsure of what to do, whether to charge her or assist him.

She raised her arm, not to fire another dart but to finish him for good. Before she could, he flung out his own arm. Briefly, she caught sight of the wystic artifact that had taken control of her stones. Then it penetrated her shield without the slightest resistance and struck her in the temple, and she knew no more.

CHAPTER TWO

"Let go of me!" Isemay yelled at the winged man as he carried her toward the looming forest ahead. "Let go, I have to help her!"

"Please stop squirming," he replied shortly, his voice strained from effort. "I don't want to drop you."

She glanced down, saw how high they were, and promptly followed his advice.

The child clutching him whispered in a voice filled with fear, "Are they going to get us, Salukis? I promise I'll never disobey Deespora and sneak to the Thallorn for nightcaps again. I promise on my talisman I won't."

"Shh, it's okay, Neeka. We got away."

As he spoke, they descended toward the edge of the forest, and Isemay could see it more clearly. It wasn't a forest at all, not in the way she thought a forest should be. Rather, the hilltop had given rise to a forest of stone towers, all as tall and thick as the oldwood forests in Vinnr, stretching beyond her vision. Far in the distance, she could just make out a glow over their tops, as if sunrise was on its way.

Salukis gave his wings a milder flap, and they reached the ground. Under ordinary circumstances, Isemay knew she'd find his flying ability extraordinary—but not at this moment. He released her with a sigh of relief, and Isemay ran forward a few steps, just as happy to be free of him. The other Rheunosians had all gathered to wait for them, and the older woman scooped the child named Neeka from Salukis's chest.

"Oh thank Mithlí you are safe, little one," she crooned, hugging the girl. "I would never have forgiven myself if… Where are Cylli and Onni? Where are the twins?!"

Those gathered began to look about them frantically, calling the names the woman had said. Isemay pressed her back to one of the tall stone columns, dejected and scared. Facing the meadow below, she could make out the swirling mass of cerulean klinkí stones her mother wielded. She took a determined stride forward, but a strong hand came down on her shoulder. She whirled and faced the woman, who was still holding Neeka. Her flashing green eyes were filled with compassion, yet stern.

"Please," the woman said, "don't. We can't protect you from them. The Minothians will imprison you, and you'll never be free again."

"But my mother!"

"I'm sorry. There's nothing we can do for her now. Nor for Cylli and Onni. Deespora can help. Please come with us."

Isemay stood undecided, then turned back to the meadow to watch, helplessness making her feel weak, afraid in ways she never knew fear could manifest.

"Mura, that stranger, she killed a…a Deathless," Salukis said.

"What?" the woman said.

"A Deathless Guard was after Neeka, and the stranger was protecting her. When the Deathless came after me, she threw those blue stones, and they went through him like a spear and killed him."

Repeating him, Mura said, "She killed him…" and her voice trailed off ominously, causing Isemay to glance back. The two Rheunosians were eyeing her warily, as if they feared she might attack them. Confused, she felt as if she needed to defend herself.

"They were coming after us. He drew a sword. My mum saved your lives," she chided.

One of the other winged Rheunosians, no more than a child, said quietly, "Mura, we should get back and tell Deespora what's happened."

Neeka added, "I'm scared. What are they going to do to Cylli and Onni?"

Isemay could feel their fear, and something deeper, a helpless sadness, like the cold sea mist that had surrounded the funeral party at a burial she'd been to as a child. The deceased, a teacher of hers at the Conservatum, had died by accident, and all had wept as he was sent to sea wrapped in gray fog. Isemay felt that sense of no return again, and of irretrievable loss. She looked back to where her mother stood alone against a troop of hostile soldiers, and this time she saw only a handful of lights moving back toward the mountains that rose on the other side of the starpath valley.

Everything in her went numb. She felt like a dead tree, erect, unaware of its death, too insensate to even know to fall over. Someone was speaking, maybe to her, but the words couldn't penetrate. Her mother was gone, her father too, fighting a battle she knew nothing about, one or both of them maybe dead. She was in a strange world with no one familiar to rely on.

"What is your name?" These words, repeated who knew how many times, slowly came through.

"Isemay," she responded through cold lips.

"And you're from the realm of Vinnr?"

"Vinnr," she acknowledged.

"Isemay from Vinnr," Mura said. "I don't think they will harm your mother. The Minothians still honor life, just as we do." She paused, as if uncertain of what she'd said, then continued. "Come with us to speak with Deespora. She may be able to help. Isemay, can you hear me? Please try to understand."

"I'm going down there," Salukis said.

"No!" Mura said. "You can't."

"We need to know what's going on, and someone needs to look for the twins. They might still be there, hiding." He glanced sideways at Isemay, then said in a lower voice. "There are too many questions we still need answers to, Mura. Why have these other-worlders come here? And why now? What if their arrival has something to do with the Equifulcrum?"

"That stranger saved Neeka," Mura responded. "Do you really suspect them of harm? This one is still a child. What realm sends a child to create chaos? Besides, she said they're from Vinnr, not Battgjald."

At the mention of Battgjald, Isemay began to listen closely. Knight Evernal had said something, some kind of warning, about the Verity from Battgjald, whom Isemay's father had gone to face him. Isemay had been barely paying attention, too excited about the festival in Ivoryss and the visit from the foreign Verity. She blurted, "What do you know of Battgjald?"

The two Rheunosians fell silent. Then Salukis said, "What do *you* know of it?"

"My da, he is the Stallari of the Knights Corporealis of Vinnr. My mum is a Knight too. Our realm was visited by the Battgjald Verity right before we…came here. My father went to…to—Vaka Aster's eyes, I don't know! It all happened so fast." She wanted to kick herself for paying so little attention. For being obstinate and impetuous and ignoring her parents one too many times. She finished more quietly, "If I had listened to Da and not gone to Aster Keep, none of this would have happened."

Salukis was quiet, and Isemay could feel his considering stare as he spoke to Mura. "I think a Knight Corporealis must be like an Archon." He looked to her. "Are your parents watchers of the vessel of your Verity and protectors of your realm?"

Isemay nodded.

He and Mura shared a look. "It explains much," she said simply.

"Yes." He returned the focus to his plans. "We should try to find out what we can before they take the Vinnric all the way to Everlight Hall. If the Menace is visiting other realms, he may be returning to ours."

"You'll get caught," Mura said, her voice strained.

"I've never been caught before. I swear, I'll only go as far as the Aktoktos Gate, then come back. Wait for me here until midday? I'll be fine."

The woman fell into a disagreeable silence, clearly seeing no point in arguing further.

"Take me with you," Isemay pleaded through her nerveless lips. "I need to look for Mum."

"I'm sorry, but I can't. It will endanger us both. If I'm going to help your mum, I have to do this alone."

He bent his knees, and with a single flap of wings, he rose. Mura called after him, "Midday, Salukis! See you're not late." Then she turned back to Isemay, seemed to want to say something, but merely gave her a look of pity that did nothing to soothe her fears.

CHAPTER THREE

Symvalline smelled the crispness of fresh mountain air along with dry stones mixed with hints of unidentifiable herbs or plants. Underneath these were notes of unwashed garments or people, not overpowering but still detectable, as if the scents had settled into the space around her long ago and fallen dormant. Her temple throbbed, but she didn't yet reach for her head to see if blood had been drawn.

Consciousness had come abruptly moments earlier, but she kept still. She needed to listen before acting, try to learn what she could about her captors before they turned their own questions on her, and try to discover Isemay's fate.

She heard breathing, two people. Likely whoever was guarding her. Cold stone beneath her told her she was indoors, so they'd left the meadow. Though she could not see it, she sensed light, perhaps from a window. Was it daytime? How long had she been unconscious? Distantly, she heard the sound of boots on stone, coming from somewhere below her.

One of the guards whispered, "Straighten up. It'll be the Archon."

Risking it, she opened her eyes but only to slits. She could see two sets of booted feet. Their footwear was not leather, but some kind of rigid and unusual fiber. Her guards were on the far side of the room near a doorway, as far from her as they could get. In the corner of the room sat a small wooden table, no chair. She could also make out a door near the guards, which swung outward as she watched. Someone with large booted feet entered.

"Is she awake?" the now familiar voice of the Rheunosian Archon asked.

"Not yet, Archon. She hasn't moved at all."

Another set of feet entered behind him, and the Archon turned. "On the table."

The person, not a soldier but someone dressed in what seemed to be common clothes, hurriedly set a tray containing a pitcher and four goblets atop it, then turned and left quickly, almost scurrying.

"She's slept enough. Get her up."

"But, Archon, if she carries the plague—"

"She is not a plague-bringer," he said shortly. "Get her up."

The guards approached her reluctantly, and while their backs were to the Archon, she saw him pull a flask from a pouch at his waist and quickly let a drop of its contents fall into the pitcher. Her gaze was blocked as one guard knelt and poked her in the chest with the tip of a wooden bludgeon. "Wake up," he commanded.

To avoid any unpleasantries, she immediately opened her eyes, startling the guard. He stood again as if on a spring, and they both took a step back. Symvalline pushed herself to a seated position and finally reached for her bruised head. It was tender, with a thumb-sized goose egg, but no blood. With her Verity spark, she would be healed within the day. She had already sensed that her wrist crossbows had been removed. Next, she reached for her Mentalios.

Gone.

Along with her medicine bag of herbs and concoctions, a small kit she went nowhere without.

Her eyes darted back to Tuzhazu. He smirked knowingly. "You two, wait outside while I speak with our guest." The two guards began to exit, but diverted first to the table and goblets when he said, "Take some mead with you. For your diligence."

The Archon regarded her closely as the guards grabbed their

drinks, and Symvalline was afforded a view of their extraordinary wings. They were membranous and covered with a felt-like down, two or three heads higher than the crowns of the guards' heads, and sweeping down just short of reaching the floor. The guards wore a kind of armor made from some dense material over their chests that were designed to fit around their wings, and buckled at their waists, and shirts and trousers similar to clothes of Vinnr beneath. When the door was closed behind them, the Archon stepped forward and she rose to her feet, taking a preparatory stance.

"So, it seems my guess was right," he began. He produced her Mentalios lens from the same pouch. "This is more than just a pretty pendant. Why are you here, fellow Archon?" He tucked the lens away as he waited for her reply.

The Vinnr Scrylle had sparse details of this realm, but enough that she knew it had three moons, which she'd recognized upon arrival. Archons were its name for an order like the Knights Corporealis. "In my realm, servants of the Verity are called the Knights Corporealis. And if you guessed I am one, perhaps you can guess why I came, as well." She spoke slowly, drawing out her answer as much as she could in order to take in her situation.

The chamber was modest, no larger than the main room of a small house. In a corner lay a heap of old textiles, the source of the unwashed smell. High atop two of the walls were open frames that let in outside air. Too high to see through, but wide enough to fill the interior with daylight. The air was cool, but not cold.

"A lack of cooperation will not go well for you," Tuzhazu said evenly.

"An expectation of cooperation from someone you attacked without provocation and nearly killed me is foolish for anyone who likes to think of themselves as an Archon." She looked at him squarely for the first time, the challenge in her eyes equal to her tone.

Not as tall as Ulfric, but stout like him, his beige skin was striated with a web of darker lines along his face, arms, and what she could see of his chest. The lines looked natural, not decorative, like the Dyrraks' skin adornments. Symvalline couldn't quite ignore her curiosity. He was the first being of another realm she'd had time to truly observe—if you didn't count the gangling people of Battgjald she'd encountered on Mount Omina. And Vaka Aster, of course. Besides these markings, the wings, and the ears, which were longer than Vinnrics' ears, he appeared much the same as her own people.

Her tone provoked him, and he took a menacing step forward, spreading his wings halfway. She gasped, unable to hold it in. Unlike the guards' membranous wings, his were ragged and skeletal, with bits of dried flesh attached to them in places that looked like the skin of a desiccated carcass. The wings rose over his head and curled forward, the visible bones tipped with gleaming metal hooks that looked like a hornet's stinger, but hundreds of times bigger. The man's wings were incapable of flight and horrid to look at, reduced to remnants by either accident or battle. And he now brandished them as weapons.

"I can hurt you, Archon, despite your Verity's gifts."

She pulled her gaze from the appendages, suppressing a shudder. "Try it, if you dare. We'll see which of us suffers more."

"Is that a challenge?"

"Consider it a test of endurance."

He stared at her silently for a moment, then his face broke into a wide, though not friendly, grin. "You're a fierce one! If I only had five soldiers with your verve, I'd have enough to finish the Zhallahs for good!"

She let him enjoy the moment, then continued with a slight blunting of the edge in her tone. "You used a Fenestros to disarm me, thus showing me you are a servant of the Verities too. Why, then, are you threatening me? We are in the same service, with the same purpose. You should be coming to my aid."

His smile dissipated and he blinked, revealing another difference from her own people. His eyes had two sets of lids, the inner set closing from side to side, like a bird's, before the outer set. At the speed at which the Rheunosians had shown they could fly, she could see the need for the protective layer.

Her mouth was dry and made dryer by the anxiety the Rheunosian was no doubt pleased to be causing her. But she'd seen his suspicious vial and wondered what he'd put in the pitcher. She looked to it, noting he had not drunk any either. But, she reasoned, if he'd offered it to his own guards, it must be harmless.

"Thirsty?" he said, catching her glance.

She pulled her eyes from the tray. "The only thing I would request from you, my fellow oath-taker, is to be set free." She paused, remembering the meadow. Had they caught others? "Both myself and the other Rheunosians I was with. If you'll grant me use of your Scrylle and a Fenestros so that I may take safe passage back to my own realm, I will be gone and trouble you no more. Will you?"

"Other Rheunosians? You mean the Zhallahs"—he spat a word in a language Symvalline didn't know, and not a kind word—"you were protecting?"

She eyed him, giving no hint of her thoughts.

"Why chase frightened mice when you can catch the courageous cat? But"—he turned aside and paced toward the table to pour another gobletful—"you killed one of my soldiers. I think first we shall establish why you're here, and it seems, unable to leave. I can see you're not from Battgjald. That leaves Vinnr or Himmingaze."

He came back and held out the cup. She refused it silently. He began to circle her. She stayed rigid, watching him from the corners of her eyes.

When he again stood before her, he said, "Vinnr, I think, based on the clothing you wear and the fact that you speak the Verity tongue. I've heard Himmingaze is a watery world now and has a language of its own."

"Why would you assume I'm not from Battgjald?"

"Are you?"

"You seem eager to know. I saw your…unusual soldiers, and I know their kind. Raveners from Battgjald. Does that make you a Knight with loyalty to this realm, or are you a puppet of Balavad's?"

"'Raveners'? No, we don't call them that here. And 'puppet'… interesting term. Am I to understand that your dealings with Balavad have been less beneficial than our own?"

He tried to pass her the cup again, and again she refused, watching his face closely. She sensed something was coming and didn't like her chances of coming through it unscathed. But whatever happened, she would not drink what was in that goblet.

With a deliberately unchallenging tone, she answered, "Your dealings with Verities are yours, and I don't seek to interfere. I simply seek aid in returning to Vinnr."

His patience seemed to have reached an end. "Who sent you here?"

"I cannot say. That's the truth."

"Why have you come?"

"I can't say."

He stepped close enough that she could feel his breath on her face. "Who follows you?"

Looking into his red-rimmed emerald-gray eyes, a color like tarnished silver, she gave a slight shake of her head. "I don't know. But if you let me go—"

Abruptly, he hurled the clay goblet into the wall behind her, smashing it to bits. She quelled inwardly but didn't flinch. He had no visible weapons except the ghastly metal-tipped wings. If he attacked, the only weapons Symvalline had were her own strength and training.

He collected himself, his nostrils still flaring with anger, and stepped back. "I have time to learn your secrets, *Knight*. The Equifulcrum is still days away. When it comes and I take my place as leader of Arc Rheunos, I promise you'll no longer need to concern yourself with the Zhallahs we've captured. Until then, how would you like to meet a new Verity?"

She said nothing, unable to gauge his intentions. There was a trick in his question, but she would have to play along until she understood it. Something about his eagerness for this Equifulcrum, which she knew from Scrylle archaneology was the syzygy of their three moons, an event that occurred only once every three hundred years, told her it would be better for her and Isemay to be gone from this realm before it happened.

To answer him, she said flatly, "It would be my honor to have an audience with Mithlí, Verity of Arc Rheunos."

He smirked at her one last time, then spun and paced from the room, giving her a better look at his wasted wings. She could see where they sprouted from his back, their bases made of thick, denuded, yellow-white bone. Where the bones thinned, more shining metal had been wrapped onto the skeletal framework, piercing through the flaps of skin still hanging here and there, creating a frightening armature that epitomized suffering. The healer in her wondered if he still felt the pain of whatever had done this to him. Darkly, she wondered if he enjoyed it.

The door slammed, and Symvalline was left alone. Already, her headache had lessened, and she easily ignored her thirst. Refusing to give in to the frustration at having gotten no useful information from the Rheunosian Archon, she began to pace the chamber rapidly, touching every stone, digging her fingers into every cranny, looking for any hidden asset that would help her either escape or protect herself. He'd said nothing about Isemay, and she was sure her daughter and at least some of the Zhallahs had escaped. This was her only comfort. And with her mind free to focus, several more things surfaced that she desperately wished to know: Where was Ulfric and was he safe? What was happening now in Vinnr?

"Heyo."

The word was whispered, barely audible, and coming from above her. She wheeled around, looking first to one window, then the next. A face was framed there, looking down at her. Amber-skinned with markings similar to the Archon's, locks of copper hair dangling beside his cheeks. She recognized him and her heart froze.

"You're the Rheunosian who took Isemay," she said.

"Yes, I'm Salukis."

"Where is my daughter?"

"She's safe in the Churss with the other Zhallahs, my people."

Her relief was so great, like a weight suddenly ripped from her, that Symvalline nearly staggered. "Thank you," she said. "Thank you."

"I overheard most of what Archon Tuzhazu was saying. They're taking you to Everlight Hall, in the middle of the Tyrn Mountains. That's where Mithlí is being—"

They both jumped at the sound of something rattling on the other side of the door. Symvalline cut in. "Can you get me free?"

"No, there's no way. The Minothians have too many guards at the gate to the mountains, and the Deathless prowl the valley. I have to go before they see me. I'll tell your daughter you're unharmed. Archon Raamuzi will think of something to help you."

"Wait, before you go, can you tell me what Tuzhazu meant about the Equifulcrum? What's happening then?"

"At the Equifulcrum, Tuzhazu will be the next living vessel of Mithlí and ruler of Arc Rheunos. Then—" He glanced away quickly, distracted by something outside.

"What?" she pressed.

"He may come for the Zhallahs. I have to go."

"Wait. What does he want with your people?"

"To bury the truth of what he and the other Archons did forever. And I think he means to bury all the Zhallahs with it."

His eyes darted to the side, and in the next breath, he was gone.

CHAPTER FOUR

"Is it a boy or a girl?"

"A boy, of course. Look at the hair."

"But he doesn't have wings. Is he a mutant?"

"Mura said he's from another realm. Maybe they look different there."

The whispering from the children trying to decide what she was had been going on for some time, but Isemay had tuned it out. The party had moved inside the rock towers, a feature of their world they called the Churss, to wait for Salukis. The sun had long since risen and begun its arc across the sky, turning the night's cool air into a comfortable warmth. They seemed to believe the soldiers from across the valley couldn't reach them here, though Isemay couldn't see why a bunch of towering rocks were much protection. She sat apart from the six children, sullen and unwilling to speak to them, as close to the edge of the Churss as she could get to watch for Salukis and news of her mum. Never in her life had she been so miserable.

"Hush, Neeka, Ballion," Mura chided. "She is a girl, obviously, and our guest. Try to be nice."

"But she's got hair!" one of the children said, as if Mura might be missing an important factor to the argument. "And her skin is all wrong."

"Shh!"

Her tone quieted the group, but Isemay hardly noticed. She heard steps behind her, then Mura sat beside her. When Isemay gave no sign of having seen the Rheunosian, Mura sighed.

"Isemay," she began. "I know what you're going through. I lost someone to the Minothians too. My brother, and now maybe Onni and Cylli too. But I haven't given up hope that I'll see my Dwoon again. You shouldn't give up hope, either."

She wanted to seem grateful, though her heart felt dry and withered, and attempted a weak smile that faded quickly. Her thoughts had been bounding between her mother and father since the dawn. Her mum's nurturing warmth, her da's adoring praise. Symvalline's stern but caring lessons, Ulfric's stoic but devoted indulgences. But despite their love, they had never let her get away with things. She was taught from birth to be a diligent, assiduous, and upright citizen of Vinnr, the kind who might someday become a Knight, a worthy servant of Vaka Aster. Nevertheless, Isemay was naturally stubborn, if precocious. "Impish" was her mother's word. And the traits of strength and wisdom hadn't yet developed in her, because, as her parents so often reminded her, she was still a child.

But that time was over. She had to grow up. Right now. It was up to her to be of service to her parents rather than the other way around. Somehow, she swore to herself, before another night passed in this foreign realm, she'd find a way to help her mum.

Mura spoke again. "It's just past midday. The children are hungry and scared. We need to return to our homes in Maerria and get them to their parents. And we need to meet with Deespora. She'll be able to help. She's an Archon and knows more about the Minothians than anyone."

Through dry lips, Isemay said, "I thought you were going to wait for Salukis."

Mura sighed again and put a comforting hand on Isemay's forearm. From the corner of her eye, Isemay saw the hand change colors to match her own pink-tinged walnut-brown skin. If she hadn't been so upset, and so deeply tired, she would have been astonished. Yet instead she noticed how warm Mura's hand was, and the way she somehow felt a bit of her worry and fear evaporating, as if she'd received news that all would be well. It was a distraction from her distracted state, and she gave in to it, if only briefly.

"He's late," Mura said, "but he'll be on his way. He's too hardheaded to get caught."

"I'm not moving until I know what's happened to my mum."

Mura was silent for a few moments, then said, "I understand. I'll wait with you. Just a moment." She rose and walked back to the children. "Young ones, you should get back to Maerria. I'm going to wait with Isemay a little bit longer for Salukis. Get to the Churss Circle and tell Deespora what we've seen. If you start to get lost, ask the Churss and they will guide you. We'll return by nightfall. Neeka, Ballion, you're in charge. Watch the younger ones."

There was rustling as the children gathered their things, and quiet feet once again approached Isemay. The little girl, Neeka, stood beside her without speaking until Isemay turned her face to look at her.

"I'm sorry about your mother," the little girl said, and the hue of her face, which had been a light, pale tone, shifted like Mura's hand had to match Isemay's own. "You can have my nightcaps." She held out a sisal-like pouch, and Isemay took it.

"My thanks," she mumbled.

The child gave her a sad smile and rushed off to catch up with the rest, who had begun to walk deeper into the stone forest.

Curious, Isemay opened the pouch's flap and reached inside. She pulled out a handful of button-sized bulbs that smelled unlike anything she'd ever come across. Not bad, maybe a bit musty, but with a hint of a spice similar to what the Vinnrics used in sweets.

Mura sat beside her again, and Isemay asked, "What are these?"

"They're nightcaps, and delicious. They only grow by the river we found you and your mother at, and only during the vernal season. That's what we were doing there, though it's forbidden. My people, the Zhallahs, are never to leave the Churss. But we didn't think anyone would see us in the middle of the night. Usually the Minothians don't leave their gatehouse at the entrance of the Tyrn Mountains unless they see someone in the valley. But when the starpath opened, it must have drawn them out, and we were there. So stupid. Deespora is going to have me and Salukis weaving textiles until the next Equifulcrum for this…"

Isemay's stomach rumbled, and she realized she hadn't eaten since the day prior, before everything had gone wrong. "So, do you just eat them raw?" she asked.

Mura nodded, and Isemay popped one in her mouth, chewing cautiously. After a moment, she said, "It's like a mushroom, but sweet."

Mura's expression said she didn't understand exactly what Isemay had said—they must not have had the word "mushroom"—but she nodded again. "See? Delicious. You see why I let the children talk me into risking coming down here."

Isemay wouldn't have called them delicious, but they were edible and took the edge off her hunger. As she ate more, she asked, "What happens if Salukis doesn't come back?"

Mura's eyes, a brilliant green and large like a nocturnal cat's, grew hard, and she didn't look at Isemay. "Deespora will know what to do."

"Mura, why are the Minothians taking your people? Where do they take them?" Isemay was trying to think like her parents, ask strategic questions that would lead her to the answers she needed to find them.

Staring into the distance, Mura reached for a pendant hanging from a fiber band around her neck and began to fiddle with it. "It is complicated, and I'm not sure Deespora would approve of me talking of it. Maybe a story for another time."

Isemay couldn't very well force her host to tell her, and besides, she was too spent to be angry. They returned to silence and she looked closer at Mura's pendant. It was made of stone, the same kind as the Churss towers all around them, with a naturally occurring hole through the center. The edges of the stone had been carved into a delicate design similar to scrollwork.

"That's like mine," she said and drew the memory keeper Ulfric had given her from inside her white, though now very dirty, tunic and over her head.

Mura looked at her own pendant, then to Isemay's. "A Churss talisman. We treasure them here. They bond us with the Churss and remind us of Mithlí's gifts."

"Mine reminds me of my da," Isemay said miserably.

"It's very pretty," Mura offered. "What is that creature it's carved to look like?"

"We call them dragørflies. They are favored by our Verity, Vaka Aster."

"And that crystal in the center, what's it for?"

"My da is a lens maker. He made this for me to show me my memories."

Mura looked confused. "Your people can't remember things without a crystal talisman?"

Isemay half smiled. "No, I mean, it shows me whatever I want to remember if I think about it and focus my thoughts. See these two stones?" She pointed to the klinkí stones, one from each of her parents, that made up the eyes of the dragørfly. "These were my parents' and contain a bit of their Verity spark. It's what we call wysticism."

Mura nodded. "That is very like the Churss. The stones of this forest share Mithlí's vitality, her 'spark,' I think you called it. They protect those who are devoted to her and keep out those who have forgotten or denied her."

Isemay looked sideways at the towering formations and considered this. "Do you mean they can…think?"

"I don't know if that's the right word. They can understand and they can act."

"But I am not of this realm. Or devoted to your Verity. Why am I able to enter the Churss?"

The ridge of bare skin above one of Mura's eyes went up, as if she were cocking an eyebrow. "I don't know. Perhaps they sense something in you they approve of."

Isemay let her gaze fall back on the meadow below them, to the last spot she'd seen her mother. Stone trees that could feel and defend their residents. Men with wings and women with skin that shifted in hue according to either whim or emotion. A sky with three moons and mushrooms that tasted more like sweet bread than plant. It was all so different from her home. Yet one thing was the same. There was still enmity between different peoples. And Isemay and her mother were now part of that strife, like it or not.

She turned the memory keeper over in her hand. Looking into the crystal, she thought about calling up some memory of her family to make her feel better. As she considered it, a light suddenly flared within it, brilliantly blue and yellow, swirling.

"Huh?" she squeaked. She'd said no focusing charm nor called up any memory.

The crystal's inner light began to brighten. Then, as clearly as if he stood before her, she saw her father's face. Isemay shot to her feet.

"Isemay?" he said, looking directly at her.

"Da! Is that you?" she cried. "Is it really you? Not a memory? How… where are you? I was so worried you were—" But she couldn't give voice to that fear, the fear he might have been dead. Because he wasn't. He was safe! He could help her and Mum!

She saw his hand reaching toward her, so tiny in the crystal, yet she almost reached back just to feel the safety of his rough fingers and hardened palms holding her own hand.

"Are you safe, Crumb? Where is Symvalline?"

"I-I don't know. Mum and I are in Arc Rheunos. There are people here who've helped me, but Da, Mum was-was taken." But the face of the crystal grew cloudy, and he was fading. "Da!" she cried, but he was gone, and the light inside the memory keeper vanished.

She held the pendant tightly and shook it, hoping somehow it would bring him back. She could feel tears welling in her eyes, her heart seeming to swell into a hot, painful stone in her chest that threatened to drag her to the ground. Gritting her teeth, she promised herself she would not cry, not in front of this stranger in this strange realm. She became like her heart, stone, still burning but resolute.

"Salukis! Thank Mithlí, he made it back."

Mura's voice cut through the tenuous control Isemay wrestled with, pulling her from her pain. She looked out over the meadow and saw his form coming toward them, his wings making him look uncannily like a bruhawk. He landed beside them moments later.

After a brief quizzical look at Isemay, he spoke to Mura. "Is she okay?"

Mura shook her head faintly, and after a moment, Salukis went on. "We need to get to Deespora. I overheard Archon Tuzhazu speaking with the Vinnric woman. Deespora is right, after the Equifulcrum the Minothians are going to attack us."

"You saw my mother?" Isemay jumped in. "Is she hurt? Is she in danger?"

"She was unharmed, but the Archon did not seem to like her much. They're taking her to Everlight Hall to meet Akeeva."

"Don't worry too much, Isemay," Mura tried reassuring her. "Arc Rheunosians, even the people of Minoth, do not believe in harming other living things. Your mother may be held captive, but they won't hurt her."

She saw the uncertain look Mura shot Salukis. "Then why," she asked, "did he just say they were going to attack you?"

Both the Zhallahs' faces grew uncertain then.

Without answering her, Salukis said, "Let's get home, Mura."

CHAPTER FIVE

The light outside had brightened and darkened twice while Symvalline was carted by wagon toward her next place of imprisonment, Everlight Hall, which lay somewhere within the mountain range. She could see very little through the narrow cracks between the planks of the wooden sides, back, and roof of the wagon bed. Locked away tight, her time was occupied by nothing but waiting to arrive.

For nearly the entire journey, the rolling of the wagon wheels and murmur of voices when her captors spoke outside had sounded closed in, as if they were traveling along a narrow tunnel. A ravine that led deeper into the mountain range, perhaps, though it had seemed endless. She'd overheard her Minothian captors call them the Tyrn Mountains.

Only one thing distracted her from the tedium of her captivity. She wasn't alone. Her two companions, also prisoners, were a woman and her little girl. On occasion, she heard the Minothian guards speaking of another prison wagon as well. These mountain-dwelling Arc Rheunosians seemed to be quite adept at taking others captive. Tuzhazu had been vague when she'd fished for information about the

Zhallahs she'd met in the valley. Had some of them been caught after all?

The woman and child with Symvalline had spent most of the first day and night huddled as far away from her in the wagon bed as they could get, as if she would infect them with the plague everyone in this realm was so clearly terrified of. Symvalline, too troubled by circumstances, had not tried to speak to them before, but as the ordeal went on, she decided there was no reason to let the silence continue.

"Lady Rheunosian, please understand, I am not going to harm you," she said, trying to reassure them, troubled to be anyone's source of fear. "I'm just a traveler from Vinnr, and a Knight Corporealis, duty-bound to serve the Verities and makers of our different worlds. Long before that, I was a healer. I don't know what our captors have told you, but I am not a plague-bringer or anything like that. You don't need to be afraid of me."

She caught the woman's eyes beneath the hood of the cloak she wore. They shone brightly, studying Symvalline, though she clasped her child a bit more tightly. After a moment, she said, "You're a healer?"

"I am, trained by the Resplendolent Conservatum, though you probably don't know what that is."

The woman pushed her hood back, giving Symvalline a better look at her. Her skin was sallow, the same brown hue as the wood of the wagon, but tinged with a pale yellow. Even her irises shared the sickly color.

"Are you ill?" Symvalline asked.

The woman shook her head, then pulled the wrap that covered her child from the child's head and shoulders. "Tulla is feverish. I fear she has..." She trailed off, but Symvalline knew exactly what the woman feared.

"May I?" she asked, beginning to scoot toward them.

The woman hesitated, then nodded assent. Symvalline put her wrist to the child's forehead, then checked her breathing, looked into her eyes, and even had the child show her the inside of her mouth. The lighting was bad, but there was no doubt the child was ill. Her skin was yellowish as well, flushing red wherever Symvalline laid her hands.

Unusually, different colors cycled along her body, too, from a weak blue to an orange-white, as if the child's skin were a prism through which light was refracting into its many unique colors, though the little girl seemed to have no control of it. Along her cheekbones and in the hollows below her eyes, a redness that didn't change color even when her hue shifted elsewhere was blooming, the edges becoming scabbed. Symvalline guessed this symptom would manifest on other parts of her body too.

"How long has she been like this?" she asked.

"Since just after the Deathless caught us outside the Aktoktos Gate. Three days ago. I've tried to tender her, but it doesn't last. I took Tulla away from Minoth because…" She stopped herself, glancing guiltily at Symvalline, then went on. "Archon Tuzhazu questioned us about whether we'd had any contact with the Zhallahs, and Tulla grew sick shortly after that. They would have brought us back to Minoth sooner, but you arrived." The woman gently caressed her child's head, worry creasing the skin around her eyes and mouth. "I swear, we never saw a single one of those plague-bringers. I don't know how Tulla could have caught it. And I haven't got it."

"Do you mean that the Zhallah people are the ones who spread this illness?" she asked.

"They are cursed. That's why they're exiled beyond the Aktoktos Gate."

"I don't understand," Symvalline said kindly. "If the Zhallah can make you sick, why did you leave your home and make for theirs?" *And why did the Zhallahs think Isemay and I were these plague-bringers?*

"I wasn't going to Maerria, where they live inside the Churss. I would have gone north, away from Minoth and the Zhallahs to raise Tulla myself."

"Why can't you raise her in your own city?"

That guilty look passed over her face again. "Because Mithlí the Everlight takes all the children to raise herself. Maybe I deserve to be punished for breaking the Everlight's law, but I just wanted to be Tulla's mother forever." She grimaced sorrowfully. "Instead I've condemned her to death."

The woman began to sniff, hiding her tears and hugging her listless daughter. Symvalline sat back, giving the woman room for her grief. She badly wanted to do something for the little girl, but there was nothing she could do without her medicines or a Fenestros. She watched the two for a moment, then decided she had to try something and began banging on the wagon's wall.

"Guards. Guards!"

The wagon came to a slow stop, and a small round port in the wooden walls of their cage was opened in the front. A Minothian woman looked at her. "What is it?"

"This child is sick. She needs water and I need my medicine bag to try to give her ease."

The woman eyed her for a moment, then slid the portal cover closed with a snap. The wagon bounced a bit as the guard stepped down from the front, and footsteps trailed away. Symvalline couldn't make out the words but heard the murmurs of a nearby conversation. Soon, two sets of booted feet approached, and the lock and bar holding the rear wagon door were removed. The mother pulled her child forward to sit beside Symvalline. She seemed less afraid than cautious of her captors.

The Archon stood there, his face in full sunlight, making the dark umber lines crossing his skin contrast starkly against his lighter complexion. His eyes gleamed at them, their color a silvery green unlike any Symvalline had seen beyond the hue that sometimes swirled in the bruhawks' eyes when under Safran's sway. His stare drilled into her, and despite herself, she was intimidated by the cruelty she could see in their depths. Or was it something worse, like a twisted and insatiable hunger?

"You want this, Vinnric?" he asked, holding up her herb pouch.

"This woman's child needs treatment, she's very unwell. I have things in my bag that could help her."

"So, you're a healer and a Verity servant?"

"I am. Please, there is nothing in that pouch that can harm anyone." This was altogether untrue. Many of the powders and herbs, if properly mixed, could create effects that would lead to all sorts of unwanted outcomes—unwanted to the recipient. Such as the poison that tipped the darts of her arm-mounted crossbow. But they wouldn't know that.

"That child has the Waste and is as good as Cosmos dust. Her mother"—he looked pointedly at the woman—"should have known better than to travel outside the safety of our boundaries. The Zhallahs are crafty and spread their disease in hidden ways." He beckoned to someone unseen. "You can have water."

"Please—" she tried, but the Archon had already paced away. She looked to the child's mother. "I'm sorry. They are taking me to see Mithlí when we reach our destination. I will beg the Verity to remedy her. You have my word."

Two small wooden drums of water were passed to them and the wagon door closed and barred. As Symvalline helped the woman pour a cup, she heard another conversation outside, held in quiet tones. The wagon jounced as the driver mounted the bench, then they began moving again. A short time later, the port to the driver slid open. A woman's hand reached through, holding a stoppered container about the size of Symvalline's finger.

The driver's voice slid to Symvalline's ears like a secret. "Give the girl a few shakes of this in water. It will make her sleepy but should help her suffering some. And say nothing about it. Nothing, understand?"

"I will not," Symvalline promised.

The journey continued.

CHAPTER SIX

Walking through the Churss gave Isemay plenty of time to feel her sorrow, but the stone forest struck her with awe and took some of the sting out of it. The towers of rounded stones, glittering with flecks of a different shimmering substance, rose like monoliths, thick boulders at their bases and tapering toward the tops. Vines and other flowering flora climbed the stone towers, creating a canopy of green and gray and multicolored blooms that was unlike anything she'd ever seen. The Churss was alive with birdsong and the hum of different insects. It could have been a treed forest for all its growth and life, but for the fact that these "trees" were nothing but rock.

"Should we worry about any dangerous animals?" she asked the Zhallahs, not really believing anything threatening could live amid such a strange and beautiful landscape.

"We try to stay away from the urzidae when they're rearing their cubs. They are protective," Mura said. "But the Zhallah live harmoniously with the Churss and its other creatures. It keeps us safe, and we are grateful."

Salukis, who seemed to travel on foot grudgingly, asked, "What is the Churss like where you're from?"

"Our forests have trees," Isemay said. "And in the Howling Weald there are still dragørs who will eat anything that's smaller than they are, which is everything, but we don't have anything like this in Vinnr. At least, not that I know of."

The farthest she'd been from Asteryss was Magdaster, in the north, which was bordered by the Howling Weald, a vast forest spanning the entire north of Vinnr. But she'd been too small then to remember it and had spent the last few years begging her parents to take her back. The rigor of studies at the Conservatum had kept her in place, however, and her parents had grown too busy to take Isemay traveling and more and more preoccupied with maintaining cordial diplomatic relations with the problematic Arch Keeper Beatte, who pressed all the time for more access to Vaka Aster's vessel.

But I'm traveling now, farther than I could have dreamed, to a place even more fascinating than even the Howling Weald, in its way.

They crossed a wide stream using a series of perfectly placed boulders in the water as their bridge, then their path bent to the right into a denser stand of stone towers, where the foliage grew thick and heavy and the light dimmed. In the gloom, Isemay's toe hit an unseen rock.

"Oof!" She stumbled forward, planting a hand accidentally against one of Salukis's folded wings. Its velvety texture felt smooth as water under her palm. "Sorry about that," she murmured.

He looked over his shoulder to check on her. "All right?" After she nodded, he looked toward the sky and said, "Bit of light, please."

A slow grinding sound, like a knife sliding across a whetstone, began above them. Startled, Isemay looked up and gasped. Above and around them, the tower had begun to move. First the capstones arched sideways away from the path they were following, the tangle of vines and mosses clinging to them shifting with ease, then the base stones too began to slide across the forest floor. Isemay gave out a squeak of fear and pushed her back against Salukis's, staring wide-eyed as the living rock forest went about complying with his request.

He took a step away and turned to face her. "You really don't have Churss, do you? Don't worry, Vinnric, they are friends to those who are friends to the Verities. And to us Zhallahs, of course."

"S-so Mura told me. I just didn't imagine...*this*." She had no trouble now understanding how the Churss protected the Zhallahs. Any people who could command the very stones of the realm would have, it would seem, nothing to fear.

Light flooded their footpath, and Mura led on. Isemay quickly got over her fright and reached out tentatively, then eagerly, to run her fingers over a few of the boulders as they passed. The stones felt like nothing but stone, except for a faint tingle in the tips of her fingers, like one felt when touching something recently lightning-struck. Or something consecrated by a Verity.

"It's wonderful," she whispered.

The Arc Rheunosian sun, not terribly different from Halla, was directly overhead when the spaces between the stone towers began to widen, and Isemay noticed more and more footpaths branching from the one they were on. Soon, she could hear the sounds of people, voices, instruments, typical village sounds of banging, cutting, building. They passed a few sparsely spaced stone huts that were arched like phanx mounds, with open window frames and doorways hung with woven screens. This must be the outskirts of their village of Maerria.

Before they reached the village proper, three more Zhallahs could be seen coming from ahead. Once they saw Mura and Salukis, they rushed toward them. Isemay grew still behind Salukis, trying to prepare herself for becoming the object of inquiry she knew she was bound to be.

The trio had two animals unlike any Isemay had ever seen with them, standing about knee-high with ropey black fur so long and thick it was hard to tell where the things' legs attached to their torsos or even where their eyes were in the lumpy mat. Horns curled down the sides of their heads in a corkscrew pattern, and stumpy, fluffy tails whisked behind them. The creatures spotted Salukis and bounded to him, jumping up excitedly and making noises that sounded to Isemay like sheep choking, but Salukis responded to them by smiling and scratching their heads between their horns.

A woman hurried to Mura and wrapped her in a relieved embrace, and a tidy, neatly dressed older-looking man stopped short, eyeing Salukis. "Reckless, son, very reckless," he said.

The other man spoke up. "Your mother wants me to clip your wings, Salukis Engzu. You had us all worried to death."

Salukis grew sheepish, at a loss for words, and for the first time, Isemay realized he was nearly her age, not the confident adult he played at being.

The woman, her skin a mellow sunflower color, released Mura, whose own color had changed to match. "Neeka and Ballion and the other children told us what happened." She gave Mura a glance that spoke of something deeper than disapproval. "After Dwoon…I don't know how you could do this, Mura. And now Onni and Cylli…"

"I'm sorry, mother, I am. I know better. But it's just…I don't know how to explain it. I feel closer to Dwoon when I'm out there. Like maybe someday…someday he might come back."

The woman hugged Mura tightly, neither of them speaking. Isemay looked away, feeling as if she were infringing on a moment she had no business in.

"But you're home safe now," Mura's mother said after a moment. She let go of Mura and turned to look curiously at Isemay. "Please, introduce us to this young, ah, woman?"

Mura held her hand out to Isemay. "Mother, Browan, Drevor, meet Isemay of Vinnr. Daughter of two members of the Archons of her realm and protectors of their Verity, Vaka Aster."

Their eyes fell on her, and with a deep breath, she stepped forward. "Hello."

The one named Browan, Salukis's father, stepped forward and held his hands up with his palms splayed before Isemay. She didn't know what to do. Mura stepped forward and pressed her palms to his, intertwining their fingers, then looked to Isemay. "It's our way of welcoming each other."

She let go, and Isemay, a bit shyly, copied the gesture. His hands were very rough.

"Welcome, Vinnric," Browan said. "We Zhallahs are very sorry to hear about the circumstances in which you were introduced to Arc Rheunos. But come with us. We've been waiting for you so you can meet Archon Raamuzi."

He turned and began to walk up the path. Isemay looked uncertainly to Mura, who gave her a reassuring smile and beckoned her to follow. As they passed the man called Drevor, he reached out a hand and pinched Salukis's ear, tugging painfully. "You have some very serious apologies to make to your aunt."

Salukis groaned. "I had to do something to try to help the Vinnrics!"

"And now you'll have to do something to build a new wall around Phaemee's garden," his uncle promised.

Salukis groaned louder and followed behind.

As they walked, the village grew around them. Assorted rock homes and other structures rose from the ground and protruded from the Churss at all levels in ways that seemed as if they were as natural as any other part of the stone forest. Some of the structures soared so far overhead that Isemay had to crane her neck to see them. She wondered if the rocks that seemed to be their primary building material were "living" in the way the towers seemed to be. Did they actually have to build or did they simply ask the rocks to create homes, a smithy, and various storage structures and other buildings? Based on Salukis's groan at his uncle's promise he'd be building a garden wall, it appeared probably not.

Zhallahs bustled about the town, some flying amid the high structures, some walking along the earth, the men all winged and the women all smooth-skinned and multicolored. Everyone stopped to stare curiously at Isemay as she passed, and she did her best to remain stoic like her father, to seem as if she were more than a frightened and isolated foreigner. She assured herself that their leader would know how to help her mother. And if the leader, whom they called Archon Raamuzi, didn't, she would return to the valley that separated her from her mum and keep going into the mountains beyond until she found a way. They wouldn't hold her here against her will if she chose to leave, would they? If she was lucky, her father would speak to her again soon through the memory keeper. The moment she had a chance, she would try to contact him. She hadn't known the pendant was capable of such a trick, but it was a thin string of hope she now clung to.

In the village's center, they came to a circular open-topped wall that spanned wide enough to contain the whole party she now walked with and then some. Churss towers crowded the wall at every angle, and platforms jutted out from their sides, rising up their heights, giving even more people the option of viewing inside the wall from above. Birdlike creatures, most feathered but some not, of many varieties lined the top of the circle, facing outward like sentries. A round entryway made of a massive Churss boulder containing a natural hole through its center served as an entryway.

Isemay's party passed inside, and she found the ground was covered with a densely woven mat of living vines, creating a soft, spongy surface to walk on. A woman sat in the center, surrounded by several older Zhallahs. At the entrance of Isemay's group, everyone turned to them.

"The visitor from Vinnric," the woman in the center said and rose from her seat on the ground, using a stout wooden staff to assist her.

Isemay's eyes fixed on the staff. Its head contained a single perfectly round orb. It was the color of alpine water and shot through with lines that looked like lightning. It was a Fenestros, it had to be.

The woman began walking toward her, and Isemay noted her coloring was the same as the orb's, her hue steady, not shifting like most of the women Isemay had seen. It gave her a wystic aspect, as if she was a Verity's living vessel. Isemay hoped for a moment that she was, but she knew it was unlikely.

"Don't be afraid, young Vinnric. We are a peaceful people," the Archon said, still approaching, and Isemay realized she'd come to a halt.

She made herself move forward again and met the woman in a few strides, then held out her hands the way Browan had shown her. Deespora grasped them with her free hand, staring into her eyes. "They've told me your name is Isemay. You may call me Deespora."

"Are you…just a person?" Isemay asked and instantly felt foolish. What kind of question was that?

To her relief, Deespora gave her a small grin. "No more, no less," she confirmed. Her voice was as cool as the tone of her skin, but not unfriendly. "I see my appearance may have led you to think I was the vessel of Mithlí. Sadly, I am not."

"I'm sorry if that was rude," she said shyly. "The Fenestros..." She looked meaningfully at Deespora's staff.

The Zhallah leader followed her gaze, then nodded. "Come, sit with us. Everyone here would like to know more about how you came to be in Arc Rheunos."

She led Isemay's group to where she'd been sitting, and they took their places among the other Zhallahs. Salukis was rubbing his ear, and Mura looked stricken with sadness and perhaps guilt.

Isemay had the impression that the assembled Zhallahs were a kind of council. At Deespora's prompting, she told them what she knew about the goings-on in Vinnr: the attack by an airborne enemy that came after her da had met with Balavad of Battgjald, Knight Evernal's warning that the Knights protect Vaka Aster's vessel at Mount Omina, the avalanche that had nearly overcome her and her mum followed by the menacing Battgjaldics who'd been about to attack them, and then their sudden starpath trip to this realm. The Zhallah council members asked her many questions about Balavad, none of which she could answer, and she chided herself inwardly again for paying so little attention to important affairs. What kind of Knight would she be one day if she couldn't even focus on what mattered?

One of the council members spoke up when her story was through. "The Menace is threatening realms beyond ours now."

"So it seems," Deespora agreed. "Salukis Engzu, tell us what you learned when you followed the Vinnric woman, Isemay's mother."

Salukis sat up straight. "The Minothian guards were so distracted that it was fairly easy for me to sneak up to the tower on the outer gate walls, where they were holding the Vinnric. They're about as smart as—"

"Don't inflate the story with hubris, Lukis. Just tell us what happened," his father warned.

Salukis's face flushed red to match his ear. He went on, this time humbly. "Archon Tuzhazu came to question her, but she didn't tell him much. She asked him to release her and to let her use the Arc

Rheunos Scrylle and a Fenestros so she could return to her realm." Salukis paused, thinking. "He was on edge about something, I couldn't tell you what, and when she wouldn't tell him what he wanted to know, he threatened her"—he looked quickly to Isemay—"but he didn't hurt her. He just said he had time because the Equifulcrum was still days away."

With a weight of seriousness in his expression that made him appear older, he looked at Deespora. "Archon Raamuzi, I think it's true. Tuzhazu is going to use the changing of vessels at the Equifulcrum to make the Minothians believe he's the new living Verity, and then he's going to spread more lies among them about us. The Minothians are too foolish—they'll believe he's the Everlight and follow any command he gives, even if it's to harm us here in Maerria." His voice cracked as he finished.

The assembled Zhallahs listened in silence, and Deespora regarded him steadily. "Did you hear Tek Det say they were going to attack us?" she asked.

"...Not in those words," Salukis said.

"Salukis, we will be safe in the Churss, as we have always been," she assured him.

"Deespora," an older Zhallah man said, "what if the Minothians find a way to overcome the Churss or to control it? What if the Menace has given them a new weapon?"

Another man nodded in agreement and said, "Eventually we will need to unite our peoples again. It is not fate's wish that we hide forever. Does the Scrylle offer any ideas on how to protect ourselves from Balavad or other Verities who mean us ill?"

Isemay caught the glance the man who was speaking shot her.

"No, Poolan," Deespora said. "But what more could we need but the Churss and all the life of Arc Rheunos to assist us? Life will always face death. If it is the Verity's will that we be subsumed by the Minothian throne-sitter, then that is our fate."

"But it is *not* the Verity's will," a woman objected. "And more of our children have been taken. We can't just forget them, we must—"

Deespora held up a hand, cutting her off. "We shall discuss that at another time. For now," she looked to Isemay, "we will see how we can assist our guest."

Seeing her opportunity, Isemay didn't hesitate. "Help my mum. Get her out of that place so we can go home."

The Archon looked at her sadly. "I wish we could."

Desperately, Isemay cast a look toward Mura, whose own expression looked stricken.

Mura said, "Her mother saved Neeka from them. Isn't there something we can do?"

"And she killed a Deathless," Salukis blurted.

Everyone looked at him.

"Killed a Deathless Guard?" Deespora said, her tone grave.

"Yes, he was going to attack us. She—she did it to help us get away."

"The Vinnric should have submitted before she took another's life. The Arc Rheunosians do not kill. That is our deepest, most cherished law."

Isemay didn't like the accusation in the Archon's tone. "My mum and I are not Arc Rheunosian. When someone tries to hurt us, we stop them in whatever way is necessary." As she said it, she could feel the judgmental stares of the older Zhallahs.

Deespora's mouth turned downward, carving deep lines in her face. "That leads to one thing. War. And war is death and suffering. Does your realm accept suffering as a way of life?"

"No! But how is submitting any better than suffering?" Around her, the group peppered each other with mutters and grumbling, driving home how foolish her hasty words were. She flushed and tried to backpedal. "I'm sorry, but I'm just trying to understand why you won't help someone who helped some of you..." She trailed off, feeling slightly ill. These people weren't going to help her. They seemed not only unwilling but possibly incapable.

Deespora's tone evened out as she spoke. "Understand, Isemay, that your ways and our ways are not the same. We are a peaceful people. Even the Minothians, though their peaceable ways have become warped since the Menace visited our realm. Fighting them won't change them. Nor will we allow ourselves to become the violence we shun, even to live. You're too young, and not one of us. It may be that you don't have the wisdom to grasp what I mean. Nevertheless, our only masters are time and the Verities. Refusing to submit to them leads to suffering. Accepting them allows us to live in harmony with them." She reached into an embroidered bag that was slung over her shoulder. "Now, there is something I can do for you." Her hand emerged holding a narrow silvery scepter.

"Your Scrylle," Isemay said, confused.

"Yes. It would be for the best if I help you return to Vinnr by starpath, the same way you came here."

"But what about my mum?"

"As I said, there's nothing we can do for her."

Isemay went cold. "No. I'm not leaving without her."

Deespora eyed her, then seemed to come to a decision. "We will not refuse you hospitality. You may stay with us for a time. Perhaps the Minothians and your mother will send for you. Or maybe they'll release her to join you." She turned to Mura's mother. "Lysis, would you be willing to provide our guest with a safe haven for now?"

Lysis nodded her consent.

Deespora tucked the Scrylle away and rose, once again using the staff bearing the Fenestros to aid her. "We shall adjourn for the day. Tonight, we'll celebrate our visitor from another realm and give thanks that she is among us to shine the light of knowledge from distant corners of the Great Cosmos. This is fortuitous. As we Zhallahs know, we are not alone in the Cosmos. We all share the gift of being part of the Verities' creations."

CHAPTER SEVEN

Symvalline knew they'd arrived at some kind of plain or valley based on the way the clatter of the Minothian party and their mounts had stopped echoing against close walls. And with the change in geography, she sensed a quickening of their pace. They must be getting close to Everlight Hall.

The child had shown no improvement, but neither had she worsened. The two Minothian prisoners had remained on their side of the wagon, saying very little since they'd been given water. Food was also provided, but Symvalline had given all her share to the woman. She could go much longer without eating than an average person, thanks to the endurance provided by her Verity gifts. She hoped the extra portion would give the woman and her child the strength they needed to face what was coming.

After a time, the wagon ventured onto a stone-paved road, eventually coming to a stop. Heralds called from somewhere above, and someone among her captors' party returned the call. She heard the crank of a giant winch and the grind as a ramp was lowered or a gate raised. Then the wagon continued inside what she assumed from the sound was the curtain wall of a fortress or castle.

As their journey neared its end, she reconfirmed her promise to the woman. "What is your name? I will speak to the Verity on your and Tulla's behalf."

"Agatha Pahzi."

The wagon stopped and the wagon door was unbarred. A guard beckoned to Agatha. "You two, come with me." To Symvalline, he said, "Wait."

Then they were gone.

She was not left alone for long. When Tuzhazu came for her, he had her hands bound behind her and a blindfold tied over her eyes. Fury burned within her, but she kept it under control. Without her klinkí stones and Mentalios, she could do little to change the situation in her favor, other than keep her wits and use her skills of reasoning and negotiation. She wished for Safran, who had so much more practice at the latter part. She wished for Stave and Eisa, who would likely have already broken this wagon to pieces and perhaps defeated the entire troop of captors singlehandedly. She wished for Roi and his calm calculation. But mostly, she wished for Ulfric. He was her heart and the greatest leader the Knights Corporealis had ever had.

By now it was apparent that some kind of rift had taken place in this realm. The Zhallahs had called her and Crumb "plague-bringers" but seemed to quickly realize they were not a threat. Tuzhazu claimed the Zhallahs caused the plague, or the Waste, as she'd also heard it called. Whatever the disease was, it seemed to be the cause of the strife and division of this realm.

What troubled her the most, however, was not the divided kingdoms. Vinnr itself had broken into three during the War of Rivening. It was inevitable that anything large enough would eventually fracture under its own weight, and that included kingdoms. It was the fact that the Arc Rheunosian Knights, or Archons, themselves were also divided.

The Zhallahs they'd met, mostly children, had intended to take her to someone called Archon Raamuzi for help. They had shown her and Crumb kindness and offered sanctuary, and Symvalline's instinct told her such people's leader would also be honorable and compassionate, the kind of Archon who would not shirk their duty to serve and protect their Verity, while also capable of benevolence and sympathy to the Verities' wider creations. But the Minothian Archon served the Arc Rheunosian Verity directly here in the Minothian stronghold. And he had so far demonstrated far less benevolence. He gave her the impression that Minoth, and the Archons who lived here, were callous, possibly even corrupt, people. And if it was true their Verity was here, she could only conclude one thing: Mithlí was, like Balavad seemed to be, at best a cold and detached Verity. And at worst, a cruel one.

This did not give her much hope for her meeting with the celestial creator.

"Move along, Vinnric. Your audience with Mithlí awaits." Tuzhazu's tone had a sardonic grate to it, setting Symvalline further on edge.

She stumbled forward, finding it difficult to keep her balance on the unfamiliar ground while blindfolded. As she slowed her pace, a guard nudged her in the back, and the second time it happened she fell forward to a knee, bruising it. Someone yanked her up, and she cursed at them.

"Verities fiery eyes, if you keep pushing me, I'll forget I'm a healer. If you want me to move faster, remove this troghopping blindfold."

Tuzhazu grumbled. "Kaneas, take her to the Everlight's balcony and hold her there until I arrive."

"Yes, Archon."

Symvalline felt thick arms reach beneath hers and grasp her around the chest. There was a gush of air and a sudden jerk, and her feet left the ground before she could demand to be released. She was being carried upward by a winged soldier, the sensation disconcerting and unwelcome.

Moments later, her feet once more struck solid ground. "Get off!" she yelled and took several paces forward to escape the guard's grasp.

"My maker," she heard him say reverently.

Then a new voice spoke. "Unbind her, then leave us, Kaneas."

Symvalline's blindfold and the rope on her wrists were removed, and the guard swiftly retreated over the side of the balcony. She blinked away the haze from being blindered, then looked to the speaker. "And who are you?" she asked.

The woman who stood before her was much more distinct than those she'd met thus far. Brawny, tall, the colors of her skin a constantly shifting rainbow that grew so pale in places she looked like white marble. Her eyes, too, shifted colors, swirling in an entrancing dance that Symvalline had trouble looking away from. She wore a richly embroidered sleeved tunic with a belt that fit snugly over wide hips and carried no visible weapons.

"Don't you know a Verity when you meet one, foreigner?" Her words were clipped, but not a challenge.

"I do. And you aren't." Symvalline realized she was already losing her clutch on diplomacy and amiability, but she was teetering on the brink of not caring.

The woman smirked, an expression that reminded Symvalline of Tuzhazu. Everyone here seemed to find something funny about Symvalline's ignorance.

The woman paced closer to her, unhesitant and deliberate. Symvalline stood her ground. What choice did she have? She was not one to cower, and if seven hundred years as a Knight had taught her anything, it was that she could endure almost any challenge that was thrown at her.

"An Archon from Vinnr," the tall woman said, eyeing her. "I know little of your realm, but based on your appearance, we are not so different."

Symvalline, in no mood for chitchat, moved the conversation to where she most needed it to go. "You'll forgive me if I seem curt, but I've been held against my will and treated like a criminal for over two days, with no reason and no explanation. I was told I'd have an audience with Mithlí. May I impress on you how important the matter is? There are lives at stake, and I must speak with your Verity."

"And what do you want of me?" the woman said.

Confused, Symvalline fumbled for a moment. "You? Nothing. You're an Archon, if my guess is right, not—"

"I am what the people of Arc Rheunos believe me to be."

What was going on here? Was she implying—? "You mean, you pretend to be your maker? But...why?"

Steps approached from outside the chamber's large set of doors, and a Minothian woman entered, her head bowed reverently. The Archon turned. "Food and drink. Enough to welcome our Vinnric"—she turned to Symvalline—"Knight? That's what you call yourselves, isn't it?" After Symvalline nodded, the Archon finished, "Now."

The servant departed, and Symvalline found herself once more under the Minothian's scrutiny. The woman said, "Let me ask you a question. How long has it been since you spoke with your Verity?"

"It has been hundreds of turns," Symvalline replied simply, assuming subterfuge would be pointless. The woman's eyes seemed to see straight into her, a sense similar to looking into a Scrylle. They were wise, but deep inside their shifting layers, there seemed to be a darkness or a pain that Symvalline could almost feel.

"So Vaka Aster has abandoned you." It was a statement, not the smallest gap at its edges for argument. "And since then, what calamities and troubles has your realm faced?"

Now Symvalline did hesitate. There was no doubt where these questions were leading, but she saw no point to them. "The Verities do not interfere in the lives of their creations. You imply they should, that troubles we bring on ourselves should be resolved by our makers. That's ridiculous. If people faced no consequences for our mistakes, we would forever be helpless and ignorant."

The earlier servant and another returned and laid several things to eat and drink on a small table they brought with them. When they were gone, the Archon gestured to the libations. "You must be hungry after your journey. I have never traveled by starpath and am curious if it is taxing."

Symvalline remained in place. "And you call yourself a Verity."

An authentic smile crossed her face. "My name, my true name, is Archon Akeeva Raamuzi. I've been a guardian of our vessel for lifetimes. It doesn't matter how many. But I have been Mithlí to my people since the last Equifulcrum." She gestured to the far end of the chamber, which opened to the outside balcony. "Follow me."

They crossed the room and stepped out. For the first time, Symvalline was able to look over the vista of her surroundings. She wanted to stretch and bend her cramped muscles, to complain about her rough treatment, but there was no point. Instead, she stood stiffly beside the foreigner and took in the vast valley spread out before her. It encompassed a village twice the size of Asteryss. In the distance, she could make out farmlands and rolling foothills that rose to more terraced farms growing up the mountainsides. Two of the moons, one red the other blue, stood out faintly in the sky, and she could make out just a hint of the third, like a ghost on the horizon. They were closer to each other than the night she and Isemay had arrived.

"The Equifulcrum is twelve days from now. In our tradition Mithlí changes vessels then and will take the form of one of the Archons who volunteers for the honor. This was our way for as far back as we Arc Rheunosians existed, until…" Her eyes shifted toward the faint outlines of the realm's three moons. "The last Equifulcrum."

She stepped back inside to the table and poured herself a cup of amber liquid. With her back to Symvalline, she said, "Our world was ending, our people were dying in great numbers. We called it the Great Waste. A sickness with no cure. Families rent apart. Children dying in their parents' arms." She paused, then gulped the drink.

Symvalline took one last look over the balcony handrail. The court-yard below was too far. Even if she survived a jump, she'd break and rupture too many things to walk away from it. Then she'd be useless to Isemay for an untold length of time. She would have to find another way to escape the Minothians. Walking away from the railing, she stopped just inside the chamber.

Akeeva placed her cup down and faced Symvalline. "And where was Mithlí as her creations suffered and died? I'll let you guess." She watched Symvalline closely, the colors of her face and hand flushing from magenta to burgundy to a dusky gray, like the eye of a hurricane at twilight.

The reason for the pain she'd seen buried in the woman's eyes came to Symvalline. "How old was your child when you lost her?" she asked.

"Children, Vinnric. I lost three children. One after another. And all I wanted was to die with them. But Mithlí even took that option from me."

Symvalline observed her quietly. An Archon who led the people of her realm to believe she was the living vessel—it seemed inconceivable. The fiction would crumble the moment the true vessel or the Verity in her celestial form chose to appear. The price for such a betrayal would be equally inconceivable. So why would Akeeva take such a risk, betraying not only her maker but her duty and oath as well? Her children would never come back, no matter what Akeeva tried or what disloyalties she was willing to commit.

And where was Mithlí's true vessel?

"The people of Arc Rheunos were once much more numerous than just those who live in this valley," Akeeva went on. "We were spread across the realm. But the Waste took it all away. Hundreds of thousands died. Whole families, cities. Minoth closed itself off from the rest to try to protect a few. But even with our lands barred, the mountains serving as our stronghold, the Waste finds us at times. Brought by any who come from outside. Like the Zhallahs, or"—she looked Symvalline dead in the eye—"other foreigners."

Symvalline wanted to scoff, but she held it back. "I'm no plague-bringer."

Light flashed off the steel-tipped hooks of Tuzhazu's wings as he walked into the room. Akeeva turned to him.

"You've been informed?" he asked her, not looking at Symvalline.

"The runner arrived a few hours before you. Our guest and I have been discussing her options."

"She may serve some purpose or have some ends she hasn't revealed. We must keep her locked away from the people. Who knows what diseases she may carry."

"No," Symvalline broke in. "I have no intention of meddling in your affairs, and I'm not a danger to anyone. I must return to Vinnr. I only ask for you to open a starpath and send me home after I—" She cut herself off. How could she tell them of Isemay without giving them more leverage over her?

Tuzhazu continued without even a glance toward Symvalline, as if she weren't there. "Balavad may have use for her. She said he's come to the Vinnric realm as well."

At the mention of Balavad, Akeeva's eyes flashed yellow, predatory like a bruhawk's. She faced Symvalline. "What do you know of the Battgjald Verity?"

Fighting against the cracks spreading through her composure, Symvalline took a deep breath. "He came to Vinnr in disguise, calling himself His Holiness Prime. His forces usurped my home kingdom, Yor, then started to infiltrate Ivoryss, the seat of my Order. My...our leader tried to stop him, but Balavad's forces attacked Ivoryss and besieged the Knights at the sanctuary of Vaka Aster's vessel. I was isolated and outnumbered in the attack, and then, somehow, I was sent through the starpath and ended up here. I honestly don't know who opened the starpath, why I was sent through, or where the rest of my Order is now. The one thing I do know is that Balavad is a calculating, malicious celestial. He has ends that I don't yet understand, though it involves the Syzycki Elementum. Our Scrylle is not detailed enough to show what this means or what it is, but if you return me to my realm, I can learn more. There's a chance that what I learn could be of benefit to you as well."

She stopped, drawing another deep breath. It had all come rushing out. Until this moment, she'd not had much more on her mind than worrying for Isemay and Ulfric and had not begun to question or analyze Balavad's motivations in Vinnr. Now that she'd said all that she knew aloud, the larger picture was coming into focus.

She noted the look that passed between the two Archons as she pieced things together and asked them, "What do you know of the Syzycki Elementum?"

Tuzhazu said, "We know it is a doom that will never come to pass."

Despite the frustration his evasiveness caused, Symvalline pressed on. "Then you have no need to keep me here."

"Tell me, did you speak to Balavad yourself?" Akeeva asked.

"I did not."

"Did you and the rest of your Order meet with him to learn his intentions?" When Symvalline refused to answer, the false Verity nodded her head knowingly. "Then you can't be certain that anything you've said is any more than hearsay and gossip."

"One of my Order saw him murder several members of our Arch Keeper's staff."

"Perhaps they were a hindrance to the greater good." Akeeva moved to a settee in the shade of the overhanging roof and sat. "Balavad is a Verity," she stated simply, "and his purposes and methods are beyond our comprehension. But he saved this world from near destruction and stopped the spread of the plague while Mithlí the Everlight did nothing. He put an end to the Waste and asked for little in return. Some of our own Order did not like the compromises we had to make, but with Balavad's help, we saved our people. I have no regrets."

Some of their Order disagreed with the choice to accommodate Balavad—which must mean the one Salukis had mentioned. "Raamuzi," she said. "The Archon who leads the Zhallahs?"

"Yes." Akeeva nodded. "My sister. And once, my ally. But no longer. Balavad is not an enemy of Arc Rheunos. If he came to our aid, I encourage you to entertain the possibility that he came to Vinnr's as well."

"Send me back there, and I will find out."

"No," Tuzhazu broke in, looking at her for the first time. "From what you've said, your people have angered him. It seems likely he's the one who sent you to us. Thus, he must want you here."

It was clear that these people would listen to nothing she said. They were corrupted too far by Balavad's treachery. Her patience strained, then snapped. "If Balavad was such a savior to you, why then did the child I was brought here with suffer from this Waste? He has not cured it permanently. If he were benevolent, as you seem to believe, he would have. He's using you." *But for what?* she wondered.

Tuzhazu swarmed toward her like a gale, pressing close enough she could count his teeth as they flashed. "He did more for us than our own Verity did. And if you question the choices the Archons have made further, after the suffering we've endured, you'll end up in a cage just like—"

"Enough, Tek Det."

He remained looming over Symvalline for another few breaths, his emerald-gray eyes spearing hers, then stepped away.

With nothing left to lose, Symvalline gave away her last secret. "Please, listen to me. I didn't come through the starpath alone." She had their attention. "My daughter, her name is Isemay, she was with me when the starpath drew us in. She…she's with the Zhallah people." Her voice broke, the despair she'd been holding back creeping from her stomach to her heart, threatening to drown her from the inside. "If you won't help me, at least let me go to her. She's alone, frightened, too young to know what's going on. Please. Don't be cruel to those who've done you no harm."

Akeeva stood and walked closer to her. "A child. How old?"

"Sixteen turns around Halla, our daystar."

"And does she carry the spark of your Verity?"

"No, she's just a frightened girl who's already been through more than a child should."

Akeeva paced back toward her seat and settled in. "Then we do have use for you, Vinnric. I've been told you're a healer. Our own tenders can do nothing for the Waste. So until your Verity retrieves you, you'll stay and work with our healers to find a perpetual cure for the plague. If you do, we'll release you." Akeeva's eyes turned toward the distance, her stare as remote and unfeeling as her voice. "If you don't, it won't matter if you see your child again. Her death from the plague is as good as assured."

CHAPTER EIGHT

Mura and Lysis lived in a four-room dwelling on the edge of the village that extended from the side of a massive Churss tower like a stone bubble. Green and purple vines twined along its outer walls and roof in a dense mat that almost hid the home within. Inside, the main room that served as kitchen and dining room, workspace, and sitting room was cool and comfortable. Mura showed Isemay the sleeping room they'd share. Another room was where her mother slept, and the final room was for storage and private business.

Isemay asked her first question: "If these rock towers can move, what happens to your house when this one does?"

Suppressing a grin, Mura assured her, "Oh, it won't."

Lysis seemed glad to have the company, but Isemay couldn't miss the slight wrinkle that creased the space between her brows every time she looked at Isemay. She just didn't know if the woman's concern had more to do with Isemay's situation of being lost and alone, or if it was about her being a foreigner, with all the unknowns that status carried.

She was generous, though, and gave Isemay a plate of fruits and something vaguely breadlike, and she began consuming them as fast as she could. She'd barely taken note of her hunger until now, but after the first bite, the hunger established itself as a ravenous beast that would not be tamed until it had its fill. The food was unusual but at least better than the nightcaps.

While Lysis made tea at the hearth, which Isemay noted did not burn wood but rather was composed of flat stones that were heated through some unseen means, she said to Mura, "Erli Detzu came to visit with you last night."

Mura's face flushed a rose pink, and Isemay realized she was blushing. Unlike a Vinnric, her whole face and head were overcome, and ordinarily Isemay would have giggled at how hard the emotion was for Mura to hide. Yet, at the moment, she could not feel a trace of amusement, not while her mum was in danger.

Lysis's first statement came out with a tinge of playfulness, but the next was serious as she leveled a dark stare at Mura. "I didn't know what to tell him. Mura, at your age you should know better than to leave the Churss. And to take children out there—what were you thinking? What would I do if I lost you the same way we lost Dwoon?" Before she finished speaking, the anger in her tone gave way to sorrow that seemed to live just below the surface, and Mura quickly reached for her mother's hand.

"I know, and I'm sorry. It won't ever happen again," she promised. "I miss him too. I just…it was just something he'd take me to do when I was still young. I thought it would be like being with him again. And the other kids, they're too young to know the danger. I just wanted them to realize that Arc Rheunos isn't the scary, horrible world it sometimes seems like—"

"But it is dangerous. Far too dangerous, as you've proven. Cylli and Onni's mother is distraught. She might not recover. The only safety we have is here in the Churss."

Mura's color washed to a pale blue-tinted gray. But her feelings of guilt and sorrow didn't need to be illustrated by anything but her stricken expression. "That can't be true, Mother. We all know the story of how Deespora saved many by bringing them here after the last Equifulcrum, but we can't hide in the Churss forever, just like Salukis says, and even Councilor Poolan agrees. Eventually, we have to face the Minothians and reclaim Arc Rheunos, or at least mend the division between us. Hiding is the same as imprisonment. It's not fair to us, and it's not fair to the children after us. Worst of all, it's not fair to the children we've already lost."

"Salukis Engzu is reckless and foolish," Lysis snapped, slamming down the tea mugs she held. "You are not, Mura. You know better than to treat your life like a bargaining piece to be thrown at whims like hunting for nightcaps…"

As their argument continued, Isemay felt like she was intruding. This rift in beliefs seemed to be among more than just Mura and her mum and was much more pressing to them than her and her own mum's troubles. She slid through the outer entryway with all the stealth she'd learned from her Knight foster family and emerged outside into the peaceful Churss without them noticing her go.

She looked around, taking in the fresh air, the last glints of a setting sun that dappled the tops of the massive towers, the chirrups and whistles of songbirds and hum of insects. The rock forest felt…safe. Like living among giants whose every impulse was to ensure you had nothing to fear. It was as different to the wide streets, thriving and widespread markets, and looming buildings of Asteryss as she could imagine. And she found she liked it.

But she could not stay. Pushing the moment of respite behind her, she peered about for a footpath that looked like it might lead to somewhere quiet where she would not be interrupted as she tried to reach her da through the memory keeper. If she had luck reaching him, he could help her decide what to do next. Maybe he could even come and get her. Her hand rose to her neck to touch the jewel.

It wasn't there.

Frantically, she patted herself up and down, searching in every fold of her clothes for it, then she began to scan the ground.

"Did you lose something?" a familiar voice asked.

She looked up and saw Salukis approaching from the main path. "My-my memory keeper. A pendant my father gave me. I was showing it to Mura, but I haven't seen it since…" Since they'd been sitting at the edge of the Churss. Had she dropped it there or somewhere along the path?

He stopped before her, and the two black-furred creatures that he'd greeted earlier planted themselves on either side of him contentedly. "Since?" he prompted.

The wending paths inside the Churss were growing dark as evening fell, but she couldn't wait another day to try reaching her da. She had to get back to the forest's boundaries. Alone, she'd get lost. But with help…

"Salukis, you have to take me back."

"…Back where?"

"Where Mura and I waited for you. I have to find that pendant. It's my only link to my da."

"Sure, I'll take you back."

She was about to press the argument, but then realized he'd agreed to go. "You will?"

"Why not? Believe me, I'm not in much hurry to return to my own house. My father is…let's just say, he's got designs on a garden wall that will be thick and tall enough to surround a forest before he's through making me build it. My mother and Uncle Browan are pretty excited about it, too. What's one more day of waiting before I get started?" He muttered sullenly, "Especially since it'll probably take me my whole life to finish it. First though, he sent me over here to apologize to Lysis for being involved in a trip that put Mura and the other kids in danger. Even though it *was* Mura's idea. Not that they believed me. Just give me a moment." He looked to the two furry creatures, "Juz, Tekl, I'll be right back. Stay here."

He rapped against the rocks that formed the entryway arch of Mura's home, then called, "Heyo?"

The sound of a raised voice cut off abruptly, then Mura's voice came from within: "Come in, Salukis."

He started to part the woven screen covering the entrance, then turned his head back to Isemay. "Don't go anywhere, okay?"

She nodded impatiently.

While he was gone, his two pets turned their heads toward her. "…Hi," she said, unable to resist her curiosity about them.

Her voice seemed to be taken as a kind of invitation, and suddenly they were circling her, each pushing their wet black snouts up close and sniffing her as if she were an irresistible morsel of the unknown. She supposed she was, being from another of the Cosmos's five realms. She reached down carefully and scratched one behind its horn. "Good...boy?"

At her touch, the creature lunged up and placed its front paws on her chest, and she saw the length of its claws for the first time. They looked sharp enough to gut her. "Okay, yes, good. I, uh, I like you too."

Its muzzle opened, revealing teeth that were, if anything, sharper than its claws, and panted in her face. Its breath smelled a bit like fish.

"Nice boy, good boy," she stammered, trying to back away.

Salukis stepped outside, rather hurriedly. "Ugh, that's that. It's a good thing Lysis isn't my mother. Juz, what are you doing? I know she's a wonder, but get down, boy." To Isemay, he said, "Ready? We better go before she decides she needs a new garden wall too."

CHAPTER NINE

Symvalline considered fighting her captors as Minoth guards arrived to escort her from Akeeva's quarters. But though she was stronger than many, she was not stronger than a kingdom. And she couldn't risk being killed when the other option was only captivity. Not when Isemay's life depended on her.

"Summon all the healers we have in Minoth and bring them to the Knight," Akeeva told the guards.

"Yes, Everlight." They dipped their heads to acknowledge the command and began shepherding Symvalline out.

They passed first through the anteroom of Akeeva's chamber, which was filled with children, who by her estimate were all under ten or eleven turns. They were well-fed, clean, and boisterous as any children their ages. From what Agatha her fellow captive on the way here had told her, these girls and boys were separated from their parents and kept here in the palace, yet none seemed overly distressed by their situation. Seeing this lightened her heart the smallest bit. It meant there were limits, then, to the Minothians' cruelty and heartlessness.

Everlight Hall was vast, and the guards escorted her through without her blindfold. Small victories. Each glimpse she had through windows showed her steep, soaring mountains in every direction. The hall and the city outside its gates were in a wide valley, every side hemmed in by terrain it would take her months to walk through if she escaped. And that was only if she could find a map to show her how to get back to where she'd started. And if she could shake off pursuit by flying guards. And...

The puzzle grew ever more complex as she thought it over. To make matters harder, her immediate situation contained an even more complex puzzle. How could Akeeva seriously believe Symvalline could cure the disease that cut straight into the hearts, both literally and figuratively, of this realm's people? She knew nothing of their bodies, or their plants and animals, much less the diseases that could fell them. She had barely even practiced healing in her own realm in the last centuries. Knights hardly needed much aid from her or any source but their own inherited vitality. There'd been the times she'd ministered to Isemay, her broken arm from stealing and crashing a set of prototype wings Ulfric had built, her concussion from falling from Vigil Tower when she'd tried to climb it without aid of ropes. But little beyond that. The people of Ivoryss had healers of their own, and her primary duty was to her Verity, not their ills.

The thing her new obligation did give her was time—and, if she was lucky, access to enough natural elements to concoct more than medicines. As the guards led her down what she hoped was the last staircase to wherever she would be held, she wrestled with the part of her mind that argued: How much time did she really have? If Isemay was susceptible to this world's ailments, and if this Waste was as widespread and virulent as they all seemed to believe, Isemay's time could be short indeed.

At the base of the last stairs, her guards pushed open a heavy wooden door and escorted her into a spacious chamber the size of a modest eating hall. It was filled with every manner of vial and bottle, basin and box, mortars and pestles, and numerous fireboxes for setting contained burns. Shelves, tables, and trunks were spread throughout, holding what she assumed were to be her experimental materials. The space was loaded with the accoutrements of not just any healer's laboratory, but with enough necessities for many, many healers to work together. Ulfric, with his love for craft and experimentation, would have been agog at what she'd been granted access to.

Smiling inwardly at the possibilities that lay before her, she turned to her guards. "I'll start immediately. Leave me, lock me in if you must, but please take my assurances to Ak—the Everlight, that I will do everything within my power and experience to carry out her will."

The female guard shook her head. "We're to stay with you until your assistants arrive."

The other nodded agreement, and they took positions in front of the door. These two, she noted, wore light swords and armor.

So, not quite as easy as she'd hoped it would be. But that didn't mean she was completely handicapped. One did not live as many lifetimes as she had without learning a few tricks about stealth—or how to make potions that could make the liveliest person fall asleep when needed.

Looking around, she thought about where to begin. First step, inventory. And it would go much faster if she had help. "Guards," she said, "when will assistance arrive? I assume the Everlight doesn't expect me to start from scratch with this task."

Both eyed her, saying nothing. Either they didn't know, or they'd been ordered not to speak to her more than necessary.

Fine, then.

It had been midafternoon when they'd arrived at Everlight Hall, and by the time her first visitor arrived, she'd had to light several lamps to keep the gloomy shadows of the large chamber at bay. Her afternoon's discoveries had revealed a few dozen herbs, leaves, powders, and tinctures she mentally catalogued as potentially useful, along with several books that were written in Elder Veros to refer to.

The bookshelves in the room stood taller than any typically sized Arc Rheunosian could reach, soaring all the way to the vaulted ceiling six times higher than her own height. But then, with half their population able to simply flap wings to gain access to the top shelves, it made sense. She, however, had required the aid of one of the guards to bring down every book she couldn't reach alone or with the aid of a ladder. Hundreds lay in neat piles on the floor now.

But one had been pulled down that held her attention longer than any other. Though thick, it was a smallish book and bound with a plain fibrous cover that was flexible and worn. More like a journal than a tome on medicine or botany, and when she flipped it open to a random page, she saw that's what it was. The first words written, scribbled really, in the corner of the first page were odd: "Only the maker can unmake the cage."

The single line was strangely compelling, and she flipped through the rest quickly. Informal handwriting and detailed but disorganized drawings adorned each leaf. A quick scan showed her none had anything to do with the business of healing. This book contained musing and theories about Verity lore. More than one page discussed the archaeology of Verity vessels and their Fenestrii at great length.

Furtively, Symvalline tucked this book aside where no one else would see it. When she had the chance to study it in depth without being observed, she would.

Based on her early research of a handful of the remaining voluminous stacks, she felt closer to being able to concoct useful potions of her own, but it would be some time before she was ready to break free of this place, and she would need more than potions to aid her in finding Isemay. Patience had always been one of her attributes, but she knew the next few days would try hers more than any other in her life.

When the chamber's main door was pushed open in the evening, she assumed it would either be dinner or her promised help. It was neither.

"Both of you, we have three more Waste victims. Go up to the main hall and help bring them down to our new"—Tuzhazu's gleaming eyes shot to her as he nearly sneered the word—"healer."

She could read the thoughts of her two guards on their faces as if they were more books. They were equally distressed at the idea of handling victims of the plague as they were at wanting to defy their commander's orders. Their fear of Tuzhazu turned out the greater, and they left the room without a word.

Tuzhazu meandered around the space, his gaze lingering for a moment on everything she had touched it seemed, measuring her actions and guessing her intentions. She'd rarely felt so exposed, as if she were a child who realized that she was nowhere near as clever at sneaking about and getting into things she knew she shouldn't as she'd thought.

After a bit, he said, "How are you settling in to your new role?"

"You know as well as I that I'm as useful in this *role* as a tree. How could you or Akeeva—"

"The Everlight," he corrected her.

"Yes. How could I be expected to know the fundamentals of your natural world?"

"I know you're useless."

His admission caught her by surprise. "Then what am I doing here?"

He returned to the entryway and pulled the door shut, then said, "Akeeva still believes in a cure. I'm not so…idealistic. But she runs the kingdom, for now, so appeasing her is what the people of Minoth do. As they should. And you, for reasons we shall soon learn, are a Minothian for now."

"I'm a Vinnric."

"Believe whatever suits you."

A knock came at the door and Tuzhazu called, "Enter. Lay the sick on those planks." He waved to a side of the room with several sleeping platforms.

Symvalline was dismayed to see the child, Tulla, being brought to her for care. She'd failed to help the girl before. What could she possibly do now?

Yet another sight that was even more disturbing followed. Two winged guards, whom she recognized, were laid side by side, their flesh a watery gray, their cheeks sunken. Like Tulla, the skin over their cheekbones bore an angry, crusty rash that looked painful to the touch. In just under three days, they'd declined from the robust, healthy men who'd been guarding her at the gatehouse to the mountains to husks of their former selves.

Her healthy guards quickly retreated at the flick of Tuzhazu's hand and shut the door behind them.

Symvalline went immediately to the child's side and began to feel her cheeks and test her pulse. It was as light as the brush of a dragørfly's wing. She sensed through her healer insight that the girl's life was ebbing to a close, and Symvalline could do nothing about it.

"Why haven't you used your Fenestrii on her?" she asked Tuzhazu. "And all those who suffer from this disease? Try to heal them with the vitality the celestial stone contains." Her voice remained composed, but inside she was frantic. How could they be so cruel as to put this child in her care, knowing she could do nothing for her?

When Tuzhazu didn't answer, she looked to him. The hard lines of his face convinced her not to push too hard to get answers from him. Instead, she asked, "Where is her mother? She deserves these final moments with her child. They both do."

"Pahzi broke our laws. She and her child pay the price." His tone betrayed nothing, no feeling, no hint of care or conscience.

The child was unconscious, her limbs as limp as a dead flower. Symvalline gathered what shreds of professional sobriety she had and forced herself to examine the two other victims. They weren't as far along in their sickness. Maybe there was a chance she could ease them in some way.

"I know these men," she said as she leaned toward the first. "They were guarding me at the gate tower…"

"The Aktoktos Gate," Tuzhazu said. "Built to keep watch over the starpath valley and the damnable Churss. We have too many visitors from outside Arc Rheunos," he added, clearly galled by the stone forest. "Any Minothian who passes through it knows the risk. The Waste is out there. The Zhallahs hate and fear us, hate and fear their own maker, and they curse us with the Waste because of it. So the Minothians believe."

"But these men were never near a Zhallah person. They were with the party who caught me, but the Zhallahs had already run into the forest."

"Nevertheless, the Zhallahs cursed them."

"That's ridiculous," Symvalline said, adjusting a blanket to serve as a pillow under one of the men. He groaned, his eyelids fluttering. She felt his skin. Hot, boiling hot. She moved to retrieve a decanter of water for him from beside a full basin. As she passed Tuzhazu, he reached for her arm, taking her wrist to stop her.

"I have something to show you." He began to tug her back to the soldiers, but she yanked free and stood in place. He seemed unconcerned. Leaning over the taller of the guards, he said in a quiet voice, "Kaneas Viddzu," and to the other, "Kaneas Toranzu. Do you hear me?"

Both men opened their eyes and tilted their heads toward his voice. "Yes, Archon."

"You know what's happened to you?"

Their nods were miserable, painful looking.

"And you know you will die?"

Again, the stricken nods. The man called Viddzu sucked back a whimper.

"I have a choice to offer you. You will meet eternity soon, that is certain. Either it will be as nothing but food for the slimes and grubs that crawl under the mountains. Or it can be as one of Minoth's most glorious protectors in the ranks of the Deathless, forever a vigilant servant of our Everlight and forever honored by all Minothians."

The other guard, Toranzu, stared at Tuzhazu wide-eyed, a spark of new and fervid life in his gaze. "I would serve Minoth to the end, my liege."

"Good." Tuzhazu nodded. "And you, Viddzu?"

Viddzu's stare had drifted to the ceiling, and he did not look back at Tuzhazu.

"Make your choice," the Archon ordered.

Viddzu's voice was barely a whisper. "I will serve in the Deathless Guard until, Everlight willing, I am called to peace."

Tuzhazu gave a curt nod, then looked over to Symvalline, ensuring her attention was on them. He reached into his ever-present pouch and pulled out a new flask. It differed from the one she'd seen him use previously to pour something into the guards' goblets at the Aktoktos Gate tower, the glass tinted dark blue instead of black like the last one.

"Open your mouths," Tuzhazu ordered.

Carefully, he let a single drop fall from the flask onto the tongue of each man. She could see that the liquid, blue in color, was what gave the bottle its color. Toranzu grimaced sourl, but swallowed and lay still. Before Viddzu accepted his dose, he reached out and grasped Tuzhazu's wrist.

"Tell my son…tell Inder I love him," he begged in a voice that cracked.

With barely a nod, Tuzhazu pulled his wrist free and administered the drop. He shot Symvalline a look that bordered on glee—at least as much glee as one as hostile as he'd shown himself to be could muster.

What happened next disturbed her more than anything she'd seen in her long life. A low moan started in the back of one of their throats, she couldn't tell which, a sound like a wind through a distant underground tunnel. The noise was so haunting that she feared she would hear it in her nightmares. Another sound joined, a grunt of pain, followed by Viddzu crying out. She started to pace toward them, wondering what Tuzhazu had given them to cause such pain, but stopped abruptly. Before her, the men began to thrash. But worse, they began to…change. The sallowness of their flesh grew more so as their skin, and the bones beneath, seemed to…to stretch.

Their cries rose in pitch, becoming screams, as their bodies grew into abnormal proportions. The howls even disturbed the nearly unconscious child, whose eyes fluttered as she whimpered. The guards became gaunt as their height increased, every ounce of flesh and fat on them being shaped into something new, something ghastly.

In moments, it was over. They stilled and grew silent, as if dead.

Symvalline found she couldn't make her feet move closer. "You're creating these, these…abominations."

"They are not abominations, Vinnric. These are more gifts from Balavad. The Verity of Battgjald knows that our fragile peace is fleeting. Perhaps just between the Minothians and Zhallahs." He looked into her face, his expression hinting at inquiry. "Perhaps between others in the Cosmos. Balavad gave us an advantage, soldiers who feel no fear, who are obedient to the end, and who can't be killed easily, except perhaps by a Verity's chosen. But there are only so many of our kind, those who've been chosen, aren't there?"

Our kind. She wouldn't give him the satisfaction of seeing her cringe at the association. "It was my understanding the Arc Rheunosians were opposed to spilling blood."

"Bah. It's a law that has served its purpose. Even you said it, you aren't from this realm. What will we do when others come, others who are not as well-meaning as you say you are? Are we required to give up everything and be overtaken, or is it better to give up just one thing, just one law?"

Symvalline understood the logic and could think of no reason to disagree. Her own world wasn't without violence and war, but planning for an attack from another realm? The possibility had previously been too remote to even consider. Yet Balavad had come to Vinnr with a skyborne army, the Raveners, who invaded mercilessly. And he'd come here, too.

But the difference was night and day. Balavad had attacked Ivoryss. Yet he'd apparently given the Minothians an army of their own, or at least a means to raise one. Why the difference? What were Balavad's ends?

She had to get back to Vinnr. Everything was at stake.

Tuzhazu had approached the guards and was looking them over. He returned his flask of—was there a better word for it?—poison, and brought out the Fenestros he'd used to strip her of her klinkí stones in the meadow. Its color was as black as a cave, but the lamps in the room glanced off tiny runes etched into its surface. The Fenestrii of Vaka Aster were a swirl of blue and yellow, making this one's darkness even starker.

In defiance of gravity, he spun the fist-sized globe around his hand and spoke to the guards. "Rise, Deathless Guards. Your new duties await."

The two men's eyes opened. No longer typical, they had become a solid flat gray. Were they sightless? They stood, and Tuzhazu smiled genuinely for the first time she'd seen.

"Your first task will be to guard this foreigner," he told them, and they moved to either side of Symvalline, not exactly listlessly, but almost as if they did not know the bodies they inhabited. She noted the disappearance of the red blotches that had begun to cover their cheeks. The transformation had cured their disease but infected them with something much worse.

Tuzhazu looked over the still child and spoke aloud, more to himself than to Symvalline. "Their ascension in the ranks will be lauded, but it's a pity an example had to be made of this one. Akeeva would have treated her well."

An example had to be made... And Symvalline suddenly understood a fact she'd have preferred never having discovered. Tuzhazu was causing the Waste. He infected any he could claim had been exposed to the disease with whatever was in that other flask he carried and blamed their deaths on the Zhallahs to keep the two sides divided and the Zhallahs feared by the Minothians.

She didn't want to believe it. Why do something so horrible, so corrupt? Yet he stood before her all but demonstrating his power and then admitting to it. He didn't know what she'd seen back at the tower at the Aktoktos Gate. She could be in worse danger if he did. Was Akeeva part of this monstrous ploy? Was this Balavad's doing?

She was trapped in an intrigue she wanted nothing to do with. But clearly innocents were being hurt, killed even. And Tuzhazu seemed to have a greater plan in mind. A plan that had something to do with the Zhallahs, people now keeping her own child safe. Like it or not, she couldn't ignore his treachery. She was too vulnerable to accuse him, though, so she'd have to wait and watch for a way out of this scorpion's den.

"You're not going to provide me with any assistants, are you?" she said numbly.

He turned to her, his expression betraying what he thought of her: she was a nuisance, and one he'd prefer to be rid of sooner than later. "It would hardly be worth the effort. You do what you think you can, *healer*." He did sneer the word this time. "And when the time comes, your true uses will be discovered."

CHAPTER TEN

"So," Salukis said, "walk or"—he spread his wings impressively and waggled the tips—"fly?"

Distracted with worry, Isemay responded, "Walk. I don't want to miss my memory keeper if it fell on the trail somewhere."

"Oh, yeah. Of course."

His disappointment was hard to miss. Just as they turned toward the trail to go, Mura stepped out. "Isemay? Are you all right?"

She couldn't very well lie to Mura, not after all the help she'd given her, so she said simply, "I've lost the pendant my father gave me. Salukis said he'll help me look for it."

Mura appraised her for a moment, then said, "I understand. But the village is preparing a celebration for you tonight. If you're not back in time..." She let the statement hang.

She was stuck. These people, especially Mura and her mother, and even Salukis, had been more than kind to her, even if they weren't going to help her with the one thing she needed help with most. Still, to rebuff their kindness...well, she hadn't been raised like that. Her mum would be disappointed in her, as would her da. But she couldn't see any way around the issue. That memory keeper was her lifeline right now. She had to find it.

"I'm sorry, Mura. I can't lose it."

Mura gave her a decisive nod, her cheeks and chin filling with a soft, calm lavender that reminded Isemay of her favorite flower in Vinnr, the dalla. "I'll tell the council where you've gone and why if you're not back in time. Which"—she glanced toward the darkening sky—"I'm guessing you won't be."

"Thank you, Mura, thank you so much. I owe you everything."

Mura glanced over her shoulder, then looked at Salukis meaningfully. "Better go before my mother comes out."

"Follow me," Salukis said quickly and motioned to Isemay as he turned up the path.

Before she followed, Isemay reached a hand out and placed it on Mura's arm. "Thank you again. I don't know what I'd do without you."

Mura's lavender hue warmed to a deeper purple, flushing even her lips as she smiled softly. "It is our way, Isemay. But even if it weren't, your mum helped us and saved Neeka when she didn't have to. It is a privilege to be able to help you now. I'm sure Deespora will think of a way to aid your mother." Her brows drew together in a small frown as she said this, sending waves of gray rippling from the crease. Then she took one of Isemay's hands and squeezed it. "Besides, it isn't every day you get to talk to a woman from an entirely new world. I'll look forward to when you get back. Good luck finding your pendant."

When she let her hand go, Isemay loped after Salukis. The forest quickly dimmed, and they hadn't gone more than a few steps beyond sight of Mura's home when Isemay asked, "Do you have a torch or something we can use to help us see by?"

"A torch?"

"Yes, or an illuminate orb?"

He seemed puzzled by her request, then nodded as if it suddenly made sense. "Oh, we don't need those. We have the Churss. Watch." He breathed words, or perhaps simply hummed, so quietly she couldn't quite understand which. Around them on every side, a dim glow began at the bases of the Churss towers, sparkling slowly one by one from the shining flecks of another kind of rock that spread throughout the greater stones until each individual light combined and suffused the area. The effect stole her breath.

"How do they do that?" she half whispered.

He smiled at her wonder. "Starlight. The Churss absorbs it and shines it wherever we need it. Works with sunlight too. Ready?"

They took a path that skirted the village, Salukis reasoning that if someone inside the village found her pendant, they would know it was foreign given the unique representation of dragørfly, something Arc Rheunos had never seen, and give it to Deespora. She noted he didn't suggest they go and ask the Archon if anyone had found it, but she supposed he'd say so if he thought it likely. And perhaps he preferred the adventure to staying in Maerria. Isemay would have. Soon, they'd wound back to the main path, close enough to the village that Isemay wasn't concerned they'd missed too much ground.

The Churss lights followed them. Isemay glanced back once and saw how they dimmed behind them once the lights were no longer in range of the duo. Juz and Tekl came along as well, their paws soundless in the still night. The sounds of the village faded away, leaving only the occasional unfamiliar tweets and hoots of what she assumed were birds and buzzes and hums of what she hoped were small insects. She felt almost protected by the mellow Churss light in this strange place, as if it kept any fears of the dark and unknown from finding her.

As they walked, she scanned the ground ceaselessly, internally berating herself for being foolish enough to lose such an important and precious gift. What if Da tried to speak to her while it was lost? What would she do if she didn't find it? The memory keeper could be the only chance she had to get her mum back from the Minothians, and she'd lost it as if she were a stupid, inattentive toddler.

"You're pretty quiet, Isemay. But then, you must have a lot on your mind."

Salukis had been very helpful, keeping her on the right path and looking as hard for the pendant as she was. Though her temper was short and her worries long, she didn't want to be rude. "I do. But if you'd prefer to pass the time by talking, I don't mind. I'm grateful for your help."

"And I'm grateful for your mother's," he assured her. "And once we get Onni and Cylli back, Mura and I will never make that mistake again." He closed his mouth abruptly and looked back to see if she was listening.

Intent on keeping her focus on the forest floor, she didn't realize she'd failed to respond until he spoke again.

"So, what's it like?"

"What's what like?"

"Where you come from, Vinnr. Is it like here?"

She thought a moment. "It is. And it isn't. No one has wings, for instance. And we definitely don't have those." When he glanced back to see what she meant, she pointed to Tekl and Juz.

"Churss cave snoozes? Do you have Churss?"

"No." She shook her head emphatically. "The closest type of stone we have that has been touched by our Verity is the ore of Mount Omina and the Fenestrii. And there are only five of those."

"It's the same here. That's true in all the Cosmos, Deespora says."

"Yes, that's right. I've been a student in the Conservatum to become a Knight Corporealis like my parents since I was twelve turns—longer really, if you count having been raised by the Knights themselves. The Fenestrii and Scrylle lore are part of our lessons. But, of course, no one but a Knight can look in the Scrylle. That's where I learned to speak Elder Veros too, the first gift of the Verities to their people."

"What we're speaking now? We call it Varitika, and everyone in the Cosmos must know it, because even the Minothians all speak it."

Earlier, when he'd whispered to the Churss, it had sound like words she didn't understand, not spoken in Elder Veros, and she'd overheard other Zhallahs speaking in the same unusual tongue. That must be the language of the Zhallah people. Curious why they spoke differently if they knew Elder Veros, or Varitika, she asked him, "Why don't the Zhallahs always speak the first language?"

She saw his shoulders and even his wings stiffen, and she wanted to take back the question. But he said, "The Minothians don't know our speech. It makes it easier to…keep things from them when we need to."

She let the conversation go quiet after that, feeling a deep unease in her stomach at the thought that an entire people spoke their own language for little more reason than because they needed an advantage over an enemy.

Salukis said nothing more for a while, either. But eventually, his curious nature came back. "We don't have that here, a Conservatum," he said. "Our Archon Order is gone, and the Everlight can't replace them."

"Why not? Does your creator need no guardians for her vessel?"

"It's nothing like that."

He was silent again, and Isemay sensed there was something he feared to tell her. She wondered if she should press the issue. It wasn't really her concern, though distantly she'd been curious about Archon Raamuzi. She seemed to be unique among people, with no vessel to protect.

She let the silence linger as long as she could, but this time her own curiosity about his tight-lipped response overcame her. What if whatever he was withholding held some clue or detail that could aid her own needs? What would a Knight do? Would they dig for more answers?

Eventually, she said, "What do you mean?"

"...Mura would clip my wings if she knew I was telling a stranger this."

"What does it matter if I know? Who would I tell?" she urged.

He stopped and turned toward her with a smirk that she found to her surprise oddly...cute? Its playing-with-fire twist was like looking into a mirror.

"It's the reason the Archons split and the Minothians and Zhallahs are divided. During our last Equifulcrum, some of the Archons made a compact with the Menace, Balavad the Battgjaldic Verity. All except Deespora. This was three hundred years ago, and Arc Rheunos was suffering a wasting plague that had killed many thousands."

"The plague you thought my mum and I had?"

His smile turned sheepish. "Yes. And, uh, I apologize for my hasty accusation."

His tone was so sincere that any lingering resentment she may have had instantly dissolved, and she shrugged it off. "What was the compact?"

He began walking again and spoke over his shoulder. "Deespora tells us the Archons were angry with the Everlight for allowing so much suffering and death, and for doing nothing to stop it, no matter how much they pleaded. Balavad came to us then—us being the united Arc Rheunosians, before we split—and promised the Archons he could cure the plague if the Everlight was sapped of her power. Deespora was alone in refusing him, but in their desperation the rest of the Archons overruled her. They did something, something Deespora won't speak of, to the Everlight's vessel at Cosmoculous Tower."

"What's that?"

"It's in Minoth near Everlight Hall, the tower where the vessel resides, and at the top is a Churss crystal as big as, well, it's massive. At the Equifulcrum, when the moons align with the daystar, their light shines through the crystal and...something."

"Something?"

"Some great event that only an Archon can fully comprehend. Anyway, that's how the Archons managed to take control of the vessel. Whatever the Menace showed them required the Cosmoculous, and they somehow trapped the Everlight in her vessel. It's not something I really understand. Afterward, Deespora stole the Scrylle and the last Fenestros and fled here, to the Churss, with as many of our people as would follow her, knowing she could not fight the rest of the Archons or the Menace."

Chills dotted the back of Isemay's neck. This story sounded so familiar...Balavad's visitation to Vinnr, a realm that wasn't his own, his plots to subvert Vaka Aster...

Her mum had not told her much about what was happening in Vinnr in their quick flight to Mount Omina before being transported here, but what she had now reminded Isemay closely of what Salukis was saying. She wanted to hear more. "I don't understand how you can trap a Verity. Do you know why Mithlí can't escape?"

He shook his head. "I can't grasp it either, I'm no Archon. Not that I wouldn't like to be, maybe. But the worst part was that Akeeva was supposed to be the next vessel, and after the Archons turned against the Everlight, she's been pretending she is. The Minothian people know none of what the Archons did, and Akeeva and Tuzhazu now rule Minoth. They're lying to the people and have been since the Equi-fulcrum. They've even made the Minothians believe it's the Zhallahs who caused the plague and that we ran away before the Archons could punish us. We are all exiles..."

Even the histories of Vinnr she'd studied had no tales of such treachery, and it shocked Isemay to hear that a people could turn so thoroughly not only against each other but against their Verity as well. She thought about what he'd said, the similarities to Vinnr's current crisis. As it had been happening, she'd thought it was all balderdash—because how could a Verity be shackled? It seemed impossible. But she wasn't a Knight, not yet anyway. What did she know?

Something else came to mind. "Then where did the plague really come from? Does it still afflict people?"

"We have to be careful. The Waste still strikes occasionally. Deespora has even wondered if it came from somewhere else, outside Arc Rheunos. We don't know its cause or how to cure it."

"Salukis, why do the Minothians take Zhallah people captive? What happens to them?"

"I'm not sure. No one has ever come back from Minoth. But they are not harmed," he added hastily.

"But how do you..." Isemay let the words wither. She didn't want to scratch at a wound that was already too deep.

He understood her question anyway. "How do we know? Because the people of Arc Rheunos value life. We live in peace with all living creatures, causing no harm, including to each other. Even the Archons' compact with Balavad was to prevent further death: caging the Everlight in exchange for a cure for the Waste. Akeeva and the other Archons only took the Menace's offer in order to save lives. Why would they turn against that law now?"

Isemay fell quiet, considering all he'd said as she continued hunting for the memory keeper.

"Oh look!" Salukis said and hopped upward, using his wings to thrust him into the brush beside the trail. "Wait there, be back in a moment."

"Do you see it?" she asked breathlessly, but his voice had trailed off.

He returned quickly with a pouch full of thumb-sized deep red berries. "Govels," he said. "Have one. They'll fill you up fast, but they might make you need to…er, don't eat too many. Even though they are delicious."

Disappointment at the false hope he'd triggered swelled in her chest. She almost refused his offer but stopped herself. It would be petulant. Besides, she was still hungry.

After she took one, no sooner had the berry been squished between her teeth and its juice splashed her tongue than she completely agreed with him. They were the best thing she'd ever tasted. Before she'd swallowed the first, she was reaching for the second.

"They might affect you differently, you being from Vinnr. Just keep that in mind," he warned ominously.

When she realized what he was implying, she stopped herself after the second one. He was right. She hadn't considered what affect food from another realm might have. As if the suggestion itself were infectious, she felt a tug and roil in her belly. "We better keep going."

They'd covered about half the distance to the edge of the Churss, and Isemay had fought herself every step from either slowing to a crawl so she could scan every blade of grass, twig, and stone, or speeding toward the border where she suspected she'd dropped the pendant and possibly missing it. It could have fallen off anywhere, but the dragørfly stone was heavy. She'd have noted the change as its weight fell from her neck while walking, she was sure. But she and Mura had been seated at the edge of the Churss, and it might not have been as noticeable. Perhaps she'd simply misconnected the clasp that held it and it had fallen then. She held out hope like a shield, willing this possibility to be the right one.

After a while, her eyes began to unfocus as weariness made its presence known. To keep herself sharp, she decided to keep Salukis talking and asked, "If Deespora is an Archon and she has the Scrylle, why don't you all just confront the other Archons in Minoth and demand they let your people come back to Maerria? Surely Deespora can work strong wystics with the artifacts, at least strong enough to protect a…a delegation."

"Sure," he merely said.

When he didn't continue, she pressed, "So…?"

"Many of the Zhallahs want to do exactly that. But Deespora refuses. She says she tried to reason with Akeeva in the past, and it came to nothing. She will do anything to avoid a confrontation with the Minothians, but many of us think it's just delaying the inevitable. Maerria and the Churss is our home, but so is the rest of Arc Rheunos. It's like being in prison…well, you heard the discussion in the Circle."

"Mm-hmm. Can't some of you go there, like by stealth, and try to rescue the captured Zhallahs? I mean, what would Deespora do? How could she punish you for saving your own people?"

"Because of the labyrinth."

"The what?"

"The Tyrn Mountains are vast, steep, with unpredictable weather. Dangerous, basically. Everlight Hall and the lands of Minoth are in a valley deep in the mountains. Depending on the season, it could take a month or more to traverse them, and there's no way to get a large caravan through at all. The only way to Minoth is through the Aktoktos Gate. But between the gate and Minoth, a labyrinth of stone channels is cut into the mountains themselves. No one in Maerria knows how to get through it but Deespora. And they are heavily guarded."

"But you can fly."

"Sentries everywhere, day and night, and they carry nets and water cannons."

"Water cannons?"

"We can't fly if our wings are wet. If we're netted or wetted while in the air, we'll fall just as fast and hard as anything land-bound. We'd never get enough people past the sentries to do any good, and carrying back those who've been captured, who maybe can't fly, would make us even easier to catch. Believe me, we've talked it through."

"Of course," she said, troubled by how tied the Zhallahs' hands were from rescuing their own. She wondered who the "we" he spoke of were.

"Well," he said, shifting their talk to a new topic, which she found she was glad of. "The good news is we'll be at the border soon. The bad news is we haven't found your pendant yet. But it'll be there. I'm sure of it."

"Me too," she said, trying not to notice how unconvinced her voice sounded to her ears.

CHAPTER ELEVEN

Tulla was dead by morning.

The Deathless Guards had remained with Symvalline in the healers chamber all night, watching silently, chillingly still. She'd done her best to ignore them while keeping watch over the girl and doing anything she could to ease her. The child hadn't awakened at all, not even long enough for Symvalline to provide her with more of the green powder the wagon driver had given her in secret on their journey to Everlight Hall. Now, as dawn light filtered in through high windows, Symvalline teetered on the edge of exhaustion, not of the body but the heart, the pain of a child's death, even a child she hardly knew, far deeper than any wound she'd ever suffered herself.

When Archon Tuzhazu arrived some short time later, he said nothing to her as he walked to the deathbed and looked into Tulla's face, which, Symvalline noted with gratitude, was now peaceful.

"Her mother will be informed," he said flatly.

Standing quietly to the side, conscious of staying out of his reach, she tested the limits of what she could imply in order to pry more information from him. "I wish there could have been some way to avoid this tragedy. The cure to the plague itself could perhaps lie within the Scrylle."

Tuzhazu's voice was low, grating as he spoke. "Do you really think we didn't look? When the Waste swarmed throughout Arc Rheunos years ago, what do you think the Archons did? Run? Hide? Lock ourselves into a fortress with the vessel and ignore what was happening to our people?"

The simmering anger in his tone was a storm, but it was still on the horizon. She had some time still to pry further. "I'm sure you did everything you could within the limits of your duty to protect Mithlí's vessel. But if not even your wysticism could affect this disease, why does Akeeva consent to you holding me here? I'm no more powerful than any of you."

As his eyes wandered around the room, probably searching for hints that she might have been planning something clandestine, he answered, "She is a fool who still wants to believe this is a natural disease, and still too blinded by grief to see the truth. But that will change at the Equifulcrum. Arc Rheunos will benefit from a strong leader again when Akeeva's mantle passes to me, and I'll do what's necessary to ensure Arc Rheunos is never threatened by devastation again. Or is subject to the whims of an uncaring Verity."

She had an idea of what the Equifulcrum was but needed him to be specific. Exactly how long did she have to escape? "The Equifulcrum?" she asked.

He glanced to the high windows. "Syzygy is in ten days. And my army should be here by then as well." He caught her eye and smiled wryly. "When I was informed the starpath had opened, I thought your arrival was the army promised me. Your coming here is more than just a curiosity to me."

No more than it is to me, she thought. Then: *Army?* Looking to Tulla, she asked, "What will you do with her body?"

"Burn her."

Symvalline gasped.

He seemed to repress a grin. "At night where the celestial lights can't be sullied by the stain of the Waste."

"But her mother..." she whispered in horror.

"She's lucky she doesn't receive the same treatment." His dispassionate response was like a bucket of freezing water thrown in her face. She knew his type. Not just uncaring but unwilling to imagine a *need* for sympathy or care. People like him were dangerous. Much too dangerous to lead a kingdom.

"And what shall I do now?" she asked, trying not to show the wrenching pain she felt thinking of Agatha.

"Akeeva will not come to the healing chambers, so there's no need to keep you here."

She braced herself for whatever foul dungeon he had in mind, but what he said next surprised her.

"But that dart you stuck me with—that, I found interesting. Something like that would aid greatly in my efforts."

Seeing what he was getting at, she hedged. "But your materials are new to me. To make the agent in my darts, or something similar, I would have to be more familiar with the composition and matter in this realm."

"You have a wealth of books and materials to work with, and ten days to become familiar."

"And if I create the substance, you'll release me to find my daughter?"

"If you make it, and it's effective, you'll see her again."

He left her alone then, sending an awaiting guard from outside to retrieve Tulla's body. Tears slid down Symvalline's cheeks as the girl was taken. The guard, not one of the Deathless, at least had the decency to wrap the child's body gently in a shroud and carry her away with genuine sadness in her eyes.

The two Deathless returned, glaring at her with their disconcerting eyes. They neither slept nor seemed to need to eat—though that must be impossible. She wondered what malignant wysticism made them into such inanimate nightmare creatures.

Wishing to sleep herself, but knowing she could not, Symvalline approached a shelf and pulled a random book down. As she feigned reading through it, her thoughts whirled.

Then again, it was no mystery what was creating the Deathless. This was Balavad's doing. For some reason, the malice-bent Verity had

Tuzhazu doing his bidding. Balavad must be providing him not only with the means to transform Arc Rheunosians into these Deathless ghouls, but also the means to spread the plague in whatever strategic vector Tuzhazu chose. Did that mean Balavad had brought the plague originally? And what army had Tuzhazu meant? Was he not making his own army with this vile Deathless toxin? What "efforts" was he referring to? Was Salukis the Zhallah correct that Tuzhazu wanted to destroy his people? But why?

Endless questions marched through her mind, many of them involving the current false vessel's role. Was Akeeva part of whatever plot Balavad and Tuzhazu were bringing to boil? Unlike Tuzhazu, she had seemed to retain some sense of compassion and empathy. She seemed to not know Tuzhazu was the plague-bringer everyone feared, or rather the plague-spreader, as Balavad seemed to be the one bringing it.

It was clear that not only Isemay's but many others' lives depended on the answers to these questions. She needed another audience with the Minothian leader, one without Archon Tuzhazu. But given that he commanded all the soldiers, and any message she tried to send would first reach him, how would she get that audience?

CHAPTER TWELVE

Isemay stumbled along the final steps to the boundary of the Churss. Night had spread in full force across the sky, the three moons high above seeming to hoard the illumination of every star to themselves, and even the wystic Churss lights seemed to grow more muted with each step closer to the edge. Salukis slowed down for her, and their conversation trailed to silence. The idea of sitting down, just for a moment, became a constant drumbeat in her thoughts.

"I'm exhausted," she finally admitted, and hearing it out loud seemed to instantly double her fatigue.

Salukis whispered something, and a perfect tunnel of lights bloomed along the Churss before them far off into the dark. She could almost make out a glow at the end.

"It's the edge, we're almost there. If you want, I can carry you."

"No," she blurted, the suggestion awkward enough to wake her up a bit. "I'm fine. I'll make it." And she would. To be a Knight Corporealis, one had to learn to control and rise above simple things like fatigue. How many times had her trainers told her that everyone was capable of so much more than they knew if they learned to tap into the reserves they had deep down? But then, how long had it been since

93

she'd slept? Didn't matter. She'd push herself as far as it took to find that pendant. Even if she walked her feet off.

Her competing fatigue and willpower consumed her, the war between the two things enough to make her forget how far they'd come—twice—in one day, how much she missed her parents, how scared she was. And before she realized it, the meadow and valley in the distance were spread out before her.

"Made it," she whisper-panted. "Now, where were Mura and I sitting?" Looking around, she soon thought she recognized the familiar base of a Churss tower. Its foundation boulder, half as large as Mura's entire home, had a slight concavity at ground level. It had been perfect to lean up against as they'd sat waiting for Salukis.

She rushed to the stone—

And there it was, her memory keeper. Collapsing to her knees, she swept the pendant up, feeling unnervingly like she was about to burst into tears like a child. *I'm just tired,* she told herself.

The wystic stone eyes of the dragørfly glinted silvery blue in the light of the three moons, almost as if they were flashing some message at her. With it lying in her palm, she stared down at it, her breath rushing out in a relief so profound that she felt light-headed. *Am I...I'm fainting?*

A moment later, her cheek hit the ground, and she felt the cool stone against it.

"Heyo, are you okay?"

Salukis knelt beside her. When he came back into focus, his eyes were darting nervously around her face. Isemay blinked the spots away from her vision and pushed herself up on arms that felt as loose as wet string.

"I'm fine, just light-headed. It's been a long day." Embarrassed, she scooted back into the shelter of the concave boulder and put her back against it.

Salukis eyed her closely for another moment, long enough for Isemay to grow self-conscious. Blushing, grateful for the darkness that hid it, she dropped her gaze to the pendant in her hands.

He cleared his throat. "Well, we did it. I'm really happy you got that back. It's quite, um, pretty."

"Yes," was all she could manage. It felt so good to be sitting that she quickly stopped caring about her embarrassment.

Salukis settled cross-legged beside her, the bottom halves of his wings draping out on either side behind him. Juz and Tekl joined them, Juz lying next to Salukis and Tekl relaxing into a contented sprawl against Isemay's outstretched leg. Startled, she grew stiff, but Tekl made a huffing sound through his wide mouth, then rolled onto his back, sticking his rear legs nearly into her face. His tongue, as black as his fur, lolled out.

"I'd say you better scratch his belly before he starts licking you with that tongue," Salukis said. "Consider yourself warned. Snouz drool really stinks."

Hesitantly, Isemay reached for the beast's ribcage and gave a light pat. Tekl's back legs kicked, nearly braining her, as if to urge her on. Taking the hint, she dug her fingers into the mat of his belly until she could feel skin, then started scratching harder. It was like massaging a bearskin rug, but it seemed to be doing the trick. The snouz twisted from side to side, still on his back and emitting snorts of what she hoped was joy.

Salukis watched, amused, and leaned back on his hands. They sat quietly for a time, Isemay keeping up her not entirely voluntary task of keeping the snouz entertained. With her hand busy, her eyes drifted toward the strange sky. Three moons: the largest a pale, colorless glow, much like Archon Deespora's skin tone; one red as the haze of the sun setting against a smoky horizon, and the smallest one a sparkling liquid blue, the same color as her father's eyes. The orbs fanned out above them. If Isemay spread out her fingers and put her hand in front of her face, all three moons would fall within their span.

"Salukis, do your realm's moons have something to do with that thing you mentioned? The Equiful-Equifil...?"

"Equifulcrum. Yes, they do. The three come into syzygy once every three hundred years. The Equifulcrum refers to when it's a solar eclipse. In our tradition, that's when the Everlight takes a new vessel, someone who volunteers. It's always been an Archon, since as long as Deespora's been alive. But she tells us it doesn't have to be. It can be anyone who chooses to offer themselves and the Everlight accepts."

He pointed to the largest. "Znopho the White Watcher." Then to the red: "Maiztos the Life Giver." Then the blue: "Kahros the Seeker. We just call them the Watcher, the Giver, and the Seeker. Parents tell their children that the Watcher and the Churss know whenever they get up to mischief in the night. Neeka and Ballion are probably getting that lecture right now from their folks, come to think of it." He looked to her. "Anyone who marries when Kahros is full, they say, will stay married for eternity."

She quirked an eyebrow at him, and he looked away quickly, clearing his throat once more. Tilting her head down to conceal her grin, she asked, "And what is the Life Giver's lore?"

"The Life Giver controls the tides of our blood. Without it, our bodies would grow still and die. Anyone born when Maiztos is full will live an extralong life. Or, you know, that's what they say. What are your moons called?"

"We just have one, and we just call it the moon." Fascinated by the richness all around her, she suddenly had a sense that Vinnr was a dull world. Only one moon, and no forests of stone that lit up and walked around if you asked them to politely. No women with marvelous skin tones that flowed through the colors of the rainbow like lights shining through a crystal prism. And no nice-looking boys who could fly. Dull indeed.

"A lunar eclipse at the syzygy is called the Distalfulcrum," he added quietly.

"Does your Verity change vessels then, too?"

He gave a short shake of his head and added after a pause, "It's a time of shadow and reflection, to think about our past so we can ensure we don't forget the lessons we've learned. People stay indoors during the Distalfulcrum or meet in the Churss Circle just to be together. Deespora tells us of the last war between the people of Arc Rheunos, dozens upon dozens of lifetimes ago. She says the worst slaughter was during the Distalfulcrum, and since then, Arc

Rheunosians have avoided repeating that mistake. It nearly wiped us out. And the rumor is that the Waste started during the last Distalfulcrum, too."

At his words, and the shade of subtle fear that tinted them, Isemay thought twice about how dull her own home seemed. Maybe a world without wars of annihilation and wasting plagues wasn't so terrible after all.

"But that's all ancient history," Salukis went on, attempting a lighter tone. "Arc Rheunos hasn't seen war in over six hundred years. And the next Distalfulcrum is another three hundred from now. Maybe things will be much different then. It's not a destiny or anything. Just coincidence."

Who was he trying to convince? She decided to change the subject, but before she did, he gripped something in the grassy turf and lifted it until the combined light of the moons and Churss gave him a clear look. "Ah, broken. See?" he said, and held something up for her.

The pendant's heavy copper chain dangled from his outstretched fingers, the clasp's hook snapped in half. As she reached for it, he assured her, "We have plenty of smiths who can repair that for you, even make it stronger so you won't lose it again."

"Thank you." Then, because the moment had grown solemn, she added, "Thank you for everything."

"Of course. Don't mention it." He gave her a smile that had her blushing again.

After giving Tekl a final pat, she held the pendant in the bowl of her palms so she could look straight into its crystal heart. "Salukis, I'm going to try something. If you wouldn't mind, could you stay still and quiet for a little while?"

With a shrug and a quizzical raise of the eyebrow, he nodded and leaned back again, angling his face toward the moons.

Despite being on the edge of exhaustion that seemed to have added pounds to her bones and made even her skin feel heavier, she took a deep breath, then murmured the chant her da had taught her to bring her mind fully into focus.

"Cæcra ad resrs, boromcad bea dord, kucik kea kesrs, emsu kæ loekra." *Cycle of light, balanced by dark, focus my sight, into my heart.*

Shutting her mind against all distractions took a few iterations of the chant. As she focused, the feeling of the night air surrounding her fell away, along with the coolness of the Churss at her back, even the movement of the snouz breathing against her leg, until her sight, her hearing, her every intent were aware of nothing but the memory keeper's crystal.

Da, she thought. *Can you hear me?* The pendant worked by her simply thinking about memories, rather than speaking of them aloud. She hoped reaching out to Ulfric could work the same way. She would have felt silly calling to her father out loud with Salukis sitting right there.

For a moment she thought she saw light swirling in the lens, but the next it was gone. *Da? It's me, it's Isemay. Are you out there, somewhere?*

Nothing happened. She stared into it for some amount of time, losing track, but there was nothing. *Maybe thinking of a memory of him would help,* she thought and allowed herself to conjure the first one that came to mind.

She was eight, bored, precocious, and in her own mind quite cunning. She'd pilfered the key to one of her father's smaller crafteries. Small by *his* standards, anyway. The room was the size of five of her own sleeping chambers, but unlike her chamber, it was filled with marvelous bits and baubles, tools and artifacts, materials and metals, shelves and tables and benches cluttered with the stuff. A room filled with *treasure*, and it finally became all too clear why her father banned her from his crafteries—oh, the things she could make, or try to. Her reputation for mischief had been well earned and was known to all the Knights, who were like an extended family of aunts and uncles, and in Mylla's case, practically an older sister. And this room had more options for creating mischief than a gimgree sloth had stink.

She'd puttered around the craftery, taking in everything. Some things she knew their purposes, some things were foreign or unusual to her. Running her fingers over the innumerable items as she moved along, she forced away the increasingly insistent voice in the back of her mind telling her to leave before she got into big trouble. But how could she disregard all these wonderful treasures? Her parents thought she was with Safran studying Elder Veros. Safran thought she was going to the market with members of the Conservatum who attended to the Knights. Ulfric and Symvalline were likely to be gone for hours teaching the Prelates at the Conservatum about topics pertaining to boring subjects like history or medicine, as was usual. She had the whole day to explore, and she planned not to waste it.

And soon she discovered the best thing of them all—a rudimentary set of wings that to her young eyes looked just like bruhawks' wings. Was her da building something people could use to fly?

Isemay's memories skipped forward to a few hours later. She'd managed to sneak the heavy set of wings, one at a time, to her sleeping chamber, where she'd figured out how to strap them on, then hopped around in the high-ceilinged room for a time, trying to figure out how the wings worked. Frustrated with her lack of progress, she'd gone to look for Yggo and Urgo, who were at ease in their usual roost among tree-sized perches in the fortress's great courtyard. She loved the bruhawks. They were wild and vicious, but also loyal and intelligent beyond, she sometimes thought, even some of the Ivoryssians. She'd been raised to be respectful of them, but when she spoke to them, she knew they understood her, and their heads would tilt as their great yellow eyes fixed on her, making her shiver. Their talons could shred a person with hardly an effort, but she'd never feared them. Well, not enough to stay away from them, anyway. Yggo and Urgo were Knights, or at least ordained like the Knights, and she was going to be a Knight too, someday. They may as well have been kin, and you didn't tear up your kin and eat them for lunch.

Using fresh-killed hares, she'd coaxed the bruhawks into showing her their secret of flight, assuming that once she understood how to launch from a perch, the rest would be as easy as it appeared when they did it. After an hour or so of lessons, she felt ready and returned to her sleeping chamber. Its second-story balcony would be perfect for the first step: takeoff.

Overlooking the courtyard, she'd stood on the balcony with the wings tucked to her sides, her arms through the straps along their central frame, and called to Urgo and Yggo to join her in her maiden voyage. The bruhawks had flapped up to her, watching her with sharp curiosity.

"Da made these so the Knights would finally have your backs the way you've always had theirs. Ready to go?" she asked them.

Yggo uttered a high-pitched cheeping sound that Isemay had never heard before. Interpreting it as encouragement, she drew in a deep breath, stepped back a few paces, and ran up and over the balcony's bannister using the ramp she'd created of a table (which she already knew she'd be chastised for breaking, but that was later), and off into midair.

The broken arm and untold number of bruises and abrasions she'd suffered on landing weren't the most frustrating part of her failed experiment. The severity of the fallout that followed—the scolding her mum had given her once she was certain Isemay would recover; the way Stave had outright laughed at her undertaking of, as he'd put it, "the kind of instructive lesson nothing but one's own dumbassery can teach"; and her father's unnervingly quiet scowl that had told her he was not only aggravated but disappointed by her breaking of his rules —wasn't even beyond her ability to get past, eventually. It was the fact that the experiment hadn't even worked for one fleeting instant. She hadn't even glided, just crashed to the ground like a dropped rock. She would never have told her parents that the lesson she learned wasn't to not do as she been told not to, but rather to get better at figuring out how to do it without getting injured—or caught.

The sound of muffled laughter yanked Isemay sharply out of the memory, and the darkness of the Arc Rheunos night jarred her after being so immersed in a memory that had taken place under the bright light of Vinnr's daystar.

"You should have had me there to show you how it's done," Salukis said, midchuckle. "A girl flying. It takes a bit more than some fake feathers and clever straps."

"You...you saw that?" she said, her embarrassment flaring like a petard. She'd been too deeply focused to think her memory would be visible to others through the peculiar wystic way the memory keeper worked.

"I did, and it was wonderfully funny."

His amusement at her expense—and her embarrassment—set off the temper Isemay's family would sometimes joke she'd inherited from her "aunt" Eisa. "Is it an Arc Rheunosian trait to laugh at other's suffering, or are you just a mean-spirited slackface bahooky?"

His mouth snapped closed at her cutting tone. "I'm sorry. I shouldn't have laughed. It's just, I mean…" His top lip trembled as his mirth returned.

Her anger evaporated like steam in sunlight. She was too tired to be mad. And disheartened. The memory keeper remained stubbornly quiet. *Where is my da? What am I going to do if I don't hear from him again?*

Something warm and wet slipped over her hand, and she looked down to see Tekl staring at her face, panting expectantly. Sighing, she scratched between his spiral horns. "Salukis, I'm not sure I have the energy to walk back to Maerria tonight. Do you think we'll be safe if we just stay here and sleep a little while?"

The air at the edge of the Churss was cool, but she'd noticed that the temperature within the stone forest's confines had never seemed too hot or cold, just comfortable, and she suspected the Churss had something to do with that, too. If they found a leafy nook to curl up in, she doubted the chill would reach them, and she might feel better after a few winks.

"That's a good idea," he said. "I'm supposed to start the garden wall tomorrow anyway. I'll be happy to put that off for a good cause." The smile he gave her this time was warm, not teasing. "I know the perfect spot. Come on."

CHAPTER THIRTEEN

The morning of her third day in Maerria snuck up on Isemay. A light breeze lifted wisps of her curly hair and fluttered it across her eyelashes, tickling her. Brushing them away, she opened her eyes to light. She'd fallen asleep tucked into a hollow inside a Churss tower, and the first sight greeting her was the meadow below and the valley farther off with the meandering river wending away in both directions. It looked so serene, but she felt anything but.

Reflexively, she gripped her tunic pocket and found the dragørfly pendant tucked inside. She wouldn't lose it again, on her life. A grumble and huff beside her brought Tekl and Juz to her attention. Both snouzes had curled up with her and pressed against her as tightly as a cocoon.

"Hello?" she called after not seeing Salukis nearby. "Salukis?"

There was no answer, so she gently pushed against the snouzes to help her stand up. They didn't budge, and Tekl huffed again and shifted his big head on his wide paws.

"Snouzes," she said quietly. "Come on, you have to make room so I don't squish you."

Juz, on her left, raised his head and looked at her, the beast's glittering eyes barely visible beneath thick hanging ropes of black fur. He nuzzled her hand, then pushed one horn into it. She scratched around the base of the bony protrusion and could have sworn from the way his lips curled back that he was smiling. After a moment, he started panting. Isemay realized she should have been concerned with Salukis being out of sight and hearing distance, but she found she wasn't. The snouzes put her at ease in a way the bruhawks, though she'd spent her childhood treating them like pets, never had. It was probably because they didn't seem to have any long talons or sharp, pointy beaks that turned flesh into dead strips of meat.

She scratched for a few more moments, then decided to try once more to reach her da through the memory keeper. After several frustrating and fruitless minutes, she gave up. Impulsively, in her frustration she wanted to chuck the pendant away, but of course, she wouldn't do that.

Juz had lain his muzzle on her thigh, and she commenced rubbing again, though halfheartedly this time. "Where's your master, boy?" she asked the extremely contented beast.

"She."

Isemay startled at the voice, then relaxed when Salukis stepped from behind the tower. "There you are," she said.

"Just went to get us some water and these." He opened his fist to reveal a handful of what she assumed were a kind of Arc Rheunosian nut.

Juz and Tekl loped to his side and received scratches from his free hand. "I figured you wouldn't want to be left alone, so I left the snouzes with you. But Juz is a girl. They're from the same litter."

"Ah. Well, at least I'm starting to be able to tell them apart." Tekl had one horn whose tip jutted out slightly backward like a hook. And Juz's tail was a bit bushier. Other than that, they were twins. She stood, reaching her arms over her head and emitting a long groany squeak as she stretched. "How long ago did I fall asleep?"

"A few hours," he said. "I didn't want to wake you up. You've been through a lot."

That was far too true, and she wished it weren't. She'd always enjoyed risks and excitement, but not like this. Not when everywhere she looked and everything she saw was unfamiliar, strange, and, worst of all, utterly devoid of friends or family. She wasn't safe. For the first time in her life, she wasn't safe.

Suddenly, she felt weightless and light-headed. The world swayed side to side, then tilted as she crumbled to the ground.

"Isemay!"

This time she stayed put, fighting against sudden nausea that was working its way through her guts. Her mouth filled with spit. She didn't have much inside her, but she was on the verge of vomiting, nonetheless.

Salukis knelt by her side, his expression indicating how uncertain he was about what to do. "Here." He passed her a hollow gourd of water. "Drink something."

"I don't feel well." She groaned. "Don't want to drink."

"Uh…" He looked around the space, as if he'd find something that might aid her. "What can I do?"

She pulled her legs up to her chest and clutched them, like a child hiding under her bed in fear. But it wasn't fear she felt, just a sense of overwhelming exhaustion, worsened by the nausea, and topped off by a rush of dismay. She was never going to see her parents again.

"Maybe…uh, maybe I should go get help."

She remained silent, holding her knees. She wanted to cry. Like she had when she was six and broke her favorite wooden toy bird or when she was five and Knight Eisa had reprimanded her for touching Vaka Aster's vessel with food-stained fingers. In other words, like a child who needed her mum.

Salukis put his warm, smooth palm on her forehead. To comfort her? A moment later, he pulled it away. "You're running a fever. Verity's mercy, do you have the—"

The plague. That's what he'd been about to say. And what if he was right? What if she died, and no one in Vinnr would ever know?

"Isemay, I'm going to carry you back to Maerria. You need to see Deespora. She can help."

Deespora? She hadn't bothered to try helping Isemay before. Why would she now? His hands found her wrists, and he began tugging her up. It was annoying. She just wanted to lie here. But as she began pulling away from him, a strangely adult realization washed over her. Fighting him would be silly. He was kind, and nice looking, and he just wanted to help. And besides, she was going to be a Knight someday. She had to be tough. And if things got too hard to do alone, she had to be wise enough to accept help when it was offered.

She relaxed her arms and sat up. "I'll try not to retch on you," she promised meekly.

"It isn't the Waste making her ill," Deespora said to the brave three who'd joined Salukis and Isemay at Deespora's home. These included Mura and her mother Lysis. No one knew the third was there but Isemay. It was the young girl Neeka, who stood outside peering in through the open window frame, the child's curiosity stronger than her fear. Deespora added, "She is very sick, but she has no plague symptoms. None need fear."

Isemay lay on a hastily created bed of blankets and pillows near the hearth, which was wood- and ashless like the one in Mura's home, shivering. Memory of the flight back from the edge of the Churss was spotty. She mostly recalled the cool wind blowing against her, which had been simultaneously a relief from her fever and had grated at her like ice pellets, and occasional glimpses of the snouzes keeping pace below. She remembered Salukis had stopped once or twice to catch his breath high up on ledges in the Churss towers, and the silhouettes of the three moons in the sky above fading behind the brighter daystar.

She sat up and coughed and someone patted her on the back. When the cough subsided, she asked, "Do you know what it is? A cold maybe?"

Deespora's heartmatch was also present, or so Isemay assumed him to be, and he leaned down and handed her a stone mug. He was a shortish man with a belly that pushed against his thin, loose vest. She could barely see the striped markings it seemed all the Arc Rheunosian men had, their color blending almost perfectly with the mellow brown hue of his skin. His wings and hair, which were both a black-streaked gray, stood out against his youthful smooth skin. Otherwise, she'd have guessed him to be much younger than their color suggested. The only wrinkles he had were around his eyes and mouth, which looked like it never went a day without laughing.

She took a cautious sip of whatever the mug contained and immediately followed that with a deep swallow. It was thick and warm with a sweet, milky flavor, and reminded her of hot chocolate but tasted even better.

Oh. Ugh. Don't retch, don't retch, don't do it. Not in front of...them. You'll die of embarrassment. She'd managed not to lose her stomach contents on Salukis during their trip, and had even forgotten about the nausea for a bit, but now it reared up once more, and black spots peppered the backs of her eyelids. She almost didn't set the mug back down in time before sinking back to the floor. "This doesn't feel like a cold."

"No, it isn't," Deespora said, her voice sounding hollow and tinny in Isemay's fugue. "It isn't even what we'd ordinarily describe as a sickness of your body, I fear."

"It most definitely feels like it's my body." What did the Archon mean? This was too awful to be just something in her mind.

"Isemay, you were not created for this realm. You're not adapting to it. I don't think you can. Your body fights our world, and our world fights your body, the same as either would attack any foreign matter."

"What does that mean?" Mura asked.

"Think of it like this," the Archon said. "What would happen if you stuck your hand in a bizzle hive?"

"They would get very cross and sting me until I pulled my hand out."

Salukis cut in. "So you're saying Arc Rheunos is a bizzle hive, and Isemay is a hand?"

"She is foreign to us. I can see she is a woman of some strength, but she is not strong enough to win a fight against the rules of the Cosmos," Deespora said simply.

Isemay let out a mix of a moan and a half-swallowed sob as another flash of heat spread over her. Sweat broke out on her forehead, behind her ears, all along her back and chest.

Through ears that felt stuffed with straw, she heard Lysis say, "Is there anything you can do to help her?"

Robes rustled and footsteps receded to a far corner of the room. Whispers slipped to her, but she was too miserable to even try to understand them.

Deespora returned and settled beside her. "Isemay, there is one thing I can do to assuage the discomfort you're in, but it will only be temporary. The only thing that will help you is if I send you back home. You cannot stay here forever without eventually succumbing."

She pried her eyes open and looked into Deespora's face, close to her own, the Archon's eyes shining with sympathy. "But my mum..."

The Archon nodded but said nothing.

"Is my mum sick too?"

Deespora's brows creased and she took a moment to think it over. "I can't say, but she is not like you, child. She carries the spark of a Verity, and I believe that will protect her. All the realms are safe to those who've received the celestials' touch directly."

Relief must have shown in her face, because Deespora went on. "You do not have to worry about your mother. She is powerful. She saved many in this room already, and I'm sure she can save herself as well."

"If we could help her, the way you're helping me..."

Instead of the exasperation Isemay usually caused in adults with her relentless debating, Deespora's expression smoothed into kindness. "Quiet now, let me use the Fenestros to make you feel better. Then we'll talk about what to do next."

Nodding—anything to make this illness bearable—she closed her eyes and slipped her hand into her tunic pocket to grip the memory keeper, as though it were a lone tree limb keeping her afloat in a vast, deep lake.

Moments later, a slight weight settled on her chest and a blazing warmth began at her sternum, spreading up and down her body, a feeling like slowly sinking into a hot bath. It was the most soothing sensation she'd ever experienced, and her hand tightened even more on her pendant as she felt the warmth push away first her nausea, then the aches that had begun to sink into her muscles and bones. The feverish heat of her cheeks grew milder. Deespora spoke over her, but she barely heard the words as her body slowly began to feel not just normal but stronger, healthier, infused with an uncommon vitality. She began to feel as if she could stand up and rush from Maerria to the Aktoktos Gate in a single unbroken run.

"Open your eyes."

She did. Deespora was sitting cross-legged beside her still, examining her with an avid, questioning expression.

"I feel like I could compete in every sport in Ivoryss's annual Aster Games and win them all," Isemay marveled.

The Archon smiled pleasantly. "You must remain calm. The less you do, and the less you worry and fret, the longer you will feel better. But it will wear off."

"You mean I'm to sit still until I'm sick again?"

"Or until you go back to Vinnr."

She shook her head vigorously, not wanting to defy the Archon but adamant that she had to stay in Arc Rheunos. "But I can't."

"Yes, I know. You can't leave your mother. But, Isemay, you must understand, I can't do this for you forever."

"I-I am grateful." She tried hard to remember to be polite and show the gratitude that was very much owed, adding meekly, "Then just for a bit, please, help me stay well. My mum will free herself, I know it, and she'll come find me."

Deespora dipped her chin, indulging Isemay once more, then rose and went through the doorway to speak to the others, who waited outside. Isemay caught sight of Neeka at the window again. When the child saw her looking, her face flushed a light lavender and she smiled, then gave Isemay a small wave.

"You glowed like a Churss boulder full of Znopho light," the little girl whispered. "It was so pretty!"

Isemay couldn't help but return her exuberance. "Well, it felt as brilliant as it must have looked."

Neeka disappeared as fast as fish snapping up a gnat as soon as Alvar, Deespora's heartmatch, entered, followed by the others.

"Feeling bouncy, bloopie, and full of bizzle nectar again, young one?" he asked her.

When it was obvious she didn't know what to say, Mura supplied, "He means are you feeling better?"

"Yes, very much."

Mura smiled, and Isemay could see her worries lifting away. She was touched at how concerned Mura must have been about her, and realized again how much she had to be grateful for. These people had taken her in without argument or hesitation, they'd provided all she needed to survive, helped her get back her memory keeper, saved her life more than once, and had asked nothing of her in return. As reluctant as she was to admit it, the adult side of her mind recognized that Deespora had her reasons for not wanting to step into the Zhallahs' enemy's lands and sacrifice her own people for one foreign woman, even a Knight. The Archon had to keep the Zhallahs safe, and yet she'd taken Isemay in. Isemay needed to be patient and do whatever she could to repay their unearned kindness. She needed to put aside her selfishness, and her loneliness, trust that her mum had probably faced harder challenges and gotten through them without Isemay's paltry and inexperienced contribution, and start pulling some weight in return. To become a Knight, she would need to learn gratitude as well as wisdom.

She pushed herself to her feet, paused as the last lingering flush of Fenestros-induced warmth rushed away, and said, "While I'm waiting for Mum, is there anything I can do in return for all you've done for me?"

CHAPTER FOURTEEN

I t was the sixth time the sun had risen while Symvalline was in this world, the sixth day that had passed since she'd seen her daughter, and the seventh since she'd seen her husband. She didn't know which of these was the most burdensome to her heart and nerves, but she would soon be pushed past the edge of reason and into making desperation-driven choices.

Each time she sat, her skin felt as if it were igniting in a million tiny fires as her restlessness spread. Each time she paced, she grew frantic at her whirling, repeating thoughts that were getting her nowhere. Only the strange little journal gave her a reason for hope, a thing to focus on that gave her a glimpse of how she might escape.

Within its pages were many passages discussing the Equifulcrum and historical accounts of the dealings of the Archon. Whoever had kept the journal had chronicled the events of hundreds of past turns.

One doodle was drawn in random margins over and over. A tower with some kind of orb or lens atop it whose crystalline nature had been perfectly captured by a skilled hand. Its use or reason for being such a focus of the artist wasn't clear, however. More disturbing, several of the book's final pages seemed to be an in-depth study of a spell combining all five Fenestrii. One drawing showed them spinning around an ill-defined figure, as if holding the figure inside. Was this the cage that the journal's first words spoke of? *Only the maker can unmake the cage.* Her attention was drawn back to this spell again and again, though she could see it was incomplete. But why would the book's owner have been so interested in the idea of holding someone captive through the use of the celestial artifacts?

Symvalline suspected the book had once belonged to an Archon. How it had wound up forgotten on a shelf in the healers chamber was something she would never know, but she scoured every word, every diagram, looking for clues that would reveal Arc Rheunos's secrets and perhaps lead her to the celestial artifacts, the Scrylle and Fenestrii, she needed to get her and Isemay home.

After Tulla's death, her first day and night were consumed by pacing, reading, pacing, and more reading. No amount of pleading or arguing with the Deathless Guards, who acted like stones, or the servants who brought her food and water, got her any closer to a meeting with Akeeva. So, she soon reasoned she would have to find another way to escape this prison. Through force. Or rather, through the healing arts that she could use in her own secret ways.

A new idea had occurred to her. The powder she'd attained from the sympathetic wagon driver…

Late on her second afternoon in Everlight Hall, acting with as much nonchalance as she could contrive, she put aside the mysterious journal and paced to the stacks of medicinal books, hunting through them for the recipe to make the sedative powder. The guards would assume she was doing as she'd been told, creating more of the toxin Tuzhazu wanted. With enough of the sedative, and crucially with the right ingredients to enhance its effects, she may be able to knock out her Deathless watchers and begin her escape from this dungeon. She'd already ruled out trying to beat them in a hand-to-hand attack. Her first encounter with one of these Verity-enhanced fighters above the starpath valley had more than illustrated why they were called "deathless," and she doubted she could overpower two of them. Before they'd been changed, they'd seemed reasonable. But one look in their lifeless gray eyes, and she knew hoping for reason from them was a dangerous indulgence.

She found the right books and dove in, focusing for who knew how many hours, not even stopping to eat when food was brought to her. All the while, her tireless sentries watched, motionless. And in the back of her mind, she fretted at the days passing with her daughter unprotected in a hostile realm and the love of her life and her family of Knights fighting a world-scale battle in Vinnr.

Over the next two days, Tuzhazu made a practice of surprising her with random visits to check on her progress, and, she suspected, to see if he might catch her in the act of sabotage or trying to escape, but Symvalline was ready for such interference. She wouldn't have trusted her either if the tables had been turned. And his instincts were, of course, on target.

The irony of the whole situation was that the substance she'd set out to create was the very thing Tuzhazu wanted from her—in a way. Only she had no intention of giving it to him but of using it *on* him.

Once she'd found the recipe for wagon driver's medicine, she researched, extrapolated, and combined several new selections of the substances stocked in the healers chamber to come up with what she hoped was what she needed to not only knock out a Deathless Guard and potentially an Archon, but to knock them out for a very, very long time.

Time enough to escape this chamber, find Akeeva, and retrieve the Verity artifacts, which she reasoned must be within this fortress and were her best chance of fending off Tuzhazu if he caught her. And of course, she needed them to get herself and Isemay home. A compound to end their lives would have been much more direct and certain, but she didn't want to kill anyone. It was contrary to her nature as both a healer and a mother. And she'd seen firsthand that those who'd "chosen" to be made Deathless hardly had a choice at all.

So she did as she had done countless times in her role as healer in Vinnr, and after testing small doses on herself to determine the effects of her new toxin, she was ready to put it to a real test.

Over the top of a wooden bowl containing a few drams of her

concoction, she eyed the Deathless Guards surreptitiously, pondering how to get them to ingest the powder. She didn't think they'd be gullible enough to be coaxed into drinking it if she mixed it with a liquid, nor would they simply agree to be her test subjects. After rejecting several courses of action, she decided on the most direct.

Out of their view, she clasped a couple of spoonfuls worth of powder in each fist, then walked out from behind the worktable and announced, "I am leaving this room, guards, and you can't stop me."

Alerted, they closed ranks and took defensive postures. She ran straight toward the left one, Toranzu.

They'd never been issued weapons, but she didn't doubt they'd been trained to fight. This didn't concern her. She just needed to get close.

Before she made contact, she turned to one side as if to shove her shoulder into the guard's chest. Toranzu reacted as expected and side-stepped before she hit him. She thumped into the door with her shoulder, her other hand already reaching for Viddzu's face as he tried to grab her. Her palm smashed into his mouth and nose, and she threw an arm around his neck to hold him close. Toranzu yanked her away by the back of her tunic, ripping it to the waist, and she let go of Viddzu, flung herself around, and heaved her other palm into Toranzu's face in the same way.

Viddzu sneezed loudly once, then again, then began grappling her from behind. The two guards seemed ill-equipped for dealing with a woman who seemed to be simply trying to hug them, but it didn't matter. She released Toranzu and ceased struggling completely, letting Viddzu pull her free. He shoved her toward the ground, and she let herself fall limply to her back, then propped herself on her elbows to see what would happen next.

They loomed over her, their faces comically dusted with what might have been common bread flour, albeit greenish. Neither made a move to harm her, and she hoped it would stay that way. Tuzhazu had plans for her that required her to be alive, and she wouldn't have put it past the Minothian to have given orders that the only one with permission to hurt her was himself.

Toranzu began to sneeze as well, and both men began swiping

roughly at their noses, as if gnats were infesting their nostrils. Viddzu was the first to stagger, then he suddenly fell forward, not even trying to catch himself with his arms. Symvalline pushed herself out of the way as he struck the stone floor, and Toranzu followed a breath later.

She stood up, watching them, breathing in short, sharp gasps of anticipation. When they didn't wake up instantly, she lunged to the doorway, turned the handle, and pushed.

It didn't move far, and she felt the telltale resistance of a bar locking it closed from the other side.

Cursing, she rammed the same shoulder she'd hit it with before furiously into the door. It didn't budge, and she cursed more, this time at herself for her stupidity. Why hadn't she known there was a bar? She'd never heard it being slid into place, testament alone of how thick the wood was. She'd never break through it, not without her klinkí stones or an emberflare petard.

She'd have to try her second plan. Materials she'd covertly set aside would when combined and ignited by a rushlight create a heavy spark and sudden blaze—maybe enough to burn through the wood surrounding the door's hinges.

She rushed to her worktable to gather them when, from somewhere above her, a child's high-pitched voice said: "Did you kill my father?"

Symvalline stopped in the middle of the floor, scanning the space, unable to pinpoint where the voice had come from. "Who's here?" she asked. There was no response. "If you mean the guards," she went on, "I haven't harmed them. I've just put them to sleep for a while. They'll be fine in a few hours." *If even that long,* she thought. Gently, she said, "And I won't harm you either. Where are you, child? How did you get in here?"

"They said you're an Archon from another realm…Vinli or Vine. Is that true? Was that Archon wysticism you used on the Deathless Guards?"

His voice placed him between the ages of six and nine turns, she guessed, noting that the fear she'd heard when he'd first spoken was already being replaced by curiosity. *His father...?* She shuddered at the thought that the boy was looking at his own kin and glanced about the room in search of him. The Deathless had not stirred, but that didn't mean they wouldn't. She didn't want a child present to witness what might happen when they did.

And, if he was in here, that meant there was another way out.

The chamber's walls and floor were bare stone and about twenty feet high, with cloudy glass-covered windows on the west side at ground level. She hadn't tried to climb up to them, but the frequency in which pedestrians passed by outside told her they would be a poor exit. They opened to a courtyard or bailey, and a courtyard of a fortress this size was never without traffic. The windows were still as tightly closed as ever. The child hadn't gotten in that way.

A massive hearth, which she hadn't needed to light, adorned the south wall, near where the pallets of the sick were. Could he have crawled down through the chimney? She stepped closer to examine it, and when she did, a small fall of ash and pebble sifted down from somewhere above, pattering the cold hearth's floor. The mantel stones formed an arch over the opening whose apex fell several bricks shy of the ceiling. Among those bricks, she finally spotted something. There were darker spots, gaps in the brickwork. They were too far above her head to see inside, but from their vantage, the entire healers chamber would be visible. There must be a space between the outer wall and the chimney, or some kind of alcove inside where the child was perched, watching her. For how long?

She stopped far enough away that whoever was up there could see her. "That's right. I am an Archon from the realm called Vinnr. Is your name, by chance, Inder?"

"How did you know that?" he blurted, caught by surprise.

Her guess had been right. "Your father, Viddzu, wanted you to know he loves you. He asked Archon Tuzhazu to make sure to tell you before he was…enlisted into the Deathless Guard."

"…The Archon never told me. He only said my dad's great honor would outlive even me."

She barely kept her calm at that statement. *What a monstrous thing to tell a child whose da was just turned into a monster himself.* Every new revelation of Tuzhazu pushed Symvalline's regard for him further toward contempt. She'd met a few cruel people in her life, but Tuzhazu turned cruelty not just into a practice but nearly into an art form.

But back to the child and the potential escape he may have to offer. "Inder, Tuzhazu doesn't want me to leave this room and won't let me speak to the Everlight. That's why I had to put your da and his fellow guard to sleep, but the door is barred from the outside. It's very important that I speak to the Everlight. Vaka Aster, my own Verity, has given me a message to deliver. Can you help me get to Mithlí?"

"The Everlight's been too busy to spend time with us kids lately. She's planning the Feast of Future's Hope for the Equifulcrum. We've been stuck in drills all day long on the proper way to eat and sit and sing, and all that dumb stuff. It's *soooo* dull." He stopped for a moment, and as Symvalline was about to try again, he said in a softer voice. "Tulla was supposed to stand next to me in the choir. I kept telling her she squeaks like a mouse when we were practicing. But she's gone now, isn't she?"

She felt her throat start to tighten at the boy's obvious pain. "I'm so sorry, child. She has left this world, but her spirit will remain in the Cosmos eternally. No one is ever really gone for good."

"Do you think she knew I was only teasing when I made fun of her? I didn't mean it!"

"If she didn't, she does now. And I'm sure she's forgiven you."

He went quiet again, and she could hear him shifting around in the space behind the hearth's wall. More ash filtered down, reminding her of sands falling through an hourglass and her limited time.

"I saw what you did for her, how nice you were as she was sleeping. Before her mom, her real mom, not the Everlight, took her and she got the Waste, she cried a lot. She really missed her mom. Some of the kids don't get to see their folks. But I had my dad here in the hall, so I didn't cry when I first came here. Do you think Tulla thought you were her mom?"

Symvalline, seething in anger at how heartless it was for Akeeva to take children from their parents so young, answered slowly, "She was sleeping very soundly, but I have a child too and I tried to comfort

Tulla as I would my own little girl. Her name is Crumb, my daughter." *And I should be comforting her right now instead of trapped in these walls of deception and delusion.*

"Crumb? Like a piece of bread? That's a funny name."

"It's not her real name. Her father started calling her that when she was a little girl." She got lost in the memory for a bittersweet moment. "He told her his true age—the Knights, or Archons, live an extraordinarily long time—and she laughed and called him a crusty old man. 'If I am a crust,' he told her, 'then you must be just a tiny little crumb,' and we've called her that since then."

"Like we all call Mithlí the Everlight."

"Yes, just like that." She spared a glance over her shoulder to check on the Deathless, who were still motionless. But for how much longer?

"Will they be mad at you when they wake up?" he asked, confirming he could see all she did.

Symvalline was doing her best to keep up with his constant change of subject, but she worried her patience might not last as long as the sleeping powder at this rate. She had to try to persuade him to help her somehow.

"I'm not sure," she said. "If I had a place, perhaps, that I could hide if they did get angry, it might help give them time to calm down before they found me. What do you think, Inder? Do you sometimes hide when you're worried you might get in trouble? Maybe the place you're hiding now?"

Much too clever for his own good, he seemed to see what her line of questioning was intended for and responded, "If I show a grown-up the tunnels we use, my friends will be cross with me."

The child's craftiness reminded her, achingly, of Isemay. His mention of "tunnels" was intriguing, though, especially since he seemed to think they were unknown widely among adults, thus well suited for being a means of both escape and evasion. How could she get him to show them to her? Simple bribery usually worked with children. "Would they be cross if you told them I promise to show them some Vinnric wysticism? Do they like to see Archon tricks?"

"You mean like what they say you can do with those blue stones Archon Tuzhazu has now?"

Her heart beat harder. "You mean my klinkí stones. Those are gifts from my Verity. Inder, this is important, do you know where they are? And a pendant, a lens set within an eyestone that I wore around my neck?"

"The Archon keeps them in his chambers. Could you show us how you make them fly around?"

"I can show you, yes. But"—she didn't want to dash his hopes but sensed he'd know it if she lied to him—"you have to be an Archon to use them. And I have to get them back first."

"…It's too bad your Archon tricks couldn't save Tulla."

"Oh sweet boy, sometimes it's time for people to move on, and no tricks can help them."

"…I have to go now. Mistress Hertha will swat me if she finds out where I've been."

"No, wait—"

"All us kids see the Everlight for evening meal. I'll find out if she will see you. But don't worry, Archon, I'll make sure it's our secret. Then maybe you'll show me the blue stones."

Symvalline gritted her teeth against the demands she wanted to make of him, but he was gone before she had could have.

CHAPTER FIFTEEN

After the child Inder had gone, Symvalline was left with a choice: try to find a way into his secret tunnels or remain in place and wait for the Deathless to awaken and Tuzhazu to return. She guessed she had under three hours until the evening meal, where Inder would be able to convey her request to Akeeva for an audience. By now, she knew to expect her own dinner would be brought sometime later, but that didn't mean Tuzhazu wouldn't surprise her with a visit.

One thing that had to be done, and quickly, was binding the two Deathless before they awoke. She couldn't know how they'd react to what she'd done, and she preferred not to find out the hard way.

Using strips of cloth torn from the bed linens on the patients' pallets, she quickly had the guards trussed. They were still alive, she could tell by the movement of their eyes behind their closed lids, like someone in deep sleep. A distant sense of self-satisfaction tickled her thoughts when they didn't awaken during her endeavors. Whatever else she was, there was no doubt she was a good hand at potion-making.

What next? Leaving was out of the question. Even if she could access the secret passages, what then? They could be vast or limited, and she had no way to know. If all she ended up finding was a passage to the kitchens, which seemed a likely enough place for children with a taste for sweets to wend their way to, she'd be no better off. And if the tunnels split and multiplied and advanced beyond her own frame of reference, which was cripplingly limited, she could get lost in the fortress walls. Worse, they could be filled with dark shafts or crevasses that would swallow her whole and forever. If she was going to escape that way, she needed a guide. And knowing children as she did, she suspected she hadn't seen the last of little Inder.

That left the last option. She would wait for Tuzhazu and face the consequences. Therefore, she needed a good bluff—and a good backup plan.

Tearing further strips of cloth from the linens, and using pieces from her own now damaged tunic, she created a set of small rags. Once she had a handful, she quickly mixed a bowlful of the ingredients she'd assembled that would create small explosions, took a few rushlights from the collection she'd found for lighting the room, and tied the bundles up with twine with the rushlights sticking free to be used as fuses.

These primitive petards could be useful, but not if they were found. Nowhere in the chamber was safe from a determined search by Tuzhazu or someone under his command. Except...

The hearth gaped wide and rose high over her head. She barely had to duck to step into its cold mouth. Holding up a rushlight, she saw only blackness, the walls caked with soot from untold hundreds of hours of wood burning. Pulling a stool inside, she was able to rise high enough in the chimney to see something flat and square set into the wall over her head.

Cursing her inadequate height, she pulled a wooden ladder, about six feet tall and used by those without wings to retrieve higher-shelved books, into the hearth, then climbed up, as careful as she could be not to brush against the sooty walls and thereby give away her explorations.

The thing she saw was a door, really only cupboard-sized, made of a metal that might have been iron, though it was too blackened to really tell, flat and featureless, except for two hinges on the left side.

She tried wedging her fingers into the cracks around each side, but even her small hands were too big. The fire poker just barely fit, but she could not get it deep enough to crank against it and lever the door open.

Pressed for time, she decided to make what use of it she could. Returning to her worktable, she stored all the makeshift petards in a burlap sack, then added a container filled with most of the sedative powder she'd created. She returned to the ladder, climbed up, and tied a loop of the twine around a hinge and knotted it around the mouth of the sack. If Tuzhazu looked up into the chimney with a light, he might see it. But why would he?

After returning the ladder to the wall and hiding the scuffed, soot-stained side, she then took the remainder of the sedative ingredients and fed them into a firebox, destroying them.

Then she set herself to the hardest task she had before her yet. Waiting.

CHAPTER SIXTEEN

The amount of time Symvalline had to wait until Tuzhazu came crashing down on her like a giant wave was mercifully short. A meal was delivered shortly after the rays of the Arc Rheunos daystar dimmed through her windows. The attendant took a single glance at the tied-up Deathless, who had begun to twitch with the first signs of regaining consciousness, said not a single word, and hurried away, leaving a bowl of steaming stew and a cup of something that smelled a bit stronger than Vinnric wine.

Symvalline knew it was a matter of moments until Tuzhazu would be notified, and she'd barely touched food since this "adventure" had begun. She needed to keep her strength up, so she dug in. The stew had no flavors she immediately recognized—unsurprising in a new and different world—but she noted there didn't seem to be anything that resembled meat within it. Still, it filled a hollow spot within her that she hadn't noticed, and she felt a hundred times better almost instantly. She would have to remember to be better about taking sustenance.

She was more hesitant about the drink but eventually decided that if Tuzhazu wanted to poison her, he'd be more likely to force it down her throat than disguise it in beverages at this point. The liquid warmed her insides enough that she only had a few sips. It wouldn't do to be drunk and malleable when he arrived.

The door didn't precisely crash open, but it swung with a power behind it that announced the Archon's state of mind as clearly as a herald. He strode in and spied the Deathless Guards, who had begun to writhe and flop like angry landed chelbeifin sharks. They started to screech in their ghastly voices, making her wish she'd thought to add gags to the restraints.

She decided to give an explanation before Tuzhazu asked. "I did nothing but what you asked. The sleeping agent is ready. And I needed to test it somehow, obviously." Her hands clenched into fists, which she held rigidly to her sides. She didn't exactly fear him, but no one in their right mind wanted to invite the wrath of someone who observed people suffering with the flat dispassion of a flounder. "It works, by the way," she added.

Tuzhazu threw a look over his shoulder at the Deathless and commanded, "Silence!" Then he eyed her, a twitch in the crevasse between his heavy brows. "What happened to your overshirt?"

Nonchalantly, she pointed to where she'd balled the remains of her tunic and laid them on the worktable. If he picked the bundle up, he'd see it was missing pieces and would probably question her about that. "The guards were less accommodating to my experiments than I was hoping they'd be." Let him think she'd managed to overpower one, or even both, of his toughest soldiers. That might put him in a contemplative rather than aggressive mood and stave off any attack he might be inclined to.

"Do you think you're clever, Vinnric?"

The hostility in his tone was unmissable. "All I want is my freedom," she assured him as calmly as she could. "What must I do to attain it?"

How wrong, dangerously wrong, she'd been to think she could convince him she had that much physical strength. He lunged toward her, and one of his hands circled her throat. Before he could set his grip, she raised both arms and brought her elbows down on his forearms, breaking his hand free. Then she spun, ready to take flight. Her hair, which she'd merely tied into a single loose plait, was her downfall.

He grabbed the plait and yanked her from her feet. She landed on her back, the wind knocked out of her, yet still rolled to her hands and knees and scrambled under the worktable. She'd left a bowl of the narcotic powder on the table as evidence of her success. If she could grab it, she might just have a chance of stopping, or at least slowing, Tuzhazu before he wounded her too severely.

His useless wings served as an advantage for her, making his body too bulky and cumbersome to come under the table after her. She reached the other side and hesitated, watching his booted feet. He remained motionless.

The sound of him rummaging through the pouch he wore came to her, then the telltale glow of serene blue light filled the room and reached under the table.

"Verities fury—" she whispered, but her words were cut short by the sudden whip-like streaks of her own klinkí stones surrounding her and creating a net. She heard him speaking under his breath as the net closed, the stones enveloping her in a shroud of blue light. Then she was being tugged from beneath the table as if she were inside a sack, helpless to stop her own Verity weapons from being wielded against her.

He stepped back as she was pulled out. Though she struggled, she couldn't seem to penetrate the web of light. At his command, the stones lifted her from the floor and bore her up to float in front of him. In one hand, he held the Fenestros, the conduit through which he controlled her klinkí stones.

"You are becoming more of a problem than you may be worth," he stated, then reached his free hand easily between the stones, this time grasping one of her wrists. Within the tight enclosure, she couldn't move enough to yank it free.

His crooning chant began once more, the words spoken quietly with his heavy accent, making them difficult to understand. Not that she would have bothered trying, for the simple fact that she suddenly felt as if she couldn't draw in enough air. The incantation he was speaking seemed to be not only cutting off oxygen to her lungs but also to her very spirit. An aching weakness dashed through her, filling her with sudden, intense exhaustion. What malevolent wysticism was this?

Her eyes bulged, and she realized she was no longer even trying to draw breath. Her struggling arms fell limp. Her will to fight began to wither like the fruit of a lind tree in the desert.

As she began to lose consciousness, he released her from the net, dropping her on the hard floor pavers. She lay there, shrouded in a mist that neither sight nor sound could penetrate. The hollowness food had filled earlier was back, but this time it overpowered her.

His booted foot slid beneath her shoulder and pushed her over none too gently. She gasped in a breath and stared up at him. His looming shape came into focus, almost as if surrounded by a halo. In his hand was the Fenestros, but to her wavering sight it looked more like a ball of black light—an impossible thing, but it was the only description her mind could conjure.

"You'll be easier to control this way," he mused, allowing the Fenestros to bob back and forth across one of his palms and holding her klinkí stones to hover over his other. He had used the artifact to draw her vitality from her like sucking water from a glass through a reed. It was a tactic she had no counterforce for. He had made it clear: between them, he was the only one with real power here.

With her breath restored, her senses sharpened a little at a time as he crossed the room and cut through the Deathless's bonds. They rose, but docilely, without wills of their own, and at his command, they retrieved her and placed her on one of the stripped pallets.

"Now," Tuzhazu said, standing over her. "Where is this concoction you've created? It may be different from what you brought from your realm, but it should do, and I'll need a great deal of it."

She lay motionless, less from obstinacy than from sheer weakness. He paced to the worktable and looked it over, then glanced around the room. All there was for him to find was the single wooden bowl of the stuff.

He returned to her side, and his tone was that of a man grudgingly explaining his plans to one he doubted had sense enough to under-stand them. "I can see you have no fear of the Deathless Guards and likely nothing else in my power. Perhaps what you need is a more persuasive reminder about how fate works here in Arc Rheunos.

"I want you to imagine this, Knight of Vinnr: I will lead the Minothians and the full might of the forces under my command to subdue the Zhallahs and the traitorous Archon Raamuzi. We will encounter your child, if she even exists."

He paused there, letting her fill in the blanks of what he was getting at. A fountain of hate sizzled in her chest, being held back only by the spirit-deep malaise he'd inflicted her with. Feeling as if the rage would tear her apart, she willed herself to concentrate on the deep V-shaped wrinkle between his brows and the blazing green of his eyes that were filled with the promise of death. A promise, she swore to herself, she would keep—to him.

He smirked at her expression, which was no doubt easy to read, and reached out, sliding his fingers almost gently through a lock of her hair. Its coppery color perfectly matched the striations crisscrossing his forearms. "And instead of simply being subdued, maybe even returned to your own realm, your child, your little girl, will be struck down. By a sword, maybe, or a cannon. These are the weapons my army will use if you fail to make the substance I seek. Or, maybe she'll be ripped apart by an urzidae. You saw them, yes? My urzidae mounts, remember? Their teeth are as strong as stone, and their jaws can shut with the force of a mountain coming down."

The hand still twined in her hair suddenly yanked, pulling her face closer to his. She blinked at the sharp pain, then opened her eyes and gazed into his, refusing to let him see into her, see the way she quelled inside.

"Does she also have these tresses?" he went on. "What would it look like, I wonder, her little head crunched inside an urzidae's muzzle, her blood-colored hair even bloodier? Can you imagine it? Would you avoid that outcome if it were in your power?"

"You-you would die a thousand deaths if you hurt her." It took what little energy she'd recovered to force the words out, but she'd been more sincere in her life of many lifetimes.

He watched her steadily for a moment, then released her. "You'll do as you're told and cause no more delays, and you'll cease playing these little games with my Deathless. Or what I described will only be the beginning of the torments to come. Yours, your child's, and the Zhallahs'. You understand torment, don't you, Vinnric?"

He spoke to the Deathless Guards as he exited, and they followed him. Just before shutting the door, he turned back. "Imagine how many will die if you refuse me. The children. *Your* child."

She lay on the pallet long after he was gone, even the weakness that pooled inside her very bones not complete enough to keep her body from shaking in rage and fear. It would take time, but eventually, as long as she stayed fed—and he didn't suck the life out of her again—she would recover.

But how much time did she and Isemay have? Whose army was coming?

Balavad's, of course.

CHAPTER SEVENTEEN

Along a lightly trodden, little-used footpath beyond the outskirts of Maerria, Isemay sat on a platform of stone high above the Churss forest floor, sullen, frustrated, and most of all, lonely.

It was evening and the three moons overhead shone with a mixed intensity of pale, red, and blue light that turned the sky and stars into a fluid rainbow nearly too beautiful to look at. They were visibly closer to each other than they'd been on her arrival, some eight or nine days ago. Sleeplessness and anxiety, along with her failing health, made keeping track hard. The magnificence of the foreign sky filled her with both inspiration and anguish at once. She loved the beauty and strangeness of everything she'd seen in Arc Rheunos. But then, every new and amazing thing also reminded her of the fact she was not home and was without even her mum to share the endless fascinations with.

The memory keeper crystal flashed with a shimmer of red light from Maiztos, the Life Giver, drawing Isemay's gaze back to her palms where it lay. Again, she'd called to her da this evening. Again, he hadn't responded. For all the meaning Life Giver might hold to the Zhallah people, the words and the moon meant nothing in the empty face of the crystal. It lay as dormant now as it had since she'd recovered it, neither life nor her father's face in it.

Da, why won't you speak to me? Where are you? A tear hung from her lower lash, but she swiped it angrily away. *What am I going to do if you and mum don't come for me soon?*

By yesterday afternoon, illness brought her near the point of collapse again. She'd hidden her flagging health from everyone, not wishing to be a burden. But she'd fallen to the ground while helping Mura grind grains, and Lysis had summoned several people nearby to carry Isemay back to Deespora's. The Archon once more used the Fenestros to assist her in recovering. It was very hard to read the unusual older woman, but when Isemay looked into her pale eyes, she thought the pity she saw there was barely masking a growing resolution to send her home. She was an unexpected ward, and, she suspected, becoming an unwanted one.

But more than anything, she did not want to be sent back to Vinnr. Not without her mum, and not into a milieu of danger she didn't understand with no idea of what to expect when she got there. Would anyone even find her on Mount Omina? Was there anyone still there?

So she'd made herself scarce and untroublesome over the past days, lying down but not sleeping much of the time at Mura and her mum's dwelling and trekking through the nearby Churss, or climbing it. The stone trees seemed to understand when she wanted to get away and subtly created a foothold or handhold wherever she needed them. The Zhallahs had forbidden her from doing anything too strenuous to help them in daily life, knowing every strain and chore further taxed her easily compromised health. It was maddening to want to help but not be allowed to.

But she'd had to swallow her dissatisfaction and restlessness and be grateful nonetheless. A Knight would control their emotions and do what was necessary, not what she wanted. But she would be slagged if she was going to sit around like a dead, useless log much longer. If she was wearing out her welcome, then she'd have to leave, go find her mum on her own.

"Thought I'd find you up here."

Startled, she jerked around. Salukis had risen through the Churss like a silent bizzle and now leaned carelessly against the tower behind her on the rocky shelf. Despite her embarrassment at the possibility he might have seen her nearly crying, a now familiar spark of excitement whipped up her spine at seeing him. He wore a cheeky half-grin, one she'd grown not quite grudgingly fond of.

"Pah! I told you not to sneak up on me, Salukis!"

"My father tells me that if you're good at something, practice it until you're the best. Are you asking that I go against the wishes of my father?" he asked, all false innocence.

"Do you mean go against his wishes *this time*, or again?" she returned. Of the traits she'd observed in the intriguing Zhallah, a penchant for willfulness and mischief were two of his most pronounced. She imagined her father's voice saying, *Just like you, Crumb. You only do as you're told when it suits you.*

Thinking of her da, and the fact that he wasn't here and she couldn't reach him, sapped the surge of joy at seeing Salukis from her as quickly as a drop of water on a hot pan.

He must have seen it in her face and asked, "Heyo, you okay?"

"Just thinking about my da." She sighed, dropping her eyes back to the pendant.

He was silent a moment, then after shuffling around with something, he touched her shoulder. "Have you ever heard one of these?"

When she looked back, he held up an instrument of some kind. It appeared to be a double set of gently curved vines with finger holes, adorned with fine, intricate carvings all along its two hollow bodies. For such a simple instrument, it, like most things she'd seen in this realm, was beautiful. Many of the Zhallahs played instruments of various sounds and styles, usually in the evenings to pass time until sleep after their day's work. The Churss forest echoed with the warm and inviting tones at night, making her feel as if she'd been taken in by a troupe of traveling minstrels.

She grasped the bait eagerly, grateful to have something to take her mind off her loneliness. "We have something similar called an aulos. Will you play?"

He placed the reeds to his lips.

If the timbre of a soft wind blowing over the swirling riffles of a fast-moving river could be transformed into music, it would sound something likes the tune he began. Melodious, wistful, punctuated now and again with a brisker light-hearted tempo, the song seemed to reverberate in her heart instead of her ears. She listened intently, unwilling to move or even breathe, careful not to offer the slightest disturbance to the music. She didn't want him to stop. For the first time since coming here, she lost track of the dozens of worries and fears warring within her. As she watched his fingers move lightly over the finger holes, occasionally daring quick glances into his deep brown eyes, which were always lingering on her own, her thoughts turned to the idea of what it might be like to live here among these harmonious, welcoming people, with their wystic forest and peaceful village. With Salukis.

Before she was ready, the tune came to a slow, quiet end, clasping hands with a puff of breeze that cooled the perch they sat on and dancing off into the night. She blinked.

"That was…" she whispered, then with more strength, "Can you teach me to play like that?"

He lowered the instrument and smiled gleefully. "Of course!"

Scooting closer to her, he wiped the instrument's mouthpieces with his sleeve, then passed it over and began explaining the process. The wood of the two bodies was smooth and finished with a mellow gloss. As she got a closer look, she saw the designs better. Tiny facsimiles of five- and nine-pointed stars burst from the reeds down toward the base of each pipe, as if the sky itself was being blown from the user's mouth.

After getting the hang of controlling how much air to send through the pipes and how to direct it with her tongue, she tried a simple tune. At first, Salukis attempted to help her by pointing out which holes to cover with her fingers from his seat beside her. She wasn't a clumsy girl, but she wasn't picking up the pattern easily, given that his placement of his own fingers to show her was from the front instead of from her own vantage. Realizing this, he pushed himself around to sit behind her, extending his legs on either side of her and reaching under her arms to hold the pipes up to her mouth and guide her fingers as if his and hers were the same. The technique reminded her of how her father had taught her to hold a pen and write when she'd been small.

Except this wasn't her da—and everything about the young Zhallah man suddenly had her feeling…quite warm.

She utterly lost focus on what he was saying, conscious only of his warm breath tickling her ear, his warm hands over hers, and his warm thighs pressed on the outsides of hers. The words he spoke were lost to the breeze, but the low timbre of his voice, like the melody he'd just played, vibrated deep within her. Gooseflesh, hot instead of cold, peppered her arms and she became aware of feeling too light, as if she would float away if she didn't do something, and fast.

"Salukis, wait," she barely managed to mumble.

"Sorry, should I slow down?"

"No, it's not that. I just…" She just what? Oh fate's fickle fury, how could she be feeling this way? Was she actually starting to *like* him, in *that* way?

Embarrassed and still light-headed, she pushed away his hands and stood. "I can't do this right now," she said, then realized how silly that sounded.

"The lesson? But you asked…"

He was genuinely confused, and it rattled her further. "I know, I just mean…I have too much on my mind."

She expected him to be hurt, or at least perplexed enough at her sudden change of mood to leave, but he didn't. "I understand," he said instead. "Do you mind if I play some more?"

Surprised, she nodded.

He crossed his legs and leaned back against the Churss trunk, appearing to think about what to play next. After a moment, he said, "Listen to this."

The new tune he began was deceptively simple, a lilting tremolo followed by a slowly blown deeper note, then repeated. She wondered why he would play something so basic after the beautiful song of moments ago. As he repeated the short melody, she heard a grating, rolling sound below her. Curious, she glanced over the shelf's edge and saw a boulder, easily large enough that she could fit inside if she were a chick and it an egg, rumbling its way up the base of the Churss toward them.

"What? What's it doing?" she blurted.

Salukis stopped playing, and the boulder, against reason, came to a halt midway up the Churss. "Its frequency. All the Churss has a frequency. The Zhallahs learned how to call them a long, long time ago. I've learned a few of their—well, 'songs' isn't the right word, but it fits. That song works on round Churss stones, particularly very large ones." He put the flute's reeds back to his lips and played the notes in reverse. The boulder rumbled back down the Churss tower and found its indention in the ground and grew still.

With a humble snort, she said, "Well, there is no end to the fascinations in Arc Rheunos, is there?" Inwardly, his explanation was ringing a little bell in her mind. The klinkí stones were similar. The Knights attuned the stones' to their own Verity spark, thus giving them control over them. Were the Churss stones and those that the Knights in Vinnr used for klinkí stones made of the same stuff? It seemed likely, as all the Cosmos was shared among the five realms.

"Want to learn it? If you stay in Maerria long enough, I can teach you all of them. All the ones I know, anyway."

Growing gloomy once more, she cast her eyes back to her feet. "I can't stay here, Salukis."

It was as if the words had been hiding behind her teeth for days, ready to spill out at any opportunity. She didn't know she'd been needing to say them, to let them off her chest, but now that she had, she felt a sudden sense of being deflated. But in a way that felt freeing, as if a poison had been released.

She glanced up as some expression she couldn't quite read passed over his face, and slowly, he lowered the pipes and laid the instrument down beside him. "I know."

The darker lines crisscrossing his face reminded her of the streaks of light in the night sky left by shooting stars during a meteor shower, the way they were broad near the center of his brow and his nose, but narrowed as they reached his hairline and ears. Funny she'd never noticed it before. "You do?" she asked incredulously.

"I'm amazed you've managed to sit still this long. I'm not sure I could have."

She couldn't believe it, but he understood, she could see it in his face. And it made her feel less alone. "I just don't know what to do. If I try to get to my mum, I'll get sicker and Deespora won't be able to help me. But if I stay, I know she'll send me back to Vinnr, whether I want her to or not. I've never been so...so helpless. It's doing my head in."

"Why don't you want to go home? Do you have other family there who could come back to help your mother?"

"Yes. I mean, the Knights and my da, they could. But I don't know what's happened to them. Everything was so chaotic when Mum and I came through the starpath. There was an avalanche, and Balavad's Raveners, and we lost track of Mylla and her Dragør Wing friend on Mount Omina when the avalanche struck—I...I don't even know if they're still alive. And I can't just leave Mum alone in Arc Rheunos in the hands of that other Archon."

He listened quietly as she began to pace on the short shelf: two steps to the broad Churss tower, two to the edge overlooking the dark forest floor, then back.

After a bit, he asked, "What would your mother want you to do?"

She sighed deeply. "Stay put. Wait for her. But I don't know how much longer I can. What if she's hurt? What if I'm the only one who can help her?"

His hand reached out and clasped one of hers, putting a stop to her frantic pacing. He stood and looked her in the eyes as his wings wafted gently back and forth, shifting night air toward her that smelled of herbs. The scent reminded her of chamomile and melissa from home, the effect calming.

"Isemay, I don't know how to make this easier for you, but I wish I could. The only thing I can tell you..." He took a breath, as if considering what he was about to say, then continued, "Is that the Equifulcrum is in seven more days, when the moons are aligned. Many of the Zhallahs are preparing for it, and for what might happen if Tuzhazu tries to enter the Churss...if he tries to harm us. Deespora doesn't know this—and you have to promise you won't speak of it to her or anyone but who I tell you…"

He paused, waiting for her to signal agreement. But she was torn. Deespora was the only thing standing between her being sent home against her will or staying here. If Isemay crossed her, and the Archon found out, the last shred of choice she had would be taken from her. What would she do then?

He held her eyes, quietly waiting for her promise. And she realized she would give it, despite her debt to Deespora. His kindness toward her was only part of it. It was the way her skin flushed when he was near, the way his smooth voice sounded in her ears the way velvet felt, the way she had watched his fingers play his flute and wondered what they would feel like on her cheek or her waist. And yes, even the way his pets Tekl and Juz had adopted her as if they belonged together.

She nodded.

His shoulders relaxed, and she realized how much he'd wanted her to agree. "Many of us are ready to do what we have to protect ourselves and stop the Minothians from taking our little kids. In seven days, things are going to change. With your help, we might be able to find the people who were stolen and your mother. Will you help us?"

CHAPTER EIGHTEEN

After two days, Symvalline was back on her feet. The first day had seen her crawling across the floor like a rodent to reach the food and drink that had been routinely delivered. She thought she could see sympathy in the eyes of the serving woman, the same person each time, but the servant didn't speak to her, nor she to the servant. The Deathless accompanied the serving woman inside Symvalline's prison when she brought in meals, and she could see her fear of them in the way she cowered and squirmed out of reach of their clawlike hands.

She knew why the Deathless hadn't been left to watch over her inside the chamber any longer. What more incentive did she need than the threat of Isemay being brutalized and murdered? Tuzhazu knew how to keep her in line. Causing torment was an instinct in him, honed like a favored sword. And perhaps he wanted to ensure Symvalline didn't interfere with the guards any more. If she learned something about their nature that would give her an advantage, well, Tuzhazu appeared to be enough of a tactician to know when it was better to ensure secrets were kept.

The first night was the worst. The darkness of the chamber was unmitigated, and she'd been too drained to even spark a rush alight.

She lay shivering on the pallet, her bones feeling hollow and fragile like the thinnest crystal. It wasn't pain, but rather an emptiness so deep it felt like oblivion that scraped her insides away. After a while, she'd slept, but awoke again and again from nightmares. Isemay, her skin sallow and loose, her eyes sunken, lay on the floor of a forest somewhere. The nearby foliage was unfamiliar, and in the recurring dream, it was as if a ray of light shone directly on Isemay's pallid face, leaving everything around her in the dark. As if Symvalline was being forced to bear witness to her daughter's suffering. Isemay never moved, never blinked, maybe wasn't even breathing. She simply lay still, lifeless, alone in a strange place, and Symvalline knew she could do nothing to reach her.

The dream tormented her and came back the following night. In her weakened and exhausted state, Symvalline had only her mind to occupy her, and ample time to plan her next steps, which were cuttingly obvious. She didn't have the luxury of biding her time here any longer, not in hopes of reasoning with Akeeva, not to seek out the Verity artifacts. Tuzhazu had made his plans clear: he was going to attack the Zhallahs, and indirectly, her Crumb. She had to warn them and come back for the artifacts when time permitted. If it ever did. And she had to find Isemay. The dream was not simply fantasy. It rang through her spirit like a warning bell.

On the third day, when her first of two daily meals came, she broke her silence.

"Mistress," she said to the serving woman, "may I speak with you about something?"

Startled, the woman drew still and her face and hands flushed a pale green.

Symvalline went on, "If you would be so kind, I've run low on a few supplies that I need to complete Archon Tuzhazu's request. I have a list. Would you take it to him for me?"

Tuzhazu had not bothered to check on her since his attack. She'd burned all the materials for the sleeping agent he wanted, but he didn't know that. She still had other materials to work with, things capable of doing more than putting a person to sleep.

The woman nodded, and after she'd lain Symvalline's meal on a table, Symvalline handed her a small package she'd wrapped in paper and tied with twine.

"This contains the list and a sample of what the Archon requested." She placed it in the woman's waiting palm, then, as the woman closed her fingers over it, Symvalline enveloped her hand with both of hers and stared intently into the woman's face. "Take this to him, and only him," she stressed. "It's important that neither you nor anyone else opens this, do you understand? Tuzhazu could be angry if it's been tampered with."

She disliked using the woman's fear of Tuzhazu this way, but Symvalline's package was special. It was meant for no one but the Archon.

Her plan could easily fail. There was no way to ensure it would succeed. But if it did, she'd just made it a bit easier to keep the promise she'd made herself. And she'd never have to stare into the sea of cruelty in his gray-green eyes again. No one would.

The serving woman and the Deathless left. Though still somewhat short of being fully recovered, Symvalline wasted no time. She had to leave this chamber, now. Rushing to the ladder, she strained to maneuver it in place below the access hatch to Inder's hidden passage. She knew he'd been watching intermittently as she recovered slowly on her sickbed. She'd called to him a couple of times, but he hadn't responded. And Akeeva hadn't come. She didn't blame the child, either for his hesitancy or for not having been able to persuade the imposter Verity to see her. He was too young, too blameless to be expected to carry the burden of Minoth's many troubles. She regretted asking him in the first place to help her. But she'd had no choice.

The task of pulling herself up the ladder drove home how weak she was. She'd forgotten what fatigue was, so used to being bolstered by her Verity-given vitality. Lifting the small haversack she'd found in the healing chamber and the few supplies it held taxed her, and she took a moment to gather her strength. Inside the sack was the small bit of bread and nuts she'd set aside, a flask filled with fresh water, a few herbs and simples that could be of use, and the Archon's journal. She didn't know a reason she'd need it, but her instincts demanded she not leave it behind.

Atop the ladder, she began to reach for a petard from the makeshift bag she'd tied to the hatch, intending to use it to help her break open the small door. But she paused, then reached for the simple ring welded to the hatch like a handle, slipped her finger in, and gave it a tug.

This time, it opened.

"Inder, thank you," she breathed, realizing he must have decided to help her in the only way he could think of.

The space inside was dark, and she lit a rushlight to help her get oriented.

What she saw lying on the floor gave her the first drop of hope she'd had since first laying eyes on the Ravener Minothian in the meadow outside the Tyrn Mountains.

CHAPTER NINETEEN

Isemay counted the twenty-four Zhallah men and women who had been gathering clandestinely under the triple moon an hours' walk from Maerria. She and Salukis had arrived first, shortly after the evening meal, to wait for the rest. Since last night, after he'd asked her if she'd help them, he'd been tight-lipped on what exactly she would have to do. They'd gone back to their homes for the evening right after, and he'd told her to meet him tonight at the same Churss tower, then they'd come here to wait for the others.

The Zhallahs had been trickling into the clearing over the last three or four hours, so as not to make the exodus obvious to those who remained in the surrounding villages. Twenty-four was a fraction of their actual numbers, Isemay had come to learn. The group she lived among had the nearest set of homes to the border of the Churss overlooking the Thallorn River valley because Deespora wanted to be the first alerted should the Minothians ever try to breach the Churss. But the population spread out in the other directions farther than she'd have imagined.

By Isemay's loose estimate, there were perhaps five to eight hundred total Zhallahs throughout the Churss. She'd learned the stone forest ended at a sea far to the south. Maerria had seemed small to her at first, but then she'd realized that the narrow and little-used foot-paths were only regularly traveled by half the inhabitants—those without wings. Upon seeing the many unfamiliar faces that churned by her throughout her day, coming from farther away than she'd yet walked, she soon realized her first impression was skewed by her limited knowledge and experience of these people, this realm. Their true population suggested they had more than enough people to challenge a force of Minothians if they chose to. So why Deespora rejected the idea was still a mystery to Isemay. She'd been raised among people who faced adversity with either wisdom or weapons or both instead of hiding from it. But the Zhallahs faced adversity with, it seemed, their absence. She had a hard time understanding this.

A girl, younger than Isemay, brushed by her and Salukis, pulling her from her thoughts.

"Rusa, does your mother know you're here?" Salukis asked, stopping the girl.

She turned and her face flushed a dark violet tinged with hot red along her cheeks and neck. "She doesn't," she said. The stubbornness in her voice hadn't yet matured to defiance, but Isemay recognized the timbre already growing strong. She'd been hearing it in her own voice since she was younger than this one.

"You know it's my wings she'll clip if…"

Salukis didn't finish. The "if" didn't bear thinking about. Their purpose for this meeting would not be well received by those who believed Archon Raamuzi's strategy of dormancy and retreat was best. But of one thing Isemay wasn't yet sure: What kind of punishment did the Zhallahs dole out for those who rebelled against Deespora's rule?

And that's what were they doing here, wasn't it? A rebellion? A defiance of an order? Or was it more of a final gambit by frightened and proud people to ensure their families would not be taken from them anymore?

With no counterargument to offer, Salukis shrugged at the young woman, who was surely no more than twelve or thirteen years in Arc

Rheunosian age, and she moved off to find a seat by another girl closer to Isemay's age.

An older woman, much older if the sagging flesh around her neck and beneath her arms was an indication, stepped amid the gathered people. Isemay recognized her from the council in the Churss Circle on Isemay's first day. The Zhallahs quieted down immediately at the woman's gesture.

"Let's begin this discussion before the night grows any older. Salukis Engzu, you said you had something to tell us," she said.

His usual swagger was absent when he stepped to the woman's side to address the group. "Yes. Er, I think I know how we can create a map, of a sort, to get us through the labyrinth quickly."

He was direct, Isemay thought. A quality that reminded her of her da. She looked over the group. Most were held rapt but wore skeptical expressions. Salukis glanced toward her at her seat along the outskirts of the circle, then continued.

"Our foreign friend, Isemay of Vinnr, carries a unique eyestone. Her parents, the leader of the Vinnric Archons, created it with Verity-inspired properties unlike anything we have here."

Others glanced curiously in her direction, but she barely noticed. What was he getting at? She'd had enough embarrassing slips through her memory keeper. Surely he didn't expect her to show all these people her thoughts.

"I can't explain how, but Isemay's memories are part of the stone. Whatever she sees or experiences is captured within it, and she can then recall these at will." Salukis paused dramatically. "And even make them *visible* to others."

Now everyone was looking at her. She arranged her features to appear impassive, a look she'd practiced from observing Knight Nazaria, though her insides felt a bit stormy.

The elder woman was quicker to understand his intentions than Isemay. "You're proposing to take the Vinnric through the labyrinth and have her commit the way to memory, then bring this map back to Maerria for us to transcribe."

"Yes, that's exactly right, Kalisk."

Kalisk turned to her. "And what do you think of this idea, young Vinnric?"

What did she think? It was exactly the kind of thing a Knight Corporealis would do, and she thought it was a wonderful idea… except it would never work. The task was inconceivable, yet she didn't want to make Salukis look foolish. "I'm-I'm sure the idea is sound and Salukis has thought through all the steps on how we might get it done," she said blandly. Safran would be proud of her diplomatic lack of a real answer.

Salukis flashed her a half-grin. "Yes, I have. Isemay and I will follow a supply wagon from the Aktoktos Gate through the maze. Once we've discovered the route, I'll fly us back to Maerria. I'm fast, and I've already studied the guard posts. I know how to avoid the Minothians. Their wagons are slow, so it'll take maybe two days to get through, but I can get us back in under one."

Isemay wanted to shout, *Are you feebleminded?!* Follow a wagon through a vast labyrinth—she'd heard it described in words like "impassable" and "treacherous"—guarded by hostile Minothians? As if they wouldn't be noticed? And those giant, wooly beasts they called the urzidae, surely those would sense them. Isemay considered herself good at hiding and sneaking—she'd practiced her whole life trying to outwit her Knight family—but she didn't think she was ready to do the same when the stakes were real.

Was she?

She felt something warm on her hand and looked down to see Tekl nuzzling it. The snouz must have felt her anxiety. She patted the beast, then reached for her memory keeper, once more secured around her neck on the mended copper chain.

"She's not Arc Rheunosian, Salukis," a man was saying. "She's not a yielder. They'll spot her easily."

"They won't be looking for us—no one goes into the labyrinth," Salukis argued. "We have the sheer impossibility of anyone daring what we're about to dare to help hide us. She is trained in stealth by her own Archons, and my wings will mostly conceal us."

Kalisk put a hand on Salukis's elbow. "There is a great deal of danger in this, Salukis, and much risk. Are you prepared for the consequences if you fail?" She looked at Isemay. "And is the Vinnric?"

He wrapped her wrinkled hand gently in one of his and took a breath before addressing the crowd. "I know the risks, we all do, but there are always risks. We're not going to find our families, your grandchildren Onni and Cylli, Kalisk"—he turned to a nearby man—"or your daughter Eleni, Bunefer, if we're not willing to take risks. Isemay's and her mother's coming here is not just a coincidence. It's a…a chance, and possibly a sign from the Cosmos. What if we are meant to try? If we don't use the advantages Isemay brought us, we'll never be free of the Minothians or the Churss. And what happens when Archon Tuzhazu rules Minoth?"

Before Isemay's spellbound eyes, the boy only a couple of turns older than she transformed into a man, and she listened intently. Salukis's ardent speech, the line of his jaw as he spoke, the flash of the wystic Churss light in his eyes, the way the muscles in his forearm bunched as he clenched his fist to emphasize his words, all held her attention like no Conservatum lesson on Verity lore or wondrous wystic trinket ever had. His confidence and sincerity not only made her think he may truly have a viable plan, it also made her forget its folly and know she would follow it, and follow him, to whatever end. She felt drawn to him, but more than that, she felt admiration.

Salukis finished with: "Isemay can give us a map. And she has the courage to help us. We have to find the courage to let her."

His eyes met hers, and it took her a moment to realize he'd caught her staring back into his. She blinked, then nodded to the rest in the gathering. "I'm…" She had to clear her throat. "I'm willing to do what it takes to find my mum and get back home. If I can help the Zhallah people get back your families, too, I will. It's the least I can do for all your kindness to me."

Kalisk gave a short nod. "When would you leave, Salukis?"

"Tomorrow morning. The sooner we go the better." He looked to Isemay again and added, "If you're ready."

How could I be ready for this? she thought, but nodded mechanically. She would have to be, for her mum's sake.

That quiet but urgent adult voice in the back of her head added, *Be smart, Isemay. Don't let this crush you have on him make you overconfident. You're only a kid, don't fool yourself. And so is he. But those Minothians aren't playing a game. You better not treat it like one.*

CHAPTER TWENTY

Like a beacon of light hovering over an abyss, Symvalline's Mentalios lens lay just inside the alcove behind the hearth in the healing room. Inder had somehow pilfered it from Tuzhazu's possessions and left it for her in this spot. He was a clever child, she'd give him that. But his unlooked-for gift had done her more of a favor than he'd possibly have guessed.

With the Mentalios restored to her, calling her klinkí stones back was her first impulse. But this was no time to be impulsive. The stones would be of little use to her while Tuzhazu held the Fenestros, and if someone saw them traveling at her summons through Everlight Hall, it would simply be a matter of that person following them to discover her, thus burning her only advantage to ash.

She donned the pendant and breathed the words that would make it glow, illuminating the space before her. The alcove was much too small to stand in, requiring her to stay kneeling. But a tunnel led off from the left, and it looked big enough to crawl through.

But to where? She still had no guide.

There was little doubt these tunnels would be known to the Minothians of Everlight Hall, and she wouldn't be able to rely on their concealment of her for long. The moment Tuzhazu received the "sample" she'd sent, he'd send a force after her—if he was still able. She needed two things desperately: a map, either of the labyrinth or a way through the mountains to the Zhallahs; and a means of concealing herself long enough to get from the hall to the village outside and then through it. She could cover her tracks in mountains, and possibly the labyrinth, so long as she could get to them.

She suspected she would fulfill both her needs in Tuzhazu's chambers. He was the military leader, after all, and no military leader was successful in any campaign without maps. And perhaps, as a side benefit, she'd get the chance to watch him pay in some small measure for the suffering he caused.

She pushed her haversack into the alcove and clambered in behind it. Before shutting the hatch, she pulled the ladder up and wedged it inside the chimney shaft, out of sight of anyone taking a cursory look into the hearth. It wouldn't buy her much time, but the habit of hiding her tracks may as well start now.

Holding her Mentalios out, she found the tunnel to be as tight as she'd guessed. It would be a long trip on her hands and knees, though she'd have to either push her haversack before her or drag it behind. The noise it made could be an issue, confirming that the less time she spent in this space the better.

She yanked a bit of twine free from the bag and tied the supplies to one ankle, then began her passage. Immediately, she spotted chalked arrows along the walls pointing onward. *This must be how the children keep from getting lost. If I follow these, I'll likely end up among them in their own chambers.*

This didn't sound like the worst place she could go. Children would not be heavily guarded and would be easier to subdue—if she had to— than adults. And, if her luck held, she'd find another exit before reaching them.

The secret passage was well-used, she could tell. The air though close was fresh, and no cobwebs or the marks of other insects, or worse, rats, if Arc Rheunos had them, were obvious. That alone was enough to make her trust her luck a bit more. Scorch marks on the walls and the occasional discarded end of a rushlight showed her the manner in which the tunnel's usual inhabitants lit their way. Keeping her own wystic pendant aglow cost her energy but little of it. Amazingly, she realized, she already felt stronger just at having found it. How much of her weakness had come from what Tuzhazu had done, and how much simply from evaporating hope?

She pushed on through the passage for some time, though she had nothing to gauge it with, then a hole opened in the wall to one side that was just wide enough to squeeze through. Cautiously, she peeked out and found she'd come to a small room. Its size suggested it must have been some kind of storage room at one time. She'd lost her sense of direction quickly in the tunnel and now knew only that she was at least on the same floor as the healing chamber. She had to find a way up.

She considered whether leaving the cramped tunnels here would get her closer to the main hall faster—and with fewer blind corners, which were beginning to get to her—and whispered a brighter flare from her Mentalios. With the added light, she saw a doorway at one end of the room that had sometime in the past been bricked over. It appeared to have been hastily done, and even from here she could see that the small bit of mortar used to keep the bricks in place had been poorly mixed. It looked like she could pick apart the crumbling material with her fingers. The brick blockage sagged on one side and seemed likely to topple from a single heaving breath. It might be a viable way out. Or it might be a good distraction from pursuers.

The problem was that the opening to the room from the passage was above her head. If she jumped down, she'd have trouble getting back up. Not even an old crate lay about the floor that she could stand on. Yet, if she could break through the blockage and make it appear as if she'd escaped from the tunnels and gone this way, it could throw any searchers off her trail for a time.

The question was, would she have more chance of remaining hidden in the tunnels or in the hall at large? She believed the tunnel would lead upward eventually. Inder hadn't entered from this room, and her guess was the children lived near the chambers she'd met in Akeeva in. Likewise, the children wouldn't bother drawing arrows to help them find their way if the tunnel was a single passage with one start and one end. And it provided much more concealment than the hallways were likely to.

Also, if someone was on the other side of the blocked door, they'd hear her dismantling it, which would end any chances of using either the tunnels or escaping through the hall.

Tormented by the decision that had to be made, she almost didn't notice the sound coming her direction from farther down the tunnel. Movement. Scraping.

Someone was coming.

CHAPTER TWENTY-ONE

Her decision about how to move forward had been made for her by the sound of someone in the passage, heading in her direction. She scrambled into the barricaded room before her heart beat again.

Finding weapons of opportunity came naturally to a Knight, and the closest at hand were bricks. She found she'd been right about the mortar in the hastily bricked-over doorway and dug one free swiftly, then spun around to face whoever was coming. She only wished she had enough time to dig out one of her makeshift petards and ignite a rushlight fuse. *Wishes are for romantics and poor planners,* she could almost hear Stave admonishing her. And he was right. She had planned this poorly.

The moment she'd lowered herself into the room, the sounds in the tunnel above ceased. *Curious.* She remained as still as a corpse, one brick-wielding hand raised, the other hand untying the quick-release knot she'd used to secure her haversack.

Wise? Or scared? she wondered of the hesitating stranger.

There was a chance it was Inder or another child in the passage, and whoever it was had heard her and realized they weren't as alone as they'd thought. There was just as much of a chance it was a soldier.

Even a Deathless. Had Tuzhazu received and opened her package yet? Did he know she was a fugitive yet?

The waiting became insufferable, but she was patient. She had centuries behind her; what were a few moments more?

Soon, a small, scared voice came down the tunnel. "If you had a daughter, what would you call her?"

Oh this boy, he was clever indeed. She smiled, all the anxiety and fear she'd been holding disappearing like smoke. "Crumb. Her name would be Crumb."

There was no more hesitancy in the sounds of the boy coming toward the room. A moment later, he crouched in the opening above and looked at her. "My lady, did you find your pendant? My dad always told me stealing was wrong. It didn't seem like the Archon should be stealing your necklace, so I brought it back to you."

She stepped up to him and held the Mentalios lens up, allowing its glow to spread over his face. "You are most kind, Inder. Thank you."

Fascination beamed from his wide eyes as he said, "I couldn't get your blue stones. He keeps them in a pouch he always wears. I'm sorry. Are you feeling better?"

It occurred to her then that the child may have seen what Tuzhazu had done to her with the Fenestros. That was not something a child should have witnessed, any more than he should have witnessed what Tuzhazu had done to his father. "I am. Much better. Can you help me through the tunnels? Tuzhazu doesn't want me to go, but I think you know he is…not a kind man. It's better for me if I'm not here."

Inder grew quiet, his face troubled. "He scares me," he said simply.

"Yes."

"I'm sorry the Everlight never came to talk to you. We don't see her much lately. It seems like…I don't know, it seems like something's going on but no one will tell us kids what."

"I see. And that's why I should go. Your Everlight may not wish to aid me, as she has much bigger concerns than a traveler from another realm."

He seemed to accept this without question. "Where will you go?" he asked.

"I need to find my way through the labyrinth back to the starpath valley. From there, I will search for Isemay."

"No one who leaves Minoth stays gone. The Deathless always hunt them down."

"Ah, maybe." She changed the subject. "What I need most is a map."

"The Archon has lots of maps. A room full of them."

"This room, do you know how to get to it?"

"It's easy. It's just below the children's chambers above the main hall."

"…So, that means these tunnels go near it?"

"No."

Of course it wouldn't be so easy, she thought.

"They go right to it."

This thrilled her, but only for a moment. The passages couldn't be a secret from someone as long-lived and suspicious as Tuzhazu. She had to wonder what kind of traps he might have waiting for anyone who tried entering his planning chamber. The thought made her shudder. Kids. Kids could be harmed. Did he care? That answer didn't need to be pondered.

"Inder, you never go into his rooms through these tunnels, do you? Surely the Archon and the Everlight know of them."

"Oh, yes, they know of some. But we create new ones. All the time. The lessons Mistress Hertha and Master Pitaja teach are *so dull*. We have to do something for fun."

Maybe, just maybe there was a chance…

"Will you show me?"

"You-you won't tell anyone?"

"I promise I won't."

"Then let's go."

He helped her hoist the haversack up. It took four tries, but she finally managed to get a running start and jump high enough up the wall to get her hands on the opening's edge. Though her arm muscles strained and threatened to give out, she held on and pulled herself in, then leaned back against the passageway wall for a moment to catch her breath. Inder waited quietly, almost too quietly, and she wondered if he was second-guessing his decision. She turned to face him and gave him the winningest smile she could muster, hoping she projected more confidence than she felt.

It seemed to work well enough. "Are you ready, Miss Vinnric?"

"As I'll ever be. Lead the way, lad."

They carried on through the tunnels, and Symvalline struggled to keep up. He was smaller, more limber, and not dragging supplies with him. She clenched her jaw and followed without a word, knowing how tenuous his help was.

Fortunately, the passages soon brought them to a series of ladders leading up to new floors. She supposed boys couldn't use wings in the narrow tunnels, making the ladders necessary. Now and then, the sounds of music or voices warned Symvalline that they were close to the Minothian court. She could not let her caution wander.

At one point, he said, almost casually, but in a tone that showed he was clearly resigned to the idea: "I guess this means you won't get to show us how you make the blue stones fly."

"I'm sorry, Inder. Maybe someday, but I have to find my daughter first. She may be in danger."

"I know. I-I heard the Archon when he hurt you."

Symvalline would have given up her klinkí stones altogether if she could have protected the child from that sight. This realm may have been struck with a deadly disease, but Tuzhazu was the real plague.

She didn't want to make promises or utter accusations, but she felt a need, inexplicably, to try to give the boy some kind of hope. "In my own realm, we are solicitous of how the Archons conduct themselves. All of us in all the realms take an oath to protect the vessels of our Verities. If Tuzhazu is conducting himself in a way that is contrary to the oath he took, he will someday be stripped of his title and his role as Archon, and he will be held accountable for things he's done."

It was a weak comfort, and she knew it. But this wasn't a situation she had ever expected to be in. Being a Knight Corporealis, protector and servant to her own Verity, had been a long and at times arduous deed in her own realm, but she'd never met a Knight who wasn't up to the task or who had failed their Verity. It had never occurred to her that someone might one day have to hold a misguided or malicious Knight or Archon accountable. Only the Verities could rescind the spark that each Knight was endowed with upon being ordained. A rogue Knight would be a formidable enemy if they retained their spark. And Tuzhazu was such. And worse, he would be harder to bring to justice as long as he wielded Balavad's Fenestros.

They came to a narrow place where the passage branched. One way led to the right, the other up. A rickety rope ladder that had clearly been built by a child from scraps hung from the overhead passage. Some of the rungs appeared to be little more than thick sticks, and the ropes tied to them were a motley mix of twine, possibly spun yarn, and the occasional hemp-like rope that it should have been made entirely of. She wondered if the ladder and where it led were part of a newer passage he'd said the children had built. She wondered if the ladder would hold her.

Inder didn't hesitate, clambering up it with the confidence of a child to whom it has never occurred that things break. "Come on. The next floor is where the Archon and soldiers meet to talk about things. Almost there."

She grasped a rung and gave it a testing tug. It flexed alarmingly. She was Yorish, and though not particularly heavy for her people, she was still much bigger than the boy. All she could do was hope for the best. Shouldering her pack, she followed him.

Somehow, it held, though she noticed the bit of yarn anchoring the ladder top over a ledge starting to fray. After she'd warned Inder of the danger, she looked around. They were in a narrow passage that ran between two stone walls, barely wide enough for her to stand sideways in. Even Inder couldn't square his shoulders and walk straight. Rubble, small stones, and sand dusted the floor, making her step lightly to avoid making any noise.

"Where are we?" she whispered.

"The map room," he said matter-of-factly. "And the Archon's council room. If you scale the wall there"—he waved his rushlight to indicate a spot ahead of them—"there's a gap behind one of the great maps on the wall. The Archon doesn't know about it. We cleared out this space so we could—" He cut himself off and looked away, embarrassed, but she knew what he'd been about to say.

"I promised your secret would be safe with me, Inder, and it is. Spying on your elders is certainly frowned on, but in this case, you've done an immense amount of good. Now," she bent to one knee and looked him in the eye, "it's time for you to go, and stay out of these passageways for a time. You are a wonderful boy, and you've done a wonderful thing to help me start searching for my daughter. Stay out of trouble, Inder. And steer clear of the Archon as much as you can. Your father was, and will be, proud of you."

"Okay. I hope you find her," he said lightly, as if wishing her well in something as minor as a card game. Then he dropped back down the precarious ladder, already having forgotten the fraying rope.

She watched his retreat until his light faded and whispered after him, "Stay safe, child," though he couldn't hear her.

CHAPTER TWENTY-TWO

Mura had come with Isemay and Salukis to the edge of the Churss, and now the three of them looked over the valley spread below. Morning light dappled the meadow leading down in soft waves. The River Thallorn glistened like a string beckoning a kitten far below them. Across the valley, the Tyrn Mountains advanced beyond the edge of vision, distant snow-covered tops reminding Isemay of the view of Mount Omina from Vigil Tower. Homesickness, *family*-sickness, cut through her like a thin knife edge, too sharp to feel but nevertheless flaying her feelings completely open.

Will I see Mount Omina or Vigil Tower again? Will I see anyone from home again? With an effort, she shook off the sadness suddenly stifling her. She didn't want to start off this journey feeling half-lost and half-defeated already. *You will see them,* she told herself. *Every step you take today will be one step closer to Mum, and so to home.*

Eleven days and nights had passed, and she'd heard nothing of her mother. No Minothians patrolled the Thallorn Valley or had been seen since she and Symvalline had arrived, which told her that her mum must not have escaped them. Surely they'd have sent someone after her if she had. The Zhallahs welcomed the Minothians' absence, but to Isemay it was foreboding.

Making worse the passage of time and the lingering doubts and fears she bore was the continued silence from her memory keeper. Whatever had become of her father had rendered him unable to communicate through it.

All of which simply confirmed that if anything was going to change for Isemay, she was going to have to make it happen herself. *I just have to think of it as a test, the first real test to see if I have what it takes to become a Knight someday.*

Drawing a resolute breath, she barely managed to stifle a shudder as she released it.

Mura stood beside Isemay. The woman, only about four or five Arc Rheunosian years older than she, turned and asked for at least the fifth time, "Are you certain you want to do this?" A cascade of wrinkles that belonged to someone much older and with many more cares than a woman her age should bear cascaded down Mura's forehead.

Isemay wasn't surprised she was here. That Mura was part of the group of Zhallahs who had chosen to outright defy Archon Deespora seemed inevitable. She'd lost a brother to the Minothians. What else could she do but try to get him back?

"I-I don't think I have any other choice," Isemay answered simply, the only answer she could think of.

"We'll be okay, Mura," Salukis said from behind her. He was busily going through the small collection of supplies they'd brought, packing them tightly so they'd make no sound while they were on the move. "You know I've scouted the gate a hundred times. I can get us in, and if I can get us in, I can get us out."

Mura shot him a look that said loudly, *Only a fool would pretend that makes sense,* but concealed it quickly with a wan smile. "None would ever accuse you of lacking bravery, Lukis."

She's nearly as good as Safran at concealing her true thoughts, thought Isemay, stifling a smile.

With Salukis occupied with their final tasks before they embarked, she tried to fill the moment with the few last questions still lingering in her mind. "Mura, at the gathering last night, one of the men said I couldn't hide in the labyrinth because I'm not a yielder. What did he mean?"

"Let me show you," Mura said.

She took a few steps away until she reached the base of a Churss tower, then turned and pressed her back into it. In a moment, her skin tone faded and shifted into a color closer to the tan stone behind her—then something extraordinary happened. She simply disappeared. One moment she was rock-colored, the next moment nothing was visible but the rock itself. And her clothing, of course, which was still formed around her outline.

"That's simply amazing," Isemay said. "I can't even see you except for your clothes and sandals."

Mura spoke from the illusion, if that's what it was, and the sound of her voice coming from where she no longer seemed to be was somewhat unsettling. "If you think that's interesting..." She said nothing else, but the next moment, even her garments disappeared.

Isemay's eyes widened, and she looked around despite herself, expecting the trick to be obvious if she could just spot a single tell.

"We're called yielders because we can yield our own aspect to whatever we wish."

Isemay jumped at Mura's voice, which was now beside her and speaking nearly into her ear. She'd moved without Isemay hearing her. *What the Knights would give for this kind of ability!* Looking in the direction of her voice, Isemay could see a strange wavering in the air but nothing else. It was a bit like looking at something through a distorted lens. Though she could swear she was looking directly at where Mura's voice came from, the view of the valley was still spread out before her, just slightly bent and hazy.

"You've seen how our colors change. What you haven't seen is the way we can adopt the patterns of things. We can be the color of stone, sky, or even the ground at our feet, and any combination of things we set our mind to. We yield ourselves to what we see or imagine, and we become like it. And that's not all."

Mura's cool hand wrapped around Isemay's forearm and shifted from the colorless-ness of the air it had passed through to the color of

Isemay's own bare arm, down to the dark freckles scattered over it. Only the faintest of outlines showed her Mura's fingers against her skin at all.

"Walk with me," Mura said, gently pulling Isemay forward toward the base of a Churss tower. The volume of plant life twining around and up it proved it had been stationary for a very long time. Coarse brown vines, as thick as one of Stave's thighs, wound around and up toward the stone tower's peak. Many-lobed green leaves as wide as a scholar's dictionary dangled from long stalks along the vine, ruffled by the occasional breeze coming up from the valley. When they were close enough to one of the vines to reach it, Mura shifted back into sight and gripped the vine with her other hand.

"We can also yield to the essence of things and allow it to pass through us into other things. Like this."

A sensation of warmth seeped through Mura's palm into Isemay's arm, spreading like syrup up and down it. The sensation widened rapidly from her shoulder, across her chest, to her neck and down past her waist and into her legs. She felt like she'd fallen asleep by a window and a sunbeam had slowly spread over her.

"What did you—" She broke off. This feeling was familiar. She thought she'd felt this, just less intensely, the first day she'd been in the Churss, when Mura had tried to console her. But this time, the strength of the sensation was unmissable, so similar to how it felt when Deespora used her wysticism on Isemay. "I feel…you can…heal me?" she asked in wonder.

Mura released her arm. "In a way. We can borrow life from things that have some to spare, such as this vine"—she gestured to the plant, and Isemay saw some of the leaves had wilted, but overall it still thrived—"and let it pass through us to whoever and whatever needs it. It's called 'tendering.' What I just did should give you enough time to make it through the labyrinth and back," she finished with finality.

Oh, right, that. Isemay had been feeling so well from the last time Deespora had aided her that she hadn't considered how she might fare over the next three or four days. This slow dive into languor and illness that Arc Rheunos caused could hit her hard and leave her helpless, lost in the maze. Salukis would look out for her, and she him, but she didn't want to endanger both of them with her weakness.

But now with the extra suffusion of strength from Mura, she was sure she'd make it through fine enough. As long as they didn't take longer than expected.

"But what happened to your clothes?" she asked. "Is it some kind of spell that makes them invisible?"

Mura looked uncertain about the meaning of the word "spell," but she answered, "Our Churss talismans allow us to project whatever we're yielding to onto whatever is near, such as our clothing. We call it a 'shimmer,' but it can only reach small things at a short distance."

Isemay reached out and touched her fingertips lightly to Mura's bare arm, and was surprised to note that her skin didn't feel any different than Isemay's own. She glanced into Mura's deep green eyes shyly. "I'm sorry, it's just so…so unique. I see now why everyone thinks I'm not the best person for this. You are all so much better equipped than I am."

Mura smiled. "Hardly. Your bravery is a rare gift. And none of us could hide pen, ink, and paper and sketch out a map easily, all while trying to elude the Minothians who travel and scout the labyrinth. Some have tried, and they've never come back."

Her words weren't a warning, necessarily, or meant to scare Isemay, but they did. She looked to Salukis. "Can you do that too?"

He shrugged. "No, not like her. Women have the traits of yielding and tendering, men of flying. My mother says it's Mithlí's way of spreading her gifts equally. But I never saw how flying could be equal to…" He spread his hands out and gestured to Mura and things she was capable of.

And I have barely any gifts at all, beyond the ability to fall deathly ill and become a burden to those around me.

"I can do this, though," he went on quickly, and inexplicably wrapped his wings around the front of his body. The fine down covering them seemed to wave, then he, too, shifted into a facsimile of the landscape he stood before and was lost to sight.

"So you can!"

He drew his wings back, and she saw that the rest of him was as solid as before. "Just on our wingbacks. It's enough to help us stay invisible to anyone flying over us, or blend into nooks and crannies when we need to." He raised a concerned eyebrow. "With your memory keeper and my familiarity with the labyrinth and the Minothians, believe me, we can do this. Do you trust me, Isemay?"

A glance at Mura showed her to be smiling at Salukis in a way that was somehow both sad and approving. She wondered if Mura thought of Salukis as a replacement for the younger brother the Minothians had taken. *His name was,* is, *Dwoon,* she reminded herself. *And finding him and bringing him back to his family is part of what I'm helping to do. It's a task worthy of Knighthood. And if Salukis is brave enough, I can be too.* This thought gave her the final bit of spurring she needed to face what lay ahead.

She forced herself to smile, as much as she could, and hoped the more she did it, the less artificial it would feel. "We can do this," she repeated, then bent down and retrieved her small satchel. "Okay. I guess we're ready, then."

Salukis beamed as if they were simply going on a holiday and grabbed his own bag.

Isemay turned to Mura. "Thank you," she said. "We'll see you in a couple of days, I'm sure."

Mura brought her palms together and intertwined her fingers, bringing her clenched hands to her chin and dipping her head in the Zhallah gesture for goodbye. "Like we discussed. You were distraught and wanted to visit the edge of the Churss to wait for your mother. Salukis said he'd stay with you if you promised not to go farther. I'll make sure everyone knows," she said, repeating the tale they'd agree she'd tell Lysis and Salukis's parents about their absence. "Churss protection be with you."

She patted her thigh to get Tekl's and Juz's attention. Salukis bent over and bumped his own nose to each of theirs and said, "Do as Mura says, or no govels when I get back."

The snouzes looked at Mura, back at him, then back to Mura, who waved them over. Isemay could swear she saw their shoulders sag sadly as they disappeared back into the Churss forest.

When Mura and the snouzes were out of sight, she and Salukis remained standing quietly where the meadow met the forest, looking toward the Aktoktos Gate, neither seemingly ready to take that first step toward danger.

Finally, Salukis heaved a sigh. "Walk or fly?" he asked her once again, working valiantly, it seemed to her, to keep his tone upbeat.

CHAPTER TWENTY-THREE

Creeping through Everlight Hall, Symvalline imagined herself to be a bandit, of which she'd encountered many as a Knight Corporealis and keeper of Fenestrii, the most valuable artifacts in Vinnr. Bandits always seemed to be irreverent types who believed, for some unaccountable reason, they could easily steal hallowed weapons, valuable historical items, and even a Fenestros a time or two. Old, false rumors circulated throughout the kingdoms that the Knights had mountains of lucre, which didn't help keep thieves away either. In the times she'd confronted them, she'd rarely seen past their usually grimy clothes and grimier dispositions. They were criminals and had offended Vaka Aster by offering offense to the Knights. What more did she need to see?

But now, perched before the peephole overlooking Tuzhazu's war room—this was her word for it, for what else did Tuzhazu intend but war?—she wondered if she'd been too dismissive of those many bandits and thieves. Stealth was a craft, and if her needs had led her to this type of thievery, regardless of its purpose, what kinds of needs had those men and women had that led them to such ignominious heists? Not all need was greed-driven, she belatedly realized.

She estimated the peephole was about twelve feet from the floor.

Shoddily crafted pegs that served as footholds had been wedged between the stone blocks composing the wall, and she now balanced on two that positioned her in front of a gap where two blocks had been removed. This was covered by a heavy parchment on the other side and provided an opening about a foot and a half tall and wide. Barely enough to squeeze through. Her peephole was a small slit in the parchment created to spy on the chamber outside.

Which was now occupied by Tuzhazu.

The wall opposite her held rows of wooden shelves containing a multitude of books and scrolls. She could see the shelves were labeled but couldn't read them from her vantage. One of the scrolls was a map of the labyrinth. It had to be.

The Archon, who appeared to be the only person in the midsize chamber, stood over an oblong table that could have sat at least twenty others around it. A model of the labyrinth occupied the entire surface, intricate and detailed down to the last wall she assumed. Getting through the maze's twisting corridors would not be easy, even with a map, while being pursued. But she was swift and did not need sleep. Plus, she had her powerful sleeping agent, her petards, and if her luck held, a few more weapons would find their way into her clutches before she left this fortress. And if she could retrieve her klinkí stones from Tuzhazu without alerting him, she would be nearly unstoppable. Anyone who encountered her in the maze would pay a price. She didn't think she would need to worry about Tuzhazu coming after her himself. Why would he waste his time on one person, especially one who'd caused him so much trouble?

Tuzhazu appeared deep in thought. As she watched, he placed Balavad's fist-sized Fenestros inside the maze and began pushing it through with his hand, an idle movement by someone whose mind was elsewhere. As she watched him, a grim sense of anticipation of what was to come rose up from Symvalline's subconscious. Tuzhazu had not yet received the package she'd sent him, but he would soon, she suspected. In the bedlam that was sure to follow, it would be the perfect time to take back her stones.

As if her thoughts made it so, the serving woman she'd given the package to arrived in the war room. She remained at the doorway, just a figure on the fringe of Symvalline's limited view.

"What is it?" Tuzhazu said without looking up.

"Archon Tuzhazu, the healer from Vinnr has given me something to deliver to you."

He raised his head then. "Well bring it to me."

The woman hurried forward, never meeting his eyes, and placed the small paper-wrapped bundle into his waiting palm.

"What is it?" he inquired.

"She said it's a sample of what you requested, to be given to you and only to you."

"Go." He waved her away. As she retreated, Tuzhazu lowered the package to the edge of the model table, then took a step back.

His eyes remained fixed on the bundle, and Symvalline's hopes for its effectiveness dwindled. *Of course he'd be suspicious,* she castigated herself. *It was a fool's dream.*

After a moment, the Archon looked up toward the corner to her right. She couldn't see into that space, but now realized she'd been wrong about Tuzhazu being alone when he said:

"Come here."

The sibilant sound that could only be the voice of one of the Deathless, a sound she'd come to loathe, blew to her ears. The person, if it could still be called such, to whom it belonged became visible a moment later as he approached Tuzhazu.

Symvalline recognized him. The one called Toranzu.

"Kaneas," Tuzhazu directed, referring to him by what she'd learned was a rank, "open this package."

Symvalline bit down on her tongue, holding back a shout that *he should not,* that the package was *not meant for him*! But all would be lost if she gave herself away. She couldn't help Isemay if she were caught again. So, though her entire being railed against the suffering she knew was coming, she had to strangle her desire to save the soldier from what was in store, despite that fact that he didn't deserve it. He was merely a pawn in Tuzhazu's game.

Toranzu grasped the bundle. With it held before his waist, he pulled the short twine bow. As it came free, the package emitted a subdued hiss followed by a small puff of brown smoke. Before anyone could so much as blink, it exploded in the soldier's hands, a flash of colorless fire erupting and spreading hot metal shavings that she'd painstakingly carved from nails and the fire-prodding tools of the hearth. They spread mostly upward, straight into the Deathless's eyes.

He let out a shriek and dropped the remnants of the bomb. Reeling, he screamed and screamed, his fingers clawing at his eyes and face, which gushed strange ichor blood.

Tuzhazu watched him expressionlessly. From her vantage, Symvalline saw small pinpricks of blood, colored red, on his bare forearms where shrapnel had pierced him, but the wounds were minor. The bomb was the best she could manage with her limited tools and knowledge of this world's chemistry, and while it packed a punch at close range, its most damaging effectiveness went only a foot or two. Tuzhazu looked as if he didn't even feel the punctures.

The Deathless had fallen to his knees, still grasping his face, but his screams had thinned to gravelly moans. Tuzhazu paced to a chair on the other side of the table from Symvalline's hiding place and picked up the carryall pouch he usually wore at his waist. He reached inside and withdrew—to her increasing horror—one of her klinkí stones.

"You're no good to me blind, Kaneas," she heard him say, then he sent the stone through the soldier's forehead, leaving clean holes of identical size into and out of his head.

The Deathless Guard crumbled, his last sound an abbreviated gasp. Her klinkí stone found its way back to Tuzhazu's palm, and he leaned over and polished the liquid matter from it using the dead soldier's shirt, then returned it to the carryall.

The entire time, his expression remained unchanged, emotionless. Symvalline felt a pressure rising from her guts to her gorge, but she didn't know if it was rage or sorrow. If she let it out, would she scream or cry? She couldn't afford to find out. She told herself to hold it in, turn it into a fire she would one day use to scorch Tuzhazu to cinders with.

"Archon," a man's voice near the main entrance called, and even from behind the parchment map, Symvalline could see the shock in his face.

Tuzhazu looked up quickly, and for a moment, she thought she finally saw something shift in his face. It was just a flash, there and gone. But for that moment, he had looked…guilty.

"What?" he growled, his face impassive again.

"Archon…I…" The speaker was obviously grappling with the hideous sight that lay before Tuzhazu.

"It was a mercy, Kaneas. He would have died anyway. Now what are you disturbing me for?"

The soldier tore his eyes from the corpse and said, "The starpath has opened once more."

Tuzhazu covered the distance to the doorway in five long, fast strides, stopping only when he was practically touching the soldier's face with his own. "What has come through?"

The man took a step back. "Nothing, so far as we can tell. An urzidae squad was sent there immediately, but we haven't found anyone or anything in Thallorn Valley."

Tuzhazu's hand gripped the material of the soldier's shirt tightly enough to tear seams. "Something must have come through. Some*one*. Why can't you find them? Who is it?"

His voice grew lower with each word, but somehow more threatening. Symvalline wanted to help the obviously terrified messenger, yet she was as riveted to the news as Tuzhazu.

"We have not stopped our search, Archon. We will not."

"No. You won't. When did it happen?"

"Before dawn today. I flew from the gate as fast as possible."

Tuzhazu released him and stepped back to the labyrinth model. He eyed it closely, as if in search of the answers the messenger could not give. The room stilled, the messenger seeming to sense silence was required. Tuzhazu suddenly grasped the Fenestros he'd left inside the maze, raised his fist, and slammed it down on the model.

His end of the structure shattered as if it had been dropped from a tower, the painted wood it was made of splintering and cracking and flying in pieces around the table. The destruction shouldn't have been so thorough, but Symvalline sensed the Fenestros had given his fist unnatural strength.

This act of violence seemed to calm him, and he turned back to the messenger. "I want guards positioned in Thallorn Valley itself, ten, no twenty of them, half on urzidae mounts. Not in the fortress, Kaneas, in the *valley*. I want someone there at all times."

"Yes, Archon."

"If a single Zhallah is seen coming from the Churss, I want to be notified immediately. I don't care if you or any other messenger kills themselves flying back with the news. Any news. I must know of anything that happens near the starpath immediately."

"Yes, Archon. There is something else I must tell you."

Tuzhazu whirled, his teeth flashing as if he might tear into the messenger with them. "What is it?"

"I was flagged down by a supply wagon coming back from the gates and told to give you this news. It seems they've captured the other Vinnric."

CHAPTER TWENTY-FOUR

"Close one that time," Salukis whispered as he peeked through a small gap in his wings. They were furled tightly around and over the top of him and Isemay, where they crouched with their backs pressed hard against the granite wall of the labyrinth.

"He's gone?" she whispered back.

"He was moving fast toward the gate. Maybe a messenger. We're all clear." His voice reminded her of her own when she was lying to other kids in the Conservatum about the severity of trouble they were about to get in. But she'd put her trust in him, and now, a day and half inside the daunting labyrinth, trailing a wagon and the two Minothians who directed it, she had to admit he'd been right so far.

It had been almost absurdly easy to enter the rock maze. Fewer than three or four Minothian guards had stood watch at the Aktoktos gatehouse, and they'd simply slipped past them when they weren't looking. After all, there was no reason to expect the Zhallahs should want to leave their Churss sanctuary for an ill-advised tromp to the heart of their enemy's kingdom.

The gate itself was as wide as the main road in Asteryss and half as high as Aster Keep, built to be both solid and intimidating. Made of who could tell how much timber that must have been felled and brought down from somewhere deeper in the mountains, the gate was so large it could only have been opened by harnessing dozens of beasts of burden to pull it. A smaller doorway was set into the base of one of the two towers flanking the gate, which was where she supposed the Minothians and their urzidae exited when they raided the Zhallahs.

The mountains rose steeply to the left and right of the gate's watchtowers, making the prospect of a single person attempting to scale them daunting, much less any kind of militant force.

Of course, for those who could fly, this was of no concern—except for the sentries scouting the tower tops, but Salukis had spent hours observing them and knew their patterns well enough to time a breach. Clutching her close, he'd covered them with his wings as they'd half clambered, half flown along the cliff face by the right tower when the sentries weren't watching. Once past it, they'd remained concealed on a tiny ledge above the primary branch leading to the gatehouse below until a wagon had started its journey toward Minoth. From there, they'd mostly walked along the ground, trailing the wagon outside the range of sight or sound and using Salukis's wings for cover. When they came to a branch and weren't sure which way the wagon had traveled, Salukis would risk flying over the maze until he spotted them, then come back to her and show her which direction to go to catch up. That way, she would remember only the exact path to Minoth, making the transcription to parchment easier when they returned to Maerria.

His hands were on her shoulders, holding her tightly against him, and with the danger of the Minothian overhead gone, she suddenly became aware of their weight. His fingers were long and narrow, perfectly suited for the instrument he played, or for brushing along her cheeks. He hadn't released her yet, despite the Minothian's absence, and she was getting hot—though his wings didn't look like they'd hold so much warmth inside them.

It's not his wings and you know it.

"Um, Salukis, should we go now?"

His hands dropped from her shoulders like stones, as if he'd just been caught stealing honeybread from a platter. His wings opened wide, and he took a deep breath of the stiflingly close labyrinth air the same time she did. They stepped apart nearly in sync, like magnets pushing away from each other.

Her face was flushed, and knowing it made her flush deeper. Determined not to look at him and give away what she'd been thinking, she busied herself with tightening the straps on her shoulder pack and started back down the path. After a moment, his footsteps followed, and she was again in the shade of his extended wings.

Their packs were light, holding only the essentials. Dense and hardened rounds of grains and seeds made up the bulk of their food, and water gourds they'd filled while crossing the Thallorn, two each, would be enough to keep them sustained for at least three thirsty days. They hoped to find more water en route, as they were certain wells had to exist within the labyrinth for the slower supply wagons. If needs be, though, Salukis was prepared to take side trips to the nearby mountains in search of it. Long-sleeved short tunics, hats, and a single cloak to share while sleeping made up the rest. So far, they'd only napped briefly, one at a time while the other stood watch, and Isemay tried not to think about what it would be like to share the confines beneath the cloak with him. She knew they needed to be conservative with their gear and so hadn't argued against the idea of bringing only one.

They were wearing whatever other small sundries they'd chosen to bring, along with their boots, Salukis's light and flexible and made of a thick and tightly woven grass, hers the same well-worn leather boots she'd had on when everything had gone awry in Vinnr the day her father had met Balavad. She'd still been wearing the off-white tunic and headscarf and black leggings she'd arrived in, but Mura had given her a long sheath of a nondescript grayish color to don instead, the better to blend in with the labyrinth's dark walls.

She still felt as visible as a scab on an infant's nose, though.

As they trekked on with Salukis's wings extended over them like a personal cloud, Isemay said quietly, "I've never felt more exposed in my life."

They walked close together, and his voice carried directly to her ears. It was melodious and smooth like some of the notes he played on his flute, and the sound of it made her wish they'd met under different circumstances. "I know. Me either. It's partly because of the Equiful-crum. The heavens feel so close, like they're watching us."

She glanced at him and saw him peering overhead. Kahros, Znopho, and Maiztos, visible even this far down under the labyrinth's towering walls, were limned by the light of the midday sky, their colors a hazy pastel blue, yellow-white, and red. They were closer to each other than ever, and it didn't take any imagination now to see how they would align.

"When is it?" she asked.

"Four days from now. The alignment will come at dusk, if I'm not mistaken."

She fell quiet again, listening to the slowly rolling wheels of the empty wagon they followed, still some distance ahead. One benefit of the maze was how sound carried, making the task of tracking their "rabbit" easier.

So many marvels in this unique world, she thought as they walked. For a moment, she got lost in a daydream of what it would be like to live here. She appreciated the stalwart and organized stone city of Asteryss, the neat streets, the tidy markets, the way the solid and sure walls of Aster Keep and the unyielding heights of Vigil Tower loomed like ancient guardians at either end of the city. It was home, and so much of it was different from anything she'd seen in Arc Rheunos, but not particularly better.

The realms shared many features: a vast sky, wind, mountains, animals and plants. But the city of Asteryss itself was nothing like Maerria, and she suspected the other cities of Vinnr's three kingdoms were as different from Maerria and Minoth as she was from Salukis.

The generousness and kindness of the people—at least of the Zhallahs—along with their enchanting music and close-knit, warm community stood out most to Isemay. Their peacability, which extended even to lesser creatures, was almost foreign to her, having been raised in a world where factions were always divided, communities fought almost as if it were sport, and weapons, carried by everyone who'd raised her, were meant to kill not maim. The Zhallahs revered life, so much so that they didn't eat other creatures, and even had the ability to share it through their fascinating trait of tendering.

Next to the routine and dullness of the Conservatum and ever-present undertow of strife in Ivoryss, there really was little to compare. They'd welcomed her and made her feel at home, even though Maerria and the Churss were anything but. Thinking of this sent a twinge of guilt through her, bringing her back to an awareness of the labyrinth. Archon Deespora had forbidden the activity she and Salukis now undertook, for the good of Maerria. She knew that inciting the Minothians' anger would not bring anything worthwhile to the Zhallahs, yet Isemay and Salukis were doing something sure to bring it about if they were caught. Who was she to disregard the simple rules of someone who had taken her in and saved her life? Of someone who was the same as a Knight in her realm? Such blatant disregard at home would have gotten her dismissed from the Conservatum, permanently, and she would never be allowed to be a Knight. *Every action has consequences,* she could hear her mum saying in her head. *Even good ones.*

"Salukis," she whispered, "what will happen if we're caught?"

She didn't miss the way he hesitated before answering. "We'll be taken to Minoth, at the least."

"No, I mean to the Zhallahs. What will the Minothians do if they learn what we're up to?" *And my mum? Will they harm her to punish me? Are we doing the right thing? I wish it wasn't so hard to know.*

She wished her da and mum were here, and all of the Knights. They always seemed so sure, never doubting their choices and decisions. She could think of no weakness in her parents. She'd always wanted to be like them, strong, wise, certain. But she found herself feeling as if she was none of those things. For all her show at being brave, she was frightened. And worse, she was filled with doubts that kept increasing with each step they took.

"Do you want to go back, Isemay?" His voice was calm, and to her great relief, there was no hint of reproach or scorn in it.

Of course I want to go back! her mind yelled. But did she?

She shook her head. "I mostly just don't want to feel this scared anymore."

He wrapped a hand around her back and draped it over her shoulder in a gesture that was meant to be chummy but was so much more at the moment. "I know. I've never been this far into the maze before, or this close to Minoth. But it can't be more than a day at most to the end, and then we'll be in the clear. It won't take nearly as long to get back. Plus, we've barely seen any scouts. I think…I think we're going to be fine." His arm tightened around her for a moment, then dropped. "You really are amazing for doing this, you know."

She flashed him a strained but grateful smile. "You're not too bad either."

He grinned back, and she found herself sharing his optimism. They would get through this endless, winding maze, and they would rescue her mum and the other Zhallahs. They were so close.

AND AS THE daystar rose above them on the third day, they were to get no closer.

Even though exhausted, Isemay and Salukis had forced themselves to plod on through most of the night following the wagon and its drivers, who hadn't chosen to stop. Before midday, Salukis made a quick overhead scout and was rewarded at last by the sight of the Minoth Valley Gate, their destination. The final twists and turns were few, and he could recite them to her without their need to follow the wagon any longer.

Grateful they were almost there, they moved into a shadowy alcove, both nearly bursting with equal parts relief and excitement. "We did it, Isemay," Salukis whispered, glee and fatigue making his voice hoarse. "We found the way through!"

He gripped both her hands and she squeezed his back, her grin wide enough to make her cheeks hurt. Not too long from now, she'd have the complete map! They could even turn back at this point if they wanted to. And now the Zhallahs, using their innate stealth, could come and find their kin and return to the Churss, all right under the noses of the Minothians. After all, she and Salukis had basically done it, and she couldn't even yield. The Zhallahs' success was virtually certain.

"Come on. Let's skip the final part and start back right away," Salukis said. "I have the strength still to get us home before evening."

Thrilled with the idea, she still wanted to make sure they had what they needed. "Wait, let me just check and ensure everything is clear in the memory keeper. If we don't go to the end, it's more important the rest is complete." Though she shared his enthusiasm, one trait of Knighthood was never to be rash or let excitement overcome caution.

Reluctantly, he nodded. "Not here. It's too near the gate. Let's backtrack a little way first."

Speedily, barely trying to quiet their footfalls, they reversed their path. Soon, the maze split into three passages, and they knew through Salukis's scouting that the leftmost led to a dead end not too far away, which provided the perfect quiet and off-the-beaten-path nook to review the memory keeper's contents.

They huddled with their backs to the wall beneath his wings. Isemay removed the pendant and said the phrase to help her see inside her own mind.

The images bloomed like morning roses across the pendant's crystal face. To an unfamiliar eye, they would have simply looked like a confusion of towering stone walls, where the view turned left or right at random points. But Isemay had been clever. She'd counted her paces out in her head and said the number out loud in increments of ten. As the images moved in real time, her voice could be heard. *Ten...twenty... thirty*—and when they had made turns, she also spoke the number aloud. *Thirty-seven paces, left turn.* Likewise, every misleading opening had been counted, and the ones that took them in the right direction, she'd spoken. *Fifth passage on the right...Seventh passage on the left...Forty-eight paces, right turn at the third passageway.* It would take painstaking diligence to create the map from this process, but she'd shown a level of diligence through the last three days that she knew would make her parents beam with pride. She could apply herself when she had to. Even the Resplendolent Prelates at the Conservatum had known she was capable, despite her sometimes shoddy attendance and churlish attitude during subjects she disliked.

"I think we've got it," she said, turning to Salukis.

Instead of the smile she expected to see on his face, his expression was…unusual. He stared at her softly, but with an intensity she could almost feel. Her mouth suddenly tasted of dry metal, like it did when she was nervous, and she had to swallow.

"Isemay, I just want to tell you…I've never met anyone like you. You're different from everyone here. Brave in a way I wouldn't have imagined someone from so far away could be. And so beau—" He cut himself off, and this time, he was the one who blushed. "Brave," he said again.

And like that, she wanted to kiss him. Better yet, she felt certain he wanted to kiss her too. She'd kissed two other boys, classmates in the Conservatum. But those boys had treated her like an expensive statue, something to be admired but not touched. The kisses had been brief, almost as if they feared her. She was, after all, the child of two Knights, walking the path toward Knighthood herself.

But when Salukis leaned forward and his hands came to rest on her shoulders, he didn't seem fearful at all. She leaned forward, matching her lips to his, still expecting him to retreat or divert his face aside and give her a peck on the cheek. He didn't do that either. His lips stayed put, warm, inviting, and soft like down.

The shock of kissing someone from a foreign realm hit her briefly, then was whisked away completely by the pure silky fire welling up from inside her. She didn't know how long they stayed that way, but she felt like she'd have spent an eternity kissing him if she could.

The thought of what could lie ahead of them—her becoming a Knight, him an Archon—flashed through her mind. How exciting would that be? How unique? Two servants of the Verities from different realms, crossing the starpaths to be together, lovers who transcended the Cosmos. She reached her free hand up to his chest and laid it there, feeling his strong heart. He would be a courageous and powerful Archon, she knew.

"Isemay? Symvalline? Are you there?"

Her father's voice crashed through the morning like an avalanche. Stunned, she jumped back and lifted her hand, still holding her memory keeper. Ulfric's face was there, in the glass, staring out at her.

"Da!" she cried, filled with indescribable relief—and a tiny bit of annoyance?

"Isemay? Oh thank all the Verities you're safe. Where's your mum?"

"Da, is it really you? Are you in Arc Rheunos?"

"Yes, I'm here. I've just come through the starpath. Are you with Symvalline? Are you in any danger?"

"Make him stop," Salukis said in a low voice.

For a moment, she thought he was joking, then she thought, crazily, he was implying that she should ignore her father and return to the moment they'd been sharing. But when she glanced at his face, she saw something she didn't expect.

Fear. Sharp, urgent fear.

"Make him be quiet. Isemay…"

He wasn't looking at her. He was staring toward the entrance to the dead-end passage.

Where an urzidae mount and its Deathless rider stood.

CHAPTER TWENTY-FIVE

The Deathless Guard stared at them levelly, unmoving and silent, yet Isemay had never felt fear like this. The metal taste in her mouth grew stronger, and between that and the sudden dryness that seemed to spread all the way down her throat, she felt like she might choke. The Zhallahs had said over and over that all Arc Rheunosians respected life, that they would not kill her and Salukis. But all of a sudden, she realized there were worse things than death. Merely being touched and taken captive by this horrid Deathless abomination, for instance.

"Wh-what is she going to do?" she whispered to Salukis.

"Doesn't matter. Come on!"

He'd wrapped her in his arms before she could speak and began to lift them from the labyrinth floor. At the same moment, she saw the Deathless spur her urzidae into a charge, an unholy shriek breaking from her wide-open mouth.

"Crumb, what's wrong? What's happening?" her father cried from her pendant.

"Da! It's after us!"

"What is? Where are you!? Isemay!"

"He's got to be quiet or they'll be able to follow us," Salukis said, struggling to get them higher. The long march and little sleep had taken their toll and his tired body was sluggish.

The Deathless Guard was nearly to them. She raised her arm. Isemay saw the flash of something shiny.

The object—a dagger—whipped through the air as Salukis tried to bank away from the Deathless. He cried out in pain, and she heard the clink of metal on rock, then they were suddenly listing dangerously, losing several feet of altitude.

"Oh Verities!" she cried. "Salukis!"

"I-I'm all right," he muttered, struggling to keep them aloft. "Just hold on to me."

She gripped him under the arms, embracing him the way she'd imagined so many times in these last few days. But she'd never imagined this fear, this adrenaline making her feel as if she might crush him. Somehow, miraculously, they rose to the top of the maze's walls. The ghastly shrieks of the Deathless echoed from below, making her want more than anything to cover her ears. But that would be childish. She had to try to help Salukis.

They only went a short distance, and he dropped them gracelessly to the top of a wall. The ledge was just wide enough to stand on, but he staggered a bit. She grabbed him by the arm before he could go over the lip.

He was bleeding from the upper edge of his left wing, and she realized they would never make it back to the Churss, not with Salukis injured. Not burdened by her. The Deathless would summon more sentries and they would be chased relentlessly.

Salukis regained his balance. She released his arm and held up the memory keeper to look into her father's face. "Da," she said. "Listen to me. This is Salukis, one of the Zhallah people. They helped mum and me when we got to Arc Rheunos. Go with him and get the Zhallahs. Mum and I will be in Minoth. We need your help." She looked up at Salukis, who stared at her in disbelief. "We need all the help you can bring."

Salukis started, "Isemay, I'm not leaving y—"

"Listen to me, Salukis! You can't carry me and get away. If they catch us both, this would have all been for nothing. You know they won't...hurt me."

"Crumb, what are you talking about? Where are you right now?" her da said, using the tone of the Stallari, a tone that brooked no dissent.

"Take me back into the maze," she told Salukis, finding some reservoir of calm deep within her that allowed her to make this decision, no matter what tone her father used. "Then go. I'll try to buy you time to get away. Then you and my father can tell Archon Raamuzi what's going on. If she won't listen to the rest of the Zhallahs, maybe she'll listen to my da."

His mouth opened, probably to protest, then closed again. "Isemay," he said plaintively, his eyes shining.

"I'll be...I'll be fine. And I'll be with my mum." She held the memory keeper up once more. "Find Salukis, Da. Wait in the starpath valley for him. He'll be there before nightfall." She held the pendant out for Salukis to take, and it suddenly felt as if it weighed as much as a Churss tower. Her father had finally come, but she was getting farther away from him than she'd felt before he arrived.

"Please, Lukis, quickly," she said, trying to channel some of her family's strength into her voice. "Take me down before it's too late."

CHAPTER TWENTY-SIX

Isemay. By the fires of Vaka Aster's eyes, her daughter was in the hands of the Minothians. Would they harm her?

Symvalline's eyes traveled to the neat hole punched through the forehead of newly dead Deathless on the chamber floor. No, *they* wouldn't—but Tuzhazu would.

She had to get to Isemay before he did.

A smile that held all the mirth of a worm cooked on a paver by the daystar creased Tuzhazu's face. "That's good," he said. "That's very good. Where is she now?"

"On her way to the Minoth Valley Gate with a returning supply wagon. One guard and one Deathless are with the wagon now."

Tuzhazu paused in thought. "Has the Everlight been informed?"

"No, Archon."

"Keep it that way. On your way back to the Aktoktos Gate, tell them to hold the Vinnric at the valley gate until further directed. And I want a twelve-strong squad of soldiers, including six Deathless Guards, to be scouring the labyrinth, inside and out, from the Minoth Valley Gate to the Aktoktos. There could me more Zhallahs trying to infiltrate. No one comes through those walls. Do you understand?"

"Yes, Archon. Anything else?"

"One more thing, tell the guards at the Everlight's chambers to expect me shortly, but don't say why. I shall deliver this news myself. First, there's a Vinnric healer I intend to pay a visit." He glanced back at the corpse. "She has things to answer for."

As he spoke to the messenger, Symvalline was tempted to retrieve her klinkí stones and strike him dead. But he held the Fenestros. The movement of her stones through the air would assuredly be noticed. Her mind and reflexes were quick, but the Arc Rheunosian Archon had the same reflexes she did. If he realized she was near, her only chance to save Isemay would be destroyed. She couldn't risk it.

The messenger left and Symvalline prepared to tear her way through the parchment and into the room to find the map she needed. Getting to Isemay before Tuzhazu was the one imperative guiding her now. But instead of following the messenger out, Tuzhazu paced back to the Deathless Guard's body, grabbing something from inside his carryall on the way. He then crouched beside the man, unstoppered the vial he carried that contained the foul elixir he'd given the soldier to turn him into this monster, and set the vial beside the dead man.

What could he be doing?

Next, Tuzhazu held the Fenestros in his right hand, then held his other over the hole in the soldier's forehead, palm down. He began to speak softly in the same tongue he'd used before when he'd nearly stolen the life from her. The speech of Battgjald, she was sure.

Before her eyes, the soldier began to transform once more. Instead of what had happened last time, his body growing ghastly pale, leaner, and hunched, he was reverting back to himself. A vapor began to rise from the hole beneath Tuzhazu's hand. Gray, almost oily, it slowly coalesced into a liquid ball in the air and hung there. Tuzhazu moved his palm toward the vial, and the liquid followed. When it was above the bottle's neck, Tuzhazu lowered his hand and the poison dropped in.

He was taking back the wystic elixir that had transformed the poor Minothian into a ghoul. The soldier, once more his previous self, however, was still dead.

This is why Tuzhazu wants an army sent from Balavad. He doesn't have enough of the potion to turn as many Minothians as he would need into these unnatural thralls, loyal to him. The Minothians fear the Zhallah too much to attack them, so if Tuzhazu means to, he must have an army that will follow his commands without question.

Which meant: *The Deathless can be redeemed. Under his control, they can't be held responsible for their actions. This makes them innocent.*

Tuzhazu rose and gathered his carryall, placing the vial inside. He moved to the door and was gone, closing the door behind him.

Immediately, Symvalline tore the parchment open and scrambled to the chamber floor. She was light on her feet and managed to drop nearly silently. Rushing to the dead man, she quickly searched him for whatever useful items she could carry—a small dagger, that was all—then moved to the bookshelf.

The labels were in Elder Veros, the common tongue here in Arc Rheunos, fortunately. The entire right side of the shelves was filled with scrolls, and she forced herself to carefully read each label: West Tyrns, Pass of Thossos, North Tyrns, Skaphia Caves, Cordu Valley, South Tyrns, Valley of Minoth.

It wasn't here. She found nothing that could be the maze. The top shelves were too high overhead for her to read the labels, though. It must be up there. It *must* be.

She turned back toward the table to grab one of its chairs to stand on.

And stopped. A Minothian stood inside the doorway, staring at her.

Symvalline's mouth dried up, but her heart barely changed rhythm. It was already beating too fast to speed up more.

The woman was silent. She wore an unusual long black tunic with black leggings underneath. Even her boots and the headscarf that covered everything but her eyes were black. Symvalline grasped the hilt of the dagger she'd shoved into her belt behind her back.

The woman slowly reached up, still saying nothing, and pulled the scarf away from her face.

Symvalline gasped. "A-Agatha?" Tulla's mother.

The woman put her finger to her lips to silence Symvalline, turned and closed the door behind her, then lowered the bar to lock it. She hurried to where Symvalline stood.

"Vinnric, what are you doing here?" she whispered, her pale green eyes darting first to Symvalline, then to the body on the floor, and back. "The Archon will do terrible things if he learns you have escaped."

Relief so strong it nearly took her legs swept through Symvalline. She put a hand on the table to steady herself. "Agatha, I have to get away from Minoth. Tuzhazu is planning something that I fear will endanger all Arc Rheunosians, and if I don't escape, he won't just do something terrible to me"—she looked down at the corpse of the soldier, then back at Agatha—"he'll kill me."

Agatha's color faded to ash and her expression grew sorrowful. Kneeling beside the body, she spoke under her breath quickly, the words said in a way that made Symvalline think of a benediction. She made a gesture over the man, then stood and turned back to Symvalline.

"I understand. Many in Minoth fear him."

"Please don't tell anyone I'm here."

Agatha peered at her, and her eyes were a liquid moss-green, so soft and heartsick they made Symvalline want to weep. She said, "I have been assigned to the dead rolls as a barrow tender since…my daughter…" She wasn't able to go on for a moment, and her skin grew even paler. "But I see the children occasionally. Inder has told me about you. He's told me how you tried to care for Tulla and what the Archon did with the foreign Fenestros. Where will you go?"

Aching for the woman and her suffering, Symvalline spoke barely above a whisper. "They have my daughter, and I have only a short time to reach the gate at the border of Minoth if I am going to be able to help her."

"You'll never get through the valley. You're too…obvious."

"Perhaps you could help me with a disguise?" Symvalline asked, almost pleaded.

"You'll be hunted. The Deathless have senses beyond normal. Even if you're disguised."

"I have no choice. I have to risk it."

Agatha's eyes fell on the dead man again. "There may be another way," she said quietly.

"What? Please tell me."

The Minothian hesitated, looking toward to doorway expectantly. Then continued: "There's a tunnel, of a sort, to the Minoth Valley Gate —an underground river. It flows out of the northern mountains and dives underground just before reaching Minoth. Eight wells between here and the gate provide all Minothians access to the water. I have heard it's large enough to carry a person."

Symvalline listened closely, trying to imagine what Agatha was implying. "You're suggesting I escape Minoth through this underground waterway?"

"Yes. It flows swiftly, perhaps swiftly enough that if you held your breath between wells, you could replenish it at each of them."

"Has it been done?"

"Oh no. No common Minothian could do it. But your kind, those who protect Verities, are different. Perhaps you could. It would be faster than going by foot. And you would be impossible to detect."

The prospect was terrifying, but Agatha was right. Symvalline could drown, but she could not die from drowning. Her body would simply "sleep" until it was revived or destroyed. And she could stay conscious without breath much longer than normal. Perhaps it was the chance she needed if she had the courage to take it.

"How can I get to the river?"

Agatha looked again at the doorway. "I, *we*, are to take Kaneas Toranzu to the burial barrows until his family is told of his fate. We can take you as well."

"We?" A tiny note of dread was playing in her heart. She didn't wish to drag any more innocents into her troubles.

"Widin and I—we are the keepers of the dead rolls, our punishment for betraying the Everlight's will. He's outside with the dray to take this poor one to the barrows. We can hide you both beneath the shroud that conceals the dead from others' sight. The barrows are near the

Cosmoculous Tower, and the river flows under its base. There's a well cistern inside that will give you access."

Symvalline was distracted for a moment by the mention of the Cosmoculous Tower, and her mind turned to the strange tower drawn over and over in the margins of the journal she'd found. Collecting herself quickly, she asked, "Are you…are you sure Widin will help?"

"He is old, his wife moved into the shadows several years ago. And I believe his heart wishes to join her." Her head drooped and her skin tone blanched to a somber brown-gray as she said this. Symvalline wondered if the man she spoke of was the only one who wished to join his departed family.

Quickly, she weighed the risk against the chance of escape and decided there was really no question—except one. "Why would you put yourself in harm's way to help me, Agatha? They will punish you even more if they catch you."

Agatha gave a bitter laugh. "What more could be taken from me? I only ask one thing of you, Vinnric. If I help you get out of Minoth, you help me avoid capture, at least as far as the River Thallorn. I can get you to the labyrinth, and through it. When we reach the other side, I never want to step foot inside these mountains again."

"You know the way through the labyrinth?"

"Yes, I used to deliver supplies between the gates. It's how I was able to smuggle Tulla out, and I can do the same with you."

Symvalline drew a long breath. "Agatha, I promise I will help you in any way I can. But I can do very little. I am a foreigner, hunted, as you say, and without allies except for you."

"And the Zhallahs."

Her comment surprised Symvalline. "But I thought they were your enemy."

"Are they?" the Minothian said, her tone unreadable.

Whatever Agatha knew or suspected, time was too short for Symvalline to ask. She said, "I'll do anything I can to get you free of Minoth."

After a quick nod, Agatha went out to speak to her cohort and get the cart to transport the dead. Symvalline carried a stool to the bookshelves and again sought a map of the labyrinth, but found nothing. As she waited for Agatha, anxiously, she let the practical reality of her plans begin to seep in. She'd refused to look at them when there was no other choice, but Agatha's help had given her one. Her chances of making it through the labyrinth, alone and on foot, a search party in pursuit, without her klinkí stones, all the while trying to read a map, were almost zero. But though desperation had driven her this far, perhaps cooperation would take her the rest of the way.

Crumb, you will not be captive for long, even if I have to slay Tuzhazu. Though I'll gladly do that anyway.

CHAPTER TWENTY-SEVEN

Widin peered at her through wrinkled eyelids that sagged so heavily she was surprised he could see. His eyebrows were unusually long and their edges dangled nearly to his cheekbones. His long ears were equally stretched, giving him the look of a wax sculpture that was in the process of melting. Symvalline had plenty of time to get a good look at him as he examined her with all the focus of an alchemist mixing ingredients that might very well explode in his face.

Unsure what had passed between him and Agatha, Symvalline began, "I'm—"

"No, no need. We'll help you," he cut in, then spun back around abruptly and fetched the handcart she was intended to hide within.

She looked to Agatha with questions in her eyes, and the woman said, "He's agreed to help. You don't need to worry about him."

The old man reentered, pushing a wide, tall-sided cart. His chest beneath his black robes was sunken, and he was hunched forward like a letter C. Symvalline was astonished he'd been given the laborious task of transporting the dead, but then, punishments for breaking taboos weren't meant to be easy, she supposed.

In moments, she and the unfortunate soldier lay side by side under a shroud. Being pushed along stone floors in a wooden cart wasn't a smooth ride. But it didn't need to be for the dead. Symvalline felt each bounce and bump as Agatha and Widin drew her through Everlight Hall, but she gritted her teeth and endured. She'd have willingly suffered a hundred times rougher treatment if it would have meant they'd make the trip faster. She felt every moment tick past slower than eternity.

Twice, her coconspirators stopped the cart and spoke to others to request assistance in bringing it down sets of stairs. The suffering Symvalline felt with each jolting stairstep was nothing compared to the fear that she would be found.

By some miracle, she was not discovered. When she felt the warmth of their daystar beam down onto the dark shroud, she began to breathe just a bit easier. After some time, where the jouncing of the cart grew worse as whatever path they were leading her down grew rougher, they finally stopped.

There was a moment of stillness to let Symvalline's anxious anticipation breed anew, then a gentle tug on the shroud.

"It's okay," Agatha whispered. "We've reached the barrows. You can let go."

She hadn't realized she was clutching the shroud around her face in a death grip and forced her fingers to relax. Agatha peeled it back, and Symvalline was hit with a sharp breeze of cooler air. She sat up and looked around.

They were northeast of Everlight Hall inside a steep-walled ravine. The mountain it led into formed a natural barrier to Minoth Valley. The wind blowing into the ravine was harsh and biting, and made a haunting sound as it flurried into a simple granite post and lintel entryway leading directly into a dark cave beside the cart.

This must be the barrows. It was clear now to Symvalline why the Minothians kept their dead here. The way the cold mountain wind was directed into the ravine and then into the maw of the sepulcher would preserve bodies far longer than most places. It was a place of the dead, and it felt like it.

As she stepped clear of the cart, she noted that Widin had walked back down the path to the mouth of the ravine.

"He's keeping an eye out to make sure we're alone," Agatha said, then pointed farther up the canyon. "At the end, not too far, you'll find a narrow path. Follow the right branch, not the left. The left will take you deeper into the mountains. It's easy to miss, so you must watch for it closely. It's forbidden for any Minothian to go near Cosmoculous Tower, but this path will lead you straight to its northern base. Almost no one knows about it, so you shouldn't see anyone."

"Where is the well?"

"It's inside and runs under the main floor. There are guards at the main entrance, but I don't know how many. You'll have to get past them somehow. They won't be ready for you, though. As I said, the tower is forbidden, and few would want to visit anyway. The Everlight has warned all Minothians of the danger of being near the Cosmoculous crystal. The power it draws from the Cosmos is too immense. Only the Archons can withstand it."

This was more information than she'd previously had about the crystal and its tower that were drawn in the journal, and she wished she had time to ask more about it. What did it do? How? But time was too short to indulge her curiosities.

Agatha took the shroud from Symvalline's shoulders, and the cold air bit into her harder. "Remember," the Minothian said, "once you enter the well, you will pass six more before the final one."

"Just to be clear, there are eight total," Symvalline asked.

"Yes. And if you miss the eighth one, you'll pass under the labyrinth and down below the Tyrn Mountains. I don't know what would become of you then." Agatha gave a small shrug. "But the waters do eventually reach the River Thallorn."

"How long will it take you to get to the maze and meet me?"

Agatha looked to the sky. "We have four hours to dusk. I'll be there soon afterward, but it will be dark. If you can, remain in the well until I get there."

They discussed the last details of their plan briefly. If Symvalline was successful in freeing Isemay from the Minoth Valley gatehouse, they would not be able to continue directly into the maze. The furor from both her and Isemay's escape would certainly be something to contend with, and sentries may look more closely at the maze. They would have to hide until the Equifulcrum, when every Minothian would be assembled outside Everlight Hall to witness the event and the anticipated shifting of Mithlí into her next vessel, Tuzhazu. With the populace distracted, and most importantly, Tuzhazu busy, Agatha and Symvalline and Isemay would depart. Widin did not wish to leave, citing his age as enough reason to finish his days in Minoth, so the three women would be on their own from there, using Agatha's role as a dead collector and an urzidae-drawn wagon as their concealment. The taboo against seeing the dead or associating with those who did apparently was so strong that Agatha seemed sure they would be unaccosted.

Symvalline pulled her pack from the cart, retrieved only the pouch containing her sleeping powder, and handed the rest to Agatha. She didn't need its weight pulling her to the bottom of the river, and most of its contents, particularly the book, would be ruined in this short, dangerous trip. "Can you take this, too?"

Wordlessly, Agatha shouldered the bag. The two women silently looked at each other. Though silent, however, the moment still carried voices. The voices of their missing daughters, crying for their mothers, for protection, for a comforting embrace to shield them from the dangers the world held. Symvalline yearned to hold Crumb, and she could see Agatha's yearning for her own little Tulla. Since neither of them could reach their children, she stepped forward and hugged Agatha instead. At first, the woman stiffened, but then she let herself be held. She seemed unable to return the embrace, but she did not resist it. Symvalline let her go.

"It's too late for my child," Agatha said. "But not for yours. Hurry."

Symvalline nodded, took a deep breath, and turned up the ravine.

CHAPTER TWENTY-EIGHT

Traveling by starpath well was the closest thing to what Ulfric imagined that flashing moment between living and dying would be like—rushing amid both light and dark, propelled through a dimensional rift in the Cosmos that was never made for such weak things as flesh and bone. Though there was no pain, he felt himself—or rather, he felt Urgo—being torn apart and remade anew in the space of what was simultaneously the length of a heartbeat and the length of eternity. Nothing about the sensation was mild, but at least it wasn't lasting. Having done it before, he knew to grit his incorporeal teeth and wait it out. He only hoped Urgo and Yggo would be no worse for wear by the end.

The starpath opened and shoved the two creatures and their unlikely passenger into an early morning sky—somewhere. The bruhawks, born for flight, regained their wings within moments and easily captured a rush of mountain wind blowing from their north. Ulfric sensed only the slightest jolt of what might have been confusion in his winged copilot, but that was all. The bruhawks were more resilient to the harshness of star travel than he could have guessed, and he thanked the unexpected twist of luck for having found such a hardy companion in this mad wystic peril.

Ulfric needed only one look at the sky and its three moons to know this realm: Arc Rheunos. By all the fates and their fickle furies, he had somehow been transported to the very realm Symvalline and Isemay were last known to be in.

He flashed back to the Citadel Suprima. His oldest companion's final moments, offering herself in sacrifice for the Knights' freedom, then Balavad desecrating her body and spirit, making her into a *thing*, a tool for his dark schemes. Ulfric decided it had to have been Eisa who'd opened the starpath and sent the Knights to freedom—or at least, she'd sent them away from Balavad and Vinnr. He'd seen it with his own, or Urgo's, eyes. What her last thoughts had been before she'd totally succumbed to Balavad's mutilation, Ulfric couldn't guess. He wasn't sure he'd want to know.

But he was here, so that had to mean the rest of the Knights were too.

Down to the earth, Urgo. We must find Safran, Stave, and Mallich. They can't be far.

As one, the hawks spiraled downward until they could make out the valley floor in perfect detail, down to the fish in the river flowing through it and the moss-covered rocks along its bank.

Tell Yggo to split up and each of us take one side of the river.

Urgo gave a melodious call, and the birds parted. They began to sweep downstream, but already Ulfric was feeling apprehensive. His friends had been wearing the blue and white tunics of the Knights Corporealis uniform, and given their size, neither Mallich or Thorvíl could easily blend in with such a pastoral valley that was full of little but knee-high grasses and small shrubs. No trees grew close by and only a few large boulders graced the expanse, at least to the south side of the river. Safran was smaller than the two men, but even so, there was little on the valley floor that could conceal any of them. To the south, a curious forest that seemed to be made of stone pillars rose to heights that grazed the horizon. He hoped he found the Knights before having to search there, as that landscape would be far more difficult to penetrate, even with Urgo's keen eyes.

Yggo, who'd taken the northern riverbank, let out a warning cry, and Urgo banked in that direction. Along the flank of the mountain range rising in the north, Ulfric saw a massive gate leading into the mouth of a deep ravine. A tower rose from each side, and steep cliff walls led into a mountain range that crawled into the distance as far as sight went. Figures, still small at this distance, were emerging from the base of one of the towers. Some were mounted, some seemed to be... flying?

We should stay out of sight for now, he told Urgo.

The hawks complied and swiftly shifted their flight upward, rising so steeply that it seemed to Ulfric they intended to alight on the nearest moon, a sea-blue orb midway in size between the three. It loomed so large that it actually appeared close enough to touch, and the quick ascent toward it was so disorienting that Ulfric wanted to close his incorporeal eyes and get his bearings. But, of course, if he forced his eyes closed, it would be Urgo's eyes in reality, and he needed to be able to see what was happening on the valley floor.

Without needing direction, the bruhawks rose high enough that if they were visible at all, they'd look like mere specks to anyone near the ground. They began circling over the valley like vultures as they awaited the incoming Arc Rheunosians.

It didn't take long until they were close enough to make out a party of four mounted people and three aloft. Ulfric was astounded and fascinated by the Arc Rheunosians' physical adaptation—*wings!*—and in the back of his mind, he promised himself that he'd learn more about them someday. Soon they reached the riverbank.

The Rheunosians spread out, clearly searching for something. But it was obvious what they were searching for, wasn't it? Him, or whoever had come through the starpath.

None seemed to notice Urgo and Yggo, and the bruhawks maintained their close watch as the search party scoured the area. At this height, Ulfric couldn't hear the Arc Rheunosians, but he could see they were having no more luck finding his compatriots than he had.

What could have happened to the Knights? Were they in another realm? Had he not seen what had happened at the citadel in

Dyrrakium correctly, and they hadn't been absorbed by the starpath beam? Was he the only one who'd escaped Vinnr?

If so, that meant only he and Symvalline remained as Knights Corporealis, protectors of Vaka Aster's vessel. And that meant, too, that they had failed Vaka Aster and Vinnr.

He shoved those thoughts aside. If any Knight still lived, then the Order hadn't yet failed. And he could not grieve for Safran, Stave, and Mallich, not without being certain they were dead. The only ones he could grieve were Mylla and now Eisa. For she was truly no longer a servant of Vaka Aster, and in the state he'd left her in, she was far worse than dead.

Urgo, we need to find somewhere concealed to rest. I must try to reach Symvalline through the Mentalios.

The bruhawks circled toward the mountains, familiar turf for them. Their species in Vinnr came from the northern Morn Mountains in the midst of the Howling Weald originally, and most still lived on those distant, unreachable aeries. Though Yggo and Urgo had been with the Knights for at least two hundred turns, he sensed a current of expectation in Urgo's mind, a feeling of coming home.

They soon reached the flanks of a heavily treed mountainside, and the bruhawks perched in a mat of thick branches. In the back of Ulfric's mind, the unfamiliar sights and smells of the world drew his natural curiosity, but then, through the bruhawk's senses, everything was unfamiliar. Or rather, radically enhanced to the point that each thing almost seemed new and strange. But these observations didn't hold his attention now. He settled his thoughts, prepared Urgo for what he might expect, and reached out through his Mentalios link.

Symvalline, my love, are you out there?

Urgo blinked several times, as if ruffled by the experience. Ulfric waited a few impatient moments, then tried again. *Symvalline? Symvalline, it's Ulfric. Can you hear me?*

This time, the bruhawk emitted several deep clicking sounds in the back of his throat, making his displeasure clear. The effort he was putting into reaching across this wide space was taxing the bird as it drew from his strength. *If Symvalline is here, she is too far to reach. I will exhaust Urgo if I continue to press the link this hard.*

If he was going to be any good to his family, or himself, he needed Urgo to remain hale. Yggo as well.

It had been nearly half a thirty-night since the events on Mount Omina that had launched this maelstrom of peril, after all. The starpath would have delivered them to the same valley, but Symvalline and Isemay could be anywhere in the realm by now. He longed to kick something, throw something, punch something—anything to dilute the wrath building inside him at his helplessness and impotence.

Then a thought came to him, those moments aboard Balavad's warship as Vaka Aster had tried to persuade Ulfric to release his mind to her. She had brought him, somehow, to Arc Rheunos just for a moment and allowed him to speak with his daughter—through the memory keeper pendant he'd given her.

In all the ways that mattered, the pendant was itself a Mentalios, and Vaka Aster had already shown him how to use it.

Once more, Urgo. Stay with me, boy, and we will try to reach Crumb. The hawk gave a small shiver of anticipation at his thought. Both of the winged creatures had always seemed perhaps not fond, exactly, but indulgent of Isemay.

Stealing himself against the fear that he would not find her, and the deeper fear that he would find her in peril, Ulfric sent: *Isemay? Symvalline? Are you there?*

CHAPTER TWENTY-NINE

Trembling, Isemay pressed her back against the cold, uncaring granite of the labyrinth wall. No sun penetrated the floors of this maze, and she realized how much colder it was without the reassuring warmth of Salukis beside her. She hadn't seen the daystar for two and a half days. His wings had covered the two of them most of that time, and she'd been concentrating deeply on counting each endless step nearly every moment they'd been in the maze, hardly aware of anything but his body, the sound of the wagon wheels grinding along the gravel floor somewhere ahead, and her feet.

But she wasn't trembling because of the cold. It was the sharply pointed chin, the oddly clear, needle-like teeth peeking through colorless lips, the knife-edge cheekbones, the hollows where eyes that were a flat gray color that no eyes should be were sunk, and the hissing breath of the Deathless Guard now approaching her that filled her belly with water and her heart with lead, causing her to quake.

It—Isemay struggled to think of this thing as a woman—loomed over Isemay, holding a sword, only the second she'd seen since arriving in Arc Rheunos. The weapon's lethal point was level with Isemay's throat, almost touching it. Isemay didn't speak, didn't move, did nothing to indicate she might run or fight. She wished she could melt into the wall behind her, become as solid and unfeeling as the stone, if only to end this moment of unendurable anticipation.

She'd beaten a fist-sized rock against the maze's wall to draw its attention, and the Deathless had found her moments after Salukis had returned her to the maze floor. She'd had to give Salukis a slight shove to get him to leave her, and she hadn't missed the tears that filled his eyes. He'd clutched her pendant and promised to return, then disappeared overhead. Isemay had been too petrified to cry, but not to pray. She'd beseeched all five Verities, even, irrationally, the malicious Balavad, to see him safely back to Maerria.

Now, the Deathless Guard merely stood there, not speaking either. Isemay wondered if the things were capable of talking. She'd heard them scream and hiss, but no words.

"I-I surrender," she forced through her fear-constricted throat.

The guard's flat eyes didn't blink. It showed no sign of having heard her at all. What was it waiting for?

Isemay caught sight of its urzidae mount behind it. The creature was nearly the size of a horse, but different in form. Broad in shoulder and hindquarters, it walked on all fours but looked as if it were capable of rising to two legs. Its pelt was thick, shaggy, and dark, but in an unexpected aubergine hue, like the sky over a mountaintop as night pushed the daystar away. One horn sprouted from the center of its massive head, at least three feet long. It was tipped in a wickedly sharp metal cap, more lethal-looking than the sword at Isemay's throat. Aside from the weaponized horn, though, once she looked into the creature's eyes, she thought it looked merely disinterested, not dangerous, with nothing of the Deathless Guard's malevolence.

She looked back at her captor. "What are you going to do with me?"

At that moment, a man descended. He was a Minothian, she could tell by his militant brown and purple clothing and the net-flinging bow on his back. She'd seen them carried by the other Minothian sentries at the gate, made to disable Zhallahs.

"I'll take it from here, Guard," he said to the Deathless as he eyed Isemay.

The Deathless backed up a few paces, still holding her sword point up. Isemay noted that the new Minothian didn't approach until after the Deathless was at arm's length. She understood why. She too felt relief as it put distance between them.

"So, Vinnric, you are a clever one," the Minothian soldier said. "But stupid. Why would a foreigner and a plague-bringer be trying to reach Minoth? To spread your pestilence?"

The man's question seemed idiotic to her. Surely he knew they held her mother captive. She surprised herself with her less-than-artful answer. "Only cowards have to hide behind walls and mazes. We wanted to see for ourselves what one looks like."

If she'd been trying to anger the soldier—and he was right, it was stupid of her to do so—she succeeded with the high marks of a Conservatum acolyte. His fairish umber face, nearly the same shade as Knight Nazaria's, flushed dark.

"Turn around and give me your hands, or you'll wish your Zhallah friend had dropped you instead of what I'll do."

Her body cried out to fight, but her mind told her to do as she was told. This was why she'd allowed herself to be caught, after all. She put her face toward the wall and tried a more conciliatory tone. "My mum and I are not here to threaten the Minothians. You don't need to treat us like prisoners."

"Then why did you run from us when you arrived?" he asked flatly, and she could think of no response. They'd met the Zhallahs first, and they'd treated her and her mum kindly. Not to mention having warned them against the Minothians. Running from the Minothians, and their hideous Deathless, had seemed the natural response.

The soldier bound her hands behind her tightly, then turned her back. "Now, walk. We're taking you to see the Archon."

She took a step, and the weariness that was becoming all too familiar flooded Isemay, as if it was tired of waiting behind a dam, which was cracking. She took another step, gritting her teeth against a gasp. The tiresome days were catching up to her, that was all, she told herself. They were near the end of the labyrinth already. Once they reached it, eventually she would be able to rest, to regain some strength. And she'd be reunited with her mum. Symvalline would know how to help her. She would be all right if she just held on for a few more weary hours.

Her one consoling thought was that, finally, she'd done something to help the people who had helped her. She was no longer merely a burden.

Da, please listen to Salukis. Help the Zhallahs and come find me and Mum, she thought, and to still her fears of all that had to be done before any help would come, she once more began counting her steps.

CHAPTER THIRTY

The two women standing guard at the Cosmoculous Tower were far too trusting. Symvalline, after having observed them for several minutes without them being any the wiser, came around the side of the tower's wide base, hiding her face beneath the hood of Agatha's cloak. She approached stealthily as they were looking off down the paved way to Everlight Hall, completely unaware. They hadn't expected someone to come from the rear of the tower. Gripping the dagger she'd taken from the dead guard, she prepared to get their attention. But...no. She didn't need to do that. Harming them wasn't necessary.

As they spotted her, she feigned stumbling as if she'd taken a wrong step and went down to her knees. "Please," she called from a few paces away. "I've twisted something."

The first to react started toward her before even considering there might be any danger. "What are you doing here? You know none are allowed."

Symvalline poised in a half crouch with her face still hidden. "I was sent to give you both a message."

The guard, now joined by the other, reached down to offer her assistance. "What is it?"

Instead of answering, Symvalline allowed herself to be pulled up by the arm, then blew a small cloud of dust from her other hand into the guard's face, careful not to blow all of it. The woman blinked, confused, but still held Symvalline's arm. "What—?"

She quickly pulled her arm free, holding her fist clenched tight around the rest of her sleeping powder. The second guard stopped short, confused at what she was seeing, but Symvalline was able to lunge forward and blow the powder into the other woman's face.

It was all too easy. Clearly no Minothian dared to test their so-called Verity's will and visit this forbidden place. The guards didn't know what hit them.

The second guard sneezed, and even as she reached for a small bludgeon worn on her belt, she staggered and fell. Symvalline reached out to catch her by the shoulders and soften the landing. Before she turned back, she heard the first guard drop behind her.

Carefully, she knelt and cleaned any remaining powder from her hands using one of the guards' shirts, then searched them both for a key to open the simple, unadorned doorway into the tower. She also took a short but heavy bludgeon from the waist belt of one guard.

The structure was massive, easily wide enough to house the main hall of Vigil Tower in Asteryss. Which made the nondescript entrance, no bigger than a house-sized door, a puzzle. Why build such an enormous tower if it wasn't meant to be used?

She had no time to ponder the mystery, just another in a long list. Collecting the key the guard wore in a small waist pocket, she opened the iron door and went inside.

The interior was indeed as big as it looked from outside. Unlike Vigil Tower, however, the structure was not divided into floors or even rooms. It simply rose from ground to roof in one long, empty cylinder like a bell tower, only a few arched struts stretching from one side of the tower to the other for support. She had to crane her neck back before she could see the top, which was capped by stone. The Cosmoculous crystal must have been above it. A winding stone staircase on the other side of the hall led up toward the ceiling, inviting her to explore, but there was no time for that.

As she got her bearings in the dim space, for the tower had no windows, she noted a faint sensation caressing her skin, and more. A rapid fluttering that started at the end of the hairs not just on her head but on her arms and legs as well and moved up the shafts and seemed to sink just below her flesh. It reminded her of the tiny fluttering you felt from the ceaselessly vibrating wings of a dragørfly when you held one in your hand, their rapid buzzing that you could feel just as much as you could hear, but this went deeper than merely her fingertips.

It was a sensation she felt anytime Vaka Aster's living vessel had accompanied the Knights, long ago, before the vessel had grown dormant and silent.

After marveling at the feeling for a few moments, her eyes adjusted, and she realized what little light there was inside the tower was not static. It seemed to surge briefly at moments, becoming brighter and then dimming again, with no discernable pattern.

What was this place? Was this unusual sensation truly the power drawn by the Cosmoculous? Or was Mithlí's actual vessel here?

She suspected that was the truth of it. And worse, she had come to realize what the journal was talking about. *Only the maker can unmake the cage.* The reason Akeeva and Tuzhazu could get away with their enormous deception was, with Balavad's aid, they had done to Mithlí what Balavad had tried to bring about in Vinnr. The Arc Rheunosian Verity was locked in a cage, confined through treachery.

She could not expect aid from that direction. Therefore, it made no sense to seek it.

The well, she needed to find it. Looking around, she noted the flagstones making up this level were laid in a ring pattern, the rings shrinking toward the floor's center. Somewhere, there had to be a stairway going down, and it would likely extend from the stairs on the other side. She began moving across the floor, cutting across the middle to reach the stairs as quickly as possible.

She'd have imagined her footsteps, light though they were, would still echo slightly in the confines of the stone tower, but they didn't. Instead, she heard a slight susurration, like a stream, getting louder as she moved toward the center of the floor. She hoped it was the sound of the underground river. The strangeness of the tower was getting to her, and she struggled to ignore the buzzing on her skin, the odd surging light, and the unusual acoustics.

She was nearly to the middle of the hall when a pale hand rose from beneath the flagstones, as if from a grave.

Her steps halted abruptly as a little bird of fear began to flutter in her chest. The hand seemed to have come through a metal grate, almost like a drain, centered in the innermost flagstone ring. Calming down, she realized the hand's owner must be in a room below this.

Agatha hadn't mentioned the possibility of anyone else being inside the tower, and Symvalline, in her haste, had not asked. It was an oversight that could cost her time, or worse, and she promised herself she would be more careful.

"Who's there?" she called in a quiet voice.

The hand instantly disappeared, and the barely heard sound of wings came to her ears. A moment later, the quiet susurration of the water was joined by the even quieter murmur of voices, several, but she couldn't quite tell how many. The sounds seemed to come from far below her, so the chamber under her must be quite large and deep.

Was this tower a prison? Hesitantly, Symvalline stepped forward several paces until she could look down through the grate. Far below, at least three stories down, she could see the light of a fire. Shadows moved outside the light's range. Who would be down there, and why?

She tried again. "Hello? Who are you?" And because she sensed that these were not Minothians to be feared, that, indeed, they seemed to fear her more than she them, she added, "I'm not going to harm you."

The voices hushed, and the silence filled with anticipation, as much theirs as hers. Not knowing what else to say, she decided to try one last thing. "I'm a Knight Corporealis, or what you call an Archon, from the realm called Vinnr. I'm trying to…to find a way to reach the Zhallah people."

Ages passed, then a youth's voice came up through the darkness to her. "We are the Zhallahs."

If this revelation should have been a shock, she didn't feel it. In its place was a cold acceptance. It was true, all she'd heard and surmised. The Minothians, for reasons she couldn't guess, coldly and cruelly held these captured Zhallah people in a prison, a dungeon by the looks of it. Taken from their homes and families and exiled into a dark tower far from sunlight or fresh air. Symvalline had met a handful of the people here, but aside from Tuzhazu and the delusional and possibly dangerous Akeeva Raamuzi, few seemed outright capable of this kind of malice. The real question, then, was whether this deed was truly perpetrated by all Minothians, who seemed only to fear and shun the Zhallahs as so-called plague-bringers, or was it solely orchestrated by Tuzhazu and the false Verity?

"Can you help us?" the voice asked. "Can you get us out of here?"

Faced with this sudden pull on her conscience, Symvalline wanted to think she'd do what she could to release them from such harsh confinement, despite the urgency of needing to find Isemay. But the truth was that they were between her and the way out. She would do what she could for them, yes, but Isemay was first. Her daughter was always first.

As she leaned over the edge of the grate, the face of the speaker, as pale as his hands had been, rose from the gloom and stared back at her. Startled momentarily, she quickly recovered and looked into his eyes. She was correct. He was young, perhaps sixteen or seventeen Arc Rheunosian years, Isemay's age.

"How do I get to you?" she asked.

"By the stairs, there's a door. It's barred on your side."

She rushed to the other side of the hall. The doorway hadn't been visible from the tower's entrance because it was set into the floor. Two hinged doors overlapped each other and closed over an opening to the chamber below, covered by a metal bar as thick as her arm. She shoved it free and pulled open the top door, then the bottom.

Another stairway descended into the dark. She could see nothing but the bouncing light of the fire rising along the walls like a child's nightmare. She dumped her last bit of powder from her pouch into one hand and gripped the small bludgeon she'd retrieved from the guard in the other. She did not fear these people, who, by the looks of the first boy, were only children, but she also did not believe in chancing being unprepared.

Descending carefully, feeling each step with her foot before committing, she made her way down. The firelight made distance deceptive, and the winding of the stairway along the tower wall made the trip interminable. She sent a few words into her Mentalios to give her more light, but not much. She wanted to conserve her energy. With caution on the unknown stairs dictating her speed, it would take her longer to reach the floor of the tower than it had taken her to traverse up the ravine to get here. Time ticked away from her like lifeblood, and the seeds of panic for Isemay that had already rooted in her guts began to sprout.

She was less than a third of the way down when the young man flew up to her. He was so swift that it alarmed her, and she brought the bludgeon up reflexively to protect herself. But he did not come close. Rather, he kept enough distance to study her. His eyes, somehow familiar to Symvalline, widened curiously.

"You really are from somewhere else," he said.

She lowered the weapon and glanced down to find her next step. "Yes."

The boy glanced up toward the ceiling. "And you left the door open." He stated this as a fact, but the distrust in his voice was as plain as his wings.

"I mean none of you any harm," she reassured him. "There were Zhallahs in the starpath valley when my daughter and I arrived from Vinnr, nearly half a thirty-night ago, and they came to our aid when the Minothians…didn't."

"It's true then! Onni and Cylli were right! Has the Everlight brought you here to help us?"

"Onni and Cylli?" Symvalline found her next step, carefully considering his question before answering it.

"Duripi's twins, Kalisk's grandchildren. They were taken by the Deathless the night the starpath opened. They're here with Eleni and me now."

The hope in his voice was plaintive, and it made Symvalline pause.

The poor children's fear, their parents in the Zhallah village who didn't know if they'd ever see them again, didn't even know if they lived, it wrenched at her heart. How could they? How could these Minothians do something so wicked? The danger to any Zhallahs who strayed outside the Churss was obviously extreme. But Mura and the boy Salukis, all of them, had been doing as children do, something harmless they shouldn't have been doing but couldn't resist. No children deserved this fate.

"How many of you are here?" she asked quietly.

"Four...now." He hovered beside her, searching her face for the hope she hadn't yet been able to give him. She didn't know what to say, so she brought the conversation around to what she needed. The fact was, if she ever wanted to help these children, she first had to escape Tuzhazu's reach. "Listen, child. I must try to get out of here and back to the Zhallahs. There is a well down at the bottom of the tower, isn't there?"

"Yes," he said. "And the river."

"I need to reach it. The water that feeds it runs through Minoth Valley to the labyrinth. If I can get to the labyrinth without the Minothians finding me, I'll be able to reach the Zhallahs and bring help to get you and the other children free."

She glanced up and saw him staring at her skeptically, following her slow footsteps easily. "Do you know how far it is across this valley to the labyrinth?"

"Approximately."

"And you are an Archon?"

"I am."

He seemed to be thinking, then he said, "You look light. Let me help you. It'll take you forever to reach the bottom."

She'd been carried before by a Rheunosian, and time was short enough that she consented with a nod. He crossed behind her and reached his hands beneath her arms, pulling her from her feet with wings that seemed capable of great force. The Arc Rheunosians were a truly extraordinary people. Their attributes made the Vinnrics seem almost weak and plain by comparison, and the fact that their peoples were as divided as her own realm's seemed a tragedy.

They reached the floor, and he released her lightly on her feet with a precision that said this wasn't the first time he'd carried someone. In the closer firelight, she looked around and took in the faces of three others.

Children. They were all children, and she felt her heart squeeze painfully in her chest at this inhumanity once more. The boy who'd carried her was the oldest by a couple of years, and the youngest two, twins, seemed to be about ten, two girls and two boys in total.

Her voice was hoarse when she spoke, fury at such wanton mistreatment choking her. "Why in the Verities' names are you children down here?"

None of the Zhallahs seemed to want to speak to her. They eyed her with the same fascination, well-tempered with fear, that the oldest boy had. She turned to him, hoping for an explanation.

"Archon Tuzhazu converts the Zhallahs they capture into Deathless Guards. When we're old enough," the boy said simply. "I'll become one after the Equifulcrum."

Symvalline nearly gasped. She couldn't fathom it, kidnapping children, raising them to adulthood, then turning them into those…things. It seemed Tuzhazu must have lacked for volunteers to such an "honorable" position. Or perhaps he simply did it because his mind was a twisted ball of slime.

The boy continued, "Until then, we collect the nightcaps that grow beneath the Cosmoculous for the Minothians." He waved toward the far end of the chamber, where a hinged grate opened to a rough stone shaft. A cave, or cavern of some sort. She could make out the hints of lights inside, the subdued glowing of something bioluminescent like she'd seen on the banks of the river the night she and Isemay had arrived. Were these the nightcaps?

"How long have you been here?" she asked.

"Eleni and I, almost two years. We were collecting nightcaps by the banks of the Thallorn with my sister, Mura. The Minothians—"

"Mura?" Symvalline said, cutting him off. "She is your sister?"

His face shone with sudden excitement. "You know Mura?"

"She was at the river when we arrived. She helped my daughter get away, but Archon Tuzhazu and his soldiers took me prisoner."

At the mention of the Archon, she watched the smaller children unconsciously bunch closer together, and the smaller boy and girl reached out to clasp each other's hands. They feared him, too. Every Minothian she'd met did. And they were right to. He may not have been a Deathless Guard, tainted by Balavad's elixir, but he was an abomination just the same.

But time was short, and she needed to go. She couldn't do much for these children now, but she would do what she could when she knew Isemay was safe. "What is your name?"

"I'm Dwoon."

"Dwoon, listen. The Archon is dangerous, and while he controls the Minothian forces, they are too. There is an event happening in a few days, the—"

The oldest of the two girls cut in, "Equifulcrum."

She nodded. "Yes, and I believe Tuzhazu is going to take control of Minoth, then the rest of the Arc Rheunosian people, including the Zhallahs. I'm going to try to stop him…"

Even as she said these words, she realized, somewhere deep down, she had already decided this. Once Isemay was safe, she would come back. The other Knights and Ulfric would be able to manage Vinnr and Balavad without her for now. No one who stole others' children could be allowed to rule over an entire realm. It was unconscionable. She and Ulfric may have been planning to set aside their oaths and return to a normal commoner life, but she was realizing she would never be able to live a normal life knowing there were others ordained by a Verity—others who'd taken the same oath she'd been dedicated to for so long—who could so completely and thoroughly abuse that power, that gift. She could not stand by and allow such crimes to go unpunished.

"You are going to free the Everlight?" the older girl asked, and the question jolted Symvalline from her contemplation.

"Free Mithlí? What do you mean?"

Struck with sudden shyness by Symvalline's abruptness, the girl went quiet and cast her eyes to her feet. Dwoon picked up her thread.

"The Archons hold the Everlight captive. That's why"—he spread his arms wide, as if to indicate the walls around them—"this." As if in agreement, the strange surge of light that ran through the tower's stones came again. "That's her, the Everlight. She wants to break free but can't. Her vessel is shackled by the Fenestrii in the tower."

So her suspicions were right. The book she'd found—it contained an elaborate spell to hold not just anyone entombed within a Fenestrii prison. It was meant for the Verity herself.

The child's question played through her mind. Was she going to free Mithlí? If she did, would it end this schism?

The implications shot through her mind rapidly. What would happen if the cage were undone? Would Mithlí seek vengeance, or even perceive the act as wrong? Would the Verity punish her Archons for their betrayal? Would she punish all Arc Rheunosians? But she couldn't forget the first line of the book: *Only the maker can unmake the cage.*

Was the writer of the book the maker? *I need to get it back when I find Agatha. I need to end this desecration once and for all.*

Focus, Symvalline. First things first. She looked to Dwoon. "Please, show me the way to the river. Once I know my daughter is safe, I'll… do whatever I can."

The boy pointed toward the center of the floor, where a flagstone circle surrounded a wide opening. Beneath it flowed the tributary she sought. Kneeling, she looked over the edge and dangled her shining Mentalios down to see the water. *It looks very cold,* she thought.

In the dim light, it flowed nearly black and moved swiftly. She didn't fear the darkness. Her wystic lens would give her enough light. But other fears took that one's place. What would she encounter in there? How long would she have to hold her breath between wells? Would the coldness numb sensation in her hands too much for her to arrest her passage when she reached them? Would the tributary grow too narrow at any point to pass? The unknowns were daunting.

With the strength of will only someone who'd lived her lifetimes could accumulate, she shoved her fears away. There was no time for them now.

Turning back to the boy, she said, "There are only two guards at the tower entrance, and they will not awaken for hours. You all must leave this tower. Hide in the hills or take the small path that runs behind the tower into the mountains. You'll come to a ravine, and at its end is the barrow where they keep those who've passed over. None will look for you there and you can hide until I or someone else can come for you. Take what food you can. But, whatever you do, don't stay here. It's too dangerous."

"You'll come back?" he asked, his eyes sparkling in the firelight.

She looked over all four children, seeing a wary hope in their eyes. It gave her some of her own and she grasped it desperately. "As soon as I can. Tell me all your names once more. I'll let your families know you're safe if—when I see them."

The children said their names, except for the youngest, shyest, whom Dwoon spoke for. They would be burned into Symvalline's mind. Perhaps they would keep her warm as she passed through the frigid waters under the mountains. That, and her fury, would have to do.

CHAPTER THIRTY-ONE

Urgo and Yggo flew with all the fervor and rage of a vengeful Verity, nearly frothing at the mouth like horses as Ulfric urged them onward. Isemay was in trouble, some terrible trouble that he couldn't begin to grasp. But he would be damned to the bottom of the black waters of Himmingaze's Never Sea if he was going to lose another person he loved. Not today, not again.

Her pleading through her memory keeper—*Da, it's after us...listen to me, go with Salukis...we need your help*—rushed through his mind like a flood. He knew Urgo was feeling his urgency, his wrath, and in turn was telling Yggo to go, GO!

He'd caught a glimpse of the Arc Rheunosian his daughter had mentioned. A boy, really. Salukis. His face was burned in Ulfric's brain and he would go to his grave remembering every crease, every bump, the amber skin and copper hair. The questions of why his child was with this boy and not Symvalline and where Symvalline could be ate at him, but he would find Isemay and have his answers. And Verities help anyone who stood, or flew, in his way. He and the bruhawks would cut through them like kindling if they had to.

The maze had been visible from their perch when he'd called to Isemay, and he'd seen that she was somewhere within it through the limited vantage of her memory keeper: the vertical granite walls rising to either side, and after she'd been taken aloft by Salukis, the maze below them. So he ordered Urgo forward over the maze, encouraged by the bruhawks' predator-strong sight that they'd either find his daughter or the boy who could lead him to her.

And the bruhawks' sight didn't fail him. Within moments of entering the maze's airspace, the birds spotted two figures in the distance, both flying away from him. They were swift, but they were not bruhawks. Yggo and Urgo overtook them after a short chase.

The two Arc Rheunosians were not expecting anyone coming from behind and never saw them. Ulfric had the birds cruised above the two so he could get a close look at them. They were not the boy he sought —nor were they what he'd expected.

The two men were dressed in military-style uniforms: long vests that were cut to fit around where their wings grew from their backs, undershirts of light brown, and mid-calf boots made from some material that didn't appear to be leather. But it was the swords they each carried that drew his eye. Made from a darkish metal that had the bluish-black color of a bruise, the end hooked. The same swords carried by Balavad's Ravener horde.

Ephemerally, he gasped. Could his eyes be deceiving him? Was there no end to the worlds that had already been desecrated by the malignant Verity? He'd seen the Arc Rheunosian Verity had been caged through Balavad's Scrylle, but he hadn't expected it to also be overrun with Raveners. His fears for his family nearly choked him.

Despite this, once the shadow of the tracking bruhawks drew the attention of one of the soldiers and he looked up at them, Ulfric had no trouble making a decision. These were servants of Balavad. The empty gray eyes proved it. And they would die.

He sent Urgo his command: *They are Raveners. End them.* Urgo did not need to be told twice. With a squawk, he alerted Yggo and they rocketed from the sky like meteors, the speed and agility of their coordinated attack unmatchable by anything whose primary means of travel was by mere foot. Their claws had ripped into the wings of both Raveners before either could begin to react. The monsters shrieked an unholy cacophony, and the bruhawks, as if of one mind, released the soldiers. Even if they'd had the resilience to continue to fight the birds, their now useless wings decided their fates would instead end at the bottom of the maze. They plummeted, shrill cries ringing the whole way, and Ulfric saw their bodies break against the hard path carved through the mountain before he urged Urgo once more forward. There was nothing to mourn, no regret to be felt at the deaths of these monsters.

Sometime later, Ulfric spotted a valley on the other side of the maze, still distant. Then two more forms were visible, this time coming directly at them. It was obvious one was chasing the other, and as he and the bruhawks ate through the distance, he saw the gap closing to the one in the lead. The chaser was another of the abhorrent Raveners.

The one being chased was the boy Salukis.

Yggo seemed to know what to do and flew directly toward the Ravener. The boy saw the giant bird and his face darkened with even greater fright. The bruhawks likely didn't exist in this realm, and Salukis did his best to dart downward out of the bird's path. Ulfric saw the unnatural arc of his flight and realized the boy was injured. He would never leave the labyrinth without their help.

But, as with the first two, this Ravener's time was limited. As Urgo and Ulfric dove toward the wounded boy, Yggo darted in and gripped one of the Ravener's wings, ripping it halfway off before flinging the shrieking enemy aside. He, like the others, had no chance of staying aloft and was quickly lost amid the maze's great walls.

Yet the boy continued to try to flee. His wings flapped furiously, if gracelessly, as he attempted to gain some distance on the bruhawks. Urgo came up beside him easily, and Yggo banked and glided toward them.

He doesn't know we are friends. As calmly as he could, Ulfric spoke through his Mentalios, sure the boy had Isemay's memory keeper and would hear him.

"Don't be afraid, Rheunosian. These two bruhawks are here to protect you. *I* am here to protect you."

From a safe distance beside Salukis, Ulfric could see the boy jerk at the sound of his voice, then reach around his neck and grab the pendant, Isemay's pendant. His eyes darted between the crystal in the memory keeper to Ulfric and Urgo, then back and forth.

"Yes," Ulfric said. "Speak into the crystal. I can hear you."

The boy looked doubtfully at the pendant, blinked at seeing Ulfric's face there, then said, "Where are you? How do you command these… these *enormous* birds?"

It struck Ulfric then how difficult it would be to explain the events of the last few weeks—to anyone, but especially to this stranger who knew nothing of Vaka Aster, Balavad, Vinnr, or the devastation of the Knights Corporealis. Least of all, Ulfric's habitation first by a Verity then of Urgo. And there was simply no time now to explain any of it.

"I can't answer that now. You must take us to my daughter. Now!"

In just these few moments, Ulfric could see how much more labored the boy's flying was becoming. He wouldn't last much longer. They needed to land.

Despite how frustrating it was, he needed the boy sound if he was to get answers from him and commanded him: "Boy, we must get away from this maze and into the mountains. You are wounded and won't get much farther like that. Follow me."

"No! We have to reach the Churss and Maerria. Archon Raamuzi will help us. We can't do anything for Isemay now, not without more aid."

Ulfric wasn't going to listen to this mere boy. "You'll show me where they are taking my daughter, or you'll die alone in this maze. I'm not going to protect you if you don't take me to her."

Without a second of hesitation, he had Urgo glide over the boy's back and reach his talons between his shoulders, careful not to further injure him, and grip Salukis by his clothing. The boy jerked, trying to escape, but the feeling of Urgo's hard-as-stone claws dissuaded him quickly. He quit fighting and let his wings droop.

Urgo, to the mountains. Find us a secluded place to land.

A SHORT TIME LATER, Ulfric watched as Salukis stared in unmasked disgust at Urgo and Yggo shredding and swallowing a pair of creatures that resembled Vinnr's mountain goats, which had been unfortunate enough to be in the spot the bruhawks had chosen to land. When Urgo looked up, Ulfric was able to observe the surroundings from the curious dual vantage of both Urgo's eyes and the memory keeper around Salukis's neck. It made him feel present and was surprisingly easy to sustain with the pendant so close to his incorporeal self.

Unable to watch any longer, Salukis leaned back against a boulder and buried his face in his hands, distraught. "I didn't want to leave her," he whispered. "She made me go. The only way to help her now is to get to Maerria."

He was mumbling into his palms as if no one else could hear him. Ulfric could see the boy was near his breaking point. He'd have to handle him delicately, despite the urgency and fear rampaging through his own mind.

"Boy, chin up, listen to me," he began.

He paid Ulfric no mind, continuing his subdued raving. "And that Deathless soldier. The bird killed him, let him fall…"

Ulfric was flummoxed. "Of course I killed him. Would you have preferred I let him kill you?"

"Minothians would never…" The boy looked up. "What do you mean, you killed him? It was the bird—where are you?" He began looking around the high mountainside shelf the bruhawks had brought them to.

"It's difficult to explain, and I'm only going to say this once. It isn't important if you understand or not, or even if you believe me. The bruhawk before you, the one with the grayer talons, I am—sharing his body."

As if to confirm, Urgo clicked his talons against the rocky earth, staring intensely at Salukis.

The massive bird's gaze clearly unnerved the boy, and he drew his legs tightly up against his chest and wrapped his hands underneath them. "…sharing…" he said doubtfully.

"Yes. I see through his eyes, and through that pendant of my daughter's. I am…not flesh. I'm bodiless."

With a look of doubt, Salukis pulled the pendant over his head and stared into the crystal. Through Urgo's eyes, Ulfric saw himself there. The sensation of being in a body but not his own, yet his visage visible to his own eyes, hit Ulfric like a battering ram. If he'd had legs, he would have staggered. He tore Urgo's eyes from the pendant and took a moment to catch his disembodied breath.

"But I can see you," Salukis was saying. "In this eyestone glass. You look…like a person. Is sending your spirit into others something you can do in your realm?"

"No, it definitely isn't. It's—never mind. As quickly as you can, tell me what's happened to my daughter, and do you know what's happened to Symvalline, her mum?"

Ulfric had to give the boy credit. Despite exhaustion, fear, and his obvious pain from his torn wing, Salukis was able to explain in concise and clear terms all that he knew and suspected since Symvalline and Isemay had been delivered to the starpath terminus he called Thallorn Valley. Ulfric's family was in the hands of a set of rogue Archons who ruled their people through lies and a blasphemous false impersonation of their own Verity. In a few days, there would be a shift of power, and the more ambitious of the two, Tuzhazu, would undertake some kind of hostile domination of the divided peoples of Arc Rheunos, or so Salukis believed. Only one element of his story brought Ulfric some relief: the boy was certain Symvalline and Crumb, though prisoners, would not be killed. It seemed the Arc Rheunosians held life sacred and were not naturally given to war and conflict. Though he found this surprising, odd even, he didn't dwell on it.

"What does this Tuzhazu have against your people?" Ulfric asked. "What does he gain by overcoming the—?"

"The Zhallahs. I don't know. Maybe it's because Archon Raamuzi knows the truth of the Archons' deception."

This made complete sense to Ulfric. Balavad was on a Cosmos-wide mission to stop the Syzycki Elementum, and he'd already begun his conquest here sometime before coming to Vinnr. Had destroying

Battgjald and Balavad's army stopped that conquest? Or had it merely delayed it? If this Archon Raamuzi of the Zhallahs could expose Balavad's deception and how he used the other Archons as his puppets, achieving his takeover would be more difficult. And Ulfric had already seen how easy it was to persuade people with power to follow the bidding of a Verity who promised them whatever their heart most desired. He'd almost fallen to this manipulation himself. *What did he promise these Archons Tuzhazu and Raamuzi?* Ulfric wondered.

"There are two Raamuzi Archons?"

Salukis nodded. "Sisters, Deespora, leader of the Zhallah people, and Akeeva."

Curious, but not unheard of. In his time in the Knights Corporealis, Ulfric had known a few siblings and a few parents and their children who'd taken the oath.

The more exposure to the other realms Ulfric had, the more he saw Balavad's grand plan. It seemed that either Vinnr or the fifth realm would be his last conquest. Himmingaze was a dying realm, crumbling nearly before the eyes of its people. He wondered if Balavad's meddling had also caused their doom. Perhaps Bardgrim would be able to stop him, though...

Ulfric shook his incorporeal head. Right now, Himmingaze was too distant to even comprehend. "This rogue Archon Tuzhazu, what does he look like? Where will I find him? Beyond the power of Yggo's and Urgo's talons, will I need anything else to defeat him?"

"You—you're going to Minoth?"

Ulfric blinked at Salukis with Urgo's eyes. "Where else would I go?"

"You don't understand. I want to help Isemay as much as you do. She's—" He stumbled on his words and changed course. "The Minothians intend to attack my people. If we don't warn them, they won't be prepared in time, and you'll never be able to save Isemay by yourself. They have an army, you have a...a bird."

"Your enemies have your Verity's vessel, and I assume Arc Rheunos's Scrylle and Fenestrii. Everything I need to save my family and return to my own world"—*and face the challenges of saving it...and myself*—"is there. I understand your troubles, Rheunosian, believe me, I do. But there is nothing I can do for you."

"They don't have the Scrylle."

Urgo's predatory gaze fixed on Salukis once more. The boy did not squirm, seeming to find strength in the realization of his advantage over Ulfric. "Even if you find Isemay and her mother, you'll have to come to Maerria to get back to your realm—with their army and Tuzhazu's Deathless trying to stop you." Salukis stood up, bringing the pendant level with his own eyes, unblinking. "What good will you do your family if you're all captured?"

What good...and what about the Knights and Vinnr? And Jaemus and his Glisternauts. A wave of exhaustion, not of the body but of the spirit, struck Ulfric. What was one man, Stallari or not, supposed to do in the face of such insurmountable troubles? Who was his allegiance to anymore? Verity, realm, family, Knight companions? It seemed if he did not save one, he could not save any. And it seemed increasingly impossible that he could save even one.

All I have left is fight, but do I have any more faith? he wondered.

Distracted, it took him a few moments to recognize a strange prickle spreading through him, or was it through Urgo? Somewhat uncomfortable but also reassuring, like a much-needed fire against winter-chilled fingertips. Along with it came a pressure in his mind, Urgo's own perceptive thoughts pressing upon Ulfric's. For the first time, it seemed he could understand the bruhawk, and he was pushing Ulfric not to give in, not to despair. Troubled times were always temporary—it was how we faced those moments that made us worthy of the peace and joy and love of family and friends that defined the rest. Urgo reminded him that no just fight was ever for one person's gain, and who one chose as their allies were as important as what they were fighting for. The bruhawks would fly with him, but it was up to him to find the strength, and hope, to still fly true.

He studied Salukis. The boy was young, scared, and injured, but he was not a coward. After so many hundreds of turns, Ulfric was an expert on reading people, and he could see the admirable, even coura-geous man he would become, if given the chance. And he could see his fear for Isemay, hear it in the quaver in his voice when he spoke her name. The boy cared for his daughter. Ulfric himself had seen them… *kissing*, as little as he wanted to admit his daughter was old enough to. But if anyone knew the lengths a person would go to save the ones they most cared for, it was Ulfric.

As if he could see Ulfric's indecision, Salukis spoke up. "You owe the Zhallah people nothing, but your own daughter was willing to risk her freedom to help us stop the Minothians from bringing further harm to my people. I don't think she came by such selflessness on her own. If she were here and you were in danger, I think she would do the wise thing, not the reckless one."

Ulfric snorted. "Isemay? Avoid recklessness? Clearly you and I aren't speaking of the same girl."

Salukis's face froze for a moment as he looked at Ulfric. The smirk Ulfric wore thawed his expression, and he broke into a grin as well.

"Okay, okay, you're right. But she'd at least *consider* the wiser course," he said, and both men chuckled.

Their laughter dissipated quickly, but the moment had a clearing effect on Ulfric's spiraling thoughts. His life was devoted to making hard decisions, and this was no different. *Mum and I will be in Minoth,* Isemay had said. *We need your help. We need all the help you can bring.* He asked, "You say they won't be harmed, that we have time before this Tuzhazu makes a move against your people?"

"Three more days," Salukis confirmed.

Ulfric finally relented. "Can you make it to Maerria?"

Salukis eyed the two bruhawks, who eyed him back quizzically. "I could. Perhaps with a bit of assistance?"

"It's done," Ulfric said with finality. "Yggo, would you—"

His words were cut off by the sudden shift of both bruhawks' heads as they turned toward the labyrinth below them. A dozen or more small figures were visible, men flying over the walls of the maze in a formation that suggested coordinated hunting. They all watched for a moment.

"They're searching for us," Salukis said quietly.

"There are too many of them for Yggo and Urgo to handle." Ulfric thought for a moment. "It's too dangerous, and too far, to try to go through the mountain passes. So we'll wait until dark, then make for your city. The bruhawks are swift, silent, and deadly. We'll get there one way or another before tomorrow's daystar rises."

Salukis didn't argue. Ulfric looked toward the horizon. Hours, half a dozen at least, until dark. He chafed at the idea of waiting, but there were too many things at risk to be rash or reckless. For now, they would wait.

Urgo fluffed out his feathers and settled, preparing for nightfall, and Ulfric focused on Symvalline, his love and life. Where was she? What was happening to her?

Had he arrived in this strange, unsettled realm in time?

CHAPTER THIRTY-TWO

Symvalline didn't dip her toe in before taking the plunge into the frigid water streaming beneath the Cosmoculous Tower, but it wouldn't have mattered. The water flowed as fast as a bruhawk could dive and sucked her into its depths, speeding her along in pitch-blackness. She didn't need to hold her breath—the icy river had stolen it from her anyway.

She'd ripped strips of the shroud she'd been carted to the barrows beneath into long ribbons to bind her loose leggings more tightly to her legs and the sleeves of her undershirt to her arms. The remains of her shredded overtunic, used to make the petards and small bags for the sleeping agent, had long since been discarded. But she wanted nothing loose to snag on things in the water and hold her under.

Nevertheless, the clothing quickly grew saturated and heavy. Swimming and struggling to keep near the surface of the watery tunnel, she kept her Mentalios illuminated and her eyes open, more than ready to catch sight of the first well and a moment's reprieve from the freezing journey.

It came soon. A lighter spot in the water ahead, and shortly the well cistern's rough stone lip was just above her. She barely had a chance to snag it before the water was trying to force her onward, but fortunately, the well shaft contained a metal ladder bolted into its side, which she clung to with a death grip.

Though the well shafts reached below the ground's surface, there was still a danger of being discovered. Agatha had explained that each well surfaced in a chamber that was large enough for several people to congregate, and held vessels and pails of all sizes for use by those who came for water. Though the shafts themselves were only a few feet deep, they were built wide and created small pools in the chambers so the river's strong flow could not tug the retrieval vessels out of people's hands. If she was unlucky enough to reach the well pool when someone had come for water, she would be found. All she had to defend herself was wits, her small dagger, and the bludgeon she'd taken from the tower guard. But she had no desire to hurt anyone.

She reached the first well quickly and hardly felt the lack of air. With that advantage, she pulled herself up the ladder rungs slowly, cautiously, eyes opened and fixed on the wavering light above her, searching for any sign of the chamber being inhabited. Seeing nothing, ignoring the chill settling in her limbs and fingers, she climbed until her head broke the surface and took in the space. Empty. The stone chamber was not roofed, and warmer outside air settled inside, prickling and tingling against her cold skin. She yearned to step out of the water and stand in a nearby shaft of sunlight but ignored the impulse. Drawing several deep breaths to fill her lungs, she gave the light one last lingering look, then dove again.

Six more to go.

The next three were much the same as the first. Symvalline had embarked in late afternoon, and Agatha had mentioned that most Minothians drew their water in the mornings and evenings. Undiscovered at each, her luck held on. But as she'd feared, her hands and feet were numb before the third well and the rest of her was rapidly following. Her struggle to keep close to the surface was strenuous enough to keep her blood moving, though it hardly kept her warm. As much as she wanted to, she dared not linger at any of the cisterns for any longer than she needed to replenish her breath, but even that was getting harder to hold for as long.

By the time she reached the fourth well, second from the last, she was starting to worry about her chances of remaining conscious and sensate enough to pull herself out of the last two. She would not die without breath. Her Verity spark would sustain her body for an unknown length of time. But she would lose awareness until revived—and there would be no force to revive her deep in the bowels of the Tyrn Mountains, she was sure.

At the fifth well, her luck failed. When she grabbed the underwater ladder rung to arrest her passage, the rusted metal snapped free. Scrabbling frantically at the tunnel walls, Symvalline realized her desperation, as ferocious as it was, would do her no good. She couldn't feel the walls, couldn't feel anything, and was swept onward, more than half-frozen and with straining lungs that pleaded for air.

CHAPTER THIRTY-THREE

Salukis had managed to carry Isemay a short distance back toward the labyrinth's center before she'd made him leave her. Mercifully, the regular soldier who'd bound her had not made her walk the rest of the way out of the labyrinth and repeat many of the passages she'd already traversed once to the Minothian valley. Binding her hands, he'd simply flown her back to the supply wagon she and Salukis had been trailing. Empty of anything save crates and bags, which were packed within each other, it afforded her space to sit and ride out the final leg of the journey.

When the daystar was a few hours past its midday zenith, the wagon stopped and she heard the guard shout their arrival to, she assumed, the Minoth Valley Gate guards. By then, she was so sapped of strength and vitality that she would have given in to being carried by a Deathless Guard. The idea of it made her cold, even more than she already was.

Soon, she heard a sound that could have been a heavy door opening, then people speaking outside the wagon. Lying on her side, her hands and feet bound—apparently her cheekiness had made the guard angry enough to ensure she'd enjoy no comfort—she picked up her head to listen but couldn't make out what was being said. Struggling in her awkward restraints, she managed to pull herself to her feet and look over the tall wagon sides.

The gate on this side of the labyrinth was built much the same as the other. The pass through the mountains was narrower on this side, however, and only guarded from a singular tower instead of the two at the Aktoktos Gate end. It made sense to her. The Minothians were more concerned with people coming in from beyond the mountains than they were of anyone leaving.

Now that she could see the mountains rising to either side, she couldn't help but scan them for any sign of Salukis. Perhaps he'd followed the wagon stealthily instead of doing as she'd asked. The idea both excited and vexed her. No, he had to go. Find her da and get help. He was enough of a practical sort that he would have. Still, seeing his familiar adored face would have given her at least some of the energy she was so badly lacking.

Keep that chin up, she told herself. *Help will come. Soon.*

It surprised her when she realized that she didn't feel as alone as she expected to under the circumstances. The combined knowledge that her father had arrived in Arc Rheunos, maybe all of the Knights, and that she was now so close to her mother brought more than a little comfort, even a hint of good humor. She found herself looking forward to the Minothians finally getting what was coming to them, never doubting for a second that her parents, and the Zhallahs, would more than readily mete out their deserved comeuppance.

The Deathless Guard who'd found her had departed already, likely to hunt for Salukis. Now, the guard and wagon driver were sitting beside each other, and she could overhear them speaking clearly.

"But what do you think it means?" asked the wagon driver, a woman whose drab robes looked heavy enough to keep out the mountains' chill, which Isemay was envious of. "Two people from a foreign realm coming here now, nearly at the Equifulcrum. Has the Everlight said anything about what this is all about?"

Isemay could hear the subtext to her question. Does the Everlight *know* anything? She sensed doubt in the Minothian, and perhaps something that wasn't exactly fear but more like a shakiness, like knowing that the footing you stood on could betray you and crumble at any moment.

"If the Everlight has spoken to Archon Tuzhazu, he hasn't shared it with the rest of the kaneas."

The two went quiet for a moment. Isemay crept to the front of the wagon and peeked over the edge.

The wagon driver looked sidelong at the guard and said, "It's true then, is it? Archon Tuzhazu will be the Everlight's next vessel?"

It seemed the guard's hesitation was pensive. "It's tradition. He is the last Archon. It's his destiny."

"In three hundred years, since the last Equifulcrum, why hasn't the Everlight ordained any new Archons?"

"None can say. It's the same kind of question as why does she let the Zhallahs spread the Waste? Or why did famine strike so badly at the last Distalfulcrum? None can say," he repeated.

"Some think the Everlight may not want to shift. Maybe the creator will be content to remain within Archon Raamuzi. She was a good Archon, they say, before the Great Waste."

The guard nodded agreeably. "I heard the same. Compassionate, a woman who heard all sides before judging. Then she lost all her children to the plague."

"A sadness, that. Maybe it would be best if the creator stayed put. The influence of Archon Raamuzi's spirit, whatever may remain, could be better than..." She let her thought dissipate before completing it, but even Isemay knew what she meant. Deespora's sister was undoubtedly the people's preference for leadership of the realm over Tuzhazu, who seemed to be universally feared, even despised.

She thought they were not going to speak again and had begun to crouch back down when the guard said, "Some in the kaneas worry Archon Tuzhazu will turn the whole troop into Deathless."

The wagon driver visibly shuddered and said something under her breath Isemay couldn't make out. Louder, she said, "They say it's an honor to join the Deathless. Only the finest are picked." Her tone sounded as if she was attempting to reassure him.

The guard gave a short nod, not answering. Then he said, quietly, almost secretively, "He's not really that last Archon. There's still the one in the Churss."

The wagon driver looked at him sharply, but he pretended not to notice. Then, unexpectedly, he turned his head and caught sight of Isemay.

"Sit back down, Vinnric," the guard ordered.

"Tell me one thing and I will. Do you know where my mother is? The other Vinnric I came with?"

He looked at her with a blank face, then stood and leaned forward threateningly. "Sit."

Scowling, she slid back down the wall of the wagon, awaiting whatever came next with as much bravery as she could muster. The wagon driver and guard did not speak again before the gate was opened and they passed inside.

CHAPTER THIRTY-FOUR

S *ymvalline, Symvalline, are you there? My love?*

Ulfric's voice, like a bubble, floated up from the stygian void in Symvalline's mind. She was dreaming of him. *Can I really dream?* she wondered. *Aren't I dead—or close enough that I may as well be?*

His voice again, far away, yet crystal clear as if coming through their Mentalios link. *I don't know if you can hear me, love, but I'm going to try. I'm here, in Arc Rheunos.*

It didn't surprise her. The man she'd loved for lifetimes, of course she would dream of him now, while she was eternally trapped in the depths of Arc Rheunos. She had lost consciousness before ever seeing another well shaft and was destined to remain forever lost.

All drew quiet in her thoughts for a moment—and this did surprise her. Would she be aware of a moment, of time at all, if she were truly lifeless and bobbing along the underground river toward the unfathomable depths of the mountains range, never to be seen or heard from, in any realm, again? The passage of time, even short bits of it, was something an awake person would notice. Was this what she would have to endure for eons? The endless passage of time as she languished?

I've found a boy named Salukis. He was with Isemay and is going to take me to his people, the Zhallahs. We're coming to find you, both of you. I hope...I hope we're not too late.

Symvalline jolted, but not in her mind. She'd felt her body being shoved, no, *pulled.* Something yanked on her again, as if rude hands had ahold of her. *Is there something under the mountains here with me?* If she could have shivered in fear in her state, she would have.

Then Ulfric's words hit her. Salukis, Isemay, the Zhallah people. Dreaming Ulfric was here, that he'd found the boy who'd helped Isemay and planned to attempt to rescue them—that was just a cruel trick for her mind to play on her at a time like this.

Something pushed her again, harder this time. And she did feel it, not in a distant, disembodied way, but in her bones. *Open your eyes, Symvalline,* she told herself. *You're not alone here.*

With an effort that felt like moving a mountain, she forced her eyelids to part. Everything was blurry. Blurry, *but definitely light.* If she were still in the tunnel, it would have been as dark as eternity. A form moved beside her, something large and colorless, as if a negation of the light pouring down from above. Then she was shoved, or…nudged?…again.

I'm not in the tunnel, she realized with a start. Was it possible she'd been found? With that thought, she concentrated on her lungs, consciously trying to force them to work, to draw a breath for the first time in—*how long was I under there?*

With a great gasp, she sucked in air that felt like tiny slivers of wood as it filled her lungs. The dark shape looming beside her snorted, took a lumbering step back, then returned and nudged her again. That's when she discovered she wasn't in water but on a hard stone floor. A heavy weight fell over her chest and pawed at her.

Blinking rapidly, she tried clearing the haze from her vision. Slowly, things came into focus. Stone walls, the sky above, the sound of water, the smell of—*it's like a wild animal. What in the five realms is it?*

Finally she saw it. Beside her stood one of the massive urzidae creatures, its thick snout lowered until its eyes could peer into her face.

She gasped again and found the strength through numb arms to push herself backward until she nearly fell into the open cistern behind her. The beast watched her curiously, its expression, if a bear-like behemoth could have an expression, placid.

As she shook and shivered, staring at the creature with her mouth agape, it seemed to accept her presence and stepped to the cistern's edge, lowered itself, and began to drink unconcernedly.

Near shock, she could only watch it. Awareness that the pool here was much bigger than the others and the water rose nearly to the cistern's edge came to her. Somehow, unbelievably, she must have been pushed into this cistern by the water flow from below, and the urzidae must have fished her out. It just wanted a drink, after all.

I made it, she realized. *I made it.*

And if she was awake, did that mean Ulfric's voice had not been a dream?

She sat up and reached to her chest to grip her Mentalios, the movement painful and slow like trying to bend frozen clothing. Her flesh had not recovered from its prolonged exposure to the icy waters. With nerveless fingers, she clasped the pendant and sent: *Ulfric, is that you?*

His response was instant: *Symvalline!?*

Verities eyes! she cried, and wasn't sure if she'd said it aloud. *I didn't think you were real.*

My love, is it you!? Are you safe? Are you with Crumb?

Hearing his voice sent a tidal wave of joy washing through her that nearly took away the precious breath she'd just regained. It was him, her heartmatch. He was real and he was here. If this seemingly impossible thing was possible, then anything was. *No,* she finally managed. *Ulfric, she's been taken prisoner in a place called the Minoth Valley Gate. I'm on my way to her now, and I'm very close. What's become of Vinnr? Are the other Knights with you?*

As was typical, Ulfric was quiet for a few moments, sifting through the information he'd just learned, seeing its angles, weighing its meaning. He'd never been a rash or impatient man. The only times she'd ever seen him unbalanced was the night they'd chosen to pledge themselves to each other for eternity, and the day they had decided they would ask Vaka Aster to grant them an end to their service and release from their oaths.

As she awaited his response, the urzidae—a creature that, to her surprise, was docile and unthreatening—finished quenching its thirst. A whistle sounded from above the open-topped well chamber, and Symvalline started at the realization that she was not yet safe. Anyone could look over the belowground chamber's rim and see her sitting here.

The back of the space held various vessels and vases for water gathering, some large enough to crouch behind. As the urzidae sent one more curious glance her way, then lumbered up the wide stairs of the well chamber, she half walked, half crawled to the containers and wedged herself as far into their shadows as she could. Taking pains to be as silent as possible, she pulled more around her to create a barrier to anyone who might look in her direction from within the chamber. Agatha had told her to wait here, that she would come later in the night when she arrived at the gate. Overhead, the daystar's light dimly came from somewhere west, slanting over the top of the room. It was evening, early by the looks of it. She could not expect Agatha for a couple more hours.

The Knights are not here, Sym. Things in Vinnr have taken a dangerous turn. Balavad, the one who called himself His Holiness, is the Battgjaldic Verity, as we suspected. He's undermined Vaka Aster, made her...powerless, and is now leading the people of Dyrrakium into a war against Ivoryss and Yor. We were unable to stop him. He paused to let her take in this news. Then: *There's too much to tell, and we haven't the time now. What's most important at this moment is getting you and Isemay to safety.*

It was her turn for speechlessness. Vinnr was under the sway of another Verity? A thirty-night ago, she'd have thought it inconceivable.

Yet it wasn't inconceivable at all, was it? It seemed to be the same story as was happening here in Arc Rheunos. The Battgjaldic Verity wanted power over all other Verities and their realms. But why?

It didn't matter, not right now. As Ulfric had said, there wasn't the time, and Isemay was alone and unprotected, being sought by Tuzhazu.

Ulfric, she sent, *Arc Rheunos is being threatened as well. They've been deceived by Balavad, but there is one Archon here, at least, who is willingly doing his bidding. Tuzhazu—you must be wary of him and his twisted warriors. They're called the Deathless Guards, and they're...altered in some way to be like the Raveners who followed Balavad in Vinnr.*

Yes, Salukis has told me as much. He says the Zhallah people are also led by an Archon, and this one knows of Balavad's treachery.

His treachery is worse than you can imagine. The people here were once beset by a plague they call the Waste. Tuzhazu spreads it. I believe he uses it as a weapon of fear and that he got it from Balavad.

Ulfric was quiet again, likely reining in his horror and disgust, as she'd been forced to since meeting Tuzhazu. Then he went on. *The Zhallah Archon has the Arc Rheunosian Scrylle and a Fenestros. She can open a starpath and send us...*

He trailed off. She realized that the word he was stumbling on, "home," did not necessarily mean somewhere safe. Was anywhere safe anymore?

She sent: *One more thing. I believe Tuzhazu carries a Fenestros from Battgjald. Be cautious of its power. He used it to take my klinkí stones, and to nearly kill me.*

He responded: *But you're well? You're well now?*

She wanted to snort at that. Well enough, she supposed, for someone who had just frozen and drowned. *I'm fine as a flower, my love.* She hoped she sounded reassuring. *Do you know of the Equifulcrum?*

Yes, he responded.

Those who have Isemay, the Minothians, will be occupied during the event. I'm going to free her tonight, and we'll hide on this side of the mountains until then. Then we'll attempt to pass through the labyrinth. If you can find a way to bring a force of the Zhallahs, we may be able to unite in time to overcome any resistance.

How will you find your way through?

I have help from a couple of Minothians. I can trust them.

He was quiet again, thinking through the plan. Flimsy as it was, Symvalline had to trust in it, at least until it came time to improvise something new. The Scrylle and Fenestros held by the Zhallah Archon, the sister of the false Verity Akeeva Raamuzi, and a chance to escape this peril—hearing of these should have been a relief. But somehow it wasn't. She could get her daughter to safety, be reunited with Ulfric, leave this realm, but she would always know the damage being wrought by Tuzhazu, the cruelty and deceptions that kept the people here in a form of fearful bondage. The same kind of wickedness occurring in her own realm. Where did it end?

Was the only way to stop it, in Vinnr and Arc Rheunos and the Cosmos as a whole, to stop Balavad? For good?

Again, a thirty-night ago, the idea would have been unthinkable. Impose their own wills on a Verity? Blasphemous hilarity.

But she was thinking it now. And she'd have bet her klinkí stones that Ulfric was too.

Finally, he sent: *We will be there, Symvalline. The Zhallahs and I, as soon as I can rally them.*

CHAPTER THIRTY-FIVE

Every hair (or feather), every scrap of skin, every thought in Ulfric's head screamed against leaving Symvalline behind in the clutches of the Minothians. He'd have given his last breath to press his cheek to hers right then and feel the softness of her skin and her arms wrapped around him. But that would not save Isemay, and it would not save him, either. His lot in life was to turn away from what he wanted and embrace what his realm and Verity needed. It was a bitter, bitter pill that he longed so badly to no longer have to swallow. It was the reason he and Symvalline had been planning to ask to be released from their oaths in the first place.

But today would not be the day he would finally have the freedom to enjoy what he wanted.

Evening light was about to give way to full dark as he and Symvalline finished speaking. Through the memory keeper, he focused once more on Salukis, who'd stood silently by during their conversation.

The boy's brown eyes were inquisitive. "What just happened?" he asked.

"I've spoken with my heartmatch. She is going to collect Isemay and meet us in the labyrinth during the Equifulcrum. And now, with dark upon us, we go and raise an army."

A fluid mix of excitement and more than a little dread rippled almost comically over the young man's face. He choked for a moment, then managed: "To Maerria, then."

They flew close to the mountains' flanks, darker shadows against the twilight-painted landscape, and were through the labyrinth before the three moons had achieved their full glowing might. They were now so close that their edges nearly overlapped. The Equifulcrum, the perfect alignment of all three, was in three days. He imagined what it would be like to witness.

No Minothian saw them and rang an alarm during their flight. The unique liminal lighting created difficulties for sentries in any realm, it seemed. Ordinarily, such poor security would have made the soldier in Ulfric grumble with disgust, but tonight he was thankful. If their numbers had been more than Salukis and the two bruhawks, they would have stood out.

But the threat of greater numbers was still to come—for the Minothians. They would march on Minoth tonight, tomorrow morning at the latest, if Ulfric had any control over it.

As they came over the top of the Churss, Salukis quickly explained that the Zhallah people resided amid the stone forest to protect them from the Minothians. The Churss had once been a fourth moon over Arc Rheunos, and it was loyal to Mithlí in a way Salukis couldn't explain except to say that all the oldest stones in the realm had an awareness and power they drew from their Verity. The Churss could be relied on to repel anything that endangered the Zhallah people, who'd never wavered in their loyalty to Mithlí. Fascinated in spite of himself, Ulfric marveled at the abundance of oddities in this realm.

His marveling only grew greater as he watched the stones close like a roof over the earth when Salukis began to lead their flight down to it. *They're alive!* he thought, and an idea began to take shape in his mind.

At the young man's request, Yggo released Salukis a few feet above the canopy, and he dropped atop it with a gentle sweep of his wings and pained intake of breath. He pulled a two-bodied flute from his pack and blew a short lilting tune over the stone barrier. The bruhawks, not designed to hover, took to soaring in short, tight circles above Salukis to wait for whatever was coming. A moment later, Ulfric heard the sound of stone grinding on stone, and a small opening directly beneath Salukis was uncovered.

The Zhallah turned up and waved at Urgo. "This way." Then he dove inside.

Urgo began his short descent, only to be forced to pull up sharply as the stones snapped closed behind Salukis.

What? Ulfric growled. He attempted to call Salukis through the memory keeper but received nothing in response. It seemed the Churss blocked his thoughts as well. *Look for another way in, Urgo.*

Urgo soared along the tower tops, each possible chink closing abruptly as they approached. Ulfric seethed. *We don't have time for games.* Perhaps the Zhallah boy had been planning to get rid of them from the start. *No, he seemed much too guileless for that kind of trickery.* Ulfric longed to be in his own body once more and wished he were carrying the heaviest hammer Stave had ever forged. He would show these rocks that he was not to be toyed with.

With their sweep over the Churss feeling futile indeed, Ulfric led the bruhawks back to the spot they'd lost Salukis in. Lowering themselves to perch and wait seemed their only option. Ulfric sensed the prickle of confusion in Urgo's mind. *Me too, friend. Me too.*

They were there only a moment when a stone came soaring from the left and struck Yggo in the wing. The bird let out a surprised squawk and hopped to the side. Both hawks grew instantly agitated. Urgo wanted to take flight again, but Ulfric urged him to stay, though he had no idea what could have thrown a stone at this height, or from where.

Another one struck Urgo, and this time the bird refused to listen to Ulfric and leaped skyward once more. Nothing Ulfric could do would dissuade the bruhawks, and he stopped trying as more and more missiles came toward them. The Churss, it seemed, was not going to allow any potentially untrustworthy strangers to borrow its heights for their own leisure.

Just as his frustration nearly reached a boiling point, made all the worse by his helplessness to do anything about it, Ulfric saw glistening specks of light begin to glow along the stone rooftop. *What kind of weapon...*he started to wonder.

Moments went by as the lights grew stronger, until it was as bright as day below him. Unwilling to face the unknown turn of events too closely, the bruhawks rose high into the night sky, cautiously circling the strange illuminated canopy of rock below.

Despite his anxiety over how much time was passing, the magnificent view that went as far south as the bruhawk's eyes could perceive captivated him. Ulfric had never seen anything so bizarre yet beautiful. It was like being just within reach of the surface of the daystar, but without the heat that would have charred them to oblivion instantly. He didn't know what was going on, or what was to come, but he was enthralled for the moment.

"Come down here, Vinnric, and show yourself."

The voice was deep but feminine, and it rose to the bruhawks clearly, as if amplified by some wystic contrivance. Such as a Fenestros.

Urgo and Yggo lowered themselves once more, and the intense brightness began to dim enough for them to see a handful of figures now standing atop the stone ceiling. Ulfric quickly picked out the tall figure with one wounded wing, Salukis.

The group had no obvious weapons, and Ulfric chose to have Urgo land. Urgo's hard claws clacked against the still-shimmering stone directly before an older woman with skin as pale as chalk, completely without hair, holding a long wooden staff. Atop the staff, a warm light glowed from the round headpiece, undoubtedly a Fenestros. Urgo's eyes perceived the Verity stone differently than Ulfric's did. It was lit, as if harboring an inferno inside. The woman looked up into the bird's eyes with no fear at all.

"Salukis," Ulfric said through the memory keeper. "Will you bring my daughter's pendant to me? To Urgo, rather, and drape it around his neck. I would like to speak with"—he had Urgo tilt his head to look into the Archon's eyes—"Archon Raamuzi directly."

Salukis did as asked, seeming reluctant to be letting go of the jewel.

The pendant hung next to Ulfric's Mentalios atop the bruhawk's feathery chest, nearly eye level with Salukis. "I'm sorry about not being able to bring you to the village. I didn't know the Churss would do that," Salukis said with quiet sincerity.

"It's fine. Thank you," Ulfric said, then turned his gaze to Deespora. "Archon Raamuzi, you have my deepest gratitude for meeting me. I am Stallari Ulfric Aldinhuus, leader of the Knights Corporealis of Vinnr. These bruhawks are also ordained by our Verity, Vaka Aster. They are Urgo and Yggo. We have a very serious matter to discuss."

If the Archon was surprised by the manner in which he faced her, she didn't show it. "And how long have you served your maker?" she asked.

"Nearly two thousand turns around Halla, our daystar."

Deespora seemed to take this news in with considerable thought. After a moment, she gestured to those around her, two men, two women, and Salukis. "Poolan, Kitane, Vidar, and Kalisk. And you know Salukis. As a senior member of the same Order as my own, though called by a different name, you are welcome in the Churss."

As she finished speaking, the lights shining atop the stone canopy dimmed completely, and off to their sides the stones began to open up, leaving wide gaps that allowed the moonlight and starlight to reach the Churss floor.

Relieved at the welcome, Ulfric bowed to Deespora through the memory keeper. "I'll be frank, Archon. I believe not only your realm and my own are in danger, but all of them are." He projected his memory of Himmingaze's Glister Cloud and another of its torrential sea through the pendant. "Even the realm of Lífs, as you can see."

"And what of the fifth realm?" she asked.

He shook his head. "We call it the Forgotten Realm. I know nothing of it. If our lore ever included it, the knowledge has long since been lost."

She watched him closely but said nothing.

Ulfric went on. "Salukis told me you know of Balavad here and his treacherous doings. The malignant Verity is wreaking havoc far and wide. Vinnr is under assault, possibly as we speak, due to his malevolence. And Salukis said Arc Rheunos has been similarly afflicted. I—"

She held up her hand to stop him. "I do not need a lesson on the goings-on of the entire Cosmos, Stallari Aldinhuus. We are a quiet people with a realm filled with our own troubles, as you've no doubt witnessed to some degree. What you want is our help in finding your wife and child and getting them released from Minothian hands, am I correct?"

"In short, yes," he confirmed, gladdened to be able to cut to the heart of the matter.

"We cannot help you." She tilted her head and regarded the close-set moons. "As I've told my people and am now going to tell you, it's the will of the Verities we must all bow to. We Archons meddled with our maker once, long ago, and it resulted in this terrible rift between the Minothian and Zhallah people that we now live with. I didn't help to cage Mithlí. I didn't believe it could be done. And if Mithlí had wanted things to go differently for her creations, she would have made it so." Her gaze fell on him again. "And look what has been wrought. Division, malice, one people harming another. I can't undo what was done; it's too late for that. But I can keep my people safe and leave the Verities to their own ends. You and I are not deciders of others' fates, Stallari. We are servants to the wills of our makers. And *humble*." She delivered the last word as a command, not a simple description.

Ulfric bit his metaphysical tongue, angrily parsing through the many sharp responses he wanted to launch against the Archon's speech. Before he thought of what would most aid his cause, the oldest of the Zhallahs spoke up.

The woman, who was nearly withered by age, flushed a dusky violet. "Deespora," she began.

"Kalisk," Deespora cut her off, not looking to her. "I've told you, we will not leave the Churss, no matter what my sister and her chief denizen do."

Kalisk pulled herself up straighter, the movement drawing the wrinkled folds on her neck and alongside her eyes tighter. "No," she stated matter-of-factly. "You no longer get to make that choice for the rest of us, Archon Raamuzi."

This time, Deespora looked toward Kalisk sharply, and Ulfric noted the way Salukis's gaze shot to her too.

The old woman's voice did not waver, and years of wisdom gave it an authority few younger than her could master. "We've listened to your good judgment for all our lives, as did our parents and grandparents, since the last Equifulcrum. You did what you thought was right then by guiding our people away from Minoth and the dangers the other Archons wrought. And I'm sure it was the right thing. But with each child we lose to the Minothians, with each child you refuse to aid, what wisdom you once claimed to have loses its strength."

"What are you saying to me, Kalisk?" the Archon asked. Ulfric heard the tightness in her voice.

"The Zhallah people are ready to march on Minoth and take back our children and our future. We've had enough living as prisoners in our own world, afraid to leave the Churss, a cage in its own way, and afraid to protect our own families."

Ulfric could see the Archon was not used to being criticized or second-guessed. Perhaps she'd fooled herself into believing there was no other way than to hide from the world and their enemies. He pondered what he'd have to do to change her mind, but decided to see what would come of this burgeoning rebellion first.

"You don't know what you're saying," Deespora assured her, her voice remaining calm but crisp.

"I do at least as much as you do." Kalisk faced Deespora doggedly and stretched out her thin arm to wave at the others standing with them. "We've been talking for a long time, and most of the Zhallahs want to confront the Minothians. Some even to fight them, if we have to."

The Archon stared back at her without blinking her pale eyes. "But there's no need to attack them. Even divided, we are still all one people, all Arc Rheunosians, creations of Mithlí the Everlight. You don't know Tuzhazu as I do, what he is capable of. Confronting a force he leads could end up in bloodshed, death. Could you, could any Zhallah, live with the knowledge that we brought harm upon others and ourselves? That isn't who we are or what we believe in."

Ulfric decided it was time to say something. "Balavad gave your people the means to end the plague, is that right?" he interjected. Each of the Zhallahs looked at the memory keeper. "He bought the Archons' trust with a promise to cure the afflicted if you would render your own maker powerless, I hear from Salukis, a tale you yourself tell. Did you know Balavad was the one who created the plague in the first place?" He paused to let that sink in, watching her impassive face. There was no surprise in it. She'd already drawn this conclusion herself, he realized, then continued. "And it was him spreading it among you to drive you to the brink of desperation, making the people of this realm so afraid they'd lose everyone they loved that the Archons blindly grabbed whatever hope—or what passed for it—he offered. Balavad pushed you into aiding his plans for dominion over Arc Rheunos and its people through treachery—and butchery. And Tuzhazu helped him."

Deespora, though outwardly still calm, struggled against a smirk hardening her mouth. "You're mistaken. Tuzhazu has never been overly compassionate and takes—took—his oath as an Archon to its limits, but he isn't a murderer. And how could you possibly know such a thing at all?"

"I've spoken with Symvalline, Isemay's mother, through a pendant like the one I'm speaking to you through now. She's seen Tuzhazu use a poison that causes the plague. He is Balavad's puppet and uses Balavad's tools to ensure he retains control over the Minothians. He uses fear and intimidation, lessons he no doubt mastered under Balavad himself. And he isn't even the Minothians' leader—yet. What do you think will happen to the rest of the Zhallah children if he gains control of not only the Minothian forces but the conscience and will of all Minothian people?"

Deespora had no immediate response and he pressed forward, hoping he was persuading her.

"I can see your peoples' faith in your maker is strong, and I'm sure your enemy's is too. If they believe Tuzhazu to be the living vessel..." He let that statement go unfinished, allowing those present to fill it with their own ideas. He knew that he could never hit as close to what they most feared through his words as their imaginations would on their own.

As he watched, their faces showed their disturbance. "The Archons took Balavad's offer for an end to the plague to save your people. If you don't listen to me now, Balavad will finish the task he started, and instead of saving you, he'll enslave you."

"But that doesn't make sense," the man called Poolan said. "The Minothians call *us* plague-bringers."

"That sounds like a lie that would convenience Tuzhazu to spread," Ulfric stated flatly.

Poolan tucked his wings close to his back protectively and grew quiet, considering.

Deespora spun around and paced along the top of the Churss, then turned and paced back. "Ridiculous," she said. "Why would Tuzhazu do something so foul, so profane to everything we believe in?"

"Who can say," Ulfric said aloud, but inwardly he was thinking, *Isn't it obvious? Combine fear—of death or even simply abandonment by his creator—with a lust for power, and the result will always be a corruption of that power.* "But if you refuse to stop him now, and Balavad brings an army to your realm as he did to Vinnr, the reasons won't matter. If you feel like prisoners in this rock forest now, what Balavad plans will be worse. He is a corrupted Verity, poisonous, destructive. I've seen what he can do, what he has done, with my own eyes."

Deespora stopped pacing and looked into Ulfric's jewel. "So then, even if we were to go to the Everlight Hall and somehow hold Archon Tuzhazu accountable, what would stop Balavad's army, if it's true there is one, from coming anyway?"

Ulfric stared into the woman's colorless eyes. The way the white, blue, and red lights of the moons flickered in their depths was haunting, as if they contained the Cosmos within them. Wisdom lingered there, but also a deep weariness, and pain. She'd seen too much suffering, and being helpless against it had weakened her resolve to stand up to it. He understood. He'd witnessed enough suffering of his own to last a hundred more lifetimes. The difference between them, though, was that he'd lived long enough to see an end to suffering, too, and had developed the faith to believe that if endured long enough, it could be overcome.

Instead of being angered by her obstinacy, he wished he had a hand to place on her shoulder and comfort her. But the best he could do was offer the only hope he could see. "If you were to release Mithlí, Balavad would have no more power here."

"Release the Everlight…" she said quietly, as if to herself.

"Then," he continued, seeing that he'd perhaps started to crack the wall of inaction she had built, "perhaps we can unite our realms and use Balavad's own tricks against him."

Startled, she looked at him and said, "You're suggesting we cage the Verity of Battgjald instead."

"Yes. Yes I am," he answered simply. "And—one other thing I should mention. He is no longer the Verity of Battgjald. Battgjald has been wiped from existence."

Deespora looked around at the faces of her fellow Zhallahs. All were quiet, some appearing stunned, others wary. Finally, she turned back to Ulfric. "I believe we have more to discuss."

CHAPTER THIRTY-SIX

"Let me go or I'll lay a Vinnric curse on you that will shrivel anything you've got underneath those trousers to the size of a phanx!" Isemay yelled at the Minothian guard holding her wrists behind her as another unlocked a stout-looking door to where, she presumed, they were going to hold her captive.

Apparently, the guard thought she might be capable of such a thing, and his hands dropped away so fast it was like they'd ceased to exist. She smothered an amused smirk, which was easy because she barely had the energy left to stay upright, much less gloat. Pretending to be this brave was a lot more work than she would have expected. That, and the effects of being in a foreign realm were overtaking her again, with a vengeance.

The two Minothians shoved her inside the room and slammed the door between her and freedom. Her stomach gave an uneasy lurch as they did, and she staggered, suddenly dizzy, coming to rest on her knees. She stayed that way for a moment, head down, eyes shut, waiting for the world to settle.

After a moment, she pushed herself wearily erect and looked around. Empty room. Not even a chamber pot or garderobe. She'd already heard the lock behind her rattle, so no use trying the door.

Making it a good thing she'd managed to acquire a handy little dagger, in case she needed to try to pick it.

Once she'd assured herself there was no way for anyone to see inside the room—it was basically a windowless closet—she pulled the knife from inside the front of her shirt, where she'd dropped it as she'd snuck it from the guard's sheath. Not every lesson she'd learned in life had come from the Conservatum. And the guard had been too worried about his bits to notice her deft pickpocketing once her hands were free.

Her stomach grumbled again, and it occurred to her it was as likely to be hunger as the sickness overtaking her. But they'd kept her bag and the food she'd brought. She thought briefly about making a nuisance of herself and banging on the door to demand something to eat, but the prospect was too wearying. Instead, she tried the door's handle anyway, fruitless, then pressed her back against the wall beside the door, slid down to her butt, and let her forehead sink to her sore knees.

If her mum was near, she had no way of knowing. She'd asked the tower guards about her as she'd been led inside, but they'd been tight-lipped, treating her like she was an alien who spoke another language. Surely they would want to keep the two Vinnrics together, wouldn't they? She had no idea what to expect next. The only thing she knew with any certainty was that her da had arrived, and he and Salukis were not going to let her stay a captive for long. With her da's help, Salukis could rally the Zhallahs quickly. Many, maybe enough would come. She'd seen in their faces as the secret gathering that they'd had enough. And her da could be very, very persuasive.

She flashed briefly to the moment she'd learned Ulfric was here— which led inevitably to the kiss she and Salukis had shared. Her lips felt the phantom of the breath that had spanned between them again, and her whole body grew warm. Then another thought, unwelcome and biting, came. What if Salukis hadn't gotten away?

She strangled that thought dead. Soon, something would happen, something significant enough to change everything. She just had to hang on long enough. A day, maybe two.

CHAPTER THIRTY-SEVEN

Symvalline had become a cocoon of imagined heat. For the last few hours, she'd huddled against the well chamber's wall, barricaded by all the containers found there, masked by the shadows of the waning daystar. Cold, drenched, and clinging to the hope that Agatha would be there soon.

She'd spent that time considering all the warm things in life. Hot cider, a blazing hearth fire, Ulfric's embrace, the feel of Isemay against her bosom when she'd still been an infant. These thoughts sparked a poor facsimile of heat, but it was enough. It had to be.

Only two people had come to draw water since the urzidae had drunk its fill, proving she was at the outskirts of the settled areas of the Minothian valley. The knowledge that Isemay was close, being held in the gate tower until Tuzhazu arrived, was its own kind of torture. She weighed the option of going on without the aid of Agatha and Widin but talked herself out of it. She'd have one chance at succeeding in this endeavor. Impatience and rash action could end it before it began.

Yet, if Agatha and Widin didn't arrive soon, she would have to go. She hoped Tuzhazu would be delayed by the discovery that she was missing and Akeeva the Charlatan's, as Symvalline couldn't help but label her, reaction to this news. But she was determined to mount her rescue attempt before he did arrive, if that was still his intent. Her chance of success was better without the cunning, cruel Archon's presence.

Enough time passed without her coconspirators appearing that she could wait no longer. Rising to her feet, she pushed away the vessels concealing her and stepped into the center of the chamber. Stiff, sluggish, and tired, her limbs threatened to put an end to her journey right there, and she leaned against the wall to await their cooperation. With sheer force of will, she began to run in place, lifting her knees nearly to her chest, swinging her arms wildly, doing what she had to get blood flowing to her extremities and stoke whatever tiny spark of warmth she might still have in her. The process took time, but finally, she felt ready to go.

Her first step had just hit the bottom stair when a patter of footsteps came from above her. She rushed beside the stairway and crouched, hoping she was well enough hidden in the shadows to be able to surprise whoever would be descending. The bludgeon she'd taken from the guard at the Cosmoculous Tower and the dagger she'd taken from the man Tuzhazu had killed slid into her hand almost as if by their own volition.

Before the situation came to that, however, a voice she recognized called, "Is anyone there?"

She glanced up and saw a mellow light glowing at the top of the stairs. "Aga—" Her voice, like the rest of her, had frozen. She had to clear her throat before trying again. "Agatha?"

"It's me." The rustling sound of the woman descending into the chamber followed, Widin a few steps behind. When they got to the bottom, Agatha held out a small, glowing lantern with one hand and a bundle of clothing in the other. "Change quickly. These will help you hide your face."

Symvalline took the bundle, unimaginably grateful for the feel of dry cloth under her fingers. Widin turned away so she could slide her frayed and bedraggled Vinnr shirt and trousers off and the Minothian garb on, followed by a jacket with a deep hood. Being dry brought her leaps and bounds closer to feeling renewed, once more like one of the living rather than a cold corpse.

"Thank you," she said. She wished she had more time to fully express her gratitude, but time was not a luxury. "Do you know where Tuzhazu is?"

Widin replied, "No one passed us on the main road to the maze. Don't think he's arrived."

Luck seemed to be holding. "You've done so much for me already. Now, I have to ask for a little more. Here's how I intend to get inside the tower. Agatha, you still have my bag?"

When Symvalline held it, reassured by the weight of the Archon's book, she quickly explained her plan. "These," she pointed to the makeshift petards, "are small bags of explosive powder. They will make a lot of light and sound, and be dangerously hot and destructive to anything nearby when ignited. Here's how you do that." The two listened without interruption.

After demonstrating how the rushlight fuses worked, Symvalline handed the bundle of them to Agatha. "I need you to create a diversion away from the main entrance to the tower using these, then hide quickly. Ensure you're at least twenty feet away when they go off. You should have the space of four deep breaths to get away in plenty of time. They should draw most of the guards and keep them focused on something besides the tower itself. Which," her eyes landed on Widin, "is where you'll be taking me."

The old man, almost to her shock, actually smiled as if the idea delighted him.

Symvalline ran her hand under her chin, thinking. "The question is how you'll get close enough to the gatehouse unseen to be able to use these."

"That won't be difficult," Agatha stated assuredly.

"Your dark clothing will help, but they have the advantage of height to observe..." She trailed off as Agatha seemed to disappear before her very eyes.

The woman's voice came from right where she'd stood. "It's called yielding. All women can."

Finding her voice, Symvalline whispered, "Simply wonderful." *And solves one problem easily.* This could work, she began to realize.

She quickly outlined the rest of the plan, rough and incomplete as it was. To her surprise, neither balked at the daring ploy.

SHORTLY, she was once more under a shroud inside a wooden wagon made to carry the dead, this time harnessed to an urzidae. Agatha and Widin had brought it as their means of traversing the labyrinth. She had the company of Widin lying beside her. The shroud was heavy and warm, smelling of things she couldn't identify, not unpleasant but unique to her. Spices, maybe used to prepare bodies? Or a type of mold, perhaps. Or maybe it was the elderly man who carried the odor. Either way, she knew she'd remember it long after this perilous adventure was over. If things had been different, she would have reveled in exploring this realm and learning all its unique secrets and gifts.

The cart's wheels bumped along cobblestones, and before too long, they rolled to a stop. The two barrow tenders had explained to Symvalline that this side of the valley consisted of scattered farmhouses and crops that flanked the mountainsides. Agatha had driven the cart to a barn and stables used for the supply wagons. It was far enough away from the gatehouse tower that they wouldn't be noticed, and from there she'd walk to a safe place to deploy the petards, far enough away to avoid startling the other urzidae inside the stable.

Agatha's footsteps receded toward the gate, and Widin whispered, a touch of excitement painting his voice, "That's our cue."

"Remember," Symvalline pressed, "if there's trouble, take Isemay to safety, I beg you. Her first. I can take care of myself."

"I'll do what I can, Vinnric," he assured her.

Cautiously, the two peeked out from beneath the shroud into the dark night. Except it wasn't as dark as a normal night—the uncannily bright glow of the three moons covered the landscape with a blanket of cool luster. Sneaking anywhere, much less into the guarded gate tower, would be trickier than it should have been.

Agatha had left the wagon on the side of the stable not visible from the gatehouse, giving them a bit more concealment as they climbed out. Widin jumped clear, grunting the grunt of a man with old bones that weren't prepared for being jarred.

The two snuck around the building until they could see the road. Though in daylight there would be absolutely nothing to conceal them between the stable and the tower, at this hour and with where the moons were in the sky, the tower's shadow created a road of its own of complete darkness.

Symvalline hated the exposure, but there was no other choice but to creep straight up to her daughter's prison across a relatively flat plane with sparse vegetation, in full view of the tower, while the guards' attention was occupied elsewhere.

Glancing to Widin, she dipped her chin and waited for him to acknowledge he was ready. Oddly, he pulled his wings up high and spread them overhead like someone trying to hide beneath a cloak in the rain.

"Put your wings down," she whisper-shouted. "They'll see them."

He regarded her with a puzzled look for a moment, and she wondered if his age had addled his mind. Then he gave her an impish grin. "Ah, you Vinnrics don't know much of our ways and qualities, d'you?" As if to torment her, he waggled the tips of his wings slightly. "These old leather flaps will conceal us. Got a bit of the yield to them, too. You just step under here, and I promise they'll not see a thing from up there."

She hesitated, wanting to trust but afraid to. And again, in a refrain that was becoming tiresome, she asked herself, *What choice do you have?*

As she huddled at his side, the waiting and watching for their sign to break for the tower began. After a moment, Symvalline asked him, "Are you certain you want to do this? The consequences for getting caught…"

He gave her that grin again, but the sharp impish edges of it smoothed into something kinder. "You're a strange-looker, Vinnric, and seem to be made from troubles sewn to troubles. But all I had to do was take one look in your eyes to know your heart is true and good. I've looked into Tuzhazu's eyes, and that's…not what I've seen in them. I'm not going to live forever, and I want to be able to tell my wife when I see her beyond the shadows that I ended my days doing something true and good, or at least helping someone who was."

She was too overcome with gratitude to do more than put a hand on his arm and squeeze, hoping he understood.

The night felt too quiet as they waited for Agatha to light the petards. Symvalline scanned the base of the tower, the guardhouse, the high terminus wall of the labyrinth, and the base of the steep-walled mountains to either side, wondering where the woman would perform her deed. The tower stood to the east, looking as if it nearly touched the mountain beside it. The maze wall attached to it about five stories up, and the gatehouse, the only entrance to the tower, conjoined both at the tower's base. Sentries would most likely be atop the wall, but it would be hard to see anything directly below them, which was completely immersed in shadow. If Symvalline were in Agatha's place, she'd light the petards as far west of the gatehouse as she could, just at the bottom of the wall—

There, the sharp bangs of the petards, followed by a bright bloom like a flower of blue and red fire, just where Symvalline was thinking.

"Let's go," she said.

It seemed her trust in Widin was not misplaced, and they arrived at the tower without an alarm—at least not one directed at them. Symvalline saw four figures racing across the wall toward Agatha's diversion as she and Widin approached, and perhaps three poured out of the gatehouse door. How many would still be in the tower?

The tower rose before them like a finger pointed angrily at the sky. Alarmed shouts and commands rang from the distance, but not many. Symvalline appreciated their relaxed outlook when it came to protecting the valley. Arc Rheunos, apparently, was not a realm that was on familiar terms with threats or war, the kinds of things that made building dungeons and maintaining full armies necessary.

Widin and Agatha thought the likeliest place they'd be holding

Isemay was the second story, closest to the guards' barracks and central hearth, which had several empty rooms with locking doors and no outside access. Prisoners were a rare occurrence in Minoth, so they had no need for a proper jail within the tower. Widin suggested that the best place to enter would be in the upper stories, which would be the least likely to have wandering guards, so long as they stayed out of sight of the watchtower guard.

Presently, he made a twirling motion with his fingers, and after she spun around, he placed his arms beneath her armpits and around her torso. With a vigorous sweep of his wings, they began to rise.

"Oof, didn't know your kind would be so heavy," he heaved but managed to get them aloft.

The tower walls, as straight and smooth as the labyrinth's, passed by, and Widin went directly to a window near the top as swiftly as he was able. No fire burned inside, which gave Symvalline hope the room was unoccupied. Gripping the window's right frame, she managed to crawl onto the wide sill and crouch there as she gazed through the murky glass. She could see nothing in the blackness. Carefully, she pulled on the wood frame of the left pane and felt it move slightly, but then it stopped short. Locked from the inside.

"Widin, go back down. I'm going to break the glass. It's better if you're not here if someone hears it. Find somewhere safe to stay concealed, and keep your eyes on this window. When you see my signal"—she closed her eyes and send illumination through her Mentalios for a moment—"like this, but much brighter, come back for her. Then me, if there's still time."

"I hope you find her," was all he said, then dropped back into the gloom.

Using the bludgeon, she struck the glass. It broke with a sharp crackle, but she didn't hesitate to see if it had been heard. She'd be an easy target sitting out on the ledge. Reaching in, she found the lock and undid it, then pulled the window frame out and climbed inside.

After shutting it again, she whispered the incantation to release the dimmest of lights from her Mentalios. She didn't want it to be visible from any cracks around a door. The room seemed to be storage, walls lined with crates and broken furniture. A quick glance around told her there was nothing particularly useful to her.

Once more, she carried her bag from the healers chamber, now holding only the book, the small dagger, and the sleeping potion. In her left hand, she gripped the bludgeon and crept toward the outline of the door at the far side of the room.

CHAPTER THIRTY-EIGHT

Isemay's head shot up at a noise, and she realized she'd dozed off. Shouting came from beyond her cell, guards' voices, but growing distant. She was on the second floor of the tower, at the end of the hallway near the stairway, and could hear them—some running up the stairs, some down it.

Da? she wondered. Surely it was too soon for him to reach her. *Mum?!*

She tried to jump up, found herself woozy, and rose carefully instead, using the wall to steady herself like an elderly person. A cold sweat broke out on her forehead, clammy like when she'd been feverish with the pox as a child. Using her sleeve, she wiped it away. Dirt stuck to her forehead, and she knew she must look a mess. *Won't it be a pretty reunion when Salukis gets here?* she thought.

With her ear pressed to the door, she tried to make out what could be happening. Both the voices and footsteps had receded into silence. Had they left a guard to watch for her?

The only light came from cracks beneath and above the door and through the keyhole. Crouching, she tried to see through it, and was rewarded with a tiny view of a gray stone wall across the hall. She didn't smell the smoke of torches, which made her wonder what the

Minothians used to light their interiors at night. The Zhallahs had the Churss and many permutations of glowing stones and reflective light from their daystar and three moons to provide illumination in their houses and buildings. Did Minothians have Churss stones here, too?

After several moments passed with no sound or movement visible, she risked what she'd been considering for the past couple of hours. She might be able to escape.

Using the stolen dagger, she pushed its point into the crevices of the door's lowest hinge. Wiggling it, she found the hinge apparatus was not dissimilar to some kinds in Vinnr. Shortly, she had the hinge pin removed. The top hinge was too high up to get adequate leverage, but the door was narrow enough that she could climb up, wedge her left big toe in a waist-high crack in the mortar on the wall, and hold up the bulk of her weight by her other foot resting atop the door handle. She used the free pin as a kind of grip for her left hand by shoving it into another mortar crack and pulling downward so the pressure of the angle kept it locked in place. That left her right hand free to use the dagger against the other hinge. Soon, her arms and knees began quaking, but she held on determinedly until the second came free too.

She jumped down as the door settled its weight more heavily on the lockbolt, now the only part of it attached to the wall. Whenever a guard came for her, they'd have to use force to move the door and would be caught well off guard when the whole thing came crashing in. If she was lucky, they'd by shoving hard enough that their momentum would carry them into the room and she could scurry out and find somewhere to hide before they could catch her. It seemed prudent to have a backup escape plan in case the Minothians had no intention of reuniting her with her mother—and if whatever had raised the alarm made them…angry.

Nothing happened for several minutes, and Isemay stood beside the door, still gripping the dagger in one hand and the hinge pins in another. She thought she could hear voices after a while, speaking in normal tones down on the first floor. Had whatever had caused the disturbance passed already?

She crouched once more and peaked through the keyhole. A gray eye stared back. With a gasp, she lunged away from the door in surprise.

"Isemay?" a voice whispered.

Her mum's voice.

"Mum?" she cried, her voice cracking in nearly hysterical relief.

"Isemay, shh, stay quiet. I'm going to get you out."

Scurrying back to the door, Isemay lowered herself to speak through the keyhole. "Oh Verities, Mum, I'm so…I didn't…I—"

"Shh, shh, I know, Crumb. Me too. But I'm here. I just need to get the lock open."

"I removed the pins from the hinges. Let me put them back before you open it so the door won't fall off."

"No, wait, slide them to me. I can use them."

Of course! Why hadn't she thought of using them to pick the lock? Without hesitation, she pushed them under the base of the door, and her mother's much, much more skilled hands had the lock tumblers falling in line in moments.

Her whisper came back through the keyhole. "It looks heavy. If I push it toward you, will you be able to brace it if it comes off the hinges?"

Would she? She'd have to. "Yes."

"Okay." The handle turned and the door cracked open, sliding slowly and deliberately. Isemay stepped back and got ready, but there was no need. She and her mother were narrow people, and soon the crack had grown enough that she could slide through.

"Stop," she whispered and reached outside. When her mother took her hand, Isemay could have cried with joy.

The next moment, she slipped through, and though danger was very, very close, she could not resist the impulse to throw herself into her mum's arms. "Mum, I thought I'd never…"

"Me too, darling child. I'm here now."

"Da is here, in Arc Rheunos. I spoke to him."

"I know." Gently, she pushed Isemay back. "Before you say another word, we must get back upstairs. Follow me. Stay close." Her eyes fell to the dagger in Isemay's hand. "And put that somewhere safe."

She didn't ask me to get rid of it, Isemay noted with a tremor. Nervously, she imagined what would have to happen that would make her use it, but pushed that thought away immediately. She didn't want to consider it.

Her mum paced up the tower's staircase rapidly, and Isemay lost her grip of her hand and quickly fell behind. Symvalline turned back with a question in her eyes, but immediately her expression crunched into concern. "Are you hurt?"

"No, not hurt." She panted slightly and braced an arm against the wall to catch her breath. "Just woozy, sick. It's being here that's causing it."

Symvalline scrutinized her from head to toe, then she nodded, as if she knew exactly what the trouble was. "Here," she said and put an arm around Isemay's waist. "Let me help."

Somehow, they ascended eight more stories like that, meeting no resistance. Symvalline led them into a dark storage room, shut the door, and helped Isemay sit next to the wall. She opened the nearby window and stood in the frame, holding her Mentalios lens out like a lantern. It began to glow brightly.

After a moment, she stopped but remained perched in the window, scanning the horizon.

"What are you looking for?" Isemay asked.

"A friend who's helping us."

"Where are we going to go?"

Turning halfway back, she gave Isemay a reassuring grin. "We'll hide for a short while, somewhere safe, then meet Ulfric in the labyrinth. He's coming, and he's bringing the Zhallahs. The boy we met the first night, Salukis, is with him—"

"He's with Da?" she blurted.

Her mum gave her a quick glance. "He is. And—do you know of the Equifulcrum?"

Isemay nodded. "When the three moons align."

"Right. There will be fewer Minothians guarding the labyrinth then. We'll be able to slip through as quietly as a silvflan and get you home, never to bother the Arc Rheunosians again."

Her mum said the last part under her breath, looking away from Isemay. Since childhood, when her mum had told her things she wanted to hear but weren't necessarily true, she'd done it in the exact same way. If she wasn't so tired, she'd press for the real plans for what lay ahead, but she let it go. First, they had to get away from this loathsome tower.

Isemay's eyes widened as a shadow filled the window. "Widin, thank the Verities you made it," Symvalline said, and she relaxed. "This is Isemay. Please, get her back to the stables as quick as you can."

Symvalline turned and Isemay got a better look at the man who'd joined them. He was wrinkly, with skin and eyebrows that drooped and sagged like an underwatered dalla flower. With a heavy sigh, she rose and stepped into the window.

The elderly man examined her. "You Vinnrics may not have the skin of a Rheunosian, but I can tell your color isn't so good, child. Sick, are you?"

As Isemay began to nod, Symvalline cut in. "It isn't the Waste. It's being from another realm. She can't harm you."

Widin cleared his throat. "Didn't say she would. You come here now. I'll take you down."

Isemay looked at her mum. "What about you?"

"I'll be next. You go first."

Her belly turned over again, from fear this time instead of illness. "I don't want to leave you." She sounded like a child, as if she was still four turns old and afraid of having her bedchamber door closed.

"He can't carry us both, Crumb. Hurry." She gave Isemay a small smile of encouragement and brushed her cheek with the back of her fingers. They were ever so cool, almost cold. They felt good anyway against her feverish face.

Now used to being carried by Salukis, she stood up next to Widin and readied to descend. It only took moments before she was alone, huddled against the heavy blocks of the tower's stone in the shadows, counting heartbeats until her mum was back.

Both she and the elder were quickly down again, and they began loping along the rocky field toward a structure in the distance. By now,

Isemay realized that whatever had drawn the guards' attention before must have been her mum's doing. It seemed to have worked well, as they were almost to what appeared to be a barn and nothing had gone wrong.

Yet.

CHAPTER THIRTY-NINE

The three of them waited in the dark of the stable for Agatha. Their wagon was still outside, the urzidae still harnessed to it. In the stables, close to a dozen more shaggy, enormous urzidae grunted and snuffled in their stalls. They were quiet and complacent, barely even looking toward the visitors as they had passed through seeking out a comfortable, secluded place to wait.

"I'm surprised Agatha isn't back yet," Widin mused quietly.

Symvalline wondered, as she was sure he did, whether Agatha had been apprehended. The plan was to wait here for her until just before first light. But if she didn't meet them here, she would meet them at the lower barrows, where the dead of the southern Minoth valley were put to rest.

"If she doesn't come, that doesn't mean something's happened to her. She may have felt it best to go straight to the barrow," she told Widin with a calm reassurance she scarcely felt.

Isemay leaned against her shoulder, all but empty of energy, it seemed. With effort, Symvalline put aside her concerns—as much as she could. They boiled below the surface like toxic oil, a mix of panic, anxiety, desperation, and compassion for her only child that threatened to burn her up if she didn't control it. The time-honored wisdom and strength of being a Knight could not help her now, not here in this realm, under these circumstances. She realized she'd grown complacent in the power of her position in Vinnr, being honored and even sometimes revered as a keeper of Vaka Aster's vessel. She'd forgotten what a common life was, its real threats and dangers. A simple cut that could infect the blood and kill a child. A fall that would break bones, rendering them crippled for life. An illness they could not recover from. Hundreds of turns had passed since Symvalline had experienced anything that could hinder her in these ways more than briefly.

Now, having a daughter whose makeup was still commoner, not Knight, and who could experience any of those ailments in the blink of an eye—this made Symvalline feel as fragile and inconsequential as she'd ever felt. *More*, even, than she ever had. She hadn't known to expect this fear, this feeling of impotence, when she and Ulfric had decided to have a child. Her complacence had replaced her foresight in this regard. She had felt great compassion and a desire to save the Zhallah children she'd found in the Cosmoculous Tower. But though she'd once dedicated her life to healing the sick, she would kill anyone who tried to harm her own daughter.

As the night passed, she tried to reach Ulfric through the Mentalios but heard nothing in response. The wystic link would only stretch so far, and if he was on the other side of the maze and the mountains, he wouldn't hear her. Slipping the pendant into her boot—in case she was caught and searched, perhaps it wouldn't be found there—she rested her head against the wall and closed her eyes, holding Isemay's hands in her lap and rubbing them, trying to warm away their clammy chill.

They waited an interminable time until they had to go. The urzidae were beginning to show signs of restlessness, anticipating their morning feeding, and finally Symvalline stood up.

"We can't remain here any longer. Widin, please, wait with Isemay while I look around outside."

They followed her to the barn's door and stood aside as she cracked it and looked out. She could see nothing. Even the moons had moved around to the west. Cautiously, she stepped out and searched first along the west of the building, then the east, seeing no activity from person or animal.

Returning to the door, she whispered, "It's clear. Come with me." As they emerged, Isemay shivering and pale even in the gloom, she said, "Widin, you'll have to show—"

Ice-cold hands clamped her throat closed and jerked her backward by the neck. As her feet left the ground, Symvalline's right hand went to the claw-like fingers closing off her air, but her left found the dagger in her belt and yanked it free. She brought it with all the force she could behind her, burying it to the hilt into the flank of whoever gripped her. There was a breathless hiss in her ear, and her accoster's hands loosened just enough for her to pull one free of her neck. Leaving the dagger in place, she used the other hand to try prying the second one off, too. Then she was shoved so hard from behind it felt as if an urzidae had charged her, and went sprawling a dozen feet in front of the stables, landing on her stomach and face.

She rolled over, yelled, "Stay inside!" and scrambled up.

At least a dozen Minothian guards who'd just a moment before been invisible suddenly materialized. They stood around her in a circle, none holding swords, but all carrying the bowed weapon that fired nets.

Slowly, Symvalline looked around at her enemy. Behind the guards, she saw the one she'd stabbed, a Deathless, enter the stable, heard a moment of scuffling, then he emerged, dagger still visible in his lower torso, with a hand clamped around the backs of Widin's and Isemay's necks. The Deathless pushed them outside, and Isemay went to her knees. Widin knelt beside her, reaching his hands out to her back and patting it gently.

With all the determination of a hurricane, Symvalline started to walk to Crumb, watching the faces of the guards she would have to push through. Everything she'd learned said the Minothians weren't a violent or murderous people. They had no real enemies. Even the Zhallahs left them alone, despite whatever twisted rumors Tuzhazu spread. The only people she'd encountered here who seemed inclined to use force were the Deathless and the Archon. What would these guards be capable of if she challenged them?

She didn't get far enough to find out.

"I knew you must have had some helpers, Vinnric, but even I am surprised at their...*quality*." Archon Tuzhazu sneered the word as Symvalline turned back around. He now stood revealed outside the circle of guards, who moved aside enough for him to speak to Symvalline face-to-face. Agatha cowered on her knees at his feet, bleeding heavily from a deep gash in her head. Or she had been. The blood had begun to coagulate, Symvalline noted. How long had Tuzhazu had his hands on her? What damage had he done that she couldn't see?

With deliberate, careful words, Symvalline said, "You didn't need to do that to her, Archon. Not after what you did to her child."

Tuzhazu's eyes widened. He hadn't expected such an accusation to be made aloud. Controlling the expression, he then gestured sharply with his chin to the Deathless who'd attacked her. She heard the guards shift as the Deathless jerked Isemay to her feet and pushed her and Widin to stand behind Symvalline. Symvalline reached back and gripped her daughter under one arm, holding her up.

Isemay whispered in her ear, "Your klinkí stones, mum. You can—"

"I can't. He's taken them."

Isemay glanced up at her, confused, then began to cough.

"Search them," Tuzhazu ordered.

After stripping her of her haversack, the Deathless began to pat her and pull at her clothing. Repelled by the inhuman creature, she was tempted to reach for the dagger still in his side, but something held her back. He was still a person, just cursed. She didn't want to harm someone who wasn't responsible for his actions. It wouldn't be just.

As she'd hoped, her Mentalios remained unfound, though Isemay wasn't so lucky with her own stolen dagger. The Deathless took their equipment and stepped back.

"Let them go, Tuzhazu, and just take me," Symvalline tried to reason. "She's only a child and sick, and he's an old man. Agatha has done nothing but seek to aid someone you've imprisoned for no reason. They are not a threat to the next vessel of Mithlí. Or to any Minothian."

"Are you admitting that you are?" He stepped inside the circle, pulling Agatha along with him. "What are you hiding, Vinnric?" He leaned closer to Symvalline, his tarnished-silver eyes boring into hers. "Your coming here is no accident. Where is my army? More to the point, do you have one of your own on the way?"

For a moment, Symvalline feared he knew something of her talk with Ulfric. But that was impossible. "You mean Balavad's army?" she challenged. "That force is gone, you fool. Destroyed absolutely by those of my realm who stand on the side of righteousness and faith in the gifts of our maker, who would not become pawns to the wickedness of Balavad. Battgjald has been blotted from existence. That is what happens to evil and those who bow to it."

He blinked. It was the only weakness she'd seen in him. Then he resorted to his true nature.

Reaching down, he enclosed the kneeling Agatha's head in his wide palm. Clutching the Fenestros in his other hand, he held Symvalline's eyes with his own and began speaking in the language of Battgjald again, the words low and unintelligible, foreign and breathy. Symvalline's eyes dropped to Agatha.

The woman had turned whiter than a cloud, and the veins beneath her skin, so dark blue in the dawn's light that they were almost black, nearly glowed through the translucence. Her eyes rolled back and she would have collapsed, but Tuzhazu held her up with the unnatural strength of his grip.

"Tell me the truth, Vinnric. Why did you come here? I'm not a fool enough to believe your realm or any cretinous *Knight* in it could outwit a Verity. Were you exiled? Does Balavad have grander plans I should know of? Or are you scouting Arc Rheunos for a takeover by your own kind?" His voice lowered until only she, Isemay, and Widin could hear him. Agatha looked beyond hearing by then. "Tell me now, and tell me the truth, or her death will be on your hands."

Symvalline had to do something. He was stealing Agatha's life the same way he'd once started to steal hers, using the Fenestros as some kind of life-force vacuum.

She looked around the circle of guards frantically, noting the discomfort and fear many of them didn't realize showed in their faces. "Do you see what he is?" she cried. "Don't your people regard the taking of a life as the most heinous of crimes? Is this the kind of beast you want as the Everlight's vessel? What will become of you then?"

Several looked away from her, exchanging uncertain glances with their cohorts, all avoiding the Archon's eyes completely. She was getting to them. But her flash of triumph was short-lived.

Isemay's knees buckled, and she spilled to the ground with a wounded gasp, like a bird taking its last breath. Symvalline fell to her knees beside her.

"Isemay? Crumb?" She clenched her daughter's shoulders, rigid and wracked with shudders. "Verities eyes, no," she breathed, more helpless at that moment than she'd ever been.

"Archon, a messenger," one of the guards in the circle said. Symvalline's eyes shot to her, then to where she was pointing. A winged Minothian guard was just touching down nearby.

"Archon Tuzhazu, I bring word from the Everlight," he said, bowing.

The Archon released Agatha and faced him. The Minothian woman fell face forward, outstretched and unmoving. "What does she say?"

"My liege, the Zhallah prisoners have escaped and have not been found. They could be…anywhere."

The sound of many guards drawing shocked breaths was unmissable. Children, they feared children.

The messenger continued, "The Everlight commands your presence at the hall immediately. The people of Minoth are in danger. If the prisoners spread their pestilence—"

Symvalline couldn't stand it a moment longer. "You really believe that children carry this disease? Or that the Zhallahs mean you harm? You have only to look to your Archon to see where this plague comes from. And where did you get it, Tuzhazu?"

"Be silent!" He closed the distance to her before she could blink and slapped her open-handed across the cheek. He was a large man, and the strike sent her backward several steps.

"Please, please don't hurt my mum." Isemay clung to the Archon, pulling herself halfway up his body using the satchel he carried. "Please..."

He looked at her with disgust and shoved her down with a hand to her face. Symvalline, her cheek a burning welt and her eye beginning to swell shut, ran back to her side.

"Close the valley gates, and send a runner to Aktoktos. None is to leave or enter. Under no circumstances will any gate be opened between now and the Equifulcrum."

"Yes, my liege," the guards echoed each other.

"Bind the prisoners," Tuzhazu commanded. "Bring them to Everlight Hall."

Symvalline stared up at him, and with venom that came from deep in her spirit, she promised, "You'll pay for what you've done. If I have to kill you myself, I will."

He gave her a look of contempt that matched her own, then ordered: "And gag them, too."

CHAPTER FORTY

Ulfric and Urgo stood at the edge of the Churss in the same spot Salukis and Isemay had stood four days earlier, though he didn't know it, before they'd launched their nearly successful endeavor into mapping the labyrinth. He was thinking that he should be feeling the way he'd felt before battles he'd fought in the past: resolved, ready, and filled with belief in their imminent victory.

He felt none of these things.

Perhaps four or five hundred Zhallah people stood behind him, an unprepared and untrained crew of what he'd call commoners in Vinnr who had no idea what a real militant force looked or acted like—or a real fight. They carried no battle-ready weapons, just clubs altered from farming or building tools, some nets, and heavy bags of stones tied to their waists. These, he noted ruefully, would make those who could fly heavier, less maneuverable, and therefore more vulnerable. Ulfric had seen only a few of the uniformed and, by comparison, disciplined soldiers Minoth had. And even if they didn't live up to his standards of a military force, they would easily outstrip these Zhallahs, whose lives were built on avoiding battle, not inducing it.

And then there was the Deathless Guard. He'd already seen the weapons they carried, and he'd also seen the emptiness in their eyes

279

that showed they had no conscience to prevent them from using their hooked swords, so similar to those carried by the Battgjaldic Raveners.

He feared that if the Zhallahs actually clashed in hand-to-hand combat with the Minothians, they would have no chance at anything resembling success. They would be captured and imprisoned at best, slaughtered by the Deathless at worst.

He had Urgo turn to Deespora beside him. The night before, Deespora had escorted him and the bruhawks to the Churss Circle in Maerria. There, he'd informed the Archon and the other Zhallah council members she'd summoned of everything he knew of Balavad's ultimate plans of ensuring the Syzyckí Elementum didn't come to pass, at any cost, and the susceptibility of the Dyrrakium people to the malicious Verity's persuasion. Ulfric shared with them his belief, fear really, that now that Balavad's own people were gone, he would use the Vinnric Dyrraks to subjugate Arc Rheunos, the same as he'd intended with his Raveners in Vinnr—after the Dyrraks finished taking it over first.

The Dyrraks would be used as cannon fodder in Balavad's crusade, Ulfric was certain. Not all of them would be as corruptible as the Domine Ecclesium, but most of them would be manipulable, thanks to their blind faith. The Dyrrak people were not truly enemies of Ivoryss or Yor. They were simply different, their beliefs more rigorous (to the point of foolishness, he'd thought more than once in his long life). And it was the rigor of those beliefs that had made it so easy for them, through Balavad's manipulation of the Domine Ecclesium, to fall into Balavad's trap.

Shamelessly showing Deespora the most gruesome sights he could recall of Balavad's doings, Ulfric finally persuaded her that the Churss was no longer a reliable refuge sometime near what was called Hallumbrum in Vinnr. She agreed, at last, that their realm would be defenseless against the whims of a conquering Verity and his minions from Vinnr while their own was caged, just as Vinnr had been. Ulfric suspected her coming around to the idea had more to do with the pressure from among her own people, who'd made it clear they would go to Minoth to retrieve their kidnapped kin with our without Deespora to lead them, than his tales and suspicions. The woman named Kalisk had been right: Deespora might be considered the wisest among them because she was the oldest and had been closest to the Everlight. But if Balavad was free to wreak whatever ruin and subjugation on the Zhallah and Minothian peoples he or Tuzhazu wanted, all her wisdom would not spare them one ounce of suffering.

In the end, it didn't matter why she agreed to go with him to Minoth. They now had to focus on the mission: take Tuzhazu captive, force him to unmake the cage holding Mithlí. Which, aside from rescuing Symvalline and Isemay, was what Ulfric most desired. If the fallen Archon knew how to unmake Mithlí's cage, he could be forced to show Ulfric how to do it. Therefore, of utmost importance, was that Tuzhazu be captured alive. And when that was done, they could begin to contemplate the wisdom and simple practicality of ensnaring Balavad in his own cage.

Ulfric refused to ask himself how many of the Zhallahs' lives he thought this knowledge was worth. Deespora, likewise, did not bring this question up. He sensed she held on to the notion that none would truly be harmed, that the Minothians' adherence to the belief that taking a life was the worst of evils would still be true. But Ulfric had lived through the War of Rivening and an untold number of skirmishes in service of protecting Vaka Aster's vessel. He knew that a group's values, no matter how strongly held, were always malleable under the right circumstances. Look at what had happened to the values of the Domine Ecclesium in Dyrrakium.

Their strategy was simple. With the aid of Isemay's memory keeper map, those who could not fly would traverse through the maze at top speed, and those who could fly would assist in shielding them. It would truly be a test of how closely the Minothians still held to the code of honoring life. Ulfric was betting on them reaching the end of the labyrinth with minor casualties, if any. By then, they would know whether the Minothians would stand against the might of an armed troop of Zhallahs or if they would yield. And if they didn't yield, what then? They would consider that if it came.

In the meantime, Ulfric focused exclusively on the object of the plan: if just the bruhawks and Deespora, with the strength of her Scrylle and Fenestros to aid her, made it to the Minothian stronghold of Everlight Hall, then the plan would be considered a success. Toppling her sister the false Verity and Tuzhazu, and then freeing Mithlí were the only things that could change the course of Arc Rheunos's current destiny. If Mithlí chose to punish the Archons for what they did, so be it. None could say how a Verity would react to a situation like this, which had never before happened in all the Cosmos's history—as far as any who lived knew. If Mithlí took no action against them, then their two peoples would face a period of struggle as they learned once more to live together and trust one another. Then they could begin to rebuild.

As the last wisps of night fled the horizon, he said to Deespora through the memory keeper, "Remember, we must move swiftly. We can't allow skirmishes with the Minothians to stop us. We keep going, even if we have to leave a few fighters behind to engage them and keep them away from the main body. We'll be easily targeted inside the labyrinth walls, so the Wings"—he'd taken naturally to calling the men, who would provide their air support, by the same name as the Dragør Wing Marines of Ivoryss—"will be the most burdened. They *must* not give way or be tempted to flee. They must keep their faith in the fight."

They'd gone over this a few times already during the previous night, and each time Deespora had seemed less and less attentive to his continued instructions on how they would achieve their objective. In truth, it had begun to frustrate him, but he held his tongue from delivering the admonishment he might have heaped on one of his own Knights. *Not my world, not my people. And from the Archon's perspective, the stakes for me are the least important.*

This time, Deespora turned to him and regarded him as one might watch a featherless bird try to take flight. She then said to the young woman standing next to her, "Mura, it's time."

The woman withdrew a reeded instrument with twin pipes from inside her cloak, then turned to the group immediately behind her and gave them a signal. Each carried a pipe of their own.

Salukis, too, was among the group, surprising Ulfric. He'd have expected the young man to stay among the frail and young in Maerria, due to his injured wing. He looked closer. No, that wasn't possible. The young man's wing bore no injury anymore. He looked at the other wing, sure he'd mistaken which had been cut, but it was as whole as the first.

As he was pondering this miraculous fact, as one, the troupe of musicians put their instruments to their lips. Mura signaled again, and they all began to play.

The tune was not like any music Ulfric had ever heard. It seemed to him more a collection of strange tones played out of sync and with no harmony. *Some kind of call to arms or action?* he wondered.

Then, all around them the forest of stone began to stir, the massive bases of the towers rolling freely from their entrenchments in the ground, the smaller stones climbing to the sky atop them rolling in unison to stay aloft.

As Ulfric watched, like an arcane army from some mythic tale, the entire Churss forest began to march.

<h1 style="text-align:center">CHAPTER FORTY-ONE</h1>

As Isemay leaned against her mum, horrified by the sight of the Minothian Archon and his ghastly, rotting, metal-tipped wings, the world began to swim away, leaving a black cloud in its wake.

She lost feeling in her legs and thought for a moment she was simply floating, then the hard earth smacked into her and knocked her breath away. Vaguely, she knew Symvalline was beside her, gripping her shoulders and saying something, but it was all distant. Her eyes caught on the hem of the black cloak spread out around the woman the horrific Archon was hurting, and all she wished was to have that cloak spread over her. She was so, so cold.

Someone spoke to the Archon and he released the woman, who fell next to Isemay.

"My liege, the Zhallah prisoners have escaped and have not been found. They could be…anywhere."

The man who was speaking sounded far away, and Isemay wondered if she was dying. It was fascinating, in a way, that death would feel so much like traveling through a dark tunnel, not a quick winking out of existence, but a journey to a place she couldn't quite see.

She began to grow warmer, first her hand, then up through her arm and into her shoulder. *It's odd that dying would start at my fingertips,* she thought. *It feels like when Mura had...what had she called it? Yielding. No, that's different, when they—*

Wait... Her thoughts cut off abruptly. Was someone healing her?

She shifted her head to see her hand better. It lay in the grasp of the woman in black, the one named Agatha. The woman's skin was even whiter than when Tuzhazu was harming her, as translucent as glass. Her eyes were staring into Isemay's, growing visibly cloudy as she watched.

"Stop him," the woman whispered. "Don't let him hurt any more... children." Her eyes lost focus, now completely covered by a milky cataract, and she stopped breathing.

Isemay had never seen someone die until this moment. Yet, at the same time, she felt more alive. *Did she...did she just give me the last of her...?* She couldn't finish the thought, terrified at what it might mean that another person, a complete stranger, would die so she could live.

"Be silent!"

The wicked Archon's voice rang through her bones, so filled with rage and violence it shook her. Her mother reeled backward from a blow. Isemay, acting on impulse, grabbed him. "Please, please don't hurt my mum," she begged.

The Archon pushed her down and she yielded easily, curling into a ball with her hands clutched at her belly, continuing to feign sickness. Something inside her didn't want him to know she'd been healed—or to see what she now held.

She heard Symvalline curse the cruel man in a tone of voice that would have turned Isemay to ice if it had been directed at her. She knew her mum as a firm but fair and loving parent, a calculating and thoughtful diplomat when it came to the people of Ivoryss, and a stalwart and dedicated Knight. She did not know this mien of steady, steely wrath she now heard. Her mum was promising to kill the brutal man, and Isemay believed her completely.

As the Archon mounted an urzidae and rode off at top speed, she watched the guards who remained through half-slitted eyes. They visibly relaxed at Tuzhazu's absence and began carrying out his orders.

She, the old man named Widin, and her mum were tied hand and foot and fitted with musty rags in their mouths.

"The barrow tender is…is dead," one of the guards called when her attempt to rouse Agatha failed. The guard straightened and backed away, as if the body would bite her.

"Unbind the other barrow ghoul," the lead guard said. "Old man, she is yours to deal with now. Get her covered up quickly."

Shortly, the three of them, along with the woman's body, were placed in a wagon and began their trek toward Everlight Hall. Isemay desperately wanted to speak to her mum but had to settle for nudging her with her knee. When Symvalline looked into her face, her eyebrows immediately quirked in confusion and surprise. Isemay gave her a little nod as if to say *I'm okay now.* Her mum stared at her a moment longer, then seemed to grasp if not what may have happened, then at least that Isemay was not as ill as she'd been, and her brows smoothed. But a deep sadness crinkled the edges of her eyes as she looked toward Agatha's body.

It was sometime after midday, nearing dinnertime if Isemay's growling stomach was an accurate timepiece, when they arrived at their destination. Unlike the last wagon she'd ridden in, this one had short walls that allowed her to see all around when she sat up. They went through heavy iron-barred gates in a curtain wall that flowed from one side of the valley to the other, intersecting at each end with the mountains that rose steeply to the east and west. Between the labyrinth and this northern part of the valley, all of Minoth spread throughout the vast, naturally occurring mountainous basin. It was no wonder the Zhallahs had never tried to reach their stolen kin. The natural defenses here seemed impassable.

Soon, they pulled up in a courtyard before a fortress she assumed was Everlight Hall. Two towers rose from the otherwise squat but wide series of structures. One tower stood about ten stories tall. The other, well behind the main structure, soared at least twenty stories high. If not for the mountains that provided its backdrop, it would have seemed immense, even more than Vigil Tower back home. *That must be what they call the Cosmoculous Tower. Where they keep the caged Everlight.*

Her mum's presence had been reassuring from the moment she'd laid her eyes on her in the valley gatehouse, but the sight of the looming tower brought her apprehensions raging back. Vinnr's own future was threatened with this same act that had divided Arc Rheunos, according to what Mylla had said weeks ago back when her da had gone up against Balavad. If Vaka Aster were somehow bent into submission, would Vinnr's people turn against each other, too? Living in fear, hiding in forests, kidnapping each other and subjecting them to who knew what? The idea of seeing her world, which in her lifetime had been one of harmony, at least between Ivoryss and Yor, was bleak indeed.

A guard from inside the fortress spoke to the ones watching over the wagon. "The foreigners are expected immediately in the Everlight's chambers. I'll take them."

"And what about them?" The wagon guard waved a hand toward Widin and Agatha's body.

"Has the barrow tender moved into the shadows?" the fortress guard asked, a waver in his voice. At the wagon guard's acknowledgment, he continued. "To the barrows. You watch the old man. After the body has been prepared, Tuzhazu wants him locked in the criminal stores to await his judgment."

The wagon guard nodded, her mouth downturned, and the next moment two Minothians took hold of Symvalline and Isemay and carried them aloft. They were deposited on a balcony, then ushered into an ornately decorated chamber and seated on two chairs around a central table, still bound, and made to wait.

As soon as the remaining guard turned his back for a moment, Symvalline pulled the gag down with her bound hands and leaned close to Isemay. "Are you okay, Crumb? You look so much improved," she whispered.

Emboldened by her mum, she did the same with her own gag. "I am. The woman, Agatha, grabbed my hand after I fell. She…gave me…" Her throat tightened, and she felt as if she might suddenly burst into tears.

Her mum's stare softened and she took Isemay's hands. "It's okay.

It's okay. I think I understand what she did. I have studied these people a bit. The women in this realm have a powerful gift."

Blinking against the water filling her eyes, Isemay could only nod miserably. When she felt like she could speak again, she said, "Is this what it's like to be a Knight? To see others be harmed while you are not, and for them to sacrifice themselves...for you?"

Symvalline gave her a sorrowful smile and thought for a moment before she answered. "You've grown up in a relatively peaceful time. There have been no wars between the kingdoms in your lifetime, and no vying between them for the favor of Vaka Aster. Now that I look back, I can see how comfortable life for the Knights of Vinnr has been in these last turns, and I forgot how temporary that kind of thing is."

She looked directly into Isemay's eyes to emphasize her next point. "Yes, Isemay, that kind of suffering and sacrifice *define* what life is for a Knight—whether we serve for one lifetime or many. And though I hate that you've had to endure this, I'm also glad you now know what it means to be ordained by Vaka Aster. And you will know better what you are swearing to when it comes time for you to decide if you wish to give your oath to serve her."

Isemay sniffed, thinking over what her mum said. "Is this why you and da want Vaka Aster to release you from your oaths?" At Symvalline's surprised reaction, she added, "I-I overheard you talking about it." *She'll know that means I was spying on them. But maybe she won't be mad.*

Her mum sighed. "Yes, that's part of it." She said nothing else.

Some minutes passed as Isemay considered what had been said, and not said. Finally, the chamber's doors opened, and a tall robed woman whose skin tone shifted hues ceaselessly entered. She carried a book, and Isemay saw how her mum's eyes tracked it.

"Unbind them, then leave us," the woman directed the two guards watching her and Symvalline.

When they were gone, the woman observed them wordlessly from the other side of the chamber. Isemay understood this was Akeeva, Deespora's sister who claimed to be the vessel of the Verity Mithlí.

It was Symvalline who spoke first, her tone urgent and demanding.

"Tuzhazu can't be trusted, Akeeva. You're putting the entire realm in danger if you allow him to take over."

Akeeva approached the table but didn't sit. "He will never rule," she stated simply.

Her mum cocked her head, surprised, but recovered quickly. "You're going to release your Verity from the bonds your Order created, then? You can't think to rule as a false Verity forever."

Thoughtfully, the woman raised the book and opened it, as if she hadn't heard Symvalline. She paged through a few leaves, then said, "I see you found my book. You've read it?"

Her mum's lips drew tight before she responded with her own question. "It's yours?"

"Vinnric, for some reason, you have the impression I'm less clever than you think you are." Akeeva's tone was tinged with impatience. "Do you believe I would allow something like imprisoning my own maker to occur without first completely understanding what might happen, and how to undo such a thing? I've studied the Verities for hundreds of years. And"—she glanced toward the door that the servants had closed—"I know full well that Archon Tuzhazu is not fit to rule. Measures will be taken. *Drastic* measures, if needs be. Hence, my research, which you've read, into how to free Mithlí."

"Then you are the maker of this cage?"

"No."

"But..." Symvalline glanced at the book. "It says 'only the maker can unmake the cage.'"

"Tuzhazu spoke the words to bind Mithlí inside the Fenestros prison at the last Equifulcrum, and it nearly killed him. He burned..." She trailed off, looking without focus into the distance, and Isemay thought of the ruined wings on Tuzhazu's back. That's what had happened to him?

"But he prevailed," she continued. "He was too misshapen after that to be seen by the people of Minoth for some time, while I took up the role of the vessel, and rule of Arc Rheunos. For three hundred years my people have feared only a memory of the Great Waste. I have made them feel protected, and I will continue to serve them as the mother to all if I must. As Mithlí failed to."

Isemay wasn't sure what they were talking about exactly, but she didn't miss the look that crossed Symvalline's features, that one she gave Isemay when she could barely believe how foolish something Isemay had said or done was.

Her mum said accusingly, "Tuzhazu made this cage…and he will never retract it. You must see that. You know it's he who spreads the Waste, don't you? Whatever deal you think you all struck with Balavad is only half the story. I've come to see that Tuzhazu is Balavad's puppet, and for whatever reason, he is plotting against the people of this realm. Balavad wants one thing: dominion. And he'll do whatever it takes, lie to whoever is most vulnerable or most corruptible, to have it. Balavad is probably where the plague came from in the first place, to frighten the Archons into listening to his poisonous promises and cage Mithlí to give him freedom to reign."

Akeeva looked startled, and Isemay worried Symvalline had said too much.

The Minothian's colorful eyes found her then, and she shrank a little to Symvalline's side. "I was told you were near death, little one. But you look well to me."

Isemay glanced at the mum, who looked back at her with concern. "I was healed by the barrow tender, Agatha."

"And she is now dead."

"But she wouldn't be if Tuzhazu hadn't—" She broke off, uncertain she should give voice to the accusation, and uncertain if it was even true. The Minothians valued life above all else. Even though her mum had come right out with her belief that Tuzhazu was spreading plague and killing his own people, Isemay wasn't quite as brave. To say one of their most esteemed was a murderer might be taking it too far and fray the woman's patience—even if it was true. It could equally be true that Isemay herself was to blame for Agatha's death. If she hadn't been so sick, if she hadn't let the woman heal her…

Akeeva looked back to Symvalline. "He is too powerful while he holds the Battgjaldic Verity's Fenestros. If we cannot catch him unaware"—Isemay didn't miss the word "we"—"only the Cosmoculous can strip him of it. I believe you were sent here to help me, whether you know it or not. Between us, we can change the future Tuzhazu might otherwise bring about and keep the peace in Arc Rheunos."

"Why would I help you?"

"You serve the Verities. And I can tell by the fact that you freed the Zhallah prisoners that you are compassionate. Despite the oath we all take to serve our makers, you and I have this in common—we will do what we must to aid our people. *Despite our oath.* I think you'll help me, for the sake of the Zhallahs, or Tuzhazu may—"

"What about me?"

All heads turned to the edge of the balcony, where Tuzhazu now stood, aided by two stout Deathless Guards. Symvalline rose in alarm, and Isemay followed, taking an involuntary step behind her mum.

"Archon," Akeeva said, facing him, unflustered. "I gave you your orders already. Find the Zhallah prisoners. You haven't been recalled."

The brutish Archon ignored her clear command to leave and paced to one side, then back, keeping his eyes fixed on them. His silvery gaze rooted to Isemay's face for a moment. Though his expression didn't change, she had a strong impression he was assessing her, suspicious of her improved condition, concluding that she would be dealt with when he was ready.

He spoke again to Akeeva. "What were you saying about the Zhallah pests?"

Akeeva turned away from him impatiently and paced slowly past Isemay and Symvalline. As she passed them, she raised the book she still carried and held it out in front of her with the spine against her stomach, out of Tuzhazu's sight. Just as she went past Isemay, she bent the pages slightly, catching Isemay's eye. As the leaves pulled away from each other, Isemay clearly saw an image take shape along the pages' edges, one that would only be visible completely if the pages were riffled in an exact way. *A fore-edge painting,* she realized.

Akeeva reached the end of the table, which was set out with bowls of fruits and nuts and a pitcher. She laid the book aside and began to pour herself something, speaking with her back to Tuzhazu. "Our Vinnric guest was telling me the most surprising, even unbelievable thing, Tek Det. You'll want to laugh when you hear it." She turned back and took a slow, deliberate drink from her cup. Her skin's colors swirled madly, as if tossed by a tempest. "She thinks the Waste is not being spread by those beyond our borders. But rather, by you. That is, indeed, came from Balavad to begin with and you wield it to his—and your own—advantage. Just like you do the elixir that creates our Deathless Guards."

What Tuzhazu said next shocked Isemay.

"So what if that were true? What if Balavad brought the Waste to Arc Rheunos? Tell me this, Akeeva, does it matter? The fact remains, Mithlí did nothing to stop it. Half our world died. Half!" He slammed his fist on the table. "Balavad gave us the means to save those who were left. At least *he* chose to grant our wish, instead of leaving us to wither into dust. And why? To show us what mercy looks like. Isn't a Verity who can be reasoned with, who asks for so little in return, better than one who doesn't even care?"

"You're deranged," Symvalline breathed. Her hands were clutched into tight fists, her body trembling with anger.

Isemay held her breath, fearing what was coming.

"And you, Vinnric," he spat, "are quick to find fault in something you should understand better. When you live as long as we have, and have seen as many fall into the shadow, you come to realize an important truth. That death *is* the natural order of things. You think me mad, but am I not just a tool of our creator herself, and all the other creators? Are you not, and her?" His arm rose and he jabbed a finger at Akeeva, who stood silent and horror-stricken.

"The Verities 'gave' us death. It is one of their 'gifts' to us, as a means to ensure we *earn* our lives and the choice in how we live them. And I shall ensure the Minothian way of life continues." He began to walk toward Akeeva. She took a step backward, caught short when she struck the food-laden table. "No matter whom I have to stop to do it," he finished, his voice black with menace.

Akeeva's arm rose, a dagger she'd withdrawn from somewhere in the folds of her robe clutched in her hand. Symvalline began to lunge toward them, but Isemay grabbed her.

"No, mum! Wait," she cried, pointing to the two Deathless Guards who stalked toward them, weapons drawn and held out. "Take these." She reached into her pocket and withdrew what she'd taken from Tuzhazu.

Three of her mum's klinkí stones.

Symvalline's eyes widened at the sight of them, and she swiftly grabbed them and put them in her own pocket before the Deathless could see them. "Shh," she whispered and shoved Isemay behind her, forcing them backward away from the soldiers. "Stay behind me."

"But the stones, mum. You can hel—"

Her mum shook her head emphatically, then turned and faced the two misshapen Minothians. "We are not going to resist," she promised them, as she extended her arms out submissively. "We surrender to Tuzhazu's will."

Isemay heard a groan and looked to Tuzhazu and Akeeva. Akeeva had had no chance. Tuzhazu grasped the wrist of her dagger hand, and even from where Isemay stood, she could see the veins popping out on the back of his hand at the force of his grip. Akeeva dropped the knife and clawed at Tuzhazu's eyes with her free hand, but weakly. The Fenestros, a ball of black and gray amorphous swirls whose pattern was strikingly similar to Akeeva's skin, was at work in the Archon's other hand. As Isemay watched the woman's life draining from her like water down a gutter spout, she wanted to run over and stop him, to scream that he was killing her, but most of all, to ask her mum why she wasn't helping the woman.

She did none of those things. Symvalline's cool hand closed on her forearm, and she slowly backed the two of them toward the wall, away from the Deathless and Tuzhazu, who dropped Akeeva and turned toward them. His face was a mask of malice—and promise.

"What will I do with you, now?" he wondered aloud.

"If you've killed her, Tuzhazu, how will you be able to make the people of Minoth believe you're the next vessel?" Symvalline asked. "They'll see through your ruse. They're not fools."

He smirked. "You speak as if you know us. Are you Minothian?" The question was delivered sarcastically. "Or is that you've been here for some time, spying for someone else?"

Symvalline didn't answer for a moment, but Isemay felt her arm slide down until her hand hung close to her pocket, to the klinkí stones. Isemay watched the dangerous man the way one watched a snake about to strike.

Her mum spoke, her voice calm, reasonable, the voice of a lecturer in the Conservatum sharing centuries of wisdom. "Why not stop this now, Tuzhazu? Can't you see Balavad is using you? You can reunite with the Zhallahs. Revive the Archon Order and end this pointless and harmful charade by freeing Mithlí. Return your world to balance, and to your maker. Arc Rheunos doesn't have to remain fractured like it is now. You have the power to heal everything. You simply have to choose your world over Balavad's lies."

"Did you hear nothing I just said, Vinnric? Balavad gave us a choice. Mithlí gave us nothing at all."

Symvalline's tone lowered. "There is always a reckoning. You've lived a long time, you must know that. Even if you do kill Akeeva, the other Raamuzi Archon has a Fenestros and the Scrylle. With those, she *will* put an end to your corruption."

The permanent sneer on Tuzhazu's face deepened as he approached them. "I may yet have use for Akeeva, but I believe I am done with you, and your daughter, Vinnric."

Isemay's eyes shot to his hand that held the Fenestros. It was alight with its gray and black center already whirling. Her mum's arm tensed and her hand slid into her pocket. For some reason, she'd hesitated to use the stones before, but now they were the only thing standing between them and Tuzhazu. As Symvalline's closed fist emerged, a new Minothian landed on the balcony.

"Archon! The labyrinth has been breached! The Zhallahs approach!"

Isemay could have fainted with relief when Tuzhazu whirled around to address the messenger, taking his baleful silver-green stare off her and her mum. "What do you mean they breached it? The Aktoktos Gate is unbreachable."

"The Churss, Archon, it's…on the move. It broke through the gates and is coming through the labyrinth almost as fast an urzidae runs. The stones shield the Zhallahs, and none of our troops can get through or stop them. They'll be through by nightfall or morning at the latest."

Isemay looked up into Symvalline's face, seeing her disbelief—and relief—reflected there. The Churss forest was coming. There was nothing that could stand up to something so mighty. And that meant her da and the Zhallahs would be there by the Equifulcrum.

CHAPTER FORTY-TWO

The book. Symvalline knew she had to get her hands on it. There was something important in it that Akeeva hadn't been able to say before Tuzhazu's attack.

Judging by the way Tuzhazu had ignored it, he didn't realize that it contained anything important. It shouldn't be hard to slip it past his notice when he wasn't looking—provided, of course, he didn't kill her and Isemay before she could get to it.

Symvalline had seen the way Akeeva had riffled the pages before setting the book down. A fore-edge painting. How could she have missed it before? What it might say was another mystery, but it seemed that it was relevant.

And Ulfric was close, and getting closer. She could barely conceive of what the guard had described—what was a Churss?—but had no intention of puzzling it out now. Now, she needed to hold Tuzhazu here, distract and stall him from taking any action that could prepare him for Ulfric and the Zhallahs, even if it meant he would make her suffer some new agony. The longer she held his attention, the better chance they had of carrying out whatever plan they'd devised. She trusted Ulfric to have come up with something.

"In the name of…" the guard who'd brought the news of the coming Zhallahs breathed. "Is that the…the Everlight?"

Everyone's eyes followed his, and Symvalline realized at the same moment Tuzhazu did that the guard should not have seen his false Verity in such a state. She opened her mouth to warn him to run, to *fly*, away, but Tuzhazu crossed the floor and grabbed the guard by the throat. With unnatural strength, he pushed the man to his knees. The guard struggled, but the flailing of his hands didn't last long. With his breath cut off, he weakened quickly.

"Mum, can you…" Isemay whispered, but Symvalline shushed her with a brief shake of her head. She might be able to slow Tuzhazu, but she could not stop him, not while he held the Fenestros. And then Isemay would be alone.

"Take this, Kaneas, and join the ranks of the ever-living Deathless Guard." Tuzhazu had pulled his cobalt-blue glass vial of elixir from his bag and yanked the cork free with his teeth. He spilled a single drop past the limp guard's lips. He then closed his hand over the man's mouth and nose, forcing him to swallow or choke. The man began the same gruesome transformation Symvalline had witnessed happen to the two in the healers chamber.

She dropped her glance to Isemay's face and saw horror there. "Turn away, Crumb. Don't look," she urged. But Isemay didn't look away.

As the guard's transformation took place, Tuzhazu turned back to them. When he spoke, it was to no one in particular. "Why would they come here now? What does Deespora think she's up to? She can't mean to interfere in the Equifulcrum…"

He contemplated the turn of events coldly, staring at Akeeva's body, speaking to her limp form. "Your sister has always been a troublemaker, Akeeva. And now she's back, almost as if she wants to make this easy for me. I'll relish putting an end to her for good. But I may need you"—his cold stare rose to Symvalline and Isemay—"all of you, before this is over. Guards." He gestured to the three Deathless, the newly transformed guard already emulating the empty, slavish behavior of the other two perfectly. "Re-bind the Vinnrics and watch the three of them. Don't let anyone in or out of this chamber before I return."

Symvalline stated calmly, "You can't possibly hope to stop Deespora while she holds a Fenestros and the Scrylle. She'll defeat you."

He scoffed. "Deespora is a coward, she ran away before. She will again."

Symvalline was surprised when Isemay blurted, "She's stronger than you are and cares more about life. She won't let you do...whatever you're trying to do."

Tuzhazu didn't say anything, didn't even look at Isemay, which Symvalline was grateful for. "Arc Rheunos has not seen a battle in an age. I wonder what Deespora will do when faced with a force that doesn't cower behind sentiment and cringe at the sight of a little blood. She's as limp and weak-willed as a burial shroud. I may kill her first, actually." He smiled at Symvalline then, the smile of a cunning but deranged wolf. "I am going to relish this. It's too bad, isn't it, Vinnric, that you didn't simply make the sleeping agent I requested of you. Instead of bringing the exiles gradually into submission, it will be by force. The Zhallahs' blood will now be just as much on your hands."

With that, he turned and paced to the chamber's doorway, waving the newly created Deathless Guard to follow. When the doors were shut, Symvalline heard the sounds of something heavy being dragged and then shoved into the doors from the other side.

But the book remained where it was.

The remaining two guards approached, gathering the bindings that had been discarded earlier.

"Remain compliant, Isemay," Symvalline whispered. "Just let them tie us."

"But—"

"Trust me. It will be okay."

They were bound painfully tight, and Symvalline nearly fought back when she heard Isemay's gasp of pain. But they just had to wait, just a bit longer.

They were left to lie on the floor next to the unconscious— Symvalline presumed—Akeeva.

"What are you going to do?" Isemay asked, wriggling to her side to better see Symvalline.

Instead of answering, she focused on her Mentalios lens, which, though tucked into the top of her boot, still channeled her thoughts and allowed her to direct the klinkí stones in her pocket. In her mental eye, she saw the stones' cerulean hearts come alive as they eased from her garment. Rising to a seated position, she sent them speedily toward the two guards. They were both struck in the head, too fast to react, and the blows quickly had them staggering like drunken half-agers.

Directing the stones to the bindings on her wrists, she thought of fire, of cauldrons of boiling lava, of an inferno. The stones burned easily through the fiber bindings, and they fell away.

The two guards began staggering toward her and Isemay. Concentrating on guiding the stones to wound rather than kill them, she quickly unknotted her legs, rose, and with the bindings in hand, lunged toward the nearest guard. He was dazed and slow in reacting, and she quickly had his arms and legs trussed together. The other had recovered more and lurched at her with his weapon drawn. Much to her distress, she had to use the stones to hold him back. If he ever managed to transform back into his true self, he would be scarred, but she reasoned it was better than being dead.

Using hand cloths from the table and cords she ripped from the tapestries, she bound and gagged both guards firmly, immobilizing them. Thick blood oozed from their many abrasions, and they tried to shriek through the cloths, but they would not get free without help.

Quickly unbinding her daughter, she said, "Isemay, take this sword," and held one of the guards' weapons out to her. A sickening mix of pride at knowing Crumb had the skill to use it and dread at the fact that she might have to swarmed through her. "You remember your training?"

Without answering, Isemay stepped up to her, looking as if she had to force her feet to obey, and took the weapon. Though she was only sixteen turns, the Conservatum and Stave, who took pride in his skills at readying the inexperienced for combat, had been training her in the fighting arts since she'd been small.

Taking Isemay's hand, Symvalline spared the two Deathless a sympathetic glance as she moved to the table and sat down. Their cold eyes watched them, but the men didn't, couldn't, move.

"Should we do something for her?" Isemay asked, pointing to Akeeva.

Should they? What Akeeva had wrought in this world, the atrocities she didn't do enough to stop, the Verity she was sworn to protect but had willingly undermined, these were grounds enough to show her no mercy or aid. But Symvalline didn't have it in her to leave the wretched woman crumpled on the floor in such a manner, like discarded trash.

"We'll move her over there," she said and pointed to a couch nearby.

With Isemay's help, Akeeva was soon laid out, looking far too corpse-like with her skin now cold and pale, her eyes closed. She clung to life, thanks to her Verity spark, but barely. Symvalline, like Tuzhazu apparently, didn't expect her to recover anytime soon.

She then went back to the book and pored over the fore-edge painting, a simple yet clever codex she'd previously, unreasonably, missed like a child novice in the Conservatum.

"You saw it too," Isemay commented as she examined the painting.

With a distracted nod, she studied it closely. It was a series of pictures, starting at the base of the book, wrapping around to the edge of the leaves opposite the spine, and continuing on to the top. It showed the three moons lining up perfectly over the same tall tower drawn on other pages. The tower's top bulged outward with a massive semicircular stone, painted a mix of pale red, blue, and yellow-white, like old chalk. The next image showed a column of light from the moons to the tower. The third showed another beam cascading like lightning through a darkened room and onto a prone human form with five smaller spheres hovering over it. And the final image showed the person, radiating golden light, standing beside the plinth it had previously been lying on. Elder Veros script beneath the form said, *Mithli Unshackled.*

This is the secret that only Akeeva knew, Symvalline realized. *The Cosmoculous is capable of breaking the Verity cage. Does this mean it can be done without the maker? Does the Cosmoculous somehow focus light from the*

Cosmos, like a great lens, powerful enough to overcome the wysticism that created the cage?

If her guess was correct, she now knew the secret, too. If she and Isemay could get to the Cosmoculous Tower at the Equifulcrum, they could release the Everlight and undo everything Tuzhazu and Balavad have been scheming to achieve.

Then she would be free from living for another age wondering if he'd been right, that their blood was on her hands too for selfishly attempting to escape and seek out her daughter instead of doing his bidding and creating a simple, nondeadly way to overcome his foes. *No, I'm not going to let myself believe I bear any culpability in his corrupt schemes. I've seen his face, and his mind. He would kill them anyway. He wants to.*

She turned to Isemay. "We're going to get out of here. Be ready to follow me through the door. There are secret ways around the fortress that we'll have to find."

She brought the stones, once again, into action. Instead of hurling them into the wooden door and trying to splinter it piece by piece, Symvalline used finesse and, following Isemay's example, hammered at a pin from the hinges of the left door until it came free. The door had no locking bar on the outside and fell inward, the entire process taking less time than she'd need to tie a sash.

They emerged into an even larger chamber, which was filled with the young, frightened faces of Akeeva's adopted—or appropriated— children, and one very confused and strident mistress.

The mistress watching the children was drawing a breath to scream —but a hovering blue crystal directly in front of her eyes distracted her.

Symvalline paced to the woman. "Hertha, I believe? Please, madam, listen to me closely. I am not going to hurt you, or the children, or any other Minothian. I promise. I'm trying my best, in fact, to ensure you stay safe. Go sit in that chair and don't move, don't make a sound. Don't resist or I won't be able to keep my word. Do you understand me?"

The wiry, stiff woman, skin swirling frantically between a fern green and dull brown, nodded. She fell into the chair with a wheezy sigh. Symvalline was looking around the room to find something to tie her up with when a familiar voice said, "Lady Vinnric?"

She turned. Inder stood next to her.

"Hello again," she said with a strained smile.

The boy smiled back in a much-too-old-for-him way. "Is that her? Your Crumb?" He glanced to Isemay, who dropped the sword she'd been wielding point-first to her side quickly.

"Yes, thank you. With your help, she is here now, safe. Or almost safe."

"Why did you come back?"

"Inder, don't speak to the foreigner!" Hertha chastised.

The boy gave her a haughty look. "But she tried to save Tulla. And the Archon was cruel to her for no reason. I saw it." His voice challenged the tutor to disagree, and to Symvalline's relief, she clammed up.

In her years of being a Knight, she'd often found friendship and alliances in unexpected places, but this young boy, a child from another realm, was without question the most unusual. Yet she would never be foolish enough to look askance at any ally, not at a time like this.

"Inder, can you do me one more favor? I need you to take my daughter through the tunnels and help her hide until—until this is all over. Tuzhazu is planning to do something that will put all of Arc Rheunos in harm's way, and I am going to stop him."

"Mum, no." Isemay clutched her arm tightly. "I'm going with you. You can't abandon me. Not again."

She felt as if she'd been struck. Is that what Isemay thought? That she'd abandoned her when she'd stayed to fight the Minothians in the starpath valley? She stared into Isemay's face, smooth and brown like her father's, her eyes a pale blue, almost gray, like Symvalline's. But innocent. Frightened. And nowhere near ready for this kind of conflict. The sacrifices one had to make as a Knight—why had she ever considered allowing her only child to follow this path? Why had she done it herself?

"Isemay, I'm not...not abandoning you. It's for your safety. If something happened to you—"

"I fought to get here and find you, and I'll fight to escape by your side, mum. I'm not a little girl anymore. This is my choice. Not yours."

That anguished mix of pride and dread battled in her again. She wanted neither to win. She wanted to be back in Vigil Tower, sitting by the hearth, rocking the baby that Isemay had once been, with copper curls that matched her own. Feeling her warm, little weight in her arms. Sixteen turns had passed in the blink of an eye, making the seven-hundred-odd turns before it seem inconsequential, like they'd only been a trice in life until she could meet the baby she and Ulfric had created—but who was now no longer her little girl.

"All right," she said simply. "We'll do this together. Inder, can you show us the quickest way through the tunnels out of the hall and to the Cosmoculous Tower?"

CHAPTER FORTY-THREE

Ulfric could never have foreseen the uncommon, unique even, army now on the move through the Rheunosian labyrinth, not if he lived another thousand turns. The rolling, seemingly living rock that was vanguard, defensive ceiling, and rear guard for the Zhallah people was just the beginning of it. They were surrounded by a stone fortress that was alive and nimble and could be breached by nothing the Minothians had. It was the most powerful force Ulfric had ever witnessed.

The bruhawks remained aloft, though flew low in order to dive into the protection of the Churss if needed, and Ulfric would occasionally glance below him and see only a fraction of the people he expected to. This was due to the second unforeseen and amazing thing he bore witness to. It had taken him watching a woman disappear before his eyes, then reappear a few feet forward before he'd realized the Zhallahs, at least the women, had an extraordinary ability to cloak themselves from sight. This was combined with—as Salukis had explained to him—their ability to *tender*, to let the life of one thing flow through them into another, which explained how Salukis had been healed so quickly. And Ulfric had thought the men's ability to *fly* had been incredible. An army that could move unseen and heal its wounded would be virtually unstoppable, even without an apparently impregnable shield of rock surrounding them. He imagined how differently the War of Rivening might have gone if the people of Vinnr had this ability, and it made him shudder. With these kinds of powers at hand, it was a blessing to all other peoples that the Arc Rheunosians were not a realm bent on conquering. Perhaps Balavad had even planned to overtake them because of these traits.

Inside the Churss, the atmosphere hummed in a subdued roar—stone on stone, rubbing, rolling, and often disassembling and reassembling in a new formation to plug small openings in their protective cave or to provide better platforms for the four to five hundred Zhallahs. The sound was constant, as if they walked along the floor of a raging river shoving boulders and stones along with its relentless current. If the noise hadn't been a byproduct of a perfect war machine, he'd have plugged his ears—Urgo's ears, rather—with cotton wool hours ago. But his wonder made it somehow tolerable.

Though—he'd have wagered his armor none of the Zhallahs would have approved of labeling the Churss a "war machine." But the fact was, it was an engine capable of destruction at a level he'd only seen duplicated by the vastness of the force inside the bowels of Balavad's flying warship. The way the Churss had easily crushed the gigantic gates of the fortress overlooking the Thallorn Valley was proof of it. No Minothian could have stopped them, and those who'd been assembled at the barricade for that purpose had wisely fled as the wooden doors had splintered and given way like dried leaves under the boots of a giant.

And the final unbelievable boon was how the Verity-infused Churss was able to move the Zhallah force much faster than they'd have been able to achieve on foot. Ulfric had been told it would take a minimum of two days to get through the labyrinth under the best of circumstances. But the flattest Churss stones assembled themselves into primitive platforms that were propelled by rounder stones rolling beneath, thus carting the Zhallahs along at speeds much faster than they'd have gone on foot. They'd reach Minoth's Everlight Hall by nightfall, a full day before the triple-moon Equifulcrum was in syzygy. If their luck held, they would be able to stop Tuzhazu before he took control of the Minothians.

Watching the force below him, moving with speed and a steadfast sense of purpose, Ulfric began to believe they stood a chance of not only rescuing Sym and Crumb but of righting this world's greatest wrong.

He had made such mistakes before.

ULFRIC, are you near? Can you hear me?

He started at the sound of Symvalline's voice. He'd let his mind wander for a bit, leaving Urgo to soar tirelessly over the moving Churss. If she was speaking to him through the Mentalios, then they were close now, very close.

My love. Where are you? Have you found Isemay?

Yes, and we've been captured.

He lost his focus for a split second, fear for them driving all thought from his mind. Urgo let out a low squawk, bringing him back. *Where are they holding you? Are you injured?*

It would take too long to explain everything, but we escaped. Tuzhazu has had word you're coming, and he's making preparations. He's planning to fight, so you must warn the Zhallahs about what they may be facing. The regular soldiers carry only daggers and nets as weapons, but the Deathless are well armed with swords, and Tuzhazu has the means to create more of them. I'd say not more than a couple dozen, though.

Now listen, this is important. They are not responsible for what they do, and some of them were once Zhallah children, kidnapped and converted when they grew old enough to wield a sword. Something in the elixir Tuzhazu uses to transform them makes them slaves to him. They are without will or thought of their own, completely under his control. I think it's the Fenestros he bears that allows this to happen. You must not kill the Deathless, nor should the Zhallahs. They are innocent too, no matter what they're forced to do. And we must get that Fenestros from Tuzhazu.

One last thing, my love. Our klinki stones are useless against him while he carries the Verity stone.

Ulfric swallowed the many questions he wanted to ask, hating not being there to aid his wife and daughter, just as he hadn't been back in Vinnr. He was so tired of being forced to put his family second, his life third, and his duty first. He and Symvalline had tried to leave this chaos and strife behind and settle into a normal, peaceful life that they would build from scratch once they were free of their oaths. She would have gone back to being a healer, and he a lens maker. Preferably in Asteryss, but if they couldn't find respite there, then somewhere else, a smaller village in Ivoryss or even Yor where they could fade into the background, growing older as they watched their daughter growing up. They would have been able to put aside the fear that they would see their child die of old age or illness or accident while they tarried ever on, ever in service to a maker who seemed to care little what they did or what they sacrificed on her behalf. But now, again, in another realm even, they were in jeopardy beyond measure.

And this time was worse than ever, because this time Crumb was a pawn, as well.

He pulled his thoughts together and urged Urgo to fly toward the front of the Zhallah formation. He wanted a better look at where they were.

We're nearing the far gate of the Minothian labyrinth, he told Symvalline. *I estimate we'll be able to reach their stronghold before Hallumbrum, or whatever the mid of night is called here. Sooner, if we manage to overwhelm the Minothian forces. They have almost no chance against us, and they know it. Where are you and Crumb now?*

He heard, or imagined he did, the relief in her voice when she responded. *Good. We are going to the Cosmoculous Tower. If you can keep the Minothians occupied, I think I've found another way to break the cage holding Mithli.*

You what? he cried, and Urgo made a disgruntled grating sound in his throat at Ulfric yelling in his head.

During the Equifulcrum, the Cosmoculous crystal seems to channel the celestial light of the three aligned moons. Akeeva figured out that this light, if focused, can unmake the cage. If I can free Mithlí, it will end all Tuzhazu's and Balavad's plans. The peoples of Arc Rheunos will have their Verity back, and Balavad's attempts at conquering them will come to nothing.

And what would happen to the Arc Rheunosians then? Ulfric wondered. Would their Verity seek retribution for this hubris, this betrayal? Would Mithlí even perceive it as such? There was absolutely no way to judge the Verity's reaction, but leaving her shackled was to leave Arc Rheunos vulnerable to Balavad—and the rest of the Cosmos, too. If recent and long-past history were any indication, this would be worse than being once more under Mithlí's sway.

And there was this new possibility—another way to free Vaka Aster from her own cage. *Could we bring Vaka Aster here? Could we smuggle the vessel out of Vinnr?*

He noticed with a cringe that he'd referred to his own body as "the vessel," not as himself.

He promised Symvalline, *I will do whatever I must to keep him away from the tower.* And despite the possibility of this being another way of freeing Vaka Aster, Ulfric still swore he'd capture rather than kill the Archon. He needed all options to remain viable to save himself and Vinnr.

Urging Urgo lower, he had the bruhawk perch beside Deespora and her heartmatch, an older man named Alvar. "Deespora, we've almost reached the end of the maze," he began, speaking again through his daughter's memory keeper. "I've spoken with Symvalline. There's something we should discuss, now."

Deespora stared straight ahead, outwardly stoic and calm, but Ulfric noted the subtlest hint of lavender and a subdued pink in the deep layers of her skin. She said, "Your daughter, young Isemay, is she safe?"

"She is, she is with my heartmatch. Thank you for asking."

"I'm very glad to hear it. Is she well?"

"As can be," he answered. "Symvalline discovered a way to free Mithlí without the cage maker."

This drew Deespora's circumspect gaze. "How?" she asked simply.

"She didn't explain fully, only that there's something about the

Equifulcrum's alignment that creates a celestial light capable of breaking the shackles holding your creator. Akeeva figured this out and somehow Symvalline learned of it. We must keep Tuzhazu and the Minothians distracted until after the Equifulcrum so she can see it done."

"What if it doesn't work? Then Tuzhazu will be able to carry forth his charade."

"Not if he's on the battlef—" He stopped himself. The word "battlefield" was certain to distract Deespora from the point. "Not if he's occupied, or we catch him. If he's not able to perform whatever ritual it is that convinces the Minothians he's the newly ordained vessel, it will make it that much easier for us to convince the Minothians instead of his falseness, if not also Akeeva's."

The Archon contemplated this for a moment, then said, "But he must still be stopped."

Ulfric nodded.

"And, Stallari, though you may think me meek or wavering because I'm not willing to sacrifice lives on a whim, remember that your ways are not our ways. We are a strong people *because* we value life, not despite it. The Minothians were once the same. Today, we'll find out which is stronger: our values, or our fear."

Feeling as if his thoughts were uncannily naked to the Archon, Ulfric simply said: "Understood."

"We're approaching the end gate."

Deespora turned to the troop of aulos players riding a stone platform behind them and waved her Fenestros staff. The group began playing a set of windy sounds as Deespora spoke aloud to the Churss to prepare it to breach this barrier as it had the last, her voice echoing through the enclosure and amplified by the Fenestros.

The bruhawks lifted again, and Urgo flew forward to be first past the gate. To his surprise, it was open. A dangerous invitation, likely fraught with trickery. The Minothians had either left the gates ajar because they knew the wood would be useless in the face of the Churss, or they had set a trap.

But no trap sprang as they passed through. There weren't even any guards present. Before them, a vast valley spread far and wide, farmlands near, and far ahead a haze hugging the base of the mountains rising beyond. The haze itself spoke of the industry and activity of a concentrated population, with cooking fires, smelters, and dust rising from well-trodden streets giving the air its patina. Deespora had told him most of the Minothians lived at the end of the valley, but the haze was not what one might expect in color.

The three moons of Arc Rheunos stood almost in perfect alignment above the far mountains. Their daystar was nearly hidden behind them, as well, creating a strange and ethereal aura throughout the horizon. The daystar's light struck the valley floor in wavering rays of blue and red, as if it shone through a prism, or as if the moons themselves were made of crystal. Staring at the expanse, Ulfric felt as if he'd fallen into a dream, for at no time in his long life had he witnessed such a unique atmosphere.

Drawing himself back to the present, he examined their situation. They would have to cross open country for a time, but Ulfric wasn't concerned. If the Minothians couldn't attack them in the labyrinth, they would have no better options out here. He decided to remain on vanguard as the Churss drove onward.

Before the daystar crested, they'd reached the edge of the Minothian city growing right up to the walls of Everlight Hall, a veritable fortress itself. Two towers pointed toward the heavens from within the curtain wall, the tallest up against the mountains. That would be where the Cosmoculous and the shackled Verity were. The moons were overhead, nearly at syzygy. He guessed the Equifulcrum would arrive late in the night or early tomorrow morning.

The Churss stopped at the town's edge, and the Zhallahs discontinued their incongruous piping. From high overhead, Ulfric could see hundreds of Minothian commoners running to their homes. They had seen what was coming and taken the natural action to hide and wait it out.

Urgo landed near Deespora, and Ulfric said, "We must get the stones on the move, all the way to the wall of the fortress. Then through it, if we have to."

"We will stay here and wait for Tuzhazu, and Akeeva if she dares face me."

"If we don't prove we are a threat, then they'll simply wait us out."

"We won't crush their homes and put people in harm's way. Even if the Zhallahs had your callousness, the Churss itself would not obey such an order. They, too, respect life. Tuzhazu will come. If he wishes to prove he's worthy of his Verity's ordination, he'll come." Her stare returned across the distance toward the fortress. "And if I know him, the greater the threat, the more he'll relish the challenge."

And Deespora was correct. Within moments, the curtain wall gate opened and let forth a procession of warriors, some flying, others mounted atop massive hairy creatures that resembled the great bears that roamed Vinnr's Morn Mountains, but with purple fur and a singular horn atop their heads. They fanned out throughout the city but drew relentlessly toward where the Zhallahs awaited them. Ulfric remained perched by Deespora. As the Minothians approached, she addressed the Zhallahs through her Fenestros and urged them to stand fast while she spoke with their long-time adversary.

They didn't have to wait long. Along the main road that split the town in two rode a stout, tall warrior with misshapen wings that appeared to have been shredded by beast or fire. Ulfric knew instantly this was Tuzhazu. The Archon stopped short of the Churss, eyeing Deespora and the great bruhawks Yggo and Urgo from a distance until the entirety of his garrisoned force had created a long line, three deep, spanning the width of the town to the east and west.

A group of the Deathless Guard, two dozen or so in all, surrounded the Archon in a semicircle, and it was not easy to miss how the regular Minothians beside them shied to the sides, avoiding them.

Tuzhazu's voice boomed, unnaturally loud, and Ulfric could see the familiar shape of one of Balavad's Fenestrii in his hand. "I would ask where you acquired such strange and sinister-looking feathered creatures, Archon Raamuzi, but I already know you prefer fraternizing with foreigners from other realms. First you bring your foul plague, then you bring us enemies from afar. Is there no end to what you Zhallahs will do to ruin our peace and threaten the vessel that sustains our world?"

The lies and misleading statements alone made Ulfric's ephemeral hands itch to strangle the Archon, but now seeing the man who'd threatened his heartmatch and daughter, the depth of his inner corruption made visible by his foul wings, made it that much harder to stay steady at his post.

"Lies, Tuzhazu? That's what you accuse me of while you work so hard to conceal your own and Akeeva's. What would the people of Minoth do if they knew the truth? Have any ever asked you and my sister who falsely claims to be the living Verity why you won't allow any Minothians to leave this place? And"—her eyes swept over the forces spread before them—"I wonder what has become of those who did."

"Your accusations are as baseless as the oath you swore to the Everlight. Give me back the Fenestros and Scrylle you stole from Mithlí's loyal Archons and leave Minoth forever."

"I have no plans to do that, Tuzhazu, and you know it. You've been left to run and to ruin the sanctity of our creator and her gifts for too long. We Zhallahs, ever faithful to Mithlí, have returned to take back the children you've stolen from us—and to restore our Verity to her power."

Ulfric watched Tuzhazu's crowd shift, looking at each other uneasily. They didn't know what the Archons had done to the Everlight at the last Equifulcrum, but any claim at all that the Verity was in some way hindered and powerless would unnerve them, make them question. And people with questions and without resolution were vulnerable.

As he took in the crowd and entertained the thought that Deespora's clarity and authority would win them over without need for violence of any sort, his eyes caught sight of a wagon being drawn to the front of the Minothian forces. Inside sat an iron cauldron that looked big enough to bathe in. He'd learned the winged Arc Rheunosian men would lose the ability to fly if wet, but surely a single cauldron of water wouldn't be taken as a serious threat by anyone. Which left the question, what was it for?

Tuzhazu spoke again, his voice almost conversational, despite its amplification. "I'll ask you once more, Deespora—leave Mithlí's artifacts and take your Churss and your plague-bearing exiles back where you belong. While you still can."

Deespora's response remained calm, reasonable. "We have no desire or intention of fighting you or any Minothian. We are still all Arc Rheunosians and we'll not harm our own, nor any other with peaceful intent. These birds are from Vinnr, and they come merely to aid in the retrieval of the other Vinnrics you've taken captive without cause or need. No one has threatened the Minothian people, and no one will."

Ulfric and Deespora had agreed it was best to keep the circumstances of his presence here a secret. If Symvalline were recaptured, or if he were, he didn't want either of them to be used as leverage or bait against the other.

Tuzhazu looked around at the forces spanning the edge of town left and right. A brutal smirk stretched over his face. "Do you believe her, Minothians? They bring plague and death for the last three hundred years, and now they bring a horde of stone to crush us with, and this fallen, disgraced Archon claims they mean us no harm?" The crowd remained hushed, unsure how to respond. "Well do you?" Tuzhazu roared.

It was the Deathless who started the response. Their voices all joined in a heating hissing shriek that rose in pitch and volume toward a crescendo that seemed capable of igniting the very air it passed through. The Minothians began shouting out variations of "No!" and "Banish the Zhallahs!" but their cries seemed mostly intended as a defense to drown out the Deathless Guards' unearthly screeching.

"Will you let them topple our Verity, take our homes and our children's lives, and spread the Great Waste through our haven in the mountains again, like they did long ago?"

The Minothians continued their cries of negation, voices growing bolder at his urging—and perhaps to quell their own fears of the battle that might be at hand.

Tuzhazu turned back to face Deespora, his face a mask of hate. "Then we shall stop you."

Before Ulfric could think of what to do, Tuzhazu had pulled a small bottle from a pouch at his side, yanked its stopper free, and poured its contents into the cauldron. Ulfric heard Deespora draw an alarmed breath beside him, but she gave no orders. Would she be capable of taking the necessary next step? Would the Zhallahs be capable of taking action?

Before this thought was complete, Tuzhazu did something that, though Ulfric could not guess its purpose, sent razor-like shards of ice into his veins. The malicious Archon dropped the Fenestros into the cauldron with the liquid from the vial. Then he began to speak, his voice too low and far away to understand. And Ulfric remembered Symvalline's warning: *Something in the elixir Tuzhazu uses to transform them makes them slaves to him...I think it's the Fenestros he bears that allows this to happen.*

What had Tuzhazu done?

CHAPTER FORTY-FOUR

Isemay wasn't used to seeing her mum this way. A hard woman who fought like…well, a Knight. She'd feared Symvalline was going to kill the Deathless Guards, though she wasn't entirely sure she wouldn't have welcomed it as a way to escape their vacant gray stare. But Isemay had seen enough death already. Agatha…and what had they done to the poor old friendly Widin?

As they followed the little boy her mum knew, Inder, disbelief that her mum had agreed to let her come warred with her fear at what they were facing. She wanted to be grateful for Symvalline's confidence in her. And in some ways she was. In others, though…she couldn't get Agatha's face out of her mind. The way her life bled from her eyes like melting frost. She'd died so Isemay wouldn't. A sacrifice like that, unlooked for, undeserved even—would she ever, even if she lived as long as her da, be worthy of such a sacrifice? Would she ever again be able to close her eyes and not see the Minothian woman's face staring back at her? Did she really want to spend hundreds upon hundreds of turns living just to find out?

Inder seemed to understand their urgency and scuttled through hidden passages like a silvflan through the walls, as if he'd been born in them. On one or two occasions, they'd had to cross open rooms, but fortunately, these had been vacant. The whole of the fortress it seemed was elsewhere, preparing for the coming Zhallahs and the Equifulcrum.

Soon enough, she and her mum were hurrying up a path that narrowed as it got closer to the mountains, then into a ravine, past a frightening-looking cave, and along another path that took them outside the massive stone tower where the Cosmoculous and caged Verity were. Symvalline had explained what the book meant and what she intended to do on their way.

The tower's doorways were sealed and locked but unguarded. Her mum's klinkí stones quickly disabled the lock, and they hurried inside and up the single winding flight of stairs toward a room near the top.

Isemay somehow managed to keep up with her mum, still invigorated by Agatha's gift. Veins of a whiter stone in the tower walls seemed to pulse with an inner light that made the flight upward strange, as if they walked among shooting stars. At last, they reached the doorway of a chamber, and she saw the same light pulsing irregularly beneath the door. Was it the Verity? The idea of meeting the Everlight made her hesitant. Vaka Aster had been absent from Vinnr for so long, and she'd never faced a living vessel in the flesh. What would Mithlí do or think? Could the celestial creator even act or was the cage her mum spoke of all-encompassing?

Symvalline looked back at Isemay. "Stay close behind me. We don't know what exactly we'll find inside."

This statement did not, to say the least, allay her fears. Squaring her shoulders and pretending she wasn't quaking inwardly, she nodded. "All right."

Symvalline opened the door.

The first thing Isemay saw was the ceiling, which bowed downward in a huge, perfect circle like half a kórb fruit—except hundreds of times bigger. Based on the fore-edge image in the book her mum still carried, the sphere, the Cosmoculous, was a full orb, one massive crystal. The way its millions of tiny facets glinted made Isemay think of the shining flecks of stone mixed in with the Churss towers. The orb must have weighed thousands upon thousands of pounds. Each time the light pulsed, it reflected from the massive crystal, illuminating the room as brightly as a full moon on a lake's surface.

In the center of the chamber beneath the Cosmoculous sat a stone table with four ornately carved stone legs, upon which lay a human body, male but appearing to be made of white stone—just as Vaka Aster's vessel was. And circling above his form, so fast she could barely make them out individually, were five smaller spheres. Fenestrii. Four must be Arc Rheunos's, but whose was the other? Each time the light in the room and along the walls shifted, the body itself glowed brilliantly, clearly the source of the light's pulse.

It very much seemed as if there was life within this statue, the vessel, that was fighting to get out.

"Who do you think that vessel is...or was?" she whispered to her mum.

"An Archon I'm sure, but I don't think there's anything of the person he used to be left. Like all vessels who've been so for hundreds of turns, his spirit has rejoined the Cosmos. His body is just a vault for Mithlí now."

"Like Vaka Aster," she thought aloud, remembering the Vinnric vessel was an ancient Dyrrak, apparently Knight Nazaria's own ancestor.

"Yes." Symvalline nodded.

She retrieved the book she'd packed inside a satchel and studied the art along the edges. "Strange, in this image, it is atop the tower, but I know we're still at least two or three stories below the peak. Down here, it may not be in line with the Equifulcrum." She looked around the chamber. "There must be some way to raise it. Crumb, walk around, look for any device or construct that might lift it. I'll search the book."

Isemay did as she was told and found the rest of the chamber to be devoid of anything besides the Verity. She wandered back to it and, gathering her nerve, peered into the man's face.

For being a statue, he was remarkably detailed. She could even see the colored lines that adorned his skin on his face and hands. His hands were not lying at rest on his chest or by his side—in fact, as she looked closer, she realized nothing about the body seemed at ease. Though the statue lay on a bench, there was a marked sense of movement in the form. His legs were spread, one slightly in front of the other, and his wings were as well, as if he'd been about to take flight. His hands were held up, either to beckon something or ward something off. To her, he looked as if he'd been frozen just as he'd been about to charge or run away. He'd not been caged willingly.

"There's nothing here. No mention of how to raise the crystal," her mum said, more to herself.

Isemay glanced at her, then something in the sphere, some movement it seemed, caught her eye, and she looked to it.

Just like in her memory keeper, a vision began to form just beneath the crystal's surface. "Mum, look at this," she murmured, and Symvalline looked up.

The image solidified. It showed the edge of the Minothian city and two opposing forces facing off: one long line of Minothian soldiers, another of a massive wall of Churss. The stone forest itself stood outside.

"Is this, is this happening?" she asked her mum. "Has the Churss come to fight the Minothians?" She quailed inwardly. Was Salukis out there, facing those soldiers?

"The Churss? What do you mean?"

"The stones, they can move—"

It was as if the light created by the vessel suddenly went off in her head. The Churss moved when Salukis played his reeded instrument. The Churss *listened* to the music. She looked to Symvalline. "I need an aulos."

Her mum's eyebrows quirked in a way that suggested she worried Isemay had become a little too overwhelmed to think clearly. "Why do you need an aulos?"

Before she could answer, the sound of a footstep near the doorway froze her as rigid as the vessel statue.

Isemay and Symvalline whirled to face the door. In it stood a youth, possibly just a turn or two younger than Salukis. His clothing was ragged and dirty, his skin an unhealthy pallor in the pulsing light.

"Lady of Vinnr, you came back," he said simply.

Isemay looked to Symvalline, whose face was calm and open. "Dwoon, why are you still here?" her mum asked.

"Dwoon?" Isemay cut in, surprised. "You're Mura's brother?"

He looked at her with equal surprise, then nodded. "The little ones were too frightened to leave, and I wasn't going to go anywhere without them."

"Where are they now?" asked Symvalline. "Still under the tower?"

Instead of answering, he took a step to the side, revealing two girls and a boy, all younger than him. Nearly beside herself with joy at seeing them, Isemay blurted, "Are you Onni and Cylli?"

The twins' eyes widened and the youngest girl gave her the tiniest of grins.

"They are," Dwoon responded for them.

"I know your grandmum Kalisk," Isemay said. "She's so worried about you. But she's coming, all the Zhallahs are coming." Isemay knew she was rambling, but she wanted to bring them all hope in what seemed a dire situation. "And you must be Eleni," she continued, looking at the older girl, then she glanced at Symvalline. "We'll get them out of here when this is all over, won't we?"

"We will," her mum stated matter-of-factly, and Isemay believed her.

A moment of silence fell over them, and the Zhallah children all stared wonderingly at the glowing vessel. Then Isemay had an idea.

"Do any of you have an aulos, a flute?"

Dwoon and Eleni shook their heads. "They took ours when they captured us."

"Isemay," Symvalline said, "explain what you need one for."

"The Cosmoculous is the same kind of stone as some of the Churss. The Zhallahs can play tunes that move them, or rather, that encourages them to move. It's...I can't explain it." She looked to Dwoon for help.

"Yes," he agreed slowly, uncertain what she was getting at.

Isemay struggled to keep her voice calm against the excitement trying to push the words out too fast. "We need to move the Cosmoculous to the top of the tower," she pointed up, "and we need a flute to do it." She knew this would work, she just didn't know how they'd get it to without the simple reeded instrument.

Symvalline looked to Isemay, then to Dwoon, then back to Isemay. "Give me a moment. I'm going to try reaching your da. Perhaps there's a way he can get one to us."

She closed her eyes, and Isemay let her gaze fall on the four Zhallahs. Had they been kept captive here? And…why? They stared back at her with equal curiosity, but with very different questions, she assumed.

"No, it isn't working. The lens is silent," her mum said after a moment. "I think the vessel and the Cosmoculous are interfering with it."

Isemay's hopes cooled slightly. She just *knew* this was the answer. How could the fate of a world be decided by the simple lack of a flute?

"We-we could go get one, couldn't we? I can help," Dwoon volunteered quietly. The idea captured Isemay's full attention. He seemed a bit discombobulated by the intensity of her stare—or her overall appearance—but went on. "I saw the Churss and the Minothian forces in the Cosmoculous a moment ago. Almost all Zhallahs carry a flute. If we get to them, we can bring one back."

Symvalline was already shaking her head. "The risk is too much. Neither of you is a soldier. You can't drop into the middle of…that. It may well become an all-out battle."

"You just want us to sit here doing nothing while da fights a battle and the Everlight remains shackled?" Isemay blurted and immediately regretted her sharpness.

But her mum merely looked at her, her face unreadable. She clenched her hands together in front of her, looking down at them as if she were praying, though Isemay knew she did this when thinking hard about something. After several moments, she addressed Dwoon, "Are you willing to take this risk? Knowing the possible consequences?"

The youth's focus fell on the inert vessel, surging light at rapid, irregular intervals, as if a daystar fueled by rage lay within it. Finally, he said, "If it can free the Everlight and my people, then I'm willing to take the risk."

The younger girl, Eleni, stepped up and put a hand on his arm, looking him in the eyes. "Dwoon," she said, "what if you don't make it? What about us?"

Symvalline answered, "My daughter, Isemay, will stay with you. She can help you reach safety if we don't return."

The words did not last long enough on the air to encourage the girl before Isemay said, "No, Mum, I need to be the one to go. If the Minothians come, you can hold them off."

Symvalline eyed her a moment, then reached out and pulled her into an unexpected embrace, nearly crushing her. "When and how did you get so grown, so courageous? My little Crumb…"

"Don't, Mum. Don't cry. Because then I'll cry. And I don't want to do that in front of them," she whispered, half because her mum was crushing her lungs, half because she didn't trust she'd be able to contain a whimper.

Symvalline let her go, holding her at arm's length by one shoulder. "You seek out Ulfric and bring him with you when come back, Isemay. Find him first if you can. He'll protect you." Her gaze found Dwoon. "Both of you. Once you find an instrument, don't tarry. And try to stay out of the fight if you can help it. If my senses are correct, we only have one or two hours until the Equifulcrum. We have to get that sphere raised before that."

Isemay nodded at Dwoon, who nodded back, then she extended the Deathless Guard's sword to Symvalline. Touching it had made her palms cold and foul-feeling anyway. Symvalline took it wordlessly, and she and Dwoon began rushing back down the tower's long stairwell.

CHAPTER FORTY-FIVE

In the field outside the Minothian city, what happened next turned Ulfric's anxiety into outright dread. A swirling black and gray vapor, like the heart of Balavad's Fenestros, began to rise from Tuzhazu's cauldron. It looked like an ominous storm cloud, a portent of destruction. As it rose, it grew, and soon it was a mist rising over the nearest Minothians.

The uneasy Minothian soldiers watched the mist warily, some using their wings to cover themselves. As the vapor rose, it spread and began to come toward the Churss.

Deespora cried, "Close the gaps! Everyone, inside the safety of the Churss!"

The Zhallahs were already well guarded, but those on the edges of their mobile fortress grouped together closer in the middle as the stones closed over and around them, sealing off crevices of light from outside and becoming even more cavelike. Ulfric and the bruhawks were forced with Deespora to move backward, and the last glimpse he had of the line of troops outside was the dark vapor descending around them, enclosing them within its grasp the way the Churss enclosed the Zhallahs.

There was silence. For a moment. Then, there were screams.

It sounded like a slaughter, louder than any battlefield Ulfric had ever been in. What made it worse was that there were no sounds of weapons, no clashing metal or twangs of bows. Just shrill cries, pained wails. He had Urgo look to Deespora to see her reaction. Her pale eyes gleamed with tears, her expression drawn and filled with sorrow.

"I should never have let him do this," she whispered.

Ulfric could not let her give in to guilt at a time like this. "Deespora," he said, his voice that of Stallari Aldinhuus, leader of the Knights Corporealis of Vinnr, commander. "What has happened?"

She looked back to him. "He's turned them all into Deathless soldiers. They will be unstoppable now. And there is no way to reason with them. They are mindless as well as indomitable. I never thought… I never knew he had the power to turn *all* of them."

"Can you undo it with your Fenestros?"

"If there's a way, I don't know it."

"Then that only leaves us with one choice. I've seen myself the healing abilities your people have, and we shouldn't lose many in the fight that's coming. Remember, we don't have to win this battle—we only have to keep the Minothian forces and Tuzhazu busy until Symvalline is able to free Mithlí. Once she does that, Tuzhazu will have nothing left to do but lose."

"Do you think that will make him stop fighting?"

"If he doesn't, he'll die. It's simple. He cannot win when your Verity is free. But that won't happen if we don't do something, and do it now."

Inwardly, Ulfric's mind tormented him with a vision of Tuzhazu looming over Crumb. He couldn't let his daughter be under the thrall of that man. If Deespora lost heart and refused to act, he'd already decided he would chance ordering Yggo to grab her Fenestros and Scrylle and abandon the Zhallahs to fly directly to the Cosmoculous Tower. There, he'd give Symvalline the artifacts so she could open a starpath and take her and Isemay out of this realm, perhaps to Himmingaze. The bruhawks would be a formidable force against the Minothians, even those who were now Deathless Guards, but the two of them had no chance against an army.

But the Zhallah Archon surprised him, showing the mettle that was intrinsic to every Knight Corporealis of Vinnr, the metal that had made her an Archon in the first place.

She turned and faced her people. "Zhallahs, and our time has come to right the wrongs of our people's past and bring in a new age of peace in Arc Rheunos. We do not wish to harm those we once embraced as our own kin, who once *were* our own kin, but they are not any longer. Not while they are held in a prison of lies by the Archons Tek Det Tuzhazu and my sister Akeeva Raamuzi. The Minothians have been made into puppets, ruled by greed for dominion, and the only thing that can stop them from destroying the future for all Arc Rheunos's peoples is us.

"Today, we must fight for our lives, for our children, and for our future—and the future of the realm. Are you ready?"

The Zhallahs did not hesitate the way the Minothians had. A roar of agreement and excitement boomed throughout the confines of the Churss, slamming like a physical pressure into Urgo's chest. The bruhawk raised first one massive claw into the air and clenched it, then the other, as if loosening up for a fight. Ulfric would have done the same if he could.

With the thrill that always shot through him just before a battle, he called to Symvalline through the Mentalios. He needed to know if she and Crumb were still safe and to inform her of what was about to happen here.

But as the Churss began to part to let the Zhallahs through, and the view of the mass of Minothians soldiers transformed into the ghastly Deathless ranks spread before them, only silence greeted him from the Cosmoculous Tower.

WHEN THE CHURSS had parted enough to let the Zhallahs through, the two lines of very different fighters stood facing each other. The mist that had transformed them had dissipated, and from mountainside to mountainside, the air wavered with a red and blue glow that dipped low into the valley, the colors bleeding into each other in unusual patterns, further contrasted by a paler light. It was a haunted sky. The moons—Kahros the Seeker, Znopho the White Watcher, and Maiztos the Life Giver—were nearly aligned.

For heavy moments, silence and stillness held sway in the gap that separated the two forces. Neither side, it seemed, was eager to start the battle. The thought galloped through Ulfric's mind that maybe there was still a chance they could persuade Tuzhazu to see reason.

But as the malicious Archon raised his sword, the multihued light seemed to flash on its blade and along the metal hooks that rose from the crest of his torn, widespread wings, and Ulfric knew that when the sword dropped, it would begin.

Before it did, he urged Urgo: *For the Knights, Urgo, we will have victory this night!*

Urgo and Yggo as one leaped up and swooped forth, directing their attack at the head of the snake. Tuzhazu.

The flying Deathless Guard were not slow to react. At least a dozen were already airborne before the bruhawks could reach Tuzhazu. Behind Ulfric, the Zhallahs leaped into action as well with a great battle cry as potent and powerful as any Ulfric had heard in his lifetimes.

The flying Deathless quickly diverted Ulfric and the bruhawks, and they spiraled high over the battlefield in a clash of swords, claws, and ripping beaks.

Ulfric had warned the hawks to avoid killing the Deathless when possible, as Symvalline had directed, but there wasn't much in the way of options when a ravening, mindless warrior with murder in its blood came at them. The bruhawks dodged the Deathlesses' blades and shredded their wings with their steel-like talons, but the birds couldn't mitigate the fall to the hard earth and rooftops of the closely built Minothian city, which surely hurt the Deathless as much or more than what the bruhawks could have done to them. Ulfric had to remain disimpassioned, but the reality was that it wasn't likely the Arc Rheunosian tenders would get a chance to save many before they expired.

The Minothians had the advantage of having been trained to fight, but the Zhallahs had their own advantages. The rolling Churss platforms both gave them a higher vantage and provided rock shields to hide behind when needed. Secondly, only a couple dozen Deathless Guards had the gruesome Ravener swords made for such a melee. The rest fought with pikes and daggers. Though sharp, these were also more easily countered by the farm tools the Zhallahs carried, which weren't so different.

Busy with aerial assaults, Ulfric couldn't keep much of an eye on what was occurring below. The hawks disabled and downed at least twenty enemies in short order, but there were hundreds of Minothians. After some unknown passage of time, Ulfric began to sense that more and more Minothian fighters were coming after Yggo and Urgo. He could feel the effects of fatigue overcoming Urgo as if they were his own. The constant jagging, dodging, and darting to avoid attacks was taking a toll.

The bruhawks were without doubt the best weapons the Zhallahs had, but they couldn't fight every flying Minothian. Ulfric had to get a perspective on the battle. The Deathless had twice the stamina of the Zhallahs, and if they could not stop Tuzhazu here, Ulfric feared he and the hawks would have to abandon the fight to protect Symvalline and Isemay. He had to give Tuzhazu credit. Directing a heavy assault at the bruhawks was what any commander bent on victory would order. Until Tuzhazu was stopped, the snake's head chopped off, the battle would go on.

Urgo, fall back. Get some distance from the field. We need to reevaluate the situation.

It pained Ulfric's lead-from-the-front instinct to fall back. Worse yet, he wasn't in his own form and able to yell commands and rally the troops as needed. No doubt, his long battle experience would have benefited them. The best he could do was team with the bruhawks to inflict the most stopping power. But he needed to find a tactic to get to Tuzhazu, and he couldn't do it while being harried relentlessly by the Minothian pests.

Getting to great heights quickly was a talent of the bruhawks, and they'd soon lost their pursuers in the haze of the murky air. Urgo's sharp eyes scanned the battlefield, and Ulfric's fears, ones he'd refused to consider, could not be ignored any longer.

He'd missed it to begin with, but it wasn't only the Minothian people who'd been transformed by Tuzhazu's wystic elixir. The dozens and dozens of urzidae mounts they rode had likewise been transformed.

The beasts had become hideous. Their shaggy bodies had stretched to an almost serpentine length. Ridden by Deathless Minothians, the beasts no longer lumbered. They whipped through the Zhallahs like enraged cats, pouncing and jumping with an agility nothing that size should have had, easily leaping onto the Churss platforms and wreaking disaster on those who rode them. Their claws had become swords, sharp and pointed and mortally long. The beasts tore through the Zhallahs like paper, and each blow Ulfric witnessed cut through his spirit as well.

The airborne Minothians outnumbered the Zhallahs, and their stronger nets brought them down in a constant rain. He realized the Minothians had already decimated the Zhallahs in the air, and from what he was seeing happening on the ground, it was going to become a rout. The only advantage left to the Zhallahs was the women's ability to become unseeable and fight from the shadows. The Deathless Guards and their urzidae could not catch what they could not find. One thing stood out from his vantage: it appeared few, if any, of the female Deathless fighters had become invisible. He wondered if something in Balavad's elixir was blocking this, and cheered the small advantage it gave the Zhallahs for a moment.

But even that advantage soon withered.

From the center of the melee, Tuzhazu walked forward. He'd retrieved his Fenestros from the cauldron, and it now emitted a dark vapor, which spread low on the ground like a foul, creeping rodent. As it spread, it shifted around the forms of those who would have otherwise been invisible to the eye, creating shadow outlines. Now, even the Zhallah women were targets.

His hopes seized on their last chance: Deespora, surely she could stop Tuzhazu, pitting her Fenestros and Scrylle against his lone Fenestros.

As if to answer his prayer, she suddenly appeared in the dark vapor, pacing toward Tuzhazu astride his berserking urzidae. She held both her staff with its Fenestros headpiece and the Scrylle aloft, and a soft white light like a distant star shone from the celestial stone, surrounding her in a perfect sphere that held Tuzhazu's mist and the Deathless Guards at bay.

Urgo was too high to make her words out, but Ulfric heard the tones of her speech to Tuzhazu. The Archon reined his urzidae short before her, still holding Balavad's Fenestros in his outstretched hand. Fighters all over the field disengaged. The Zhallahs who still could retreated to form a semicircle behind Deespora, and those who couldn't were assisted or carried.

As one, Ulfric and Urgo peered at the scene, on tenterhooks.

It was all over so quickly Ulfric couldn't even cry out.

Tuzhazu yelled to his mount, and the urzidae charged Deespora. Ulfric watched her crumble beneath the beast and become engulfed completely by the inky vapor.

Struck with a profound horror, he quailed inwardly. But no matter what, he couldn't let Tuzhazu get those artifacts. They were his and his family's only way out of Arc Rheunos.

Dive, Urgo, dive! he commanded, and Urgo did.

They rocketed toward the earth at such a shattering speed that Ulfric lost all sense of time and space. The world became nothing but an immense vacuum pulling at the speed of a comet, and he couldn't help but hold his ephemeral breath. The nearest he'd ever experienced to this was when barreling through the Cosmos by starpath. He feared at this velocity that Urgo would never be able to stop in time before hitting the ground and obliterating them both.

He shouldn't have doubted. Urgo was, after all, endowed with the same Verity spark he was.

The bruhawk's trajectory wasn't directly into the fray where Deespora went down, but farther off toward the south. His descent shifted suddenly from straight down to an angle, and a heartbeat later they'd begun a glide toward where she'd fallen. Through Urgo's enhanced eyes, the white light of Mithlí's Fenestros shone through the murk like a beacon, and Urgo's claws wrapped around both the stone and Deespora before anyone on the field could react. Before another breath, the bruhawk was again flapping rapidly to gain loft.

No Deathless could have reacted to that, Ulfric thought with relief, happy at least that he'd salvaged the artifacts and, Verities willing, the Archon as well.

A sharpness like icicles shot into his, or rather, Urgo's wing an instant later. Urgo gave a screech that could split eardrums and listed heavily toward his right, momentarily dizzying Ulfric. From the corner of his vision that still peered through the memory keeper, he saw something off to the left, something falling. Deespora!

But Urgo was wounded. He couldn't turn back for the Archon.

What, what is it, Urgo? Where've you been hit?

Then his senses picked up the piercing sting of a blade in the bird's right wing. He didn't think it was lethal, but it was deep enough and painful enough that Urgo was searching for a safe place to land on the far mountainside, away from the fracas.

And now, Deespora was gone, the Zhallahs were left leaderless, and the Deathless had proven the greater force in Minoth.

We've lost, Ulfric thought.

Yggo swooped in from the side, though the Deathless who'd attacked had already fallen far behind, Yggo grabbed his wings. Without losing momentum, she bent her neck and sunk her razor-like beak into the soldier's neck, ripping it outward. The hawk let go of the bloody, shredded mass, and the soldier was quickly lost in the day's waning blue-red haze below.

In moments, Urgo and Yggo found a perch on a wind-bitten ledge to set down and catch their breath. Yggo tended to Urgo and yanked the Deathless's dagger from his wing with her beak. She would not leave his side, protecting him as well as Ulfric. They'd lost Deespora and the Scrylle, but Urgo had managed to salvage the Everlight's Fenestros, still attached to Deespora's staff.

It was a small thing, and Ulfric wasn't sure what he could do with the celestial stone while sharing Urgo's form, who was now too wounded to fight.

Yggo gave a gentle squawk, pulling Urgo's and Ulfric's attention to the horizon. A form was flying at them, a Minothian or a Zhallah. Yggo wasn't alarmed, though, as if she recognized a friend rather than foe.

In a moment, Ulfric did too. It was the young man, Salukis, flying swiftly and gracefully, as if he'd never been wounded. If there was any mercy in the Cosmos, the other wounded Zhallahs would recover so well.

Yggo spread her wings partway, a gesture of welcome, though Ulfric doubted Salukis would know it. Soon, the young man landed on the shelf with them.

"I'm so glad I found you," he started, out of breath. "You saw?"

"Only a bit," Ulfric responded through the memory keeper. "What's happened?"

"The Zhallahs have retreated."

"How many were able to get within the safety of the Churss?"

"Most. The tenders are doing what they can to heal the wounded, but they won't…they won't be able to…"

Ulfric wanted to put an arm around the boy to console him, but that was impossible. He did his best with words. "Those who fell today and are not fated to rise again will live on in the Cosmos. Nothing is ever gone forever. And remember, they chose to make this sacrifice for something they believed in, something that was right. They may not have wished for death, but they faced it on their own terms."

The boy's eye shined, but he didn't cry. *Tougher than I would have thought*, Ulfric realized. *But I wish neither he nor I had to find out this way.*

"Salukis," he said, "did you see Deespora? Urgo tried to bring her from the battle, but we lost her. She fell."

Salukis shook his head. "No. I can rally a few to start a search, but the Deathless are everywhere. And the Equifulcrum is—" He stopped, shrugging and looking toward the moons.

Less than an hour. Had Tuzhazu left the field? Was he even now on his way to the Cosmoculous Tower? There was only one more thing Ulfric and the bruhawks could do, and that was meet the Archon at the door and stop him from entering. Whatever it took, even if they made the final sacrifice, Ulfric would risk it if it meant keeping him from reaching Symvalline and Isemay.

Urgo, he knew, wouldn't last long against the Archon's forces. His wing made flight painful and ponderous, and his Verity spark would take too long to heal him. Yggo would take the Archon on alone if Urgo urged her, but even so, what chance did they have? They'd been unable to penetrate Tuzhazu's personal guard, dozens to one.

They needed a fresh army, a miracle…

He looked through Urgo's eyes to Salukis. Or a trick.

CHAPTER FORTY-SIX

Isemay and Dwoon snuck through the yards of Everlight Hall as cautiously as they could. It was easier to hide beneath his wings on the ground than to remain unseen in the air, so progress took much longer than Isemay's underdeveloped patience liked. She kept telling herself, *Calm down, be careful. Be a Knight.* Fortunately, the majority of the fortress's population were missing, watching or contributing to the battle going on in the distance.

Dwoon flew them over the wall enclosing the fortress grounds, then back to the earth where they slipped through town. Every window they passed was shuttered, every door closed, as if the whole population was hiding. And the sounds of the melee continued to get louder, the cries of those who were hurt and the ghastly shrieks of the Deathless turning her blood cold.

She wanted to stuff cotton in her ears. The noise was too horrible. *I've told mum and da a thousand times I'm not a child anymore,* she thought. *But I'd rather be one forever than see what's happening ahead.*

Somehow Dwoon remained steady, and this kept her going. She wondered if he was only continuing forward because she hadn't stopped, either. Darting glances at him, she guessed he was about her age, though he looked thin for his height. She imagined how overwhelmed with joy Mura and their mum would be when they saw him again, and the thought of seeing her new friend so happy gave her the added motivation she needed.

"We shouldn't go down the main road," she whispered to Dwoon when they were about halfway through the town. "We'll have to skirt around."

He nodded, and they took the first lane to the left they found. The homes and businesses of the city were mostly constructed from wood and built two to three stories high. Even with the unique, murky light reflecting from the triple moons, they passed through the town like shadows, and she was certain they weren't seen. Or recognized if they were.

"Maybe we should just try finding a flute in one of the houses," Dwoon whispered as the neared the eastern edge of town.

She heard the fear in his voice, and in a strange way, it gave her courage to know she wasn't the only one who was scared. "I don't think that's a good idea. If someone catches me, I can't exactly pretend I'm just a miscreant Minothian. You could, though..." She trailed off, terrified that he might agree and leave her here to fend for herself. She wouldn't protest, though. That was their mission, after all.

But he said nothing and kept walking.

The density of buildings was thinning, and they had to switch their direction straight toward the front line or they would run out of cover. After they'd gone a ways, she felt Dwoon's sharp elbow in her ribs.

"Look," he whisper-yelled.

His head was tilted back, taking in the sky, and she did the same.

Then she saw it. Dozens and dozens of men aloft, fighting frantically and cruelly against one another. The Minothians were easy to pick out due to their purple and brown uniform, and the Zhallahs—

She had to look away quickly. She'd gotten to know many of the Zhallahs, and she couldn't bear to see them get hurt. "Come on," she choked out through a throat that seemed to be growing narrower. "We have to hurry."

They'd only gone a couple of paces when a man fell from the sky and crashed into a building next to them. Neither of them had seen whether he was Minothian or Zhallah. They froze in the narrow passage between two long buildings, storehouses of some sort.

"We should try to help him," Dwoon said, doing his best to keep his voice down. "He may be a Zhallah."

She nodded hesitantly, knowing she didn't need to voice what might happen to them if he wasn't.

The next second, they heard a door crash open far down the building's side. A man staggered out, one of his wings bent awkwardly and dragging behind him. From the shadow they stood in, Isemay and Dwoon could see he was a Minothian, one of the Deathless based on his gangly form. He opened his mouth and screech-hissed something that sounded like a mix of rage and pain, and the two youths needed no further confirmation.

"Shh," Isemay whispered as low as she could. "Don't. Move."

If the Deathless turned their direction, there was a strong chance he would see them. But they were lucky. He turned back toward the battle and loped off.

They both sighed and rose from the crouches they'd adopted. "Dwoon," Isemay said, "we have to hurry."

She didn't tell him, but she knew that the Zhallahs' chances for victory against troops who could shake off that kind of fall, from that height, were poor at best. The only way they would find a flute is if the Minothians were still fighting, too distracted to notice them. But if the Zhallahs had to retreat—or were all dead—she and Dwoon would stand out like, well, like they were from another world.

The two broke into a trot, paying less attention to windows and doorways now. They were nearly to the battlefield, and they could see thick gray-black smoke blanketing the ground ahead. She hoped it would help conceal them, though something about the fog made her cringe at the thought of immersing in it.

Finally, they came to the shadowed edge of the last building and took in the field before them. Isemay didn't know exactly what she'd expected, but it hardly mattered. Nothing can ever prepare one for the sight of their first battlefield.

At first, all she saw were the deformed urzidae mounts. There were at least a hundred of them, charging with riders across the open ground, many with spears and other shafted tools poking from them, though these seemed to hardly faze the creatures. Every single one of them was ridden by a Deathless Guard. *I didn't think there were so many. Mum warned me about them, but she said there were only a dozen or so.*

The fighting was so frenetic that she only caught glimpses of individuals locked in hand-to-hand combat. The flocks of men clashing above the field drew her gaze, but not for long. She watched one Zhallah man lose his hand, and the rain of blood from his wound made her feel weak and light-headed. She blinked and refused to look up again.

Across the teeming mass rose the Churss towers of Maerria. They loomed statue-still, as if to bear silent witness to the atrocity of the battle before them.

Shaking her head to clear it of the grisly sights and sounds, she wondered, *How are we going to find a flute in all this?* It horrified her to think they might have to rifle through the garments of the dead or wounded.

Something shifted in the atmosphere, and a moment later Isemay saw a white light midway between her and Dwoon and the Churss sentinels. The battlefield quieted, the combatants drawing apart. What was it? What was happening?

Then Deespora's familiar voice rang out. "Cease this violence, Tuzhazu! One drop of Arc Rheunosian blood spilled is too much! What will it take to make you end this?"

"Give me the Fenestros and Scrylle, Deespora, then submit. Your birds attacked us first. That's the only way you will walk away from this field alive."

Isemay could make them out midfield, Tuzhazu mounted on an urzidae before Deespora and the white-lit Fenestros she wielded.

"You can't hope to rule over the entire realm, turning our people into to these sickly, deformed creatures," Deespora called, her voice thick and clear in the din. "That isn't rule. It's brutality."

"Mithlí's abandonment of us when we needed her most was the brutality!" Tuzhazu yelled.

Then, as if to prove that deep down Tuzhazu truly was nothing but a monster, he kicked his urzidae and charged the Zhallah Archon, running her down.

Isemay slapped a hand over her mouth to hold in her cry. Beside her, Dwoon gaped, speechless. Tears spilled from his eyes, unheeded.

A moment later came a sight so unexpected Isemay thought she had passed out and was dreaming. It was Urgo sweeping from the sky, grabbing the fallen Archon, and just as quickly flapping into the air. He, and Yggo beside him, were gone from her sight almost before she realized what had happened.

Then the Zhallahs began to scramble for safety, running into the Churss, the Deathless in pursuit. The Churss reacted by shielding the Zhallah and blocking the Deathless. When it seemed the last Zhallah was accounted for, the stone forest closed itself over them, forming a wall of protection no simple battlefield weapon could penetrate.

In moments, the field was quiet again, only the Minothian fighters remaining. They milled around Tuzhazu, many wounded. They were a huge force, too many. The Zhallahs had been foolish to think they had a chance. And now their leader was…gone. Was she dead?

They had perhaps two hours until the Equifulcrum.

Despite the sickness of the heart overtaking her, Isemay drew on a strength that wasn't her own—she thought of her mum and da, of Safran, Stave, Mallich, and Mylla, even cold and frightening Eisa. The Knights never showed weakness.

In this moment, neither could she. "Dwoon. Dwoon!" she whispered again when he didn't answer. "We have to stay hidden. It's only temporary, the Minothians haven't won yet. Not if we can free Mithlí."

The youth faced her, tears streaking through the dirt on his face. "But Deespora…"

"Those giant hawks, the ones that took her? They are friends. They rescued her. And remember, she's an Archon and is gifted with resilience by the Verities. Are you still with me?"

He nodded miserably.

"Okay, good. Now, stay here, hide, save your strength. When it's clear, well, clear enough, we'll make for the Churss and get someone's flute." She took a deep breath, not liking what she had to say next, but knowing it was the right thing to do. "Then it's going to be up to you, Dwoon. You're going to have to fly like you've never flown before to get it back to the tower."

His eyes widened. "Do you mean leave you here? Go alone?"

"No, there are other Zhallahs there. They'll protect you if they still have some faith left in the fight." She startled herself. That was her mum and da's saying. "I'll tell them what they have to do, and they'll help. I know it. But me, I'm just dead weight. You'll be swifter if you don't have to carry me."

Dwoon settled into a thoughtful silence. She could only imagine what he was thinking, but to keep herself from falling into dark thoughts of her own, she peered around the edge of the storehouse to the field.

And saw the strangest thing.

Archon Tuzhazu was wandering through the field with a glass vial in his hand. He knelt over the bodies of dead Minothians, holding the obsidian Fenestros out and chanting. As she watched, the Minothians began to transform back into what they'd looked like before, normal Arc Rheunosians. She noted that this reversal did nothing to stanch their bleeding or restore their health. The dead stayed dead. She watched for some time, trying to understand why he was doing this, but came up with no conclusions.

She looked back to Dwoon. "Are you ready?"

He nodded, bravely, she thought, despite his clear fright.

"Okay, let's—"

Her words were cut off by the sound of a voice she'd grown more than fond of. He was shouting, "Does a coward who fights from the back of a beast have it in him to face a Zhallah one on one?"

Isemay's head jerked up and she stared wildly across the field. Standing amid a ring of Minothian Deathless was Salukis.

CHAPTER FORTY-SEVEN

"Salukis," Ulfric said, "I need your help."

The young man's face was clenched in the hard-to-define expression between defeat and determination. His youthful skin was lined and dirty, sweat streaking down his cheeks and over the bridge of his nose. But his eyes burned with vitality, rage maybe. "What else can I do?" he said. "We've lost, I think. If we can't find a way to beat Tuzhazu…"

Despair, that too was just under the surface of the boy's demeanor, about to crack through. Ulfric couldn't let him get that far. "Listen to me, I have an idea about how we can do that. We need to challenge Tuzhazu one on one. And by we, I mean, you…sort of."

"You mean to a fight?" He watched disbelief, then a hard acceptance cross Salukis's face. "All right. I will face him, if I must. But I have to be honest, I don't think that even if all five Verities smiled on me, I would be able to defeat him. Not on my own."

"You won't be on your own. Let me explain."

Ulfric didn't know if he could do it, but he wanted to give it a shot. He'd been able to make himself a part of Urgo—maybe he could do the same with Salukis. Even though the bruhawk had been endowed with the Verity's spark, and Salukis wasn't, the Fenestros might be just the conduit he needed to achieve the shift. Salukis wasn't small for an Arc Rheunosian, though he didn't have the full bulk and muscle that came with training and age. Still, he was not wounded and he was young and nimble. With Ulfric helming him like a ship, in charge of his reflexes and movements, he was sure he could fight the Archon through Salukis. And all he needed was a chance to grab Balavad's Fenestros, then he could use it to call off the Deathless just as Tuzhazu did to command them to fight.

Their advantage was that Tuzhazu would have no idea what Salukis was capable of. To get him to agree to fight Salukis, Ulfric was sure he could count on his cruel nature to prompt him to answer the challenge. Tuzhazu would see it as an easy kill and a way to personally make an example of the boy and show the Zhallahs what toll their rebellion would continue to take.

He explained this to Salukis. The youth blanched white and responded with one question, "If Tuzhazu kills me, what happens to Isemay?"

This caught Ulfric by surprise and turned his guts to stone. "I don't know," was all he could say, all he dared say. The question didn't bear considering.

"And what about you? What would happen to you?"

The honest response was, *No idea*, but Ulfric didn't want to give the boy any more doubts or burdens than he already had. "Then I'll return to Urgo," he stated coolly.

With one last flicker of uncertainty in his eyes, Salukis shrugged and said, "So what do I do?"

"Take the Mentalios, and you should have the memory keeper too, from Urgo." The bruhawk leaned toward Salukis to allow him to retrieve the two pendants, and he slipped them on. "Now, hold the Fenestros and look into it while I speak."

Salukis bent down and slowly wrapped his hand around the pale orb, reverently lifting it from between two of Urgo's talons as if he, not the orb, might break if he moved too quickly. Holding it out cupped in his palms, he said, "I'm ready."

Wasting no time, Ulfric chanted the Elder Veros phrase. *Vesr sraak*

aak, sraka aak suu kaa. With thine eyes, these eyes too see. At first, he still felt firmly ensconced in Urgo's form, the birds' strange musculature, prodigious senses, and even his painful wing also Ulfric's own. A heartbeat later, he felt an existential shift and was once again taken over by that hovering, weightless sensation he'd had at Citadel Suprima when he'd been expelled from his own body. Then it was over, and he felt...well, like a person again. His vision darkened, then his eyes opened to Urgo and Yggo perched before him.

Not my eyes, he thought. *Salukis's. Can you hear me, boy?*

His body staggered as if struck, and he reached out his hands, looking for something to steady himself with. But there was a subtle tug at his back, and a sudden lightness overcame him. He realized his, Salukis's, feet had left the ground as Salukis reflexively flapped his wings to regain his balance. *That'll take some getting used to,* Ulfric thought.

"Smoking snouz shite!" the boy yelled. "You're in my head!"

Yes, Ulfric said calmly. *In your head, and your arms, legs, and everywhere else. I can see through your eyes, hear through your ears, all of it. Do you understand? If yes, think it, don't say it.*

Waves of jangled nerves washed through the youth, then finally, he collected himself. *...Are you there?*

Yes! Good, now let yourself relax while I get accustomed to your form.

Accustomed to my...like a puppet?

Ulfric didn't answer, and he went through a few motions, learning what he could about taking over Salukis's body. It was awkward and invasive to say the least, for them both, but Ulfric pushed them through it. He'd trained hundreds of acolytes at the Conservatum in his time, and reverting to the mode of trainer made it easier on both of them. Shortly Ulfric felt he knew what he needed to. This challenge to Tuzhazu, and the deception it involved, was their only weapon, and there was no more time to search for other options.

Ulfric sent: *I'm ready, Salukis. Are you?* He felt Salukis nod.

One last question, Salukis sent. *Can you...read my thoughts?*

Ulfric had caught a glimpse of the boy's unconscious mind the moment he joined with him, but he'd quickly set up his own mental barrier to avoid intruding—and because of the thread of thought he'd apprehended that involved his daughter. He'd felt the boy's own emotions, his awe of and devotion to Isemay. Ordinarily, this would have pleased Ulfric. Who doesn't like knowing that others think highly of their offspring? But Ulfric had been a young man once, too, and he knew what lay at the end of that thread. He didn't want to see that— not in the least. As far as he was concerned, Salukis only thought of his daughter as a friend, a *plutonic* friend. There was no use in scaring the boy by telling him Ulfric knew exactly what he'd been thinking about his daughter. So he sent: *No. You're a natural at this and your mind is closed to me.*

He felt Salukis's relief like cool water flowing over a fevered brow. *All right.*

Face the bruhawks a moment, please. Salukis did as asked, and Ulfric addressed the birds through his memory keeper. "Symvalline and Isemay are in the Cosmoculous Tower. No matter what happens down there on that field, I need you to go to them, protect them. With your last breath if that's what it takes."

The birds blinked their eyes at him, a sign of acknowledgment.

"It's been an honor serving with you both."

Yggo gave a soft churr, and Urgo clucked lightly.

It was time to go. *Let's capture a traitor, Salukis, and see justice done,* he said, forcing a confidence he could tell neither of them fully felt into his tone.

Salukis answered, *Here we go then.*

CHAPTER FORTY-EIGHT

Salukis dropped toward the battlefield without meeting any confrontation. The Minothians had let their guard down when the Zhallahs ran behind the Churss barricade. Still a dozen yards above the earth, the youth hovered a moment, waiting for Tuzhazu to respond to his, or rather Ulfric's, challenge.

Ulfric's calculation had been perfect.

Tuzhazu spun like a top whose string was yanked by an eager child. "What did you say to me, boy?" he growled. His sword appeared in his hand as if by magic, so smooth and fast was his draw. He waved aside a sudden rush toward Salukis by the Minothians, and they moved back, encircling them.

U-Ulfric, he's going to cut me to pieces. Even Salukis's internal voice shook.

Not if you let me handle this. Trust me, Salukis. He's no match for me, for us.

Ulfric felt the young man struggle to relax his body, giving it over to Ulfric as much as he could, and they lowered to the ground.

Ulfric had Salukis repeat his words, buoying the boy and giving his voice power with his own courage. "You heard me. You think you've beaten the Zhallahs back through strength and cunning, but everyone here can see that your only strength is in artifice and lies. Put aside Balavad's artifact, and what are you, Tuzhazu? A wicked fearmonger whose use of the title Archon demeans everything you pretend to stand for. You're no servant of Mithlí. You're a tool of fear and malice. And if you have a single drop of bravery in your twisted bones, you'll face me—if for no other reason than simply to give your followers a shred, the tiniest shred, of a reason to continue looking to you for leadership."

Tuzhazu's face flashed with rage, but he calmed quickly and drew back his lips into his brutal smile. "Boy, you must be the most dim-witted of the plague-bringers. I'll do them a favor, then, and rid them of you. Where is your weapon?"

"Hand to hand. All Verity artifacts set aside."

With a dismissive snort, the Archon turned and beckoned to his urzidae mount. It was still misshapen and serpentine, its maw dripping with a gray froth, its eyes blank, like stones. Tuzhazu sheathed his sword in a scabbard attached to the mount's saddle, then dropped Balavad's Fenestros into a pouch at his own waist, which he removed and tied it around the saddle horn. Ulfric observed closely.

The Archon paced toward him. His silver-green eyes flashed with intention, and his hands were held up clenched in ready fists. Ulfric gauged him to be about a head taller than Salukis, and at least three-stone heavier. He drew up Salukis's own fists. *Salukis, you'll have to be the judge of how best to use your wings. That's outside my field of experience.*

Now you tell me! he responded.

Ulfric said nothing. He couldn't—as Tuzhazu crashed forward without slowing, like an avalanche of wrath.

Ulfric had been prepared to dodge the man's fists, but he'd not accounted for the metal-spiked wing tip that came directly at his face. He threw Salukis backward just in time, expecting to land flat out. But instead, the youth swung a wing, and they ended up moving to one side heavily, jerking them out of Tuzhazu's range and keeping them upright.

That was much too close, Salukis and Ulfric said in unison.

"Watch out!" Salukis shouted out loud as Tuzhazu continued rushing them, never slowing.

At the youth's words and voice, Tuzhazu's brows steepled in a question. If he guessed what was happening, it didn't slow him, though.

Dodge toward the urzidae, keep moving toward the beast, Ulfric directed Salukis as he focused on the sweep of Tuzhazu's wings. They were an onslaught of sharp metal and hard bone, slicing toward them like a maelstrom, and it took both Salukis's and Ulfric's full concentration to keep far enough away not to get skewered.

Ulfric, we'll never get close enough to fight him.

Remember, we only need to get that Fenestros. It's the key to ending this.

Then Ulfric saw his opening. Tuzhazu drew his right wing back as the left swept forward. The momentum of the metal-laden bones pulled Tuzhazu into a twist, exposing the left side of his back to Ulfric, who closed in with the reflexes of a bruhawk, thanks to Salukis's wings, and grabbed the root of the appendage with both hands. Mentally calling on strength from the Fenestros recovered from Deespora—he saw no reason not to cheat—he cranked against Tuzhazu's wing like he was trying to draw out a corkscrew. The Archon gave a deep-throated cry of rage and pain as something in the wing gave, and with a hard twist of his body, he flung himself and Salukis to the ground.

His weight crushed every ounce of breath from Salukis, and Ulfric lost his grip on the wing. Tuzhazu scrambled to his feet. His wing hung limply, dragging on the ground. Salukis tried to pull himself upright, but Tuzhazu's booted foot struck him in the ribcage, flipping his body to the side.

Salukis gave out a cry as a few ribs snapped.

Roll, roll, roll! Ulfric commanded him. In his pain, Salukis had wrested some of the control over his body from Ulfric. *Now!*

Despite the pain, Salukis managed to roll aside before Tuzhazu kicked him again, then came up hard against something immobile. Ulfric's sight through Salukis's eyes had blurred, but they cleared just enough for him to see he lay at the feet of an urzidae.

Tuzhazu's urzidae.

Heedless of where the Archon was, Ulfric got Salukis on his knees and reached upward with Salukis's hand and gripped the bag holding the Fenestros, yanking it as hard as the injured boy could. The bag's strap would not give, though, until he called upon the Fenestros again. He realized he was getting weaker, or Salukis was. This was going to end soon, one way or another.

The bag came free. Ulfric reached inside and grabbed the Fenestros.

Tuzhazu's great spike on his one usable wing speared Salukis through the back, the metal piercing all the way through his torso and emerging below his sternum. Salukis gave a breathless scream that sounded like one of the Deathless's horrid screeches.

Oh Verities, no! Salukis, Ulfric cried. *Hold on, boy, just hold on for a moment.*

He could feel Salukis's agony almost as sharply as if it were his own. Salukis's eyesight was darkening rapidly, and, panicked, Ulfric realized the boy was going to die. And when he did, it wouldn't matter that Ulfric had acquired Balavad's celestial stone. He'd have no way to use it.

Gloating, Tuzhazu drew them skyward like a trophy of war. Salukis reached for his torso with his free hand. Ulfric thought he was grabbing the spike coming through his stomach, but his hand wrapped around the Mentalios lens. He pulled it over his head and said to Ulfric, *The urzidae.* He dropped the Mentalios chain around the beast's horn.

Ulfric still gripped Balavad's Fenestros in their other hand so tightly Salukis's fingers were white. With the last of Salukis's strength, he waved the stone in front of the beast. It's empty eyes shifted to it, and he whispered through Salukis, "Vesr sraak aak, sraka aak suu kaa."

CHAPTER FORTY-NINE

Isemay and Dwoon gawked at the sight of Salukis taunting the Archon. But she quickly realized this might be the distraction they required.

"Dwoon, go now, while they're not paying attention," she whispered. "It may be your only chance."

"What about you?"

"I'll only slow you down. Your wings can hide you better than they can hide both of us. Now, do it. Hurry."

The truth was, Isemay didn't trust her legs to hold her up after seeing the way the Archon charged Salukis, his wrath like a giant that would squash the youth the way Tuzhazu's urzidae had Deespora. She wouldn't, *couldn't*, take her eyes off the fight. Salukis was managing, barely, to dodge every swipe of the Archon's torn and burnt wings, but she could see from here he would tire quickly. The torrent of the Archon's attack was relentless.

"I'll meet you back at the Cosmoculous," she reassured Dwoon through lips that felt increasingly wooden.

"Okay. Okay. Be careful," Dwoon whispered.

He steeled himself, crouched low, wrapping his wings around as much of his body as he could, and emerged from their hiding spot.

May Mithli's mercy go with you, she prayed. From the corner of her eye, all she could see was a strip of his back and his feet as he moved off, but most of her attention stayed on Salukis.

Salukis leaped like a cat and grabbed one of Tuzhazu's wings when the Archon was off-balance. She could hear the snap from where she hid as something broke inside Tuzhazu and then he threw himself backward on top of Salukis. She gripped the edge of the storehouse reflexively, barely still concealed by the shadows.

Get up, Lukis. Get up, quickly!

Instead, he took a boot in his rib cage that she knew without a doubt had wounded him. He was rolling away, only stopping when he hit Tuzhazu's urzidae. *Oh Verities, what will it do to him?*

But the urzidae merely craned its long neck to see the young man, drool spotting the ground as its head moved and its teeth were bared. Salukis was on his knees, reaching for Tuzhazu's bag—for his Fenestros!

But he's not an Archon, what can he do with that?

What happened next wiped all thought from her mind. Isemay's vision went white, and her legs turned to water as Tuzhazu's wing tip stabbed through Salukis, like a knife stuck through the middle of a bowl of jelly.

The next thing she knew, she was running, heedlessly, across the field, past Deathless Minothians lying on the ground, black pools of blood, and more Deathless who still watched the fight, their backs to her.

Then she was on the ground beside Salukis, who'd been shaken from Tuzhazu's wing. She collapsed onto her knees beside him.

"Why aren't I surprised to see you here, young Vinnric?" a voice said over her shoulder, *his* voice, the Archon's, but she paid him no mind.

"Salukis, Lukis, can you hear me?" she whispered, one hand cradling his head, the other placed over the red gash in his tunic that seeped blood, far too much of it. "Lukis, you can say something, can't you? Tell me what to do, how do I help you?"

She heard a snort behind her. "Help him? You're no tender, girl."

Isemay chanced a look over her shoulder. Tuzhazu sneered at her and leaned down to retrieve Balavad's Fenestros. It had rolled out of Salukis's hand and come to a stop nearby. The Archon stood and tucked the stone inside his tunic and said, "I don't know how you escaped the hall, but this time—"

She looked away from him, deciding that she wouldn't look back. If he was going to kill her, the last thing she wanted to see was Salukis's handsome face, that sweet, sardonic twist to his lips, even when he was unconscious. Or dead.

But there was a flash in the corner of her eye, and then she heard a *whoomp* sound, like a huge pile of laundry that had been dropped from far overhead. This did make her turn, and though her sight was blurred with tears, there was no mistaking what she was seeing.

Tuzhazu's urzidae had streaked past her and was trying to gore the Archon to death. The Archon was holding its horn in both hands, straining hard to keep the creature's head from pummeling him again. He was bleeding heavily from a puncture in one shoulder but still managed, somehow, to keep his grip.

"Guards!" he yelled. "Guards, get me away from this beast!"

Tuzhazu's one working wing swept forward, trying to gore the beast with its metal tip, but the angle was wrong. The urzidae twisted its head violently, and Tuzhazu lost his grip and was flung aside. Lying on this back, he yanked the Fenestros free of his pouch and sat up, whispering words Isemay couldn't hear. The beast lunged at him, then came to a sudden halt. It stood where it was, its head whipping back and forth as though it were trying to dislodge it from its own shoulders. It snorted with rage, great jets of froth coming from its nose and mouth.

Tuzhazu drew himself to his feet, watching the urzidae warily. He continued chanting, and within a few moments, several nearby Deathless had gathered around him and taken hold of him under each arm. They lifted him away, and the rest of the Minothian Deathless still of sound body began marching slowly after them, as if half-asleep, toward the Cosmoculous Tower.

Overhead, the triple moons were nearly aligned.

As soon as the Archon was out of reach, the beast turned back to her. In a state of resigned horror, Isemay watched Tuzhazu's blood dripping from its horn. She lowered herself over Salukis's motionless form, not knowing if she was trying to defend him or just giving up.

The beast approached, slowly, almost delicately.

"Isemay."

Impossibly, she heard her da speaking to her, right next to her ear.

"Here, around Salukis's neck. It's me."

Salukis's neck...of course, her memory keeper! She eyed the beast warily. It hadn't moved. It simply stood in place and stared back at her.

Cautiously, she moved her hand up and unfolded a blood-damp layer of Salukis's shirt. The dragørfly pendant lay there, unblemished. Her father's face stared out of it. "Da?"

"Isemay, I can't explain this to you, but I need you to crawl onto the back of this creature before you. It will take you to safety."

Her eyes shot back to the urzidae, who, though monstrously misshapen, remained docile.

"No, Da, I can't leave Salukis here. I can't...I can't tell if he's breathing."

The beast looked away in the direction Tuzhazu had run, appearing almost...sad?

"Where's your mum, Isemay?"

"She's in the tower. She'll never be able to hold them all off. Where are you, Da? Can you help her, warn her? Please, tell her she has to get out!"

"I can't reach her through the Mentalios." The frustration in her da's voice was edged enough to cut through crystal. "And this form can't fight them all..."

This form...what does that mean?

"Why are you here, Isemay?" he asked, his voice so tired the light breeze carried it easily away.

At first, she thought he was asking a real question, and she answered without thinking. "I needed a flute, an aulos. To raise the Cosmoculous." Salukis was so still, his eyes not moving beneath his bruise-dark lids. The blood coming from his torso had slowed, but there was so much. He still wore his flute tied to his belt. How was it possible he hadn't broken it? She reached for it, wanting to run her fingers along the engraved patterns in the double pipes, wanting to remember the night he'd shown her how to play it. She'd come here for this flute, or another like it, but she'd have given anything to have him speaking to her instead of having found it.

Then she realized her da hadn't meant why was she here specifically, on this field. He only meant why was she here, why were any of them here, why was any of this happening? He was as hopeless and bereft as she.

His voice cut through her increasingly darkening thoughts. "A flute? To raise the Cosmoculous? Why? Explain what you mean."

"The Cosmoculous is part of the Churss, and it's inside the tower, lowered over the Everlight's vessel. If it is raised to the tower's top, the Equifulcrum can align over it, and it will undo the shackles binding the Everlight. Mum has a book written by another Archon that explains it all. If the Cosmoculous isn't raised, the cage won't be broken. There's a song the Zhallah play that moves the Churss, and it'll move the Cosmoculous. I came to get a flute to play it."

"You know this song?"

His tone was urgent, almost harsh, as if she were about to get in trouble. But she hadn't done anything. She just wanted to go home, sit at the dinner table with her parents, laugh about whatever chastisement she'd been given by the teachers at the Conservatum that day—sometimes deserved, sometimes not. "Da," she pleaded, "where are you?"

But he wouldn't relent. "Isemay, listen, can you play this song? Can you take his instrument and play it?"

She swiped the tears of anger that had joined her tears of sadness. "Yes, I can do it," she said defiantly. "But we're so far from the tower it won't matter. Why are you pressing this?"

"Reach into his carryall at his waist."

His tone was commanding, not her father anymore but the Stallari. She did what he said and drew out, of all things, Deespora's Fenestros. "How did you—?"

"Never mind. Listen carefully. We're going to raise that stone. Take the flute and the Fenestros, and your memory keeper, and get on the urzidae."

"Da—"

"Isemay, do it. We're going to release Mithlí and save your mother. The Zhallah will come for Salukis now that the Minothians are gone from the field. But this isn't something we have time to argue about."

He was right, of course. And the Zhallah tenders might be able to help Salukis in a way she could not. After gathering the items, she leaned down to his ear and whispered, "I will find you again when this is over, Lukis. Please don't leave me for good." Then she stood, feeling a weariness that was not in her body but in her spirit, and climbed atop the frightening urzidae.

CHAPTER FIFTY

Symvalline hadn't seen anything but the wrath-red face of the approaching Archon for too long. The Cosmoculous seemed altogether consumed with him, and the scene playing across its surface followed him with a bird's-eye view.

She would have abandoned the tower when she saw Isemay run recklessly onto the stalled battlefield to the side of the poor, badly wounded Zhallah boy, but the urzidae's attack on Tuzhazu that caused him to flee showed her Isemay was at least momentarily safe. Probably safer there, in fact, than she would be in the tower with Symvalline. The Archon and his forces were now at the tower door.

And Symvalline and the three remaining Zhallah children were trapped.

Despite being made of metal, the door wouldn't stay closed for long. The Archon held a Fenestros, and he would find a way to get it open.

The lighting inside the vessel's chamber continued to pulse and wane, its light flashing stronger each time. What light from the three moons found its way down the tower's shaft and through the Cosmoculous was likewise intensifying, though still diffuse. The air held a weight of expectation. Yet no matter what angle or consideration she took trying to imagine an outcome to this that saw Tuzhazu defeated and the Zhallahs freed, she came up short. There was simply no way she and the Zhallah children could escape, not with the mass of Minothians-turned-Deathless following the brutal Archon, not with the Zhallahs all but defeated, and not with no other way in or out of the tower.

No matter how loudly she called to Ulfric through her Mentalios, it came to nothing. She hadn't seen him on the battlefield, only the bruhawks, and had no idea where he was. Even if she did, she could think of no way he could help, either.

The sound of heavy, deliberate hammering echoed up the tower to them. Tuzhazu, striking the door. It was a tolling bell, like those that played for the dead in Asteryss. She looked to the wall where the three Zhallah children huddled. The sheen of tears in their wide eyes lit up brightly each time the vessel's light pulsed. They were so afraid.

"I will keep him at bay as long as I can," she promised, hating how little anything she did would matter.

The youngest, the girl named Cylli, whimpered, and the older girl comforted her in an embrace as she said to Symvalline, "We know you did what you could, lady of Vinnr. And maybe Dwoon and your daughter will make it back. There's still time."

Symvalline smiled sadly. The girl had strength, and hope still, and Symvalline would not dampen that with her own lack of it.

Then came the clanking crash of the tower's door being thrown open, hard enough to hit the inner wall. It echoed so loudly she almost expected the building to shake. The stairway was too narrow for more than one person to climb, and when finally the sound of stomping boots could be heard on the other side of the chamber door, she was ready for him.

Tuzhazu shoved the door open. Blood coated the right side of his body from the urzidae's horn. His eyes, too, were red-rimmed and blazing with fury and triumph. He lingered in the doorway, regarding Symvalline, who stood in front of the children.

"Oh you Vinnrics, you're like the plague yourselves. Everywhere you aren't welcome," he said.

"Even if you win today, Akeeva will expose you. She knows this is wrong—" Symvalline began.

"Akeeva is dead and her head will make a pretty trophy. I sent the Deathless to finish what I started. I don't need any further interruptions to my rule. Arc Rheunos will no longer be subjected to weak leaders who refuse to do what's necessary. And now nothing else stands in my way."

Inwardly aghast, all Symvalline could think of were the children who'd been in the antechamber to Akeeva's rooms. Had they witnessed the murder of the one they thought was their maker? If so, what would, or had, become of them?

Keeping her voice calm, she said steadily, "I do." And with every bit of force she had in her, she flung her last three klinkí stones at his face.

The vessel's light pulsed, harder than ever, just before the stones found their mark. The room went white, and Symvalline was blinded completely. Her hands rose to shield her eyes reflexively, but of course that didn't help. Before her vision cleared, she heard a low chuckle.

The sound nearly drained her of her strength.

"I've dealt with these nuisances for the last time," Tuzhazu said.

Blinking away the spots, she focused on him once more. He'd taken a few steps closer to the vessel and now held her wystic stones, all of them, out in his hand as if to offer them back. Symvalline tried to call them, but they merely danced in his palm, jerking toward her, then back toward the Fenestros he held in his other hand. Tuzhazu suddenly closed his fist around the stones and clenched it. She could hear the stones cracking in his palm. And when he opened it, they were bits of dust and tiny pebbles. He shook them free, staring at her.

"I'm going to do the same to you—"

A loud but low tone filled the bore of the tower, coming from above them, snapping off Tuzhazu's words like a branch. It was a deep note, like what you would hear from a wind instrument, but hundreds of times louder than any instrument Symvalline had ever heard. Both she and Tuzhazu looked toward the Cosmoculous, neither understanding what they were hearing.

In a moment, the tone changed, becoming a lighter note, then changed again. Each note rang for several beats, evening out like a chant of some kind.

The Cosmoculous began to move.

Behind her, Symvalline heard one of the children. "It's the Churss melody. Someone is playing it."

The Churss melody? Was this the power to move the Churss that Isemay had spoken of?

"How is it moving? Why?" Tuzhazu yelled to no one in particular. Then his eyes fell on Symvalline. "Are you part of this, Vinnric? You are, aren't you?"

She wanted to spite him with a laugh but held it back, merely challenging him with her gaze.

He crossed the room, stopping briefly beneath the Cosmoculous to watch it roll upward a few more inches, then shoved Symvalline aside and gripped the arm of the older Zhallah, Eleni. "You'll tell me what's happening, girl."

Symvalline lunged at him, but he struck her hard in the chest with his fist wrapped around the Fenestros. She slammed against the far wall, feeling as if her torso had caved in, struggling mightily to breathe. It felt like the world's weight on her breastbone as she began to push herself to her hands and knees.

His eyes returned to Eleni's face, and he pulled her close enough to kiss. "Who is doing this and why? Tell me and I will spare you. I'll make you part of my Deathless Guard."

"El—" Symvalline tried to cry, but her voice couldn't break free of her wounded lungs. *Don't,* was all she managed, the word a whisper's whisper.

Eleni was terrified, too terrified to hear her. "It's a way to break the cage Archon Akeeva discovered. If-if the Equifulcrum can shine through the Cosmoculous onto the vessel, Mithlí will be free."

Tuzhazu glared at her a moment longer, then shoved her away and turned to the vessel. The other two children wrapped their arms around Eleni, crying soundlessly. Symvalline's chest burned. She couldn't straighten, couldn't stand, wasn't even sure if she could drag herself to him and make him fight her. Overhead, the long, tonal sounds continued, and the Cosmoculous had risen far enough that its bottom curve was out of sight.

"No…" Tuzhazu whispered. "No no no."

He rushed to the statue, a man he'd known in life, once an ally, surely, and then later as their maker's vessel. He gripped the man's arm where it was outstretched defensively—and began to pull it.

Catching Eleni's eyes with her own, Symvalline jerked her chin weakly toward the open door. While Tuzhazu was distracted, they had a chance to escape. Where they'd go was another concern, but anywhere but near the deranged Archon was better than here. Eleni seemed to understand and gently took the hands of Onni and Cylli. Their flight from the room went unhindered, Tuzhazu wholly focused on the inert vessel.

Even over the reverberating notes coming from outside, now rising louder and faster, Symvalline could hear stone scraping over stone. If he moved the vessel too far, the light of the Equifulcrum would not reach it, and Mithlí would remain caged. She couldn't let that happen.

CHAPTER FIFTY-ONE

Isemay sat atop the urzidae and played Salukis's flute. Deespora's Fenestros lay wedged between the instrument's dual pipes while her da spoke an Elder Veros incantation through the memory keeper she wore around her neck once more, amplifying the flute's notes through the celestial stone.

From above the ravine that led to the secret path past the barrows to the Cosmoculous Tower, the arrhythmic sounds she played were as loud as ten waterfalls, maybe a hundred, and they soared from the rocky outcrop like the summoning pipes at Aster Keep.

Below them, the Minothian Deathless Guards stood like statues in the small clearing outside the base of the tower. They looked around as the resounding notes pressed into the valley, but the sound bounced from the fortress walls to the mountains' flanks and back, making the direction they came from unknowable.

Above, the three moons were no longer visible. Now almost fully aligned, it seemed there was only one, the pale, blue, and red colors slowly melding into a single great orb, like the Eye of the Cosmos itself staring down at them.

With a heart that no longer had room for fear, or sadness, or even hope, Isemay simply closed her eyes and thought of Salukis's laughing eyes, his teasing smile, the way he'd shown her how to hold the flute and breathe through the reeds. She played the notes exactly as she'd heard him play them. She played them perfectly.

CHAPTER FIFTY-TWO

Lying on her side on the chamber floor, Symvalline spotted Isemay's surrendered Deathless Guard's sword. It still leaned where she'd left it at the end of the vessel's platform. With soft cries she struggled to hush, she reached out, wedging her fingertips into the grooves between floor stones, and pulled herself forward. Again. Once more, her own struggle matching Tuzhazu's as he continued to yank the current vessel away. He was weakened from his wound, and the vessel's weight was amplified by its celestial prisoner, but he was managing to move the vessel from the center of the platform, fingerbreadth by fingerbreadth.

Feeling the ends of her cracked ribs grinding together, she reached out and touched the sword's cold hilt. She gripped it with one hand, and with her other, she stretched to grasp the lip of the platform.

"No, curse the Verities, no!" Tuzhazu was yelling, but his voice had an edge in it she hadn't heard before. Panic.

She looked up into the bore of the tower and saw what had sparked his reaction. The Cosmoculous crystal was far above them now, lighting the space with a glow that nearly burned the eye. Faintly perceptible, a white luminance swirled inside the crystal, like the eye of a hurricane. And as she looked, two more lights joined the first, one a deep ocean blue and the other fire red. The colors grew denser and filled the orb, spinning faster and faster in the opposite direction of the five Fenestrii still hovering over the vessel. With a flash like the spark that could ignite an inferno, the spinning luminance burst from the sphere and began to spin down the bore of the tower.

Tuzhazu raised Balavad's Fenestros, screamed something in a foreign tongue, and Symvalline knew he was drawing strength from it for one final attempt to move the vessel.

With a scream of her own, she lunged to her feet, lifting the sword aloft like a candle. The swirl of celestial moonlight roared down the tower's shaft like spinning lightning as she chopped the sword down at Tuzhazu's outstretched hand.

With a flash of light off the blade, she saw Balavad's Fenestros gliding across the chamber, Tuzhazu's hand still attached to it, and the chamber exploded into soundless, shattering radiance.

CHAPTER FIFTY-THREE

Isemay's eyes rose to the three moons as she played the Churss melody, and she caught the last tiniest sliver of the farthest moon, Maiztos, as it disappeared behind the blue moon, Kahros.

Instantly, a beam of light so penetratingly bright it seemed to split the air it passed through shot from the alignment directly toward the visible Cosmoculous orb at the peak of the tower.

From her vantage along the ridgeline, seated atop the urzidae, it appeared that the tower exploded at the moment the beam struck the crystal.

The world filled with the sound of thunder, and the ground trembled beneath her as a white disc of light spread from the Cosmoculous, expanding so magnificently that she was forced to squeeze her eyes closed or risk blindness. The immensity of noise and light seemed to shatter the earth, the sky, reality itself, and a great shockwave struck her, knocking her from the urzidae. Through squinted eyes, she saw the beast's claws dig into the ground, keeping it upright, but it leaned heavily in her direction. She feared it would topple on her if the wave didn't relent.

But it did. Moments later, the last of the thunderous noise echoed down the valley. And all grew still.

Drawing a choked breath, Isemay scrambled to her feet and peered at the tower, expecting to see the massive stone monolith crumbled to pieces on the earth, her mum and the remaining Zhallah children with it.

With a relief so profound she nearly fell back to her knees, she saw that it still stood. The moons above were already parting, slivers of blue and red appearing on either side of the White Watcher. Though lit with stars, the sky had grown dark. Yet the three moons shone brightly enough that details began to emerge before Isemay's wide, shocked eyes.

The upper part of the tower where the Cosmoculous crystal had been housed above the Verity chamber was crumbling, giant pieces of stone blocks falling and smashing to the ground both outside and—*oh Vaka Aster's eyes, no!*—inward.

Her da spoke to her through the memory keeper. "Hurry, Isemay, up on the beast. We've got to get to your mum."

She barely had a grip on the reins before the urzidae launched down the side of the ravine. As it began winding down toward the tower, she cried, "Da! The Deathless Guard are surrounding it. What—"

She cut herself off when she heard a familiar chant from her father, the incantation Safran used to sightlink with Urgo and Yggo.

Then she saw the flash of light on their silvery wings in the distance, just past the tower itself. Urgo flapped oddly, as if he was wounded. As they soared toward the urzidae, the beast suddenly gave a great shake of its head, nearly tossing her off, then skidded to a dead stop.

"Isemay, grab the Mentalios from the urzidae's horn and prepare to be lifted by Yggo."

"All right," she breathed, clueless as to what might be happening but willingly following her da's instructions.

As she draped the second pendant around her neck with her memory keeper, Yggo swept down, her wings catching the lights from the moons and making her shimmer like a jewel. It was unimaginably beautiful, but Isemay only had a moment to enjoy it before the great bird had the back of her shirt gripped in her talons.

On a day of many firsts for Isemay, being carried by the bruhawk was the one she knew she would never, ever forget. The strength of the bird was impossible, and she seemed to weigh nothing to Yggo. For a moment, she fleetingly marveled at the idea that if this was what flying with a bruhawk felt like, she could only imagine how magnificent flying with a dragør would be.

The hawk carried her aloft swiftly, and as they neared the tower she looked down along the clearing surrounding it where the many Deathless Guards stood rigid, like statues. Even as stones large enough to flatten them dropped from the tower's heights around them, they didn't move. Why weren't they getting to safety?

"Tuzhazu controls them with his Fenestros," she whispered aloud, answering her own question. "If he's not forcing them to move, that must mean…"

Had her mum succeeded? Was Tuzhazu finally dead?

Yggo and Urgo reached the collapsing tower's peak. She could look straight down the center of the octagonal column, though it was too dark to see inside the Verity chamber at the bottom. The Cosmoculous had filled the tower's bore before—but it was gone. Whatever had happened, whatever had caused the wave of light and thunder and power that had shaken the earth for a moment, that wystic force seemed to have destroyed the massive Churss crystal. And her mum had been directly beneath it.

The birds hovered over the hollow tower for a moment, deciding on what to do. It gave Isemay enough time to see that the cascade of stones from the tower's walls had slowed. Pebbles and fist-sized chunks still rolled down, but the remainder of the blocks seemed to be staying in place for the moment.

The bruhawks began to descend. From Isemay's chest, her da's Mentalios lens glowed, lighting the walls. Immediately, she could tell the flecks of crystal in them no longer pulsed with that erratic light from before. Near the bottom, however, the entire floor glinted and gleamed, as if a glacier of pure blue ice had somehow found its way inside the Verity chamber.

It was the crystal, smashed into bits and pieces, some of them as large as a table. Their weight alone would have crushed anyone beneath them, let alone the chaotic jumble of their sharp edges. No one who'd been in the chamber could have survived the shower of shattered crystal.

As Yggo's descent slowed, she closed her eyes. She didn't want to see.

From the memory keeper, he da said, "Symvalline was in here, Crumb?"

She nodded, eyes still closed. "And the Zhallah children."

"We'll find her." His voice carried what his words did not, the same fear, nearly dread, Isemay felt.

Her feet brushed a surface. Yggo's talons released her, as she opened her eyes. She staggered for a moment, then found her legs. The hawk had placed her atop a wide piece of the broken crystal. Around her, the birds were gripping other chunks and flinging them toward the chamber's outer walls. The Cosmoculous rubble resembled pieces of broken obsidian, with smooth surfaces, some concave, some convex, some edges razor sharp, some jagged. The birds' talons were nearly as solid as rock themselves and could grip the sharp pieces without harm. On the whole, walking through it would be no different than walking across a scree field atop a mountain. Doable as long as your boots had sturdy soles. Realizing this, she wasn't going to just stand there and watch, and carefully she picked her way toward the center of the chamber.

"Here, there was a table at this spot where the vessel lay."

What had become of the vessel, she suddenly wondered. Had the Equifulcrum released Mithlí? It would explain why the walls no longer flashed with intermittent light. And if so, where was Mithlí now?

Yggo and Urgo focused on the space she indicated and quickly unearthed the tabletop. The vessel was not on it.

There was, however, a swath of red across one side, easily identifiable as blood.

Her da had gone quiet, and she could feel the hot streaks of silent tears falling down her cheeks as she stood on a mound of crystal beside the stone table, staring at the bloody stain.

That's when she heard it. A quiet, almost imperceptible sound. Like a butterfly's breath, barely there.

But…still *there*.

"Yggo, Urgo, come here," she said. "Can you—can you clear one side of the table so I can see under it?"

The bruhawks used their talons to rake the bigger chunks of crystal aside until a trench formed. Isemay leaned over the side of the table—and saw her mum.

Symvalline was curled into a ball under it. Her eyes were closed, and Isemay couldn't see her chest rising and falling. But she'd heard it, she knew she'd heard it.

"Mum! Mum, are you all right?" she cried.

"Symvalline!" her da yelled from the dragørfly pendant that dangled from her neck.

Cautiously but moving as swiftly as a groundhog into its burrow, Isemay squirmed beneath the table. Her mum's flesh when she touched her cheek was warm! Leaning over her body, Isemay grabbed both of her shoulders and pulled her up so they were nose to nose. "Mum!"

Symvalline's hands, which had been tucked into her belly, came free. Four matching Fenestrii rolled from her grip to the floor. Isemay eyed them only a moment, then searched her mum's body from head to foot for signs of a wound. "Da, can you do anything?"

As she spoke, Symvalline drew a sudden breath and raised her head. Her eyes opened, looking directly into Isemay's. "Crumb, my Crumb," she whispered. "I can't tell you how happy I am to see you."

Isemay felt it coming, tried it hold it back, tried to be a strong and stoic Knight like her father and her mother, but it was useless. With a shuddering sob, she threw herself into her mum's embrace. Nothing in the entire world ever felt as good as Symvalline's arms wrapping around her, hugging her with a strength that squished her lungs. But it didn't matter. Her mum was alive and her da was here.

When they finally let go of each other, her da said, "Symvalline, what happened? Has Mithlí been freed?"

Ulfric's face in the memory keeper caught her mum's eyes. "Ulfric, where are you? Can you come to the tower?"

Was there some hesitation in her da's reply? "I'll get to that in a moment. But...Mithlí?"

Isemay swiped away her tears in time to see a flash of guarded irritation cross her mum's face, the look she only ever gave Ulfric when she disagreed with him but would not bring up why until they were alone.

Symvalline spoke hesitantly. "Yes. I believe so, yes. Tuzhazu and I were struggling...I'd just gotten Balavad's Fenestros away from him. Then the chamber, it *burst*. I've never felt power like that. There was nothing but light. I don't know how long it lasted, and I don't know if I pulled myself beneath the table or was thrown there by the surge. All I can really say is that I saw both the vessel and Tuzhazu...*disintegrate*. Then I lost consciousness."

She closed her eyes as if thinking deeply. "The sight of them, like ash blown apart in a strong wind, is still burned in my mind."

When she stopped speaking, Isemay and her da were quiet. She didn't know what Ulfric was thinking, but Isemay was thinking that she wasn't just *glad* Tuzhazu was dead, she was *joyous*. A person that cruel, that wicked, should never have been ordained by a Verity. Toss the traitors with the trash, as Stave would say.

Her thoughts were cut short at that sound of the two bruhawks perching atop the table. Their talons dangled over the edge, and a moment later, something dropped to the floor next to Isemay with a thump.

It was a hand—just a hand, no body attached—at the end of a bloody, neatly severed wrist. And it was clutched tightly around a black Fenestros.

"I...I guess not *all* of Tuzhazu is gone," Isemay heard herself mumble as she fought her rising gorge.

"Ulfric," her mum said quietly, "many wrongs may be coming to right in Arc Rheunos. But you still haven't told me where you are."

Y
CHAPTER FIFTY-FOUR

Yggo and Isemay soared slowly over the battlefield. Below, the field was no longer empty of all save the dying and wounded. The Zhallahs had left the safety of the Churss and were now spread among their fallen on the field, healing those they could, weeping over those they couldn't.

Salukis was still down there somewhere, and she was going to find him. After the story her father had just shared with her and her mum... she felt her mind beginning to shut down, resisting any more shocking news that she simply could not comprehend. Vinnr under siege or soon to be by the Dyrraks, who were being enslaved into the same kind of malevolent, inhuman army for the Verity Balavad...The rest of the Knights missing...And, most unbelievable of all, her father was now Vaka Aster's vessel, yet he himself was no longer tethered to his own body...

No, she couldn't possibly listen anymore. And as her parents quietly and fervently discussed what they were going to do, Isemay had asked to leave, to take Yggo and report what was occurring outside the tower. To her surprise, they'd barely hesitated before agreeing. And just like that, she realized, she'd stopped being a child in their eyes. They trusted her, saw her as grown. The realization was an unexpected hammer blow. She thought she'd appreciate it when this day finally came. But what she really felt was the weight of knowing she no longer had her youth to rely on as an excuse for bad and irresponsible decisions. She could no longer justify *making* bad and irresponsible decisions.

As she and Yggo exited the tower, the first thing she'd observed was that the Deathless Guards had not moved from their vigil around the base, so she had the bruhawk fly to the battlefield, feeling relatively assured they didn't need to fear further attacks. After all, Tuzhazu most assuredly did not control them any longer with his foreign Fenestros. Pried out of his dead hand, it was now in her mum's possession with the others.

She spotted the area where Salukis had fallen and had Yggo take her down. A group of Zhallahs was gathered about a form on the ground, and she recognized Salukis's father Browan. The three others were Mura, her mum Lysis, and Kalisk, the old council member. The women were kneeling over Salukis, blocking him from Isemay's sight.

The moment her feet hit the earth, she ran to them. "Mura?" she asked hesitantly, not yet ready to look, not ready to see whether Salukis had lived. She didn't know if she was prepared for the chance, the *likelihood*, that he had not.

When Mura looked up, the expression on her face made Isemay's heart grow cold. Tears stood in Mura's eyes.

"Is he…" Isemay began but could not finish the question.

As Mura stood, another Zhallah approached and came to her side. It was Dwoon, and Mura took his hand. She pulled him closer to Isemay. "Isemay, thank you. Thank you for bringing him back to us."

Isemay couldn't force words from her tight throat. She could only nod, happy to see that at least Mura's family was once again whole, as her own was.

Dwoon stepped forward and put his hand on her arm. "Your mum?"

Miserably, she nodded and tried to smile. "She's all right. She stopped Tuzhazu, for good. And the vessel is…well, it's gone. Mithlí has been freed."

Mura and Dwoon exchanged a glance, and all those gathered

around Salukis looked up at her statement too. The two older women quickly went back to what they were doing. Finally, Isemay dared to look.

His face was still, his eyes closed, but there was some color to his cheeks. Alive! She rushed over and fell to her knees beside him. The women were tendering him, trying to save him.

Mura came back and laid her palm on his torso, next to the other women's, beside the great gash from Tuzhazu's wing.

Isemay grasped Salukis's limp hand. "Will he make it?"

Kalisk looked into her eyes. "We are barely keeping him from moving into the shadows. I fear he's too far to bring back."

Through a veil of tears, Isemay could see that the grass and small plants growing around Salukis were withered and brown, their life having already yielded to the draw of the tenders and passed into him. She gripped his hand harder in both of hers, feeling helpless and useless. What good was she here? Salukis had given his life for his people, and she could do nothing but watch as it ended. She squeezed her eyes closed, trying to hide her pain in the dark.

A hard but gentle hand on her shoulder made her look up. It was Browan, Salukis's father. "Your bravery and determination gave the people of Arc Rheunos their freedom, Isemay of Vinnr. You should be proud. You inspired us all, even Archon Raamuzi, to finally face the evils of the Menace. We've lost some, but we would have lost all if not for you. I know Salukis would tell you the same if he could."

Her tears came hard then, and there was nothing she could do to hold them back. She curled down and hid her face in Salukis's shoulder, weeping for both him and herself and for the sacrifices so many had to make.

She didn't notice the stillness settle around her or the way Mura and the other women removed their hands from Salukis's chest. But she did notice when a hand began stroking her hair, and she noticed when Salukis took a gasping breath.

She sat up quickly, disbelieving her own senses. Salukis's eyes blinked open, their warm brown tone shining, full of life.

"Lukis..." she breathed.

He started to smile at her, but something beside her caught his eyes. They widened. Isemay looked over and saw…

Deespora, bent down, had laid a finger on the edge of Salukis's outstretched wing. But it wasn't Deespora, not anymore.

As Isemay gawked at the woman, whose skin glittered with an aura of mellow light as if Halla shone through her, Mithlí stared back at her, her face unreadable. "Creation of my quin Vaka Aster," the Verity said.

Swallowing against the sudden tightness in her throat, Isemay whispered, "Mithlí," then immediately bowed her head, seeing everyone around her had as well.

The Verity said nothing else, and a moment later Isemay sensed her presence moving off. *She saved Salukis,* she thought. *But Da has always told me the Verities don't interfere in their creations' destinies.*

She didn't care. Salukis was alive. Gratefully, she looked into his eyes. He gave her that grin, teasing yet playful, and utterly irresistible. "Isemay," he said, and his brow wrinkled. "I think your father…"

"He what?"

"I think he saw us kissing. And I don't think he liked it."

It was the last thing she'd expected him to say, and somehow it struck her as the funniest thing she'd ever heard. With a laugh she couldn't hold back, and didn't want to, she squeezed him in a hug so tight she heard him gasp. "Oh, Lukis, I can't believe you're all right."

He hugged her back and soon their lips met again. This time, there was no hesitancy or awkwardness. This time it felt as natural and wonderful as breathing.

"Ahem," Browan interrupted. "If you're feeling so good, son, there are others who could use some help."

His da reached a hand down and Salukis took it. Before he could get up on his own, Browan pulled him to his feet and wrapped him in another embrace. Isemay looked around. All over the field, the Zhallahs were together, most smiling and supporting each other. Deespora, or rather Mithlí moved among the fallen, healing all as she encountered them. All except those who had already passed in the shadow, but even those, Minothian and Zhallah alike, even the urzidae, she stood over for a moment, as if to bear witness to her creations and what had happened to them.

Soon, the Minothians from town who'd been hiding in their homes began to creep to the edge of the field, then into it, intermingling with the Zhallahs. Wonder and awe filled their faces. No one spoke, no one cheered, but everyone seemed to have forgotten they were divided.

Mura, Lysis, and Dwoon stood together, arms around each other. They would not be parted by a foreign malice again. Isemay's eyes found Salukis again. As she looked at him, he turned away from Browan back to her, his feelings, like her own, painted on his face. She wanted to stay here, with him, hold him the way her mum and da held each other. But she could not live in his world, nor he in hers.

But a Knight or an Archon could. Her da had told her and her mum about the Himmingazian called Bardgrim whom Vaka Aster had chosen and ordained. Vaka Aster was beyond her now and shackled through Balavad's treachery. But Mithlí no longer was.

Isemay looked across the field toward the Verity, who was now walking down the main road toward Everlight Hall, her people bowing on every side as she passed. Isemay had trained her whole life to serve a Verity. It didn't have to be Vaka Aster, did it?

She glanced at Salukis, then began following Mithlí.

"Isemay, where are you going?" he said.

She glanced back. "Arc Rheunos needs a new troupe of protectors to watch over Mithlí's vessel, Lukis. And I'm going to be the first to volunteer. Would you like to come with me?"

Salukis hesitated and looked at Browan. His da smiled at him, a look that could not have contained more pride. Then he paced to her and took her hand again.

Resolute, she cast her eyes on the Verity, and they began to cross the field hand in hand. Isemay had helped to free one Verity from Balavad's treachery. The calling to free another was too strong to deny. Today, if she was worthy, Isemay would indeed no longer be just a child. She would become a Knight Corporealis.

AFTERWORD

To my treasured reader, I'm deeply grateful for your readership your presence in my wordy world. If my book has touched your heart with magic or transported you to another realm, would you consider sharing your thoughts through a review on your favorite retailer? Your voice carries immense value and can guide fellow readers to a tale that resonates with them too. Together, we can build a community of kindred spirits, connected through the power of storytelling. Thank you for your kindness and support.

Don't forget to join my newsletter at www.tammysalyer.com/news letter to stay up to date on new releases and receive a free collection of stories. Cheers!

THE FIVE REALMS

REALM OF ÆRD; THE ÆRDENS

Verity
Fimm

Characters
Ayanna (Mylla's mother)
Greven (Mylla's father)

Locations
Kaldrwoot

REALM OF ARC RHEUNOS; THE ARC RHEUNOSIANS

Verity
Mithlí the Everlight

Characters
Agatha Pahzi (Minothian)
Akeeva Raamuzi (Archon, false Verity)
Alvar (Deespora's heartmatch)
Arudara (Salukis's mother)
Ballio (little Zhallah boy child)
Browan (Salukis's father)
Bunefer (Zhallah)
Cylli (Zhallah girl; Kalisk's grandchild)
Deespora Raamuzi (Archon, leader of Zhallahs)
Drevor (Salukis's uncle)
Duripi (mother of Cylli and Onni)
Dwoon (Mura's younger brother)
Eleni (thirteen-year-old girl)
Erli Detzu (paramour of Mura's)
Gostav (Minothian guard)
Hertha, Mistress (Minothian attendant and child watcher)
Inder (Viddzu's son, Minothian)
Kalisk (female elder Zhallah rebel and council member)
Lysis (Mura's mother)
Mura (friend of Isemay's)
Neeka (little Zhallah girl child)
Onni (Zhallah boy; Kalisk's grandchild)
Phaemee (Salukis's aunt)
Pitaja, Master (tutor for children in Everlight Hall)
Poolan (Zhallah elder)
Rusa (thirteen-year-old Zhalla girl)
Salukis Engzu (Zhallah)
Toranzu, Kaneas (Minothian guard transformed into a Deathless)
Tulla (Agatha's daughter)
Viddzu, Kaneas (Minoth guard transformed into a Deathless)
Widin (elderly barrow tender)

Locations
Aktoktos Gate

Churss forest
Cordu Valley
Maerria
Minoth Valley Gate
North Tyrns
Pass of Thossos
Skaphia Caves
South Tyrns
Thallorn River
Tyrn Mountains
Valley of Minothia
West Tyrns

REALM OF BATTGJALD; THE BATTGJALDICS

Verity
Balavad; Holiness Prime

Characters
Corvus Rhafn (Flesh Caster)

REALM OF HIMMINGAZE; THE HIMMINGAZIANS

Verity
Lífs the Creatress

Characters
Cote Illago (commander of the Glisternauts)
Drustim, Flight Leader (captain of the *Deep Sea Gem*)
Fex, Ensign

Heleina Gibbaden (Glisternaut navigator)
Jaemus Bardgrim (Glint Engineer, Glisternaut)
Joburg, Flight Leader
Jovus (father of Jaemus)
Mye, Flight Leader
Sandar, Spark Engineer
Bannus, Ensign
Saxton, Ensign
Trabazan, Ensign
Vreyja Bardgrim (grandsirene of Jaemus)
Yanna, Spark Engineer

Locations
Bludghadda
Dry Quarter
Isle Stonering
Never Sea
Vann

REALM OF VINNR; THE VINNRICS

Verity
Vaka Aster the Vigil Star

Characters
Allanach (Yorish Knight before the Cataclysm)
Beatte, Arch Keeper of the Kingdom of Ivoryss
Brun, Tannir (commander of Dragør Marines)
Cympher, Chamberlain
Connaugh, Arch Keeper of Yor previously
Eisa Nazaria (Knight, Nazarian Most High, Heir of the Sixth Line)
Egsíl, Third Phase Venerate

Elinora Rekkr (Havelock's mother)

Fergus, Arch Keeper of Yor currently

Furthsom (Ivoryssian Marine)

Gara Aoggvír, Third Phase Venerate (Seldeg's niece)

Gusun Sveinungr, Fifth Phase Venerate

Griggory Dondrin (Knight, Yorish)

Gudmund Øster (Dastrart Age smith of Winter's Bite and Star Spark)

Gwinifeve Dye (Yorish Knight from Griggory's time)

Havelock Rekkr (commoner of Ivoryss, Dragør Wing Marine)

Havelock's five sisters, Lizet, Edytha, Emoni, Gelle, Hilla

Heart of Purple Might (dragør, sire is Magnificence of Oceans Tempests)

Henrick Rekkr (Havelock's father)

Irrick (acolyte of the Resplendolent Conservatum, hazel eyes)

Isemay Aldinhuus-Lutair (daughter of Symvalline and Ulfric)

Jarmand, Keeper's Guard Leader

Jimp Owers (Dragør Wing Marine)

Kòrmak, Venerate

Lillias Grannd

Magnificence of Oceans Tempests (dragør)

Mallich "Roi" Roibeard (Knight)

Mylla Evernal (Knight)

Nennus (commander of Magdastervian forces)

Ozlaus, First Phase Venerate

Peke of Magdaster, Knight

Poppy's Noble Inferno (dragør)

Safran Glór (Knight)

Seldeg Aoggvír, Chancellor of the Dyrrak Phalanx (Heir of the Third Line)

Serl (Stave's grandfather)

Sœrnec, Ambassador (Lœdyrrak before the Cataclysm)

Starkas Nazaria (Domine Ecclesium of Dyrrakium)

Stave Thorvíl (Knight, originally from Magdaster in the Kingdom of Ivoryss)

Sveinkí Edizriis, Fourth Phase Venerate

Sveinungr, Fifth Phase Venerate
Symvalline "Sym" Lutair (Knight)
Tannir Brun (Commander of Dragør Marines of Asteryss)
Ulfric Aldinhuus, Stallari (Knight)
Urgo (bruhawk)
Yggo (bruhawk)

Locations
Ivoryss; the Ivoryssians (kingdom)
Aster Keep (Asteryss)
Asteryss City; Asteryss for short (capital city of Ivoryss)
Dryft and Tarmvred (highest peaks to the north of Morn Mountains)
Gethbrond (coastal city)
Great Province Byway (runs between Yor and Ivoryss, south of the
Howling Weald)
Howling Weald
Kolga (Ivoryssian city surrounded by lakes with salt-rich lagoons)
Magdaster (northernmost city)
Morn Mountain Range
Mount Omina (Morn Mountains)
North Byway (only road through the Weald from Magdaster, links to
Great Province Byway down south)
Udunum Island
Verring Sea
Vigil Tower (Asteryss)
Wilt Mountain (Morns, where the bruhawk aeries were hidden)

Yor; the Yorish (kingdom)
Almull Sea
Great Lochanian Forest (meets Howling Weald somewhere on the
other side of the Morn Mountains)
Lake Cuffdeach
Umborough (Yor capital)

Dyrrakium, the Dyrraks (empire/kingdom; formerly Lœdyrrak)

Anzuru Desert
Citadel Suprima (Elezaran)
Elezaran (capital of Dyrrakium)
Penitence Rock (dais at the Citadel Suprima)

DYRRAKIUM CULTURE
Five Phases of Citizenship: body purification, mind purification, releasing attachments, overcoming weakness, devotion (faith and loyalty)

Six Aspects of Devotion: faith, strength, wisdom, duty, loyalty, dominion

GLOSSARY

anni-cycle (similar to a year in Himmingaze)
archaneology (lore within a Scrylle)
Archon (Arc Rheunos equivalent of Knight Corporealis)
Aster Games (annual sporting competition in Ivoryss)
barrow tender (gravesperson)
Battle of the Byways (Yor and Magdaster skirmish around 650 turns ago)
bizzle (Arc Rheunosian hive insect)
Bounding Skate (Glisternaut ship)
bruhawk (Vinnric, extremely large hawk related to dragørs)
Cæcra ad resrs, boromcad bea dord. Kucik kea kesrs, emsu kæ lækra (Cycle of light, balanced by dark, focus my sight, into my heart)
Cataclysm, the (event that left Dyrrakium exiled from other Vinnric kingdoms; when Lœdyrrak became Dyrrakium)
cave snouz (Arc Rheunosian mammal)
chelbiefin shark (Vinnric creature)
chookter (slang for commoner in Vinnr)
chuffee (drink of Himmingaze)
Churss Circle; Circle, the (gathering site for council in Maerria)

Conquestum Ecclesium (fight ceremony in Dyrrakium to choose next Domine Ecclesium)

constrained (Himmingazian word for "arrested")

cosmoscruiser (such as the *Bounding Skate*)

Council's Crest (Glisternaut ship)

cycle; Glister cycle (Himmingazian measure of time, close to a day in length)

dalla flower (Vinnric lavender-colored flower)

daystar (sun, Halla in Vinnr)

dead rolls (the dead of Arc Rhuenos)

deca-cycle (similar to a decade in Himmingaze)

Deep Sea Gem (Glisternaut ship)

Distalfulcrum (moon alignment in Arc Rheunos)

Domine Ecclesium (a title for leader of Dyrrakium)

dragør (Vinnric creature)

Elder Veros, aka Vertasian in Himmingaze, aka Varitika in Arc Rheunos, aka First Tongue in Ærd (language of the Verities as it's known in Vinnr)

Equifulcrum (moon alignment in Arc Rheunos)

Everlight Hall (Minothian stronghold in Arc Rheunos)

Feast of Five Seasons celebration (Ivoryss)

Feast of Future's Hope for the Equifulcrum (Arc Rheunos)

Fenestros; Fenestrii (*pl.*) (celestial stones)

First Tongue (Ærden term for Elder Veros)

fleech (Himmingazian flying water creature)

Flesh Caster (Balavad's warrior-priests, equivalent of Knights Corporealis)

flint glass (Vinnric type of glass made from a chemical reaction and can be sparked like flint)

flittercat (Vinnric mammal)

gimgree swamp sloth (Vinnric mammal)

Glister Bright and Glister Dim (light and dark parts of the Glister cycle)

Glister Cloud (celestial threat to Himmingaze)

Glistering Horizon (Glisternaut ship)

govel (Arc Rheunosian plant with red berries)

gramsire (Himmingazian grandfather)

gramsirene (Himmingazian grandmother)

grandling (Himmingazian grandchild)

Gusting Hall (main hall in Magdaster)

half-ager (teen in Vinnr)

Halla (the sun in Vinnr)

Hallumbrum (midnight in Vinnr)

heartmatch (Vinnric term for intimate partner)

High Halls (noon in Vinnr)

honeybread (Vinnric food)

icewine (Vinnric beverage)

interrealm well (portals to travel between locations in Vinnr)

Kahros the Seeker; Seeker, the (blue moon, smallest in Arc Rheunos)

klinkí stone (wystic stones used by Knights Corporealis)

kórb fruit (Vinnric fruit)

lifemate (Himmingazian term for intimate partner)

lind tree (Vinnric tree with copper berries)

Maiztos the Life Giver; Giver, the (red moon, middle-sized, Arc Rheunos)

memory keeper (dragør-shaped pendant made by Ulfric)

Mentalios lens (pendants used by Knights Corporealis to communicate by thought)

mindhold (mental control)

moved into the shadows (Arc Rheunosian colloquialism for dying)

muddlemind (Himmingazian term for crazy, lunatic)

Mystae (Himmingaze's equivalent of Knight Corporealis)

nightcap (Arc Rheunosian mushroom that's slightly sweet)

Octopod (Jaemus's ship)

oilfire (Vinnric term)

oldwood forests (Vinnric term)

ong fruit (Vinnric fruit like an orange)

Order of the Knight/s Corporealis; Knights, the; Order, the

phanx (insect of Vinnr)

plague-bringer (Arc Rheunosian term)

Primator (Balavad's ship)

puurite stone (Vinnric term)

Raveners of the Tooth; Raveners (Balavad's soldiers)

realm-jumper (universal term for anyone who travels between realms)

Reaper's Breath (Himmingazian plant used in funerals)

Resplendolent Conservatum; Conservatum, the (academy in Vinnr)

Resplendolent Prelates (the highest order of Conservatum scholars)

Scrylle (star-metal scepter imbued with celestial power)

shelksies (Himmingazian wrist-borne weapons)

shullet (Himmingazian ammo for a shelksie)

sight-link (how Safran sees through bruhawk's eyes)

silvflan (Vinnric mammal)

slag, slag it (Vinnric curse)

slaghammer (Vinnric curse)

slangarook (Himmingazian large dragørlike sea creature)

Song of Figments and Fables (Vinnric song)

songbox (Vinnric music box)

starpath well (portals between realms)

syke liquor (Dyrrak fermented drink)

Syzyckí Elementum (unification of the realms and their Verities)

tessalock (Ærdan device that shows the time in all realms)

tessalope; time walker (Ærden wystic creature)

thirty-night (Vinnric month)

timepath (universal term for how time connects the realms)

trogghopping (Vinnric oath of exasperation)

urzidae (Arc Rheunosian horse-size bear-like beast)

Varitika (Arc Rheunosian term for Elder Veros)

veeshock (Himmingazian animal/food)

Vigil Tower (stronghold of Knights Corporealis in Vinnr)

Vigilance (Knights' ship)

War of Rivening (the war that broke Vinnr's old kingdom into three)

Warden Temporalis (Ærden equivalent of Knight Corporealis)

Wing (Dragør Wing Marine)
wystic, wysticism (magic)
yorvic (Dyrrak large lizardlike creature)
Znopho the White Watcher; Watcher, the (white moon, largest in Arc Rheunos)

ABOUT THE AUTHOR

Tammy is an inveterate verbarian, who spends her days surrounded by the written word, both hers and others'. As an ex-paratrooper with the 82nd Airborne Division, her stories are often as gritty as a grunt's pile of three-week-old field gear. Her military science fiction Spectras Arise series debuted to acclaim in 2012, and her epic fantasy adventure series The Shackled Verities was launched in 2020. She's currently five books deep in a Weird West series called Otherworld Outlaws, featuring half-fae sawbones, a necromancer gnome, and a hoodoo cowgirl galavanting into mischief in the Old West.

When not hunched like a Morlock over her writing desk, Tammy runs and bikes silly miles with her super-cool weirdo partner in the Pacific Northwest playground and spends an inappropriate amount of time watching Henry Rollins videos on YouTube. Contrary to what-ever ideas her last name might conjure, she's never really been much of a Slayer fan.

Fantasy, space opera, satire, and snark fans will feel right at home with Tammy. Learn more about her and her books by visiting www.tammysalyer.com. She hopes you enjoy reading her works and welcomes your reviews.